DOMINION

Other great stories from Warhammer Age of Sigmar

DOMINION

DARIUS HINKS

BLACK LIBRARY

A BLACK LIBRARY PUBLICATION

First published in 2021.
This edition published in Great Britain in 2022 by
Black Library, Games Workshop Ltd., Willow Road,
Nottingham, NG7 2WS, UK.

Represented by: Games Workshop Limited – Irish branch,
Unit 3, Lower Liffey Street, Dublin 1,
D01 K199, Ireland.

10 9 8 7 6 5 4 3 2 1

Produced by Games Workshop in Nottingham.
Stormcast Eternals vignette illustration by Paul Dainton.
Dominion battle illustration by Alex Boyd.

A CIP record for this book is available from the British Library.

ISBN 13: 978-1-80026-129-7

See Black Library on the internet at

blacklibrary.com

Find out more about Games Workshop
and the worlds of Warhammer at

games-workshop.com

Printed and bound by CPI Group (UK) Ltd, Croydon, CR0 4YY

The Mortal Realms have been despoiled. Ravaged by the followers of the Chaos Gods, they stand on the brink of utter destruction.

The fortress-cities of Sigmar are islands of light in a sea of darkness. Constantly besieged, their walls are assailed by maniacal hordes and monstrous beasts. The bones of good men are littered thick outside the gates. These bulwarks of Order are embattled within as well as without, for the lure of Chaos beguiles the citizens with promises of power.

Still the champions of Order fight on. At the break of dawn, the Crusader's Bell rings and a new expedition departs. Storm-forged knights march shoulder to shoulder with resolute militia, stoic duardin and slender aelves. Bedecked in the splendour of war, the Dawnbringer Crusades venture out to found civilisations anew. These grim pioneers take with them the fires of hope. Yet they go forth into a hellish wasteland.

Out in the wilds, hardy colonists restore order to a crumbling world. Haunted eyes scan the horizon for tyrannical reavers as they build upon the bones of ancient empires, eking out a meagre existence from cursed soil and ice-cold seas. By their valour, the fate of the Mortal Realms will be decided.

The ravening terrors that prey upon these settlers take a thousand forms. Cannibal barbarians and deranged murderers crawl from hidden lairs. Martial hosts clad in black steel march from skull-strewn castles. The savage hordes of Destruction batter the frontier towns until no stone stands atop another. In the dead of night come howling throngs of the undead, hungry to feast upon the living.

Against such foes, courage is the truest defence and the most effective weapon. It is something that Sigmar's chosen do not lack. But they are not always strong enough to prevail, and even in victory, each new battle saps their souls a little more.

This is the time of turmoil. This is the era of war.

This is the Age of Sigmar.

PROLOGUE

The children had been running for several minutes before they realised they were alone. They staggered to a halt and looked back through the trees. It was dusk and every shadow seemed to be moving. They leant against each other, a boy and a girl, their chests hitching, sweat running down their faces.

'Father?' whispered the boy, not daring to raise his voice. The monsters were close. He could hear them tearing through the undergrowth, approaching from every direction, howling and snorting, shivering with kill fever. Their father had led them for nearly a mile, taking the old, hidden paths, promising them they would be safe, but now the monsters had found them. And there was no sign of him.

'Father!' repeated the boy, louder this time.

The girl held a finger to her lips, her eyes glinting in the darkness. 'They'll find us.'

'We can't go on without him!' he snapped, gripping her hand.

The girl stared at him, her eyes wide and glistening with tears.

'Keep moving!' gasped their father, bursting through a wall of bracken, grabbing them by the arms and hauling them up a muddy slope.

'You're hurt!' cried the boy. His father's face was grey and locked in a grimace. The side of his jerkin was dark with blood and he weaved from side to side as he ran, stumbling like a drunk.

He led them into a small clearing, then halted at the top of the slope and whirled around with his bow raised and an arrow nocked.

There was an explosion of branches and leaves. A monster barrelled into the clearing. An orruk. It was huge – as tall as a full-grown man but three times as wide. It was as hunched as all the other greenskins they had seen, its knuckles almost touching the ground and its shoulders bowed by scarred muscle. Its hide was as green as the forest, it had a jaw like a bucket and its eyes were crimson studs. At the sight of its prey it roared, preparing to hurl the spear it was gripping. Then it grunted in confusion, an arrow jutting from its eye socket. The greenskin let out another cry and prepared to hurl its spear again. There was a *thunk* as an arrow sank into its other eye and the creature finally fell to the ground.

'Go,' snapped the man, lowering his bow and shoving his children down the other side of the slope.

The three of them sprinted down the path, vaulting fallen trees and leaping over roots.

'Mother?' said the boy.

The man refused to look at him.

'Which way?' gasped the boy, reaching a fork in the path. They could hear greenskins everywhere, howling and blowing on their harsh, braying horns.

Their father looked left and right, then sprinted down the right-hand path, snatching a pair of hand axes from his belt as he ran, scouring the trees for signs of another attacker. The woods were dangerous even before the greenskins came. Every glade hid a predator.

'Almost there,' wheezed their father, his face growing paler by the minute.

'Almost where?' The boy was hanging on to his arm as they ran. 'We can't outrun them. Where are you taking us?'

The man led his children up another slope and then they emerged from the trees, with the valley spread out below. They had reached the edge of the forest. Fields of waving grass led down to the fast-flowing waters of a river. Corpses were scattered through the grass, their limbs wrenched into unnatural shapes, broken and butchered by the greenskins. They stared at the bodies. Fellow hunters. People they knew. Friends and relatives.

The man whispered a curse. Then he nodded towards a bridge and ran on, charging down the starlit slope as his children scrambled after him, numb with grief, trying to ignore the carnage around them.

Howls boomed from the hillside as greenskins emerged from the trees. The boy glanced back. There were dozens, perhaps hundreds of them loping into view, all massive and brutish, all brandishing weapons. Some of them were still wet with blood from the attack on the village.

'Faster!' gasped the man. 'To the river!'

The children were exhausted but terror spurred them on, dragging hidden reserves of strength from their limbs. They careered down the hillside, leaping over bodies and discarded weapons. Even in his panic, the boy was aware of distant lights, glittering at the far end of the valley. Excelsis. Home of the immortal guardians known as the White Angels. Home of god-like beings who had forged a city where people could live in safety. A place that he would never live to see.

They reached the bottom of the slope and approached the bridge. 'Quickly,' said the man, picking his way through a pile of bodies that were heaped in a muddy pool.

They were almost there when one of the bodies leapt to its feet and punched the man in the stomach.

The children screamed. It was not a corpse. It was not even a human. Its skin was the same mossy colour as the orruks charging down the hill but, where they were broad and heavy, this thing was sinewy and stooped. It had a stretched, leering face that looked like it had melted. It backed away, wearing an obscene grin, and the boy realised it had not punched his father, it had jammed a knife in him. It laughed at the sight of its handiwork, making a gurgling sound in its throat.

The children backed onto the bridge, holding each other and howling.

Their father rocked back on his heels, about to drop, but it was a feint. He lunged forwards and jammed an arrow through the creature's throat. It gasped and staggered away, dropping to its knees, clutching at the blood rushing down its chest.

The children's father shoved them forwards, sending them stumbling down the bridge.

'Run!'

It was narrow and unstable, made of ropes and planks. The boy struggled to keep his balance as he ran. The bridge lurched sickeningly beneath him. He was halfway across before he realised their father had not followed.

'Keep going!' the man cried, cutting furiously at the ropes.

The children halted and turned around.

'Keep going!' he howled.

Behind him, in the fields, the greenskins had almost reached the bottom of the slope, howling and hurling spears as they ran. He dropped his knife and took out a hand axe, hacking wildly at the rope until one of the bridge's supports snapped. The whole structure lurched.

'Keep going!' he cried again, his voice hoarse. 'Run! To Excelsis!'

The boy began stumbling back towards his father but his sister dragged him roughly in the other direction.

'Too late!' sobbed the girl, and he knew it was true. Their father was drenched in blood and he could barely stand. The greenskins would reach him in seconds.

As their father hacked at the bridge the two children stumbled away from him, barely reaching the other side before the whole structure collapsed, carried quickly away by the raging currents.

On the far bank, their father dropped to his knees, his back to the approaching greenskins as he looked across the water to his children.

'Make a life!' he cried, his voice shaking. He pointed at the distant lights. 'You'll be safe in Excelsis. The White Angels will protect you! You can be anything you want.' He gasped, struggling to speak. 'Make a new life. Make something of yourselves! Don't be–'

A blade burst from his chest and he looked down at it. Then he toppled sideways into the mud.

The wiry orruk wrenched its spear free and stood over him, blood running from the arrow in its neck. Then it did another one of its peculiar laughs, grinning at the two children before sprinting off into the long grass.

The other greenskins howled in frustration as they reached the broken bridge, looking across the river at the two weeping children. The river was fifty feet wide. The currents would drown anyone who attempted to cross. One of the orruks tried to hurl a spear across, but it faltered in the spray and landed in the middle of the river.

The children stared at their dead father, speechless, gripping each other's hands.

'They can cross at Riven Bark Ford,' said the girl eventually. 'It's only a couple of miles. They'll realise in a minute. We have to go or we won't stay ahead of them.'

The boy looked from his father to the lights of Excelsis.

'We have to do it.' He looked at his sister through his tears. 'We have to do what he said. Get to the White Angels. Make our lives count for something. He died for us.' He clenched his fists. 'We have to *be* someone.'

'We will,' she whispered.

They embraced. Then, when they were ready, they turned away from the river and headed off through the fields. As they ran, the boy heard a strange sound. It might have been the river, rippling over rocks, but he had a horrible feeling it was their father's killer, still laughing as they fled.

CHAPTER ONE

The city grumbled and lurched, almost hurling Niksar from the wall. He was perched on a broken lintel, looking down over one of Excelsis' most unwelcoming streets – a rain-lashed warren of lean-tos and hovels that looked discarded rather than built. The Veins had always been one of the poorest parts of the city and, during the tremors of recent months, several streets had caved in, opening craters and revealing the coiled horrors that wormed through the city's foundations.

Excelsis was besieged. Not just by tribes of greenskins but by the land itself. Walls groaned as grubs devoured the mortar. Sewers flooded as lizards spilled from drains. Slates tumbled from roofs, hurled by screeching, feathered rodents. Nothing was stable. The ground stirred, constantly, and every shattered flagstone revealed something repulsive. It was like being on the deck of a sinking ship. And this close to the city walls, the tremors were even more violent.

Niksar looked over at Ocella, hoping she was nearly finished. Ocella was only standing a dozen feet away but he could barely make her out through the mounds of rubbish and debris. He was sure it must be dawn by now, but the light clearly had better places to be. Niksar could sympathise.

As far as he could tell, the exchange was going as planned. The street was deserted and Ocella was talking eagerly to her contact, showing no signs of alarm. She had promised Niksar this would be an easy job. She was meeting a dockhand to buy information, tipped off by one of her pets, and as usual she wanted Niksar on hand in case there was a disagreement. Niksar almost wished there would be so he could shift into a different position, but it all seemed to be going swimmingly. The dockhand was a weaselly old salt Ocella had met on several previous occasions. He was hunched and wizened but Niksar guessed he was probably no older than thirty. Life beyond the city walls was brutal. It took its toll on everyone who sailed the Coast of Tusks.

The dockhand kept glancing up and down the rubble-strewn alley, peering through the rain, clearly nervous. Niksar could see why Ocella had asked him to hide himself up on the wall.

Ocella twitched and threw back her head. Then she laughed. Her laugh was peculiar, a kind of 'haw haw' that reminded Niksar of a coughing dog. The more he worked with her, the stranger he found her. He knew she was wealthy, but she wore filthy animal skins and a tattered cloak of greasy feathers. She looked like she had never slept under a roof. She wore a crooked feather headdress and had dozens of tiny bird skulls plaited into her hair that clattered as she moved. And she moved constantly. It was hard to be sure of her age, covered as she was in muck and feathers, but Niksar guessed she was around twenty years old. Despite that, she held herself like a palsied crone, always flinching, spitting and scratching. She leant constantly on a staff carved from a wing bone. The bone was taller than she was and as she talked it juddered in her hands, shaking rain from the beak at its head.

The meeting continued to be uneventful and Niksar's attention wandered. He had never mentioned it to Ocella, but the role of lookout did not really play to his strengths. He thought about the deal they were hoping to make tomorrow with an armourer over on Quadi Street, then his thoughts ranged into the distant future as he returned to his favourite fantasy. He pictured himself rising from the squalor he had endured for the first twenty years of his life. The city was on the verge of collapse, but his own fortunes had never been better. He was close, this time. Close to really becoming someone of importance – someone who did not have to scrape by to survive. So many of his schemes had come to nothing, but working with Ocella had gained him an incredible collection of artefacts. Strange as she was, he had to agree they were a good team. And, because Ocella thought everyone else in the city was trying to kill her, Niksar could not see their lucrative relationship ending soon. Visions of opulence and power filled his head.

His daydreams were interrupted by movement near his hand. A beetle wriggled from beneath a stone and pounced on a plump, slow-moving grub. The beetle locked its mandibles around its prey and swallowed it whole. Once it had finished eating, the beetle took a few steps, then paused, as though remembering something. Niksar leant closer, fascinated, knowing what would come next. Sure enough, the insect juddered and fell onto its side, twitching and trying to stand, then its carapace burst, revealing a mass of teeming larvae. Mature burrow grubs sacrificed themselves so that their young could start life with a hearty banquet. Niksar grimaced as the larvae devoured their host. There were so many it only took a few seconds.

The land is always hungry, thought Niksar, remembering the words of an old Thondian song.

A loud bang echoed down the alleyway, followed by the acrid

smell of gunpowder. Niksar cursed in surprise and leapt from the wall, drawing his sabre and pointing the blade into the rain.

Ocella stumbled away, and for a moment Niksar thought that his golden goose had been shot. Animals shifted under her furs and glossy eyes stared out at the drizzle, panicked by the noise. Then he noticed that the docker had a hole in his forehead. The man wheezed quietly and crumpled to the ground.

'Sigmar's teeth,' muttered Niksar. In all the times he had worked with Ocella, his presence had been a formality. She was crippled by paranoia but there had never actually been any need for a bodyguard.

The alleyway was empty, but the sound of the gunshot would have carried to all the nearby streets. Passers-by might come to investigate. Or even the city watch.

'Niksar!' cried Ocella, staggering away from the corpse, hysterical, waving her staff at the shadows.

'Damn!' he spat, rushing to her side and staring at the dead body.

Ocella looked everywhere but at him, her eyes rolling loosely in sunken sockets. 'Why weren't you looking?' She laughed, making the haw haw sound again. 'The lookout who doesn't look!' Her straining eyes made it clear that she did not really find the situation amusing. She reached under her furs, trying to calm her rodents and birds.

Footsteps echoed towards them and Niksar hauled Ocella behind a lean-to.

'It came from that direction,' he muttered, peering through the shadows. He tried to shove her further back but she gripped him like a terrified child.

'I told you,' she whispered. 'They're after me.'

'Who?' demanded Niksar, but before she could answer a figure strode into view, splashing through puddles, silhouetted by the dawn. 'It's a guardsman,' muttered Niksar as he saw a Freeguild uniform replete with a polished breastplate and a broad, feather-plumed hat.

'A soldier?' Ocella wiped drool-sodden hair away from her mouth and tucked it behind her ears. She tried to look less panicked but her mouth refused to stop twitching. 'Here? No one comes here. That's specifically why I chose here. Here is where people aren't. If you ask anyone about here, they will–'

'Niksar!' cried a familiar voice.

Ocella gasped and stared at Niksar. 'Did you sell me out?' Her eyes filled with tears. 'You? I thought I could trust you.'

Anger pounded in his temples. 'Of course I didn't sell you out. Just because I fight for glimmerings doesn't mean I'm a–'

'Niksar!' cried the soldier again, pointing a pistol his way and stepping close enough for Niksar to make out a face. It was a young woman in her mid-twenties with an angular, proud face and large, dark eyes. She was tall, broad-shouldered and powerful looking.

Niksar lowered his sword in shock. 'Zagora?'

'Who is it?' hissed Ocella, swaying and stumbling as she tried to look.

'My sister. She won't hurt…' Niksar's words trailed off as he looked at the docker's corpse. 'Zagora,' he demanded, striding out of his hiding place. 'What are you doing here?'

'Saving your life.' She was reloading her pistol as she strode past him towards the docker.

Niksar's rage was starting to be replaced by concern. His sister had forged an impressive career in one of the city's Freeguild regiments. She was risking a lot by coming here and associating with the likes of him and Ocella – never mind shooting dockworkers.

'What are you talking about?' he asked, following her over to the body.

Zagora dropped to one knee beside the corpse, avoiding the quickly spreading pool of blood, and ripped the man's doublet open. Then she stepped back, bumping into Niksar.

'What?' He pointed his sword at the corpse, expecting something to leap at him. His pulse quickened as he saw the tattoos that covered the dead man's chest.

'The Dark Gods.' Zagora made the sign of the hammer across her chest as she stared at the crudely inked symbols. She turned to Niksar, her expression neutral. 'What have you got yourself mixed up in, little brother?'

Niksar shook his head. 'That can't be right. I was just here as a–'

'There are purges happening today. Did you know? This morning. Right across the city.' She pointed at the dead man. 'Because of this. Because of him.'

There was a clattering sound behind them followed by the splash of running feet. Niksar whirled around to see Ocella weaving off through the darkness with surprising speed, her head held low. Niksar considered chasing her but his sister shook her head.

'You really don't want to be seen with that woman.' She nodded in the opposite direction, to the other end of the alley. 'This way.'

Niksar hesitated, looking at the crumpled corpse. 'My fee.'

'Do you realise how bad this is? Even for you?' Zagora waved at the crumbling buildings. 'The city is falling apart. This really is not the time to be seen with cultists. Can't you see what's on his chest? The man's a heretic. If you so much as touch him you'll be strung up outside the White Angels' tower, feeding gulls with your innards.'

Niksar stared at the corpse again. The tattoo was so repulsive it was hard to look at. The shape was simple enough – a fish-like swirl with a circle in its lower half, but it was the details that made his head hurt. The design was covered in intricately inked flames and scales that were morphing into screaming faces. The faces were partly human, but partly something else, something that Niksar could not quite explain but that filled him with inexplicable terror.

He nodded weakly and let his sister lead him away. As soon as they emerged onto one of the wider streets, Zagora stopped running and adopted a confident, nonchalant stride, ignoring the glances that came her way. She was dressed in the gold and red of the Phoenix Company, one of the regiments formed in the wake of the city's recent hardships. She cut an impressive figure and people scattered at her approach, ducking back through the doors of their crooked, tiny shacks.

'I had no idea.' Niksar's pulse was still hammering at the memory of the tattoos. People had been put in the gallows just for looking at symbols like that. 'How did you know? Ocella has always seemed like a reputable–'

Zagora glanced at him. 'Reputable?'

Niksar licked his lips. 'Reputable might not be the right word. But I'd never have dreamt she was involved in anything to do with… I can't believe she would knowingly involve herself with cultists. I didn't think–'

'You didn't think at all. You rarely do. Did you ask her where she met that docker?'

'There's not much point asking her anything, to be honest. She generally just–'

'You could end up swinging from a rope.' Zagora glanced around and lowered her voice. 'Me too, if anyone saw what happened back there. Or if that witch decides to talk.'

'She won't.' Niksar spoke with more confidence than he felt. 'And she's a fool, not a witch. And I'm the only person in the city she trusts. She won't want anything to happen to me.'

Zagora shook her head and continued down the street. 'I heard about this from someone in my regiment, Niksar. I dread to think who else has heard about it. That docker's linked to a cult called the Mirrored Blade. And then, when I heard he was selling things to someone called Ocella I remembered that *you* worked with someone called Ocella. Aren't you two partners?'

Niksar took a deep breath, trying to calm himself. 'Not partners, exactly. That's not the word I would use. I'm just her muscle, really.' Niksar was slender and wiry, but he was good with a sword and he had grown up on the streets, so what he lacked in bulk, he more than made up for in speed and nerve. 'Look,' he said, 'there's no real harm done. Thanks to you. You've got me out of a mess, Zagora. I won't forget it.'

They turned onto one of the city's main thoroughfares leading towards a large market square. The city was as unsteady as Ocella, but life continued. Lots of the traders were already setting up whalebone awnings and unloading their wares, attracting a crowd of peevish-sounding gulls that battled against the rain.

'You might not be out of the mess yet,' said Zagora. 'This morning's purges are being organised by witch hunters.'

'The Order?' Niksar stumbled to a halt.

Zagora waved him on. 'We need to put some distance between us and that body.'

Niksar shook his head as he stumbled across the square. The Order of Azyr were hard-line zealots, killers who hunted down anyone considered a threat to the Sigmarite faith. Their methods of extracting information were famously inventive and as the assaults on the city grew worse, the fanatics gained even more power, striking without censure at anyone they deemed suspect.

'And you need to stay away from that woman,' said Zagora.

They left the square and hurried through the growing light to the edge of the Veins. Finally, after walking in silence for half an hour, they left the slum stacks behind and headed out into the wider, cleaner streets of the Temple Quarter with its grand stormstone facades. The buildings here were sturdy and well-made, and they were still mostly intact. Even here, though, there were cracks in the road that revealed ominous, sinuous shapes beneath. As they wound higher, up through the levels of the city, they began to catch glimpses of the bay and the city's hulking bastion walls, lined with garrisons and siege cannons. Beyond the rain-whipped harbour and the bobbing masts of the ships, Niksar saw the Consecralium: the forbidding keep of the White Angels. It was probably the city's last hope of survival. But it might also be his final resting place if this ever got out.

Zagora saw his troubled glance and paused. They both leant against a wall to catch their breath.

'Look,' she said. 'There's so much going on at the moment that your idiocy will probably go overlooked. You've promised me you'll have nothing more to do with her. And I killed the dockhand. So he's not likely to talk. And I'm sure you weren't so stupid as to be seen in Ocella's company. As long as there's nothing linking you to either of them the Order won't come looking for you.'

Niksar frowned.

She studied him. '*Is* there something linking you to them?'

He looked at the Consecralium again, imagining the White Angels spilling from its depths, nailing the faithless to walls. 'There... Well... Possibly.'

She closed her eyes and let her head fall back against the wall.

'Ocella didn't usually pay me with glimmerings,' he said, referring to the prophetic stones used as currency in Excelsis. 'We had an arrangement. I kept her safe and then we shared the objects she... procured.'

Zagora looked amused. 'You kept her safe?'

'She's still alive.'

She laughed. 'How you've made a career as a hired sword is

beyond me. I saw you up on that wall. You were looking off into nowhere when I shot the docker. Lost in a daydream. Like always.'

'I'm not the dreamer.'

She ignored the jibe. 'Did you keep all the "objects" Ocella gave you?'

'Why wouldn't I? I knew she was odd but I had no idea she was a cultist.'

'I don't know if she's a cultist. But she certainly doesn't worry about whose company she keeps. I'll be amazed if she survives the day. This is not the time to be involved with dubious societies. Did you keep *everything* she gave you?'

'Yes. My plan was to sell them as a collection. I need to raise a lot of glimmerings, you see. I have a problem with–'

Zagora held up a hand. 'One problem's enough for now. I can imagine how many other disasters you're working on.' She looked out at the harbour and the churning clouds. 'Everything might still be fine. If you'd sold any of those things people would be talking about them. But if you've still got them stashed away, no one knows you have them. You have to get back to your rooms. Destroy everything that connects you to Ocella. What are we talking about? A couple of weapons? Some jewellery?'

Niksar massaged his temples, avoiding her gaze. 'It might be easier if I show you.'

'I don't want to see them. Just get rid of them. And quickly. If the witch hunters find you in possession of that stuff, Sigmar help both of us.'

'I can't just throw it all away. I need to sell those things, Zagora. You don't understand how much trouble I'll be in if I don't.'

She waved at the distant fortress overlooking the bay, and the bodies hung in cages at its walls. 'More trouble than being taken to the Knights Excelsior?'

Niksar slumped against the wall. 'I'm dead.'

She stood and hauled him to his feet. 'If you were, my life would be so much easier.'

'What *is* all this stuff?' gasped Zagora.

They were standing in Niksar's crowded lodgings on Sortilege Street, right on the outskirts of the Trade Quarter. It was a single room, ten foot by ten, and Niksar's furniture consisted of three items: a bunk, a wardrobe and a crooked table littered with half-empty wine bottles and dirty crockery. Next to his bunk was a pile of armour, sacks, bones, weapons, cases and books that he had just emptied from the wardrobe.

Zagora shook her head. 'This didn't all come from that witch, surely?'

Niksar nodded. Then he headed over to the table, poured two cups of wine and offered one to Zagora.

She shook her head. 'The day's barely started.'

'That's what I'm worried about.' He emptied one of the cups into the other and downed the contents. 'No,' he said, wiping his beard on his sleeve. 'Not all of this came from her.' He winced. 'Damned if I can remember which things didn't, though.'

Zagora tapped the pile of objects with her boot, as though expecting it to move. 'What were you thinking? Even I can see how dangerous these things are. Look at those markings. None of them are Sigmarite. These things were made by people who worship other gods, Niksar. The *wrong* gods. And you kept them all here, in your wardrobe? What were you going to do with it all?'

He shrugged. 'Different things.' As he studied his collection, he forgot about his desperate situation and remembered the various plans he had been working on. He nodded to one of the bottles. 'That oil can turn *anything* into amber bone.'

'Then why are you living in this hovel?'

'I don't know the correct method yet. But Ocella has a contact on Harbinger Street. He promised her he knows what to do. She has these creatures in her furs that tell her things. We just need to get our hands on a few–'

'And that?' interrupted Zagora, pointing to a mouldering, severed hoof.

Niksar grinned. 'Saltim's Talisman. A devotee of Saltim would give me anything for it.'

'Have you ever *met* a devotee of Saltim?'

'No, not exactly, but I once spoke to a man who–'

'You're deluded. You always have been. Don't you see? You're obsessed with getting rich and you're the poorest person I know. These things are mostly junk, brother.'

'You don't understand, Zagora. It doesn't really matter what these things are. They were just a means to an end. We were going to use them to acquire something *really* special. Something that would have changed everything. Ocella was talking to that dockhand about an artefact called an aetheric alkahest. A kind of alchemical talisman that would enable us to–'

'I don't want to hear it. Listen to yourself. You sound like a lunatic. Don't you see? All these talismans and *alkahests* will just land you in trouble. Like all your other ventures. They're the reason you're in this mess.'

Niksar wanted to argue but the thought of the witch hunters stilled his tongue.

'We have to shift all of it,' said Zagora. 'And quickly.'

Niksar sat heavily on the bunk. 'It's not that easy. I have debts, Zagora. Debts you can't imagine. To people you don't *want* to imagine. Some of this stuff was very expensive. If I don't sell it I'm ruined. Worse than ruined. Getting my hands on the alkahest was going to be my salvation.'

She waved at his grimy amberglass window and the streets outside. 'It's happening today, Niksar. The Order are making their move this morning. Half my regiment have been talking about it. The Grand Conclave say these tremors are because of Chaos cults – heretics working somewhere in the city. They've given the witch hunters orders to arrest anyone who even looks suspicious. What if they come here and see all this? Even I feel like putting you on a pyre.'

'What if they don't come here?'

'Ocella knew your name. I'm guessing she also knew where you lived. And there's a dead cultist lying in an alley waiting to be discovered.'

Niksar was always careful but there was no way he could guarantee his name would never come up. He looked at the pile of ephemera Ocella had given him. It was valuable stuff. Ocella seemed uninterested in most of the objects she procured and she had passed things on to him that far exceeded his normal fee. There were furs from the Thunderscorn Peaks, ivory from the coast of Kald, a feathered headdress from the Myassa Basin similar to the one Ocella wore. And there were weapons of such exotic design he could not even place their origin. This was the haul that would have made him. He had so many plans. This was going to be his chance to clear all his debts and start again.

His sister sat next to him. 'Look, I was being unfair earlier. I know how good you are with that sword.' She tapped her polished breastplate. 'Why don't you join the Phoenix Company? Captain Tyndaris is always on the lookout for good men.' She raised an eyebrow. 'We could try to convince him you are one.'

Niksar shook his head. 'Everything has always gone so well for you. You always come out clean and smiling. How? How do you do it?'

She nodded at the objects next to his bed. 'By not chasing wealth, Niksar, that's how. It's a race you can't win. I serve the city. I serve the God-King. And I let the rest go.'

Niksar wanted to mock her but he could not bring himself to. He knew her better than he knew anyone and, unlike most people, she actually meant what she said. She just wanted to do good. To lead a worthy life. Her worldview really was that simple. It was impressive and maddening at the same time.

'I'm in hock to every moneylender in the city,' he muttered. 'If I don't sell this stuff they'll kill me just as surely as the Order.' He reached for the wine bottle but Zagora moved it out of reach.

Niksar was about to argue when a scream echoed across the rooftops. Even the rain could not dampen the shrill, awful nature of the sound.

Niksar wandered over to the window and wiped some of the muck from the amberglass. There was another scream and the sound of gunfire, followed by rattling swords and the crash of breaking wood.

Zagora joined him at the window as flames blossomed across the Veins, battling against the rain, no more than half a mile from Niksar's lodgings. Birds erupted from rooftops and dogs started howling. Some of the flames bobbed away from the building and Niksar realised they were torches; torches in the shape of twin-tailed comets. As the light banked and flashed he caught glimpses of screeds nailed to boards and wooden, hammer-wielding effigies.

'Zealots,' he whispered.

Zagora nodded. 'They're already out looking. Maybe your docker friend was being watched.'

'He wasn't my friend.'

Screams rang out from another direction and flames billowed from another cluster of slums. The sounds of fighting echoed through the early morning stillness.

'We have to move fast.' Zagora turned back to the pile of objects. 'You can't be found with these things.'

Niksar felt like he was being crushed. His breath came in gasps.

But he nodded, grabbed a sack and began shoving things into it. Then he paused and looked around. 'Perhaps we could just set the place on fire? People would blame it on the zealots.'

Zagora glared at him. 'Think how many rooms are crammed into this building. And how close it is to the other side of the street. The fire wouldn't stay within these four walls. It would spread. People would die. It would be our fault. And we're *not* zealots.'

'I sometimes wish I was,' muttered Niksar, stuffing things into the sack. Zagora grabbed another bag, and within a few minutes they had almost cleared the floor.

A chorus of shouts came up through the floorboards, followed by the sound of splintering wood.

Niksar and Zagora froze, staring at each other. They ran back to the window and saw filthy, rag-wearing figures filing through the streets, carrying clubs and brands. Some were already outside the building and were hammering on doors. There was a witch hunter waving them on, carrying a pistol and wearing a tall, peaked hat.

'They have your name,' whispered Zagora. 'They must. Why else would they have come straight here? It can't be a coincidence.'

'Damn it,' muttered Niksar. 'I really am going to have to destroy everything.' Part of him had been hoping that his sister might still be wrong.

Zagora gripped his arm. 'We can't just march down the stairs with all this. Is there another way out?'

Niksar shook his head, then looked at the window. 'Maybe. There are bits of old storm-engine stuck on the walls. Old Collegiate machines. They're not in use any more but they're pretty sturdy. We might be able to climb up them.'

Zagora looked at the two large sacks they had filled. 'With those?'

He frowned. Then the sounds of fighting and yelling grew louder as people rushed into the lower levels of the building. 'It's that or the noose. Or worse...'

They quickly threw the remaining objects in the sacks and looked around the room.

'Are you sure this is everything?' Zagora nodded at some rubbish heaped under the table. 'What about in there?'

'Nothing,' replied Niksar. Then he cursed. 'Wait. There is something.' He lifted the bed onto two legs and nodded at the floor underneath. 'There. There's a loose board. There's a glimmering under it. She rarely paid me with augur stones but she said this one was special.'

Zagora crept past him and lifted the board but when she looked at the polished stone she hesitated, staring at it.

'Quick!' snapped Niksar.

Zagora muttered something, reaching out for the stone, but the moment she touched it her body jolted as though she had been kicked. She cried out in surprise.

'What is it?' demanded Niksar, trying to bend down and hold up the bed at the same time. 'What are you doing?'

His sister seemed unable to reply, muttering and gasping as though she were in pain. Then, with another incoherent cry, she dropped to the floor and curled up into a tight ball, hugging the stone to her chest.

'Zagora?' Niksar tried to see her face but it was turned away from him. 'What in the name of Sigmar are you doing?'

She mumbled something. Her voice sounded odd, more growl than speech. Then she started to shiver.

'What are you playing at?' Niksar held the bed with one arm as he dropped to his knee and reached for her. His hand was inches from her shoulder when he snatched it back in alarm. There was light coming from under her cuirass, splitting the gloom of his chamber with thin, white lines, gilding the dust motes. He shoved her over onto her back. Her eyes were wide and rolled back. Her mouth opened and closed silently.

There was a bang from the hallway outside and voices approached, shouting and cursing. A woman screamed. Swords clattered.

'They're here!' whispered Niksar, dragging his sister from under the bed and trying to hold her still. She stared past him into the dancing lights, convulsing and groaning. Niksar had never seen such a violent reaction to a glimmering. Augur stones induced witch-sight, showing miraculous glimpses of the future, but that usually amounted to little more than a vague premonition of rain, or a warning about a card game. He had never known one to light someone up. Zagora's skin was glowing. She looked like one of the aetheric lanterns made by the Collegiate Arcanum. It was cool in the room but her face was beaded with sweat.

Footsteps hammered down the corridor outside and the sounds of fighting increased. Niksar heard breathy chanting and a deep voice bellowed through the door.

'Open up! Now! For the most holy Order of Azyr!' Embers billowed through the wood as someone kicked the other side.

Niksar filled a cup of wine and hurled it in Zagora's face. She coughed and finally focused on him.

'I saw it,' she whispered, gripping his arm.

'Saw what?'

'Gnorl's Feast.' She squeezed his arm, her eyes bright. 'I was there. On the Faithful Tor.'

Niksar felt as though there was a stranger in the room with him. His sister seemed transformed. Or possessed.

'Tor?' he said. 'What are you…?' But before he could finish, more embers billowed around the door as another kick jarred its frame. 'We have to go.' He hauled Zagora to her feet. 'Can you walk?'

Her eyes clouded and she looked confused. She seemed to have forgotten who he was.

'Zagora!' he snapped, nodding to the door. 'The Order of Azyr. Remember?'

She nodded. Then shook her head, staring at him, clearly confused. 'What just happened?'

'You're asking me?' He handed her a sack and then led her over to the window. He wrenched the latch back and the hinges screeched as he pushed the window open. 'Let's talk about it later,' he said, helping her out. He glanced back at the buckling door. 'If we can.'

CHAPTER TWO

Niksar held his breath as he edged along the tangle of brass pipes outside his window, trying to ignore the thirty-foot drop to the cobbled street. They struggled over cracked spheres and bent lightning conductors and finally emerged onto the roof. The tiles were glistening with rainwater and Niksar muttered curses as he helped Zagora to the ridge, slipping and lurching as he went. They were so high he could see all the way back down to the narrow, tangled streets of the Veins, where Zagora had shot the dockhand.

Down below, they heard the clatter of Niksar's door collapsing and a clamour of voices.

'What just happened?' he said. 'What were you doing with that stone? Did it hurt you? And what was all that talk about a tor?'

Zagora was lying on her back, looking through the rain at the churning clouds. She shook her head, frowning. 'I saw something. I… It's hard to explain. I–'

There was a cry from below as the zealots reached the window and leant out.

'Give me your gun,' said Niksar.

Zagora still looked dazed and she handed her pistol over without a word.

Niksar slid back down to the eaves, shielding the firing mechanism from the rain. When he reached the tangle of brass, he found a holding bracket and fired the pistol at it. Then he lay back and kicked the pipes. The metal screamed and leant out drunkenly into the banking rain.

Niksar crawled back up to his sister, who was still staring up at the clouds.

'That should buy us some time,' he said, hauling her up onto her feet and handing the pistol back. 'They won't risk climbing up after us now I've broken the pipes from the wall. If they want to get on the roof they'll have to go all the way to Hallowstar Avenue.'

Zagora nodded but he could tell she was only half listening. He wanted to ask her what had happened to her when she touched the glimmering but they had to keep moving.

'The glimmering!' he said. 'It's still down there!'

She shook her head and patted a pouch at her belt.

Niksar nodded and began leading her slowly across the rain-slick tiles, weaving around the chimneystacks and making for the walls of a temple that abutted the building. They reached the temple's tower and dropped onto the battlements. The rain was coming down hard now but Niksar could see well enough to know there were no guards on the wall. He led Zagora around the battlements, wincing under the weight of the sack. There were steps leading down to street level but he could still hear the zealots not far behind, howling and singing as they hammered doors and tried to light fires in the rain.

'This way,' he said, leading Zagora up onto the roof of another building. They crossed a dozen roofs, edging ever closer to the harbour until, when Niksar could no longer hear the sound of zealots, he finally led them back down to the street.

They were near the Dharroth fish market, not far from the docks. Niksar had not been this close to the sea wall in months. He tried to avoid the outskirts of the city. The entire continent seemed bent on devouring the settlement Sigmar had built on its eastern coast. And the streets near the bastion walls were the most hazardous. Niksar halted at the top of a steep hill that afforded a clear, uninterrupted view of the docks. The rain was so heavy it had erased the boundary between sea and sky, creating a single, lead-grey shimmer. Most of the vessels in the harbour were moored but the wolf-ships of the Scourge Privateers were still cutting through the waves, patrolling endlessly for signs of attack.

Looming over the storm, menacing and immobile, was a stone colossus. The Spear of Mallus was a mountain-high obelisk jutting up from the sea and looking down over the harbour. Legends claimed it was a fragment of Sigmar's homeland, cast down from the sky when the God-King fell to the realms. Niksar did not believe everything priests said, but the rock was the source of countless prophecies. It was the great wonder of the realm and it drew thousands of people to the city. He stared at the shaft of storm-lashed blackness and found it easy to imagine it came from another world. Nearer to where he was standing, he could see a crowd gathering under a forest of banners. They were no more than hazy shapes in the rain but he guessed from the size of the gathering that it was one of the crusades that set off almost daily from the city, heading out into the madness of Ghur with little, if any, hope of ever returning.

'What are we doing here?' said Zagora, seeming to emerge from her stupor. She shook her head. 'I feel so strange. I remember reaching for the glimmering and then...' She frowned. 'I've never felt anything like it.' She looked around. 'What are we doing here?'

she repeated. 'The harbour isn't safe. You're not looking to board a ship, are you?'

'Board a ship? Of course not. Do you think I'd be stupid enough to leave Excelsis?' He nodded to a wharf at the bottom of the street. 'There's no quick way to destroy this stuff so I'm going to make an offering to Ozol.'

Zagora winced at the mention of the old, Thondian deity. 'Sigmar is the one true god.'

Niksar laughed, amused by his sister's piety. Then he remembered what a mess he was in and the laughter dried in his throat. He whispered a prayer to Sigmar and staggered on down the road.

There were a few dockers on the wharf when they got there, unloading cargo and wheeling it to the dockside warehouses. None of them were keen to be out in the miserable weather, however, and they paid no attention to Niksar and Zagora as they hefted the sacks to a gloomy spot between the hulls of two duardin steamships. A towering, lichen-covered statue of Sigmar looked down over the scene with a disapproving scowl, his hammer raised to the storm.

Niksar opened the sack and looked at the contents. 'This would have worked,' he muttered. 'I could have paid them all off. I could have moved out of that hovel and got myself somewhere decent to live. A place I wouldn't have been so ashamed of. This was going to be the start of my new life.'

Zagora still looked dazed by what had happened when she touched the glimmering, but she noticed the pain in Niksar's voice and managed to focus her attention on him.

'There's always another chance, brother.'

He kicked the sack and sent it tumbling into the waves. 'For you, maybe.'

The weapons and relics vanished immediately and Zagora followed Niksar's lead, hurling her bag out into the storm.

Niksar stood there in silence with brine stinging his face and the cold seeping through his jacket, then he turned to his sister. 'You still have the glimmering. That's the last thing linking me to Ocella.'

Zagora looked through the sea spray at the statue of Sigmar. She had the same peculiar look in her eyes that he'd seen when she first touched the glimmering.

'What is it?' he said. 'What happened when you touched it?'

'I saw something.'

He wanted to laugh but she was looking at the statue with such reverence that he could not bring himself to. 'What?'

'When I touched the augur stone, I saw something. I don't mean just like a normal glimmering. I mean...' She looked up at the statue's face. 'I felt someone watching me. I heard a voice.'

Niksar did laugh this time. 'What are you talking about?'

She shook her head. Niksar had never seen his sister like this. She was usually so sure of herself.

'It means something.'

'It means something?' Niksar shook his head. 'Everything in those bags meant something but we just threw it all in the sea. What are you saying? That you want to keep the stone?'

She frowned. 'There's something about that glimmering. As soon as I saw it I felt something. It seems familiar. As though it used to be mine. Or was meant to be mine. I think it came to me for a reason.'

'*Came* to you? What are you talking about? Did you hit your head when you were crawling under my bed? The stone didn't come to you at all. If it came to anyone it came to me. And I told you it was special right before you told me to ditch everything.'

Her voice regained its usual, hard edge. 'The Prophesiers' Guild need to see it. I saw something, Niksar. A place. And a moment. It was important.'

'You said I had to lose everything that linked me to Ocella. Now you're suggesting we take her stone to the Prophesiers' Guild. They'd clap us in irons and hand us straight over to the White Angels.'

'I don't think so. A glimmering is a glimmering. There are thousands of them in the city. This one is unmarked. There's nothing linking it to Ocella.'

'But why take the risk? Just because you saw something? That's what glimmerings do – they show people things. Half the time they show things that aren't even true. You know that. What's so special about this one?'

'I could feel a presence, Niksar, a soul. Something noble and terrible. Like the fury of a storm mixed with wisdom more profound than...' She shook her head. 'I think it was Sigmar. I think the God-King was showing me something. Some*where*. A holy place. He spoke to me. It's a sign. We can't just throw it in the sea.'

Niksar tugged at his beard. 'It's a special stone?'

She nodded.

'The kind the Prophesiers' Guild would place a high value on?'

'Yes.'

'And I'm broke. With debts that will get my skull ventilated. If that thing's valuable, and you think the prophesiers will want it, they can pay for it.'

She gave him a disappointed frown. 'You have a knack for making things grubby, Niksar.'

He gave her an elaborate bow.

Zagora looked up the cobbled street behind them. 'Very well. Let's try Prophesier Calabis on Vandun Street. He won't ask any awkward questions.' She gave Niksar a warning glance as she headed off through the rain. 'Try not to have any more ideas in the meantime.'

CHAPTER THREE

'Pedal,' yawned Prophesier Calabis as Niksar and Zagora watched him from across the street. He was a heavyset lump with small, thick spectacles perched on a dainty nose and a neatly plaited beard that was dwarfed by his chins. He was dressed in a rune-stitched kaftan and he was slumped in a claw-footed chair that was riveted to the insides of his machine. The machine was like something that would power a duardin ship – a brass sphere the size of a small house covered in rusty pipes, painted boards and wheezing bellows. There was an old, rusting plate screwed to the front with letters that must once have proclaimed: ORACULAR EVALUATIONS UNDERTAKEN HERE. The recent tremors had shaken some of the letters free and the sign now gave an ominous warning: LARVAL UNDER HERE.

Calabis repeated his command in the same lethargic drawl and Niksar saw that he was addressing a sallow-faced youth who was also dressed in a gold-stitched kaftan. The boy was seated at the side of the machine on a unicycle that was attached to the bellows.

When Calabis spoke, the boy pedalled harder, the bellows creaked and the machine let out a droning sound similar to Calabis' voice. There was a circle of amberglass domes around the machine's circumference and, as the bellows worked, the domes flashed with inner fire, flickering cheerfully in the rain.

It had taken nearly an hour to reach Vandun Street and the city was starting to wake up. Hawkers and pilgrims were hurrying past and there was already a queue at Calabis' machine.

'Wait,' said Niksar, grabbing Zagora's arm as she stepped out onto the street from beneath the porch where they were sheltering. 'What if Calabis has heard about me?'

'You're not a wanted man, Niksar. The Order haven't been sticking posters up. Not yet, at least. I think you're safe to cross a street.'

'They just kicked my door down. I'd say that makes me a wanted man.'

She shook her head. 'How have you got yourself into this mess?'

'Is it my fault that half the people in this city think it's fine to associate with heretics?'

'Wait here while I hand the stone over.'

'While you *sell* the stone,' he reminded her.

She raised an eyebrow and went to join the back of the queue.

'Weather prediction,' droned Calabis, gazing off into the middle distance.

The old woman at the front of the queue nodded and tried to hand him some pebbles.

Calabis shook his head without looking at her and gestured to a raw-boned wretch seated beside his chair. It was a scribe dressed in similar robes to Calabis but, where Calabis had a shiny, bald pate, his scribe had a mass of black hair that teetered on his head like a sketch of a tornado.

The scribe gave the old woman a disapproving look. Then he very slowly took a sheet of paper from a pile on his desk and wrote on it with a quill. Once he was done, he rolled the paper up and closed it with a gobbet of wax. The woman tried to hand him her stones but he gave her another annoyed look as he opened a ledger and began writing in it. Several minutes passed before he finally took the woman's pebbles, counted them out with agonising slowness, wrote out a receipt and let her leave.

Niksar watched the process with growing despair. 'This could take weeks.'

The next person in the queue was a guardsman from the Bronze Claws regiment. He dropped a glimmering into the copper tray fixed to the front of the machine.

'Pedal,' said Calabis with a sigh, and the boy's legs dragged another moan from the bellows. As the lights flickered Calabis closed his eyes and placed his hand over the stone. His hand was gloved and the glove was connected to the workings of the machine by a metal-clad pipe. Light flickered under the prophesier's palm.

'Weather prediction,' muttered Calabis and the scribe took out another sheet and began dragging his quill across it. This painstaking process was repeated several times, with the same result, until, after nearly an hour had passed, Zagora finally reached the front of the queue and dropped her glimmering into the tray, being careful not to touch it as it dropped from her pouch and clattered onto the metal.

Niksar was too intrigued to remain under the porch and edged out into the rain, standing close enough to watch.

'Pedal,' said Calabis and, as the machine's lights flickered, he held his hand out over the stone.

Nothing happened.

'Fake,' said Calabis, waving for the next person to approach.

Zagora stayed where she was. 'It's not a fake.'

Calabis stared blankly at her.

'It's not a fake,' she insisted. 'Try again.'

Calabis continued staring for an awkward amount of time, then finally sighed and nodded at the boy to pedal again.

The bellows wheezed. Again, there was no light under his palm.

'Fake,' he said, giving Zagora a pointed look.

She hissed in annoyance and reached out to snatch the stone. The moment her fingers touched it the machine gave a loud cough and juddered into life. The boy cried out as the pedals hurled his legs forward. The device shone beams across the street.

The colour drained from Calabis' face as his hand hovered over the stone, bathed in cold fire. 'Let go!' he said, staring at Zagora, and she snatched her hand back. The bellows folded and the lights died. The boy dropped from the unicycle and landed in a puddle.

Calabis stood up. 'What did you do?'

She shook her head.

Calabis sat down heavily, breathing quickly. 'A power surge?' He twisted his corpulent bulk, turning to look back at the walls of his house. The pipes from his machine were linked to older-looking storm engines that hung down over his roof. They were mostly broken and rusted but steam had started billowing from them. He frowned at Zagora. 'Back away.' He nodded at the youth in the puddle. 'I'm not paying you to sleep.'

The boy looked at the unicycle like it might eat him, but he stood, wiped the mud from his face and climbed back into the saddle.

'Stay back,' muttered Calabis, glaring at Zagora as the boy started pedalling. Just as before, nothing happened. A small crowd had gathered but Calabis did not seem to notice. He tugged at his tiny beard and studied Zagora. 'What did you see, when you touched the stone?'

'Many things. Your superiors need to know.'

He raised an eyebrow. 'My superiors?' He looked at the stone, still lying in the tray. Even now, after such a dramatic scene, he did not seem entirely awake. 'Touch it again,' he said.

Niksar hissed a warning but Zagora ignored him, stepped forward and slapped her hand down.

The machine jerked into motion, moving even more violently than before. Brass hoops turned like the rings of a giant armillary sphere and the boy's legs pounded furiously. The bellows groaned and the lights blazed so brightly people backed away, shielding their eyes.

Calabis' hand was near the stone and arcs of energy flickered between his fingers and the glimmering. His eyes strained and sweat glistened on his chins. 'Stop!' he said, staring at Zagora. 'Enough! Stop it!'

She kept her hand where it was, looking up in wonder at the light that was knifing through the machine's riveted plates.

'Let go!' muttered Niksar, but there was no way his sister could have heard. The machine was making a terrible din. Steam hissed from the frame and the whole structure shook so violently that Niksar took a few steps backwards.

'Let go, damn you!' said Calabis and finally Zagora did as asked, taking her hand from the stone and backing away. The machine's convulsions died away, along with the light. The youth toppled back into the mud.

Calabis took his hand from the glove, hefted himself out of his seat and climbed out of the machine, staring at it with the same mixture of fear and confusion as everyone else in the street. 'Take it out,' he muttered, nodding to the stone.

Zagora took the stone and dropped it back into the pouch at her belt. 'It's not a fake,' she said, stepping towards him.

Calabis looked her up and down, taking in her guardsman uniform. 'Where did you get it?'

Niksar was about to speak up but Zagora allayed his fears. 'No idea,' she said. 'It was mixed in with all the others.'

Calabis massaged his face. Then he gestured to the boy, who was still sitting in the mud staring at the machine. 'Fetch my carriage. Tell Pitara I won't be here for lunch.' Then he turned to the scribe with the wild hair. 'Record this in *both* ledgers. And in my diary. Then shut up shop for the morning.'

He gave Zagora another suspicious look.

'We're going to the Guildhouse.'

CHAPTER FOUR

The city's central square was lined with imposing, colonnaded facades but the headquarters of the Prophesiers' Guild outshone them all. The guild was responsible for evaluating every piece of prophecy mined from the Spear of Mallus and, as a result, it was one of the most powerful organisations in Excelsis.

Prophesier Calabis straightened his glasses and wiped mud from his robes as he climbed the steps to the front entrance. It was a futile effort – his kaftan was drenched and filthy – but he fussed at his robes all the same.

'Can you do something with yourselves?' he said to Zagora and Niksar, grimacing at their sodden clothes. To Niksar's relief, Calabis had not asked who he was when he climbed into the carriage next to Zagora, seeming too preoccupied to notice him. Niksar and Zagora brushed themselves down but it was pointless. The rain was hammering down now and they both looked like they had crawled from the sea.

Calabis frowned at them, then shook his head and led them

on up the steps, through huge double doors and into the auction hall.

The place was already busy. People were dashing back and forth between trading counters and machines designed to assess the divinatory qualities of glimmerings. There were dozens of prophesiers and scribes in the crowd, all dressed in the same robes as Calabis, but he marched past them, looking for someone in particular.

'We just need to sell the thing and go,' whispered Niksar, leaning close to his sister as they fought through the crowd. 'Remember what's happening outside. I need to get my head down somewhere.'

She nodded. 'We can go once I'm sure the stone is in the correct hands. Then we'll find somewhere for you to hide.'

Niksar looked at the bizarre collection of assaying machines that surrounded them. Some were similar to Calabis', although in much better repair, but others were of a completely different design. He saw one that consisted of a row of bone amber cups attached to a wooden frame that jolted and rattled each time a stone was placed in one of the containers. Others were steam engines that hissed and grumbled like hungry animals. All were surrounded by huddles of inky scribes, recording every measurement on scrolls and ledgers. Watching the machines reminded Niksar of something.

'Why did Calabis say the glimmering was a fake? Why didn't the lights on his machine come on?'

'They did, when I touched the stone.'

'But not when he touched it. All the others he examined responded to his mechanical glove.'

She shrugged and was about to reply when Calabis called out.

'Neco!' He barged his way through a group of scribes and headed for a prophesier who was standing at one of the assaying machines.

The woman looked up at the sound of Calabis' voice. She was

less than five feet tall and almost as stocky as Calabis but her face was open and cheerful where his was harsh. She threw up her arms at the sight of Calabis and, as they met, she reached up to embrace him.

'Prophesier Calabis. Spear be praised! I haven't seen you for months.'

He looked uncomfortable and glanced around at the crowds, replying in gruff tones, 'I have something, Neco.' He nodded to the pouch at Zagora's belt. 'An augur stone. But it's not like any I've seen before.' He stooped next to her and whispered something in her ear.

She continued squeezing his arms and smiling. 'Marvellous.' She looked at Zagora and Niksar. 'And who owns it?'

Calabis nodded at Zagora, giving her a wary look.

'I see.' Neco looked at Calabis. 'And you've explained that a commission will be required if we're going to present this to the ministers of the Convocation and the Lords Obscurantist?'

'A commission?' snapped Niksar. 'To show it to your superiors?'

Neco's smile grew rigid. 'I don't believe I caught your name.'

Zagora cast him a warning glance.

'It doesn't matter who I am. I just don't want you taking advantage of Zagora.'

Calabis and Neco exchanged glances. 'What *is* your name?' asked Calabis.

'Brinonnus,' replied Niksar after a hesitation that made it clear he was lying. He felt like taking the glimmering away from such obvious crooks but there was nowhere else to go: only the Prophesiers' Guild was licenced to value glimmerings.

Neco turned her smile on Zagora. 'Twenty per cent is the standard charge for assessing stones of unusual potency.' She held out her hand. 'If you're happy with the terms I'd be glad to take your stone now.'

'No,' said Calabis, tugging anxiously at his beard. 'She'll have to go with you.'

Neco stopped smiling. 'To the Convocation?'

Calabis shrugged and shuffled his feet. 'The stone doesn't respond to aetheric stimulus unless she's holding it.'

Neco stared at Zagora. 'Is that so?'

She nodded. 'Besides, I would rather hand the stone over to someone in a position of authority.'

Neco frowned. 'Can you show me?'

Calabis shook his head. 'The glimmering nearly destroyed my assaying engine. She's right. It would be wisest to take her up to the Convocation.'

Neco looked puzzled, then she shrugged and the broad smile returned to her face. 'Fine. The Convocation is always keen to hear of stones like this. They will make time to see us.' She nodded to a subordinate, who stepped behind her machine. 'Make a record of this conversation and make copies for Cyropolis and Kibris.'

Once the scribe had taken out some papers and begun writing, Neco nodded and sauntered off across the hall. Calabis and Zagora went with her, but when Niksar tried to follow, Neco paused and looked up at him with a frown.

'Your presence will not be required…' She rolled his name across her tongue, making it clear she knew he had lied. 'Brinonnus.'

Niksar was about to argue but Zagora gave him a warning glance.

'How long will this take?' she asked Neco.

The prophesier shrugged. 'An hour. Maybe two. Depends how busy they are. We will have to make sure the records are complete.'

Zagora nodded and turned to Niksar. 'Look for me at the main doors in an hour or so.'

Before Niksar could say anything else they led his sister away in a flurry of robes, calling out for more scribes as they vanished into the crowd.

A feeling of dread washed over Niksar. He looked around at the prophesiers and traders. They were all huddled together, whispering and smiling, and he had the sudden sense that they were all talking about him. About his connection to Ocella. About the objects he threw in the dock. He backed away, then turned and rushed across the hall, making for the doors, suddenly keen to be back outside.

He stumbled down the steps towards the square. The rain was still hammering down so he found a spot under the portico of a temple and pulled his hood low over his face. Once he had hidden his sword under his cloak he was sure he was dirty and bedraggled enough to blend in with the beggars. As the minutes wore on he grew more uneasy. Why had he listened to Zagora? Why had he let her take the glimmering into the Guildhouse? The Order were looking for him. And they would be looking for anything linking him to Ocella and the docker. And now Zagora had taken the glimmering to city officials and announced that it was unique. It was dangerous.

He stamped his foot on the steps, horribly energised. He tried to distract himself by looking at all the strange sights of the square. It was the central meeting point of the city and, as on every other day, it was crammed with exotically attired travellers, soldiers from distant outposts and pilgrims come to join one of the crusades. Along with all the humans, duardin and aelves milling across the flagstones, there was a noisy menagerie of animals. Sigmar had carved Excelsis from the wilds of Thondia, but the wildness remained – not conquered, only held at bay. Creatures crawled, slithered and flew into the city constantly. Some were enormous predators that butchered and smashed until they were driven back into the sea, but others had learned to live alongside the citizens of Excelsis, hunting for scraps or being domesticated for use as beasts of burden.

As Niksar sat twitching on the temple steps a gall tusk stomped by, its huge, cankerous body swaying and lurching as handlers tried to steer it, hanging desperately from ropes attached to its tusks. The thing was thirty foot tall and twice as wide, but no one paid it much attention as they rushed about their business. Barrel worms snaked through the crowds, their undulating bodies laden with parcels. Winged serpents fluttered around the heads of statues, vying for position with axebeaks and screecher lizards as bone-mask monkeys screamed constantly from the walls, their white faces locked in fixed grins.

Even such a colourful, noisy display could not drive Niksar's doubts from his mind. He knew an hour could not have passed yet, but he decided to head back over to the guildhall and see if there was any sign of his sister.

He had barely crossed the threshold when he froze and ducked behind a pillar. There were witch hunters at Neco's machine. He risked a look around the pillar to be sure. There was no mistaking them. Agents of the Order did not wear a uniform as such, but the terror they induced was unmistakeable. A pair of them were talking in urgent tones to Neco's scribes. They were dressed in a similar fashion to the man he saw breaking into his lodgings, with pistols, dark cloaks and tall, peaked hats. They had silver chains hung around their necks, bearing hammer-shaped medallions, and they were surrounded by rag-wearing zealots, all of whom were clutching clubs and maces, their skin covered in ritual scars.

As Niksar watched in horror, another pair of witch hunters swaggered into the hall, both men in their fifties with identical expressions of cold hate on their faces. They had their hands resting on pistols and more zealots entered the hall behind them. There was no sign of Neco, Calabis or Zagora, and lots of the traders had paused to watch the witch hunters.

Niksar edged back towards the doors. The second group of witch hunters was only a dozen feet from where he was standing. They were busy questioning a prophesier but Niksar had a dreadful feeling they were about to look his way. He turned his back on them, pulled his hood low and walked back towards the doors, trying to look as confident as possible.

'Wait!' The voice was deep and stern.

He stopped, his heart lurching as he slowly looked back over his shoulder.

The witch hunters were not looking his way. Whoever called out had not been addressing him. He marched on down the steps and headed back out into the crowds. Once he was away from the guildhall he broke into a sprint, dashing across the square and bolting down one of the avenues that led back to the Veins. He did not stop running until he was deep in a maze of gloomy, muddy backstreets, then he finally let himself lean against a wall and catch his breath.

'Zagora!' he gasped, cursing himself for letting her go in there. What had made her do it? He remembered how oddly she had behaved in his rooms and when they were at the docks, talking of Sigmar speaking to her. She was a staunch follower of the Sigmarite faith but he had never known her to behave like that – like one of the witch hunters' fanatics.

A few people glanced at him as they hurried through the rain but he did not care so much here. The kind of people who ended up in the Veins wanted to be left alone, and they made sure to afford everyone else the same discretion. He paced back and forth through the puddles, wracking his brains for a way to help his sister. Try as he might, the only option he could think of was a dreadful one: if he returned to the guildhall he could tell the officials the truth – that the stone was his and that he was the one they needed to talk to, not Zagora. But the thought of walking up to an agent of the Order of Azyr and admitting anything was unimaginable.

He bought some cheap wine from a stall and spent the next couple of hours wandering the streets, trying to numb the dawning realisation that he might have sent his sister to her death. Despite his best efforts, he stayed resolutely sober. Eventually, he could bear it no longer and headed back to the square. By this time, it was late afternoon but the square was still crowded with people and animals as he approached the grand facade of the Guildhouse. It was as he climbed the steps that the alcohol finally decided to take effect. Suddenly, his legs developed a will of their own, refusing to move in the way he intended. He weaved across the steps and tripped up the last few, causing people to mutter at him as he stumbled towards the doors.

There was no sign of the witch hunters in the auction hall. He edged around the perimeter, peering through the crowds but seeing no sign of them. To his delight, Neco had returned and was back at her machine, talking cheerfully to a trader. He hurried over and, when she was free, he asked her when Zagora would return.

The smile froze on her face. 'Who are you again?' she asked.

Niksar almost gave her his real name and realised he was too drunk to be having this conversation. 'Is she all right?' he asked.

The woman stared at him intently. 'Why wouldn't she be?'

There was an awkward silence and Niksar realised she was looking around for someone. She made a furtive gesture.

A pair of guards nodded and began heading across the hall, their hands resting on the hilts of their swords.

'Tell her I'll come back soon,' muttered Niksar. Then he turned and sprinted across the hall.

He heard running feet behind him but he did not stop to look, racing out into the rain and off into the maze of streets. There was no sound of pursuit but he kept running until he was far from the square, heading back down towards the docks. The terrible dread was now overwhelming. Zagora had been arrested. And all so that he could raise money to clear some debts. He cursed and spat as he stumbled through the streets. Then, spotting an inn, he ducked inside to get dry and buy more wine.

CHAPTER FIVE

The next few days were a blur of drink and grief. Niksar drifted in and out of sobriety, spending his last few glimmerings on wine and resurfacing every now and then to wonder how he had found his way to whatever grubby hostelry he was slumped in. His grief was unbearable. And he knew it was only a matter of time before agents of the Order marched into an inn and locked him in shackles.

Finally, Niksar found himself in the very place he should have been avoiding – the wind-lashed harbour wall near the fortress of the White Angels. The rain had eased a little and he could see the battlements of the Consecralium with brutal clarity. Then he realised why he had come. It was not to look at the Knights Excelsior's bastion; it was to look at their victims.

There were rusty iron scaffolds dotted along the harbour wall. They had been erected every dozen or so feet, and each one had an iron cage dangling from it. Each cage contained a body. Some were mouldering corpses, meat for the carrion birds wheeling constantly around them, and others were salt-bleached skeletons. But others were still alive – left to a horrible death by the White Angels as punishment for heresy. Niksar had heard enough stories to know that 'heresy' to the Knights Excelsior meant anything from attempting to summon a daemon to taking Sigmar's name in vain after stubbing a toe. Since childhood he had lived in fear of them: divine, terrible beings who guarded the soul of Excelsis from damnation. Like all the Stormcast Eternals, they had been sent from the heavens by Sigmar himself, forged in Azyr to reclaim the lands from Chaos. They were the heroes of the age. And they were more terrifying than anything they had come to defeat.

Niksar stumbled past the cages, peering at each one in turn. He was looking for Zagora. Trying to find her corpse. He walked for half a mile along the harbour wall and only managed to make himself feel sick. A great weariness came over him and he thought of heading back to his rooms. Then he laughed bitterly, remembering how he left them.

He was counting his last few glimmerings, wondering if he had enough left to buy one last bottle of wine, when he heard a great commotion further down the harbour wall. For a dreadful moment, he thought the Knights Excelsior were emerging from their citadel. Then he realised the noise was coming from one of the streets further into the city. It sounded like soldiers marching. He crossed the road and peered down another street, intrigued.

To his surprise, he saw that it was guardsmen from his sister's regiment, the Phoenix Company. It was dusk and he was drunk, but their flame-coloured uniforms were unmistakeable. He even recognised some of the soldiers. They were friends of his sister. It occurred to him that they might have heard some news about her fate. He followed at a distance as they marched down the street towards a square. He was torn between calling out and keeping himself hidden in the shadows.

They were still half a mile from the square when he realised what was happening. A great hubbub of voices drifted through the twilit streets and, whenever there was a gap through the houses, he saw a sea of blazing torches. The drone of prayer calls echoed towards him along with the disjointed sound of multiple drummers.

Drifting above the square, silhouetted against the clouds, were three monolithic slabs of rock – islands of granite and sandstone that were floating above the rooftops, anchored to the ground by clanking chains attached to gall tusks even larger than the one he had seen outside the guildhall. The three floating rocks were each bigger than a townhouse, trailing tree roots and soil as they swayed overhead, and they had each been crowned with a gleaming statue of Sigmar. These massive, weightless rocks were called metaliths, and they could only mean one thing.

'A crusade,' he sneered, shaking his head.

He followed the guardsmen down a cobbled street towards the crowds, wondering why the soldiers were there. The Phoenix Company was sworn to defend the city, not head off into the wildlands. Had they come to protect the city from the crusaders? Anyone deranged enough to join a crusade was declared Indulta Sigmaralis by the city's Grand Conclave. That meant they would be forgiven their sins, however heinous, for risking their life in the God-King's name. As a result, every crusade was preceded by an orgy of violence and hedonism as enthusiastic sinners took full advantage of their impending pardon.

As Niksar followed the regiment to the edge of the square he saw that the celebrations were in full swing. As the priests droned and drummed, the crusaders drank and fought, lighting fires and hurling torches. The air was filled with laughter and embers as people abandoned themselves to a potent mix of licentiousness and holy rapture. Rich and poor, native and Azyrite, the crusaders became a single, wide-eyed mob, reeling beneath the drifting rocks.

Scaffolding had been erected at the centre of the square, forming a hammer-shaped stage. It was crowded with Sigmarite priests dressed in blue and gold. One of them was calling out a litany, his voice amplified by Collegiate sorcery so that the words boomed over the celebrations. He was bellowing a rollcall of names in a deafening monotone – the names of everyone who had signed up to the crusade.

As the crowd pressed around him, Niksar felt like he was walking into a drink-induced nightmare. Flushed, sweaty faces surrounded him, howling, praying and trying to kiss him. Most were simply devout Sigmarites, ecstatic at the thought of serving the God-King, but others seemed deranged, scratching hammers into their foreheads and filling the cuts with ink, whirling through the censer smoke or even branding themselves, laughing as the smell of burning skin filled the air. Others were clearly nothing to do with the crusade at all, crawling quickly through the throng, gathering up the robes and jewellery abandoned by wealthy converts.

Niksar recoiled as people surged closer to him, praying and thrusting his hands into the air. 'For Sigmar!' they wailed, their voices cracked and wavering. Something about their clammy touch snapped Niksar out of his delirium and he realised he had lost sight of his sister's regiment. He looked around frantically, trying to fight through dancers and kneeling supplicants. He spotted a patch of flame-coloured uniform and battled on through the crush.

As he moved beneath the shadow of the floating islands, and nearer to the stage, the droning list of names became unbearably loud. Niksar clamped his hands over his ears but the sorcery amplifying the voice sent it directly into his thoughts. 'Wait!' he called, as he came within shouting distance of one of the guardsmen.

The man looked back and Niksar recognised him. It was the captain – a scarred old veteran called Tyndaris. A taut, whipcord of a man with moustaches the size of antlers and cheeks the colour of raw meat. He was leaning heavily on a cane and one of his legs was crooked from an old injury, but Niksar had seen him in combat and knew how lethal he was.

'Niksar?' he said. 'Gods, man, look at the state of you.'

Niksar let out a long, relieved breath. The captain would not have addressed him so casually if he had heard about his problems with the Order. He looked down at his sodden clothes and grimaced. He did look bad.

'This rain,' he muttered.

Captain Tyndaris only had one facial expression, the grimace of someone sniffing something rotten, but he had known Niksar for many years and there was a flicker of concern in his eyes. 'You look dreadful. And half drowned. You can't be seen with your sister looking like that.'

'My sister?' Niksar felt weak. 'She's alive?'

Tyndaris peered at him. 'Of course she's alive.'

The captain reached for a flask at his belt and handed it to Niksar. It was water. The first he could remember drinking in a while. He gulped it down and immediately felt his head clear. His sister was alive. And she was here with her regiment. He felt such a rush of relief that he laughed.

Tyndaris frowned at him. Then he noticed that his regiment was almost out of sight, heading to the foot of the stage. He took the flask and walked off, gesturing for Niksar to follow. 'We don't want to miss this.'

Niksar realised how desperate he had been for a familiar face. He followed the old soldier as he limped through the madness, weaving around fights and raging bonfires, using his cane to fend off beggars.

The crush of bodies was tightest as they neared the stage and there was a thick smell of wine, sweat and holy oil. Finally, the monotonous rollcall came to an end and the crowd noise swelled

to fill the void, roaring in a disharmonious clamour, before joining in a unified chorus. 'Sigmar!' they cried, the voices coming
together with such force that even Niksar felt moved. It was like
being caught in the swell of an ocean. Captain Tyndaris noticed
his dazed expression and nodded. He grabbed Niksar's wrist and
shoved his fist into the air. As the crusaders roared again, Niksar
let the word rush up from his chest, joining his voice to the throng.

'Sigmar!' he howled, feeling suddenly drunk again.

The crowd chanted together and, far from where Niksar was
standing, people were holding a crudely assembled effigy up in
the air. He guessed from its hammer that it was meant to be either
Sigmar or one of his Stormcast Eternals, but the thing was made
of mud and straw and its creator clearly had little in the way of
artistic flair, so it looked more like a crown-wearing vegetable.

Niksar was about to ask Tyndaris a question when a group of
figures strode out onto the stage and the crowd fell quiet. There
was something dramatic about hearing so many people holding
their tongues. An ominous quiet fell over the square, interrupted
only by the crackling of fires. Niksar shifted position, peering
between heads to see what was happening up on the scaffold.

'Stormcast Eternals,' he whispered as a row of huge, armour-clad
warriors took centre stage. They towered over the priests by several heads and their battleplate flashed in the torchlight. Niksar
considered himself a practical, down-to-earth kind of man, but
his pulse raced at the sight of Sigmar's immortals. They were the
reason the crowd had fallen quiet. They were magnificent and
dreadful. Their armour was not the pristine white of the Knights
Excelsior but a flawless, mirrored gold. Their gleaming faceplates
hid their expressions but their stance conveyed the disdain with
which they surveyed the gathering in the square.

Only two of them had their faces exposed. They stood at the
head of the group, clearly the leaders. One was a standard bearer

and he had a fiercely imperious expression on his face. He looked fairly young, perhaps thirty or so, with a short beard and eyes that burned with the pride of a great lord. The other wore armour that was more ornate than the rest of the Stormcast Eternals, with a raised neck brace that trailed a blue cloak. Rather than holding a weapon, he carried a rune-inscribed staff with a blue gem at its head. There were holy, gilt-edged books hung from his belt and metal-clasped scrolls. He had white hair, cropped short, but Niksar found it hard to make out the rest of his face. There was something odd about his eyes. As Niksar tried to look at them he found it impossible to make them out and as he tried, the rest of the Stormcast Eternal's face seemed to blur. It was like looking at a faint star. If he looked away, he could see features in his peripheral vision, but when he tried to focus on them, they slipped away.

'That one is Arulos Stormspear,' said Tyndaris. 'Their senior officer. They call him a Knight-Arcanum.'

Niksar shook his head, still trying to make out the warrior's face. 'A what?'

'A lightning mage.'

'Their armour's different,' said Niksar, looking down the line of Stormcast Eternals. 'Different from the Knights Excelsior, I mean.'

'They're a new breed of Stormcast Eternal. Forged for this war, for us. For the specific purpose of purging the wildlands.'

Niksar was about to ask more but Tyndaris held up a finger and nodded to the scaffold. More figures were walking out on to the stage. Some wore prophesier robes, but they looked far grander than Calabis or Neco. They were guildmasters, perhaps the Convocation that Neco mentioned. They were accompanied by more Sigmarite priests with shaved heads and robes of white and azure stitched with gold thread. Following the priests came some of the city's most well-known and wealthiest merchants alongside members of the city's ruling body, the Grand Conclave and even the High Arbiter himself. Niksar had never seen such a gathering of the great and good but, despite their finery, the mortals looked like scruffy children in comparison to the golden-armoured giants looming behind them.

There were several minutes of prayer and ritual as priests shuffled across the stage, scattering petals and scented oil and chanting prayers into the censer smoke. As this was happening, the Stormcast Eternals were as motionless as the statues that lined the square. None of them looked at the other people on the stage.

'They're called the Anvilhearts,' said Tyndaris. His habitual sneer faded and he spoke in hushed tones. 'They belong to the Hammers of Sigmar Stormhost.'

Finally, the most senior-looking priest nodded to the other grandees and walked to the front of the stage. She was tall with a striking, angular face but Niksar looked straight past her and stared at the person behind her. For a moment, Niksar thought that he had slipped into a stupor.

It was Zagora. His sister was up on the stage, standing behind the city's most senior prelate. And she had been transformed. She was dressed in a suit of finely sculpted white armour, and her hands were resting on the head of a gilded greathammer that looked too big for her to lift. Ocella's glimmering had been set in a beautiful, golden circlet, and it flickered at Zagora's brow as she moved. Her head had been shaved and, to Niksar's eyes, she looked like one of the holy saints who stared from frescoes across the city. Far from being dead, she looked more alive than he had ever seen her. She looked as radiant as the polished warhammer she was leaning on and, even from dozens of feet away, her white armour was dazzling.

This was why he had not heard from her. She was not dead. She had been with these priests.

'What's happening?' demanded Niksar, speaking loud enough

to earn angry glances from nearby pilgrims. Niksar's feelings of dread returned. Why had the priests shaved his sister's head and dressed her in the armour of a warrior priest? Why had they put her on a stage?

'Sigmar called!' cried the priest. Her voice rang out across the crowd. 'And you answered!'

The crusaders roared like animals. The sound of their voices was louder than anything Niksar had ever heard. It was the sound of a thousand lunatics being told their delusions of grandeur were truth.

The priest nodded slowly, eyes closed, bathing in the noise. Then she held up a hand.

'You are the righteous! You are the ones who were foreseen. You are the holy multitude! You have shaken off the fetters of your worldly lives! You have been pardoned for your sins! You! Have! Been! Reborn!'

As the crowd screamed Niksar saw his sister nodding in agreement with the priestess' every word.

'Darkness has lain over these lands for too long,' continued the priestess, speaking in more measured tones and starting to pace across the stage, looking out at different sections of the crowd. 'All along the coast our keeps have been overrun, giving the beasts of the wildlands freedom to roam and breed and to strike at our city. And if the attacks on our city continue as they are, unabated, even mighty Excelsis will fall. But now, just as the darkness seems deeper than ever, a new dawn is coming. And with it...' She paused for effect, then waved at the Stormcast Eternals. 'Comes the storm!'

This garnered the loudest cheer of all but the Anvilhearts gave no sign of recognition, remaining motionless as the noise crashed over them. Again, Niksar tried to look at Stormspear's face, but again it was useless.

The priestess continued in a similar vein for several minutes, goading the crowd to even wilder excesses as she told them they were Sigmar's chosen, drawn by virtue and fate to reclaim the wildlands in the God-King's name. Then, she gestured for Zagora to move forwards and stand beside her.

'And you will not walk blindly into the darkness.' She placed a hand on Zagora's shoulder. 'Every step has been foreseen by the God-King. As he foresees all futures. And he has placed all his vision and wisdom in the soul of this humble mortal. The wilds shall have no hold on you. Your enemies shall gain no purchase. For in your ranks, leading you to glory, you shall have Zagora the Dawnbringer!'

'What?' cried Niksar in disbelief, but his voice was lost beneath another deafening cheer as Zagora hefted the greathammer over her head. The metal flashed white, casting beams through the smoke.

As Zagora stood beside her, head bowed and hammer raised, the priestess continued.

'This devoted child of Sigmar has been granted visions that describe every footstep of your journey. She will lead you through the savagery and bring you to a great confluence of geomantic power. And there, on the night of Gnorl's Feast, you shall build a mighty fortress. You shall call it Ardent Keep. It will be glorious and impenetrable. A bastion strong enough to withstand any assault. A bastion that Zagora has seen in her waking dreams. And, along with all the other crusades that have left Excelsis these past weeks, you will form a new frontier in Sigmar's name – a bulwark against the beasts that would seek to devour this city.'

Niksar barely heard most of the priestess' speech. All he could think about was the fervour in Zagora's eyes. She believed what the priestess was saying. Every word. She believed in the crusade. Niksar believed in crusades too, of course, in an abstract sense. He believed the righteous should offer their lives to stem the madness that was consuming Thondia. But it was one thing to offer thanks to fearless crusaders, and quite another to learn that his sister was going to be one of them.

The sermon continued for nearly half an hour until the priestess led the crowd in a final prayer and left the stage, followed by her fellow priests and lords and, finally, the Anvilhearts, who maintained their grim silence as they marched into the banks of smoke.

'Zagora's going with them,' said Niksar, muttering to himself. 'She's *leading* them.'

Captain Tyndaris frowned at him. 'What's wrong with you, boy? How can you not know about this?'

As the crowds dispersed, heading away from the stage and spreading back out across the square, the soldiers of the Phoenix Company surrounded Niksar. Some smiled in recognition but he noticed that others were looking at him with a kind of wonder, as though he were as holy as his sister.

'I knew nothing about it,' said Niksar, trying to ignore the strange looks the guardsmen were giving him and focus on Tyndaris. 'I haven't seen her for days. I thought she was...'

'You thought she was what?'

Niksar shook his head.

'You're her brother,' said one of the other soldiers. It was a young woman with a wry grin and an old scar running from her collarbone to her forehead. She was one of Zagora's friends, a corporal by the name of Haxor.

'I had no idea about any of this,' muttered Niksar.

'You look like you bathe in wine,' said Haxor, still smirking. 'And you smell like it too. Maybe that's why you–'

Captain Tyndaris silenced her with a glare. 'Come and eat with us,' he said. 'You don't want to pass out in this crowd.'

'Are you part of all this?' asked Niksar, looking at the crowds. 'Are you leaving the city?'

Tyndaris nodded. 'Our orders came direct from the Grand Conclave. We are to travel with the Dawnbringer as her personal honour guard.'

It took Niksar a moment to remember that the Dawnbringer was his sister. 'Her honour guard? The entire regiment?' He looked around at the soldiers. They looked back at him with earnest, proud expressions.

Captain Tyndaris did not seem to be fazed by this reversal of fortunes. 'She has been chosen by the God-King.' He grimaced at Niksar's wine-stained clothes and hollow cheeks. 'Come on. Let's get you some food. The crusade doesn't leave until dawn and there won't be any sleeping, so we've brought provisions.'

Corporal Haxor smirked at him again. 'You're going to be the centre of attention once people learn whose brother you are. You don't want to embarrass her.'

'I have to speak to her,' said Niksar, shaking his head and looking up at the empty stage.

'Well, your best chance of meeting her is to come with us,' said Haxor, laughing. 'She's going to grant her lowly old comrades an audience once she's done with the priests.'

Niksar nodded and followed the soldiers through the crowd. The rollcall began droning out across the square again and with the stage left empty, people resumed their various forms of revelry. Niksar watched in amazement. He had never seen so many people abandon themselves like this. A madness had overtaken them. He could tell from their scraps of clothing that many of these people were respectable citizens, merchants and tradesmen, but some of them were acting like the wretches who lived in the Veins.

They reached the pedestal of a statue at the edge of the square and the soldiers shoved people aside until there was room to sit.

There were only ten of the soldiers with Tyndaris but Niksar had seen dozens more of them scattered across the square.

One of the guardsmen handed him some food and Niksar ate hungrily. The soldiers were all intent on eating their own food so Niksar was left to himself. Disjointed, drunken memories filled his head and they seemed to come from more than just a day or two. How long had he been wandering the streets, assuming his sister was dead? Assuming he had killed her?

When he had taken the edge off his hunger, he turned to Corporal Haxor. She was one of the most well-known members of the regiment. Like the rest of the Phoenix Company, she was a survivor of another, now disbanded regiment. Attacks on the city, along with uprisings within it, had destroyed several regiments so the Grand Conclave had formed the Phoenix Company to gather the remnants into a single unit. Haxor was something of a mascot for them. She was small and slightly built, but she was one of the finest duellists in Excelsis. Her skill with a sword was legendary.

She sensed him looking at her and gave him another one of her ironic smiles.

'Where will you go?' he asked, still shocked that they were intending to leave the safety of the city. 'Where's the crusade headed?'

She shrugged, wiping chicken grease from her mouth with the back of her sleeve. 'Same as all the others. All the ones that left recently, at least. North, to a distant stretch of the Great Excelsis Road.'

Niksar shook his head in disbelief. 'The road isn't safe. You'll be dead in a few days.'

She laughed. 'I see your sister got the balls in your family. We're not travelling on the road. We're going through the wilds. Until we reach a stretch of the road that has been reclaimed by the other crusades.' She nodded to the stage. 'Did you see what was up there? Anvilhearts. Hammers of Sigmar, Niksar. They've got lightning in their veins. They were born in a storm. And they're marching with *us*.' She laughed again and took a bite of the apple she was holding. 'We'll reach that damned road. And we'll become legends on the way.'

'Why would Sigmar send his immortals to help one specific crusade? To help Zagora?'

'I think the Anvilhearts have a job of their own to do. That's what Captain Tyndaris says. This is just the start of their work. Once they've got us to the Great Excelsis Road and linked us up with the other new settlements, they'll be relieved by some of the White Angels who are travelling back this way. The Anvilhearts will go east and head on to the coast. But for now they're ours. Our spearhead.'

She held out a flask of wine.

Niksar considered taking some, then shook his head. 'There are Knights Excelsior here, in the city,' he said, after a moment. 'If this crusade has been ordained by Sigmar why aren't the White Angels travelling with you?'

She shook her head. 'What are you doing? Trying to root out a lie?' She waved at the heaving crowds and the great slabs of rock drifting above the statues. 'Do you think this is all some kind of trick? The White Angels are already scattered right across Thondia trying to hold back greenskins. What would you have them do? Send their last few warriors away and leave the Consecralium empty? Would you have Excelsis left unguarded? I just told you, once the Anvilhearts have got us where we're going, there will be White Angels waiting there to relieve them. I think they're heading back from the coast or something. And they're going to rendezvous with us.'

Niksar felt annoyed without really knowing why. Corporal Haxor was talking sense but he felt an inexplicable need to argue with her. 'I counted sixty Stormcast Eternals on that stage. How can that be enough to get you so far north?'

'Sixty *Stormcast Eternals*. Do you know what that means? Do you know what they are? Each one of them is like an army.' Haxor's wry smile was still there but it was no longer reaching her eyes. 'Besides, what's the alternative? Perhaps you're the military genius we've all been waiting for. The land is trying to swallow us whole, Niksar. However drunk you've been, you must have noticed that. It wants to chew Excelsis up and spit us out. You've seen the things that keep smashing our walls down. You've seen the things that rise up from the docks and the sewers. What would you have us do? Scrap the crusades and wait to die? Should we just cower in the city and leave the land to spew out monsters in peace?'

Niksar could think of nothing to say. He had no idea why he was even arguing. Then he saw Zagora coming towards them through the crowd and realised she was the reason. The Grand Conclave was going to put her at the head of this madness. They were using her as the figurehead for the whole thing.

Zagora did not notice Niksar at first, heading straight to Captain Tyndaris, who gripped her arms and spoke urgently to her. Then the captain pointed Niksar out and she strode towards him. She looked so magnificent in her polished wargear that he was unsure how to address her, but before he could speak she threw her arms around him.

His foul mood evaporated as he hugged her back.

They stared at each other for a moment, then they sat down a little distance away from the others. Niksar looked at her strange armour and the hammer slung at her back. Then he touched the circlet at her brow, fascinated by the glimmering at its heart. The stone had been so lovingly polished that there were shapes rolling in its facets.

'What happened?' he asked.

Her expression was unlike anything he had seen on her face before. He could hardly recognise her. She was rigid with emotion, but he could not tell if it was fear or pride.

'They couldn't see anything in the stone,' she said. 'Not without me touching it. But when they placed *me* in one of their assaying machines it was a different story. I'm bonded to the glimmering. It only shares its vision with me. And this isn't the first time this has happened. All the crusades have been led by prophets who–'

'Prophet?'

He expected her to blush or laugh but her face remained rigid. 'Not my word.'

'Whose, then?'

'The city leaders. The prophesiers made me wait for hours as they wrote in their ledgers, but then they took me across the square to the lords of the Grand Conclave. The High Arbiter himself signed the proclamation. They've declared me Manifesta Sanctum. They gave me the Coin Malleus. I am a devoted instrument of Sigmar's will.'

Niksar laughed bitterly. 'I know what that means. It means they'll use you to drum up support for the crusade and they don't care if you die out there.'

She held his gaze. 'Niksar. I saw a route and a place. It was me that saw the name, Ardent Keep, hammered in gold. I saw it *before* the priests made any mention of it.'

'So you gave them the idea. They got the name from you.'

She shook her head. 'They told me they already know the names of all the citadels that will be built along the Great Excelsis Road. They call them strongpoints. Each one will stand at the intersection of Ghur's most powerful, ancient ley lines. Together, they will start to reclaim that stretch of the road.'

'They told you what you needed to hear. They told you things that would convince you to give your life for their cause.'

'*Their* cause? Isn't it our cause? Isn't it your cause? If the wild-lands are left unchecked, Excelsis will fall. You know that's true. You've seen how close we've already come over the last few years. Time's running out. And if this city falls, the whole of Thondia falls. Things will be as they were before Sigmar sent his Storm-hosts. The coast will be lost forever. Whatever gains we've made will be washed away. How can we drive Chaos from these lands if we're consumed by the beasts of the wildlands? The city has to stand. And the only way to make it stand is to tame the wildlands around it. We need to drive the creatures back into the sea. Why would you argue with that? You know this is the right thing to do. Why would you look at me like that?'

'Because you'll die.' He stared at the augur stone, glinting above her eyes. 'Because this prophecy will kill you.'

'Then you admit that there is a prophecy.'

'Call it what you like, it doesn't mean you have to go with them. You've told the lords and priests what you saw. I've no doubt the prophesiers wrote it down in fifteen different books. They all know what you know. Why do you have to leave the city?'

'That's why,' she said, waving at the crowd.

Niksar looked around and saw that dozens of people were watch-ing them talk. Some were drunk, their clothes tattered and stained, others were finely dressed nobles and others were wide-eyed children, but they were all staring at Zagora with the same rapt expressions.

She tapped the glimmering. 'I'm the Dawnbringer.'

'Do you really believe that? You really believe you've been blessed by the God-King?'

'I don't know exactly what I believe. But it doesn't matter. What matters is that *they* believe. With me at their side and the Anvil-hearts at their head, they'll be unstoppable.'

'You're play acting then. Playing a part.'

69

'I saw what I saw. And it corresponded to dozens of auguries that have been recorded at the Spear of Mallus. I saw us reaching Faithful Tor by the night of Gnorl's Feast. And, as the great conjunction fills the sky, we will–'

'Gnorl's Feast? That's less than a week away. Your visions make no sense. Are you sure you've understood them properly?'

'I understand parts, and others I don't. I don't know what exactly all of it means but I will do what I think is right. And this is right.'

Niksar struggled to keep his voice level. 'Always, you look for the way to do the right thing. What about doing the safe thing? What about the sane thing? *You* don't have to save Excelsis. There are others.'

'The stone came to me.'

'It actually came to me.'

'I won't turn away from this. I will go. And I'll get us to the tor by Gnorl's Feast.'

They both fell silent and the sounds of the celebrations washed over them. There were still people drumming and howling. Niksar's hangover was so awful he wanted to flee the square and leave his sister to her fate but he could not bring himself to do it. He thought of the last few days – of the fact that he did not even know how many days he had lost to drink and grief. He thought of the witch hunters watching over his lodgings and the wealth he had hurled into the dock. He thought of the debts he could not pay. Finally, with a lurch, he thought of the bodies dangling outside the Consecralium. A painful truth pressed down on him.

'Then I'll go with you,' he muttered.

Her mask slipped. She looked shocked. 'What?'

'What's left for me here? I'm a dead man walking. If the Order doesn't get me, my creditors will. I've no life left here.' He looked around at the deranged crowds. 'But crusaders get a new life, isn't that right? Indulta Sigmaralis. A new beginning. How did your priest friend put it? I can shake off the fetters of my sins. I'll be pardoned. I can start again.'

'You just told me it was madness to leave the city.'

'It is.' He thought of the horrors he had seen over the years – the things that crawled over the city walls.

'You're not well,' she said. 'You look like you haven't slept since I last saw you.' Then her expression softened. 'But… if you did come, I would feel less afraid.'

She looked so grand in her armour that the admission of fear was shocking. It sent a wave of emotion through Niksar so, to crush it, he mimicked the pompous tones of their dead father.

'The chain will not be broken!'

She became his sister again. Tears glinted in her eyes and a smile played at the corners of her mouth. 'The chain will not be broken.'

CHAPTER SIX

Arulos was adrift in the storm. Thunderheads crashed, filling his lungs. Lightning coursed through his eyes, revealing the heart of the land. Revealing truth.

Ghur was stirring. The realm was waking up. This was why he had been sent. Things that had lain idle for long ages were rising from marshes and mines. Things that the crusaders could not comprehend. Things that even he was yet to fully discern. The wilds had grown wilder. And there was something else; something in the tumult; a talisman that he clung to with all his strength. It was clearer every time he saw it. A glimpse of his destiny. A glimpse of his purpose. At the Siege of Delium he would join the great muster of Stormcast Eternals that had been called by Sigmar's angel, Yndrasta. He would be with them as the storm broke. He would become one with Sigmar. At Delium he would do the work Sigmar forged him to do.

He had drifted alone for hours, cherishing this taste of the infinite, but now there were faces appearing in the storm, and voices, so he dragged his thoughts back to more mundane concerns.

'Knight-Arcanum Stormspear.'

Compared to the clashing of the heavens the voice was a feeble murmur, but Arulos had learned to hear the small sounds of the discarnate world. He led his thoughts through the thunder, bringing them to bear on the speakers. They were fitful ghosts. Shadows thrown across the firmament, but he could discern their faces. It was the priests from Excelsis. They were huddled before him. Cowering in the tumult, hands clasped, trying to avoid his gaze, unaware of the divine forces that surrounded them.

'Forgive the intrusion.' One of them gestured to other figures, further back in the clouds. 'We thought now might be a good time to speak. Now that we have come to a halt.'

Arulos had learned, in the Chamber of Apotheosis, to hold two realities: the numinous storm, where all was truth, and the insubstantial domain of the mortals, where truth could be hidden. He had also learned to present himself in such a way that he appeared to reside in the mortals' reality. In truth, he was cast to the winds, blasted by lightning, but he stood motionless, holding himself with precision so that he would appear to share their dimly lit vision of reality. He nodded, gesturing for them to approach and sit.

As the mortals bustled around him, adjusting their robes and taking seats, they dragged their world with them. A command tent formed around him in the clouds, complete with rugs and flickering torches and, through the opening, a muddy, fly-harried dusk. As they painted their domain around him, Arulos felt a vague memory. He had once been as frail they were. He had once been mere skin and bone. It was always strange to be reminded of the fact. The memories of his mortal life were clasped and hidden, locked in a place where they would not distract him from his purpose. He had to be focused. The rest of his Stormhost had already answered Saint Yndrasta's call, while he had been given this errand to run.

The storm surged through him again, teasing him with another glimpse of glory. He pictured himself dissolved into lightning, obliterated by thunder as he ascended to absolute, vengeful power. Such a victory could only mean one thing. He and the Anvilhearts would help Yndrasta break the siege at Delium. It was not arrogance that thrilled through his veins, but the pride of one who had been given a worthy task.

'Knight-Arcanum.' This voice came from a figure at his side in the storm – someone as real as he was.

'Knight-Vexilor Skyborn,' he replied, turning to his second-in-command.

Varek Skyborn trod his own path, one that kept him closer to the mortal world, and simply looking at him brought more of the command tent into view. Varek was giving him a familiar look. He was warning Arulos to be more present. More like a mortal. They were not at Delium yet. There were other matters to attend to first. He needed to give the priests the sense that he was with them in their world, that he understood their trials.

Arulos fixed his gaze on them, bringing their fragile bodies into focus. How delicate they were. How vulnerable. Protecting them might be a lesser duty than breaking the siege, but he would not fail them. This task, too, was appointed to him by Sigmar. And he would not let them down.

'Have you pitched camp?' he asked.

High Priestess Chiana nodded eagerly. 'It is difficult with so much mud, my lord, and those dead things everywhere.' She glanced around for help. 'What are they, exactly?'

'A kind of squid?' suggested someone. 'The fens are mostly streams and pools. The squid must have been washed up here.'

The priestess laughed nervously. 'They're easy enough to shovel out of the way. Most of the guardsmen have already pitched their own tents and are now helping everyone else.'

There was such a peculiar contrast between the splendour of

the storm and the mundane trials of the priest. If Arulos had not endured months of arduous training in Azyr, he might have laughed. He nodded sagely instead, feigning interest in the pitching of tents and deceased squid.

He glanced at Varek and noticed that the young warrior was giving him a grateful smile. Varek was a master at this. He, too, must feel frustrated by their delay. He must be just as keen to leave these poor people behind and join the rest of the Stormhost at the coast. He was not a tempestarii. Not a stormseer like Arulos. But he was storm-born, like all the Anvilhearts. And immortal. Varek burned brighter than the lightning, and all his thoughts would no doubt be on the battle for Delium, but he would not let these people see his frustration. Arulos trusted and respected him. And he was glad to have pleased him.

'We have done well to reach the fens on time,' he said to the priestess, imagining that was the kind of platitude Varek would approve of. 'We do not set an easy pace.'

The priestess looked like she might burst with pride. 'We have Sigmar in our hearts. And to see you marching before us gives us strength. Not many of us have walked for three days, without rest, before this, but that was what you ordered and there was no way we would fail you.'

Arulos nodded. In truth, the orders had not come from him. He left details to others. But Varek no doubt wanted the mortals to believe that he, Arulos, was thinking about them. 'Sigmar sees your devotion,' he said. He was about to hand out more flattery, in an attempt to end the meeting sooner, when he noticed something peculiar. The storm was raging with the same fury as always, flickering and booming in an endless collision. But a point of calm had appeared, directly ahead of him. Arulos forgot about his audience with the mortals and peered into the clouds. He had never seen anything like it. The storm was turning around a single point, a kind of eye, a space that was immune to the energy around it. A void.

No, he realised, not a void. There was something in there. Some*one*.

He let his soul draw closer and stared at the newcomer. His excitement grew as he realised this person was linked to the destiny he was pursuing. A feeling of dreadful significance radiated from the stranger.

'Who are you?' he asked the figure in the storm. Then something even more peculiar happened. As the figure replied, her voice came to him from both realities – the heaven-storm and the dreary, mud-splattered tent.

'Zagora.'

As she spoke, Arulos saw her with shocking clarity. She looked even more vivid to him than Varek. Than the storm itself. He could see the pores of her skin, the stubble on her shaved scalp, the stone clasped at her brow. He had heard Zagora mentioned several times as a prophet but he had never stood in such close proximity to her. Never looked directly at her. He now found himself in a situation in which he struggled to know how to act. She was a mortal, the boots of her armour squelching in the squalid command tent. But she was also with him in the storm. No, more than that – she was the point around which the storm turned. Everything Arulos believed was suddenly thrown into question.

'What are you?' he asked.

The mortals were surprised by his question and looked to Varek for help.

Varek gave him another pointed look. 'Zagora is the Dawn-bringer, lord. The prophet. Do you recall that we stood with her at the ceremony?'

Arulos shook his head. He had been occupied with thoughts of Delium when they stood on the stage. He had barely registered the ceremony. He wished, now, that he had paid more attention. He kept his gaze on the woman.

'I mean, what *are* you?'

She showed none of the panic the priests were displaying. Nor did she seem as intimidated as mortals usually did in his presence. 'I am Zagora Astaboras. I am one of the reclaimed who dwell in Excelsis. My parents were Thondian hunters. I came to the city as a child after my parents were killed. I have fought in several campaigns.' She touched the glimmering at her brow. 'I have been chosen to lead us.'

Arulos stepped closer to her, causing the priests to scatter. 'But I can see you,' he said. 'Clearly.'

Zagora opened her mouth to reply, then shook her head, looking confused. She glanced at Varek.

Arulos was finding the woman's presence in both worlds increasingly confusing. She was quite unlike the other mortals in the tent. Where they were frail and worthy of pity, she radiated power. A power he could not explain. It blazed out of her. It was nothing unholy. He had fought heretics many times and the stink of Chaos was unmistakable. She was not one of the damned. So what was she?

Varek moved to his side and placed a hand on the pauldron of his armour. 'Knight-Arcanum Stormspear means that he sees the power of the Dawnbringer.' He looked at Zagora and spoke with kindness. 'He sees the potency of your vision.'

The priests raised their eyebrows and clasped their hands together, ecstatic, whispering prayers, but Arulos saw that Zagora was unconvinced. She was looking hard at his face, trying to discern his features. He began to find her presence troubling. The power in her eyes did not fit with truths he had long accepted. There was a mystery to her that jarred with the scenes in the storm.

'Leave now,' he said. 'I have matters to discuss with my brothers.'

The priests looked panicked, clearly surprised to be dismissed so quickly.

'Did we say something wrong?' said Chiana, glancing anxiously at Varek.

Varek smiled and shook his head as they all backed away, whispering prayers as Varek ushered them from the tent. Zagora looked intently at Arulos as she left and he had the odd sense that she was reading his thoughts.

Once they were alone, Varek dropped his amiable mask and frowned.

'Arulos, try to speak to them in language they can understand. Or at least in language *I* can understand. Our job is to keep these people alive. How can we do that if you make them all terrified of you? What did you mean by asking Zagora what she is? What kind of question is that? And what did you mean when you said you could "see" her?'

Arulos could barely hear his friend's words. With Zagora gone the storm was cut loose again, attacking with renewed vigour, lifting him back up into the maelstrom, tormenting him with glimpses of a destiny he could not longer quite see. Everything that had been so clear a moment ago was now obscure and mercurial. He shook his head and sat on one of the couches.

Varek headed to a table and poured them both some wine. He handed a cup to Arulos and sat on another chair, looking at him intently as he drank.

'What did you see? When you looked at her you seemed confused.'

'She is significant.'

'Of course. She is the figurehead of the crusade.'

'No, I mean she is significant to us. I have missed something. She is linked to our purpose in some way.'

Varek narrowed his eyes. 'Our purpose is clear. It has never been in doubt. We escort these people to their hill and then we get to Delium as fast as we can.' He drummed his fingers against the cup, shaking his head and looking out into the drizzle. 'We should be there now.'

Arulos focused his stormsight on him and saw the anger that boiled just beneath the surface. 'We must perform this duty with as much conviction as any other task the Lord Imperatant gives us.'

Varek lowered his voice. 'Of course we must. And we will. But it is beneath us. You know it is. Who broke the siege at Zitoun? It was the Anvilhearts. Who drove the revenants from the Kuthan Temples? It was us. We should be with Yndrasta now. We should be at the coast. If anyone can help her break that siege it is us.' He swallowed his wine in a few hurried gulps and slammed the cup down. 'There are plenty of other people more suited to this task. We were not forged to babysit crusaders.'

Arulos smiled and held up a hand, amused by how quickly his friend's passion could be roused. 'I'm not arguing with you. I feel the delay as keenly as you.'

Varek shook his head. 'I heard the tone in your voice when you asked Zagora what she is. She's triggered one of your quests for knowledge, hasn't she? I imagine you have already got half your mind in the firmament, trying to decide what she means to us.'

Arulos laughed. 'There is a grain of truth in that.'

Varek leant closer. 'We must not be drawn into their visions and prophecies, Arulos. We must not become mired in this crusade. We know exactly what we have to do. We have to reach Yndrasta. There's no need to start hunting for answers when we already have them.'

Arulos sipped his wine, wondering if he had ever been as rash as Varek. 'It is dangerous to assume one has all the answers. You know that, old friend. The realms are as strange and unpredictable as the storm itself. The hunt for understanding is an ongoing one.'

Varek's cheeks flushed with colour and his eyes flashed but, before he could say more, Arulos held up his hand again.

'Do not trouble yourself. I see something unusual in Zagora but it does not change anything. We will get them to that tor and then we will march to Delium. We will show this realm what the Anvilhearts are capable of.' He held up his cup. 'Agreed?'

Varek relaxed and clanged his cup against Arulos'. 'Agreed.' He leant back in his chair, studying Arulos with a wry expression. 'Perhaps your interest in her was more physical than metaphysical?'

Arulos laughed and shook his head. 'Do not judge me by your own low standards.' He spoke with mock-gravitas. 'I have moved beyond such worldly concerns.'

Varek laughed along with him, but there was something strained about his mirth. He sipped his drink, seemed on the verge of saying more, then looked away.

'What is it?' asked Arulos.

Varek looked back at Arulos, his expression unreadable. 'Do you remember anything of your old life? Of what it means to be a mortal, I mean?'

Arulos shrugged. 'Glimpses. Snatches of music. The scent of a forest. Just feelings, mostly, like a half-remembered dream.' He gestured to the aetherstave that was leaning against his chair. 'I have methods of protection – ways to ward myself from troubling memories. It would not do to dwell on the things I have lost, the things I sacrificed.' Varek had spoken in flippant tones, but Arulos sensed that he was masking the truth and that the question was important to him. 'Why do you ask?'

Varek hesitated. 'You have been reforged.'

'More than once.'

'More than once, yes. I suppose that is my point. I have been through the fires of the anvil only once.' Varek's tone was gruff and proud. He was trying to hide his unease. Arulos spoke in the same stern tones, not wishing to embarrass his friend with a display of concern.

'And you wonder what it is like to be reborn again and again.'

Varek shrugged, still trying to look nonchalant. 'Perhaps. It is something, after all, to be remade.'

Arulos nodded, looking at the aetherstave. 'My life is not what it was. I do not feel the things I once felt.' He tapped his chest armour. 'But I do still feel, Varek. I know what people say about us. They think we are automatons. That we have no humanity left.' He laughed. 'I suppose I do not really know what it means to be human any more, but I am no automaton. When I think of the things we have seen, Varek, the horrors we have driven from these realms, I feel a flame in my chest, in my soul. So many innocent people have died, or been enslaved. There are so many we will never reach, but for some there is still hope. For some, the storm has arrived in time. And when I think of that, when I think of what we can achieve in Sigmar's name, I feel an emotion more powerful than anything I felt as a mortal.'

He realised he had been speaking loudly, as if he were addressing a crowd. He laughed at his pompous tones and sat back in his chair, lowering his voice again.

'I've no idea if that was the kind of answer you were looking for.'

For a moment, Varek had forgotten to wear his imperious mask. He was staring at Arulos with gleaming eyes. Then he remembered himself and looked stern again, nodding as he sipped his wine.

'Perhaps. It was only an idle question.' He finished his drink and rose to leave. 'I should give them a chance to show me these squid they are so interested in.'

Arulos laughed. 'Ever the diplomat, Varek, ever the diplomat.'

It was only when Arulos was alone that he realised he had lied to Varek. He had told him he had a few vague memories left of his old life, but when he tried to summon one, he found nothing – not even the smells and sounds he had mentioned to his friend. He realised, now, that he had made those claims by impulse. Perhaps, once, it had been true, but now there was nothing. He felt a familiar twinge of pain, then he closed his eyes and let the storm carry him away.

CHAPTER SEVEN

Niksar cursed as he parried, slipping on the rocks, struggling to keep his sword raised.

Haxor strode after him, preparing for another lunge. 'I thought you were a sellsword. You might as well sell it. You use it like a stick.'

The corporal was barely chest height on Niksar and looked like she'd be toppled by a stiff breeze, but he was starting to see why she had such a reputation. She seemed to float through the dusk, gliding over puddles, leaping from rock to rock and swinging her sword so fast it blurred. He parried again, but there was still no way he could make a lunge of his own. She whirled around him, baring her teeth in a wolfish grin. When Captain Tyndaris had suggested Haxor take him through his paces, he had accepted gladly, but only so he didn't have to help pitch camp. He had not expected to find himself fighting for his life.

They were sparring on the ledge of a rocky outcrop and the rest of the regiment were down below, working tirelessly in the mud to get their tents up before dusk. It was late afternoon and the light was failing fast. All across the fens, crusaders were digging and struggling with tent poles. There were smoking torches all across the site, spitting flames and embers. In the distance, far beyond the fen's brackish pools, the faint lights of Excelsis were still visible. They had marched for three days but the city was still watching over them, glinting on the horizon.

Niksar had expected carnage as soon as they left the city gates, but there had been surprisingly few deaths – so far, at least. The creatures of the wildlands had attacked several times, but only in small packs. Less than a dozen people had died and two of those were the result of a drunken fight. The priests were already claiming it as a victory for Sigmar, telling their eager converts that the presence of Anvilhearts, combined with the blessings heaped on Zagora, had driven the beasts of the wildlands away. Niksar felt pained every time the priests mentioned his sister but he had to admit the journey was going much better than he had expected.

The three metaliths were drifting overhead, laden with building materials and supplies. They were still anchored to the gall tusks that had dragged them from the city, and with their glorious statues of Sigmar they were a statement of defiance. There were figures moving on them and he wondered if his sister was one. He had not spoken to her since they left Excelsis, watching her from afar as she led the crusade through the city gates, bathed in the cheers of the crowd. There was something terrible and wonderful about what had happened to her. Terrible, because of the danger she had put herself in, but wonderful because of the opportunities it presented. Ideas blossomed constantly in Niksar's mind as he tried to work out the best way to take advantage of his sister's newfound power.

'Get your guard up, man!' cried Haxor as she flicked her blade through the air.

'Damn you!' cried Niksar as he felt a cut open across his cheek. 'Watch where you put that thing.' He was still not fully recovered from the days he had spent drinking, but anger gave him a burst of strength and he surprised her with a backhanded slash.

She laughed, barely managing to block him. Then she backed away, lowering her sword, still grinning. 'That was more like it. You nearly looked like a swordsman. If you could concentrate for more than a minute you might almost be dangerous.'

Niksar sheathed his sword and wiped sweat from his face. 'I'm done. That's enough for tonight.' He climbed higher up the rocks and sat down, breathing heavily and gazing at the metaliths.

She sat next to him and they both took out their water flasks to drink.

'Those things are disgusting,' she muttered, nodding down the slope. They both grimaced at the pale, gelatinous lumps the crusaders were shifting from the mud. The fens were full of them, misshapen, bulbous sacs haloed by tentacles. Some were spread out like starfish but most were heaped in glistening piles that looked like the slop under a fishmonger's stall.

'How did they all get there?' said Niksar, peering down the rocky slope. The crusaders had spent the last few hours of their march wading through miles of stagnant fens and the squid-like creatures had been squeaking and sliding under their feet the whole way. 'We're nowhere near the coast.'

Haxor shrugged cheerfully. 'I once spoke to a sailor who told me that the storms along the Coast of Tusks can hurl sea creatures miles inland. Those wretched things were probably swimming happily in the sea yesterday.'

Niksar hoped the creatures' miserable fate was not a bad omen. He looked out across the lights of the camp. Hundreds of crusaders had quit within a day, heading back to the city once they sobered up, or emerged from their holy fervour, but he guessed there still were around two thousand souls spread out below him. Now that there was finally a pause in the marching, a carnival air was starting to return. Some of the crusaders were playing drums and others were gathering round campfires, laughing and singing hymns. Their voices drifted through the gloom, ghostly and strange. Niksar and Haxor were up on a rocky incline, right at the edge of the fen, but even from here he could see the peculiar madness returning to the crusaders' eyes. It was like a religious fever. Or a kind of drug that drove everyone into a peculiar frenzy. Not for the first time, he wished he could have found a way to stay in the city.

'What do you know about this Indulta Sigmaralis business?' he asked, turning back to Haxor.

She nodded to some of the crusaders. 'I know they've forgotten about it.' She was looking at a group of finely dressed nobles. 'It didn't take them long to put their fancy robes back on and start lording it over everyone. All that talk of abandoning worldly concerns does not seem to have made it beyond the city gates.'

'But things *are* different out here.' Niksar looked at a beggar hunched near the nobles. 'Indulta Sigmaralis means that anyone can become a lord of the new frontiers. We can all lay claim to land we capture. And we can leave it to our descendants.'

'Supposedly. But I'm not sure. Native-born scumbags like us might find it hard to stake claims with highborn Azyrites around to hog the glory.'

'Anyone who joins a crusade will own the places they reclaim. Own them in perpetuity.' Niksar hoped he had not made a terrible mistake. 'I heard crusaders can become masters of their own destiny out here.'

'I hear all sorts of things but I don't believe half of them.' She gave him a wry look. 'You want to set yourself up as a princeling, is that it? Is that why you're here? Not quite as devout as your sister, eh?'

'I'm devout. But I haven't sworn a vow of poverty. Why shouldn't I make something out of this? I can serve Sigmar without living in rags.'

She rolled her shoulders and stretched her back. 'My parents were hawkers. I didn't sleep in a bed until I joined the regiment. And I don't intend to stay like this. I want a way out, too. Just don't kid yourself that all the old rules evaporated once we left Excelsis. We can never totally escape our past.'

'My parents were hunters. From a long line of hunters. I'm not ashamed of my past.'

'But you don't fancy being a hunter yourself, eh?'

He thought she was mocking him but then he understood her smile. She was like him. She knew the fear that came from watching your parents slowly starve.

'People like us could make something of themselves out here,' she said. 'This *is* an opportunity. We can't reinvent ourselves but we can lay down better roots than our ancestors did. If we play this right, our children could be born into something better than we were. But we'd need to be clever.' She nodded at the nobles. 'Like they'll be. We'd need to work out who the key players are. Who holds the purse strings.' She nodded to one of the groups of crusaders. 'See those duardin?'

Niksar peered through the dusk. There were campfires flickering into life all across the field but one light was brighter than the others. A group of thirty or so squat figures were gathered around a brass furnace that looked like a metal ball cradled on copper pipes. Their bearded faces were lit by colourful fumes spewing from the pipes as the sphere sparked and turned. Lots of the duardin were wearing machinery: oily, riveted caskets; whirring clock-work mechanisms; bundles of rubber pipes. They looked like the storm engines on Excelsis' walls, or automata made from clocks and engine parts.

'The Ironweld engineers? Is that who you mean?'

'Yes. Kolgrimm Kragsson's lot. He's the cogsmith other cog-smiths wish they were. He's past his prime, perhaps, but he built half the storm engines in Excelsis. I bet even you've heard of him.'

Niksar nodded. 'The name's familiar.'

'Then make it more familiar.' Haxor leant close. 'It's all going to be about him, Niksar. I'm telling you. The Anvilhearts will get us to the Great Excelsis Road. They'll keep us alive until they're relieved by the White Angels. But then we'll be in Kolgrimm's hands. He's the one who can harness the power of Gnorl's Feast. He's the one who will turn Faithful Tor into Ardent Keep. He'll be the one that decides what goes where and who gets what. If you want to be a person of influence and power, get to know him. Impress him. If this goes well, Ardent Keep is just the beginning. From what I've heard, Kolgrimm's ambitious. He wants to build more than just a strongpoint. With the Knights Excelsior there to watch his back he's going to build us a whole new frontier along the road. Not just outposts but towns and cities. A new kingdom. And Kolgrimm will be deciding what shape the kingdom takes. He's not just an engineer. He's in a position of real power.' She laughed. 'But good luck getting near him.' She nodded to the crowd of priests and merchants milling around the duardin encampment. 'He's sud-denly very popular.'

Niksar tried to pick the cogsmith out from the other duardin but they were wearing so much whirring metal that it was hard to distinguish one from another. 'I could get his attention,' he said.

Haxor raised an eyebrow. 'Pretty confident for a man who looks like he'd keel over if he missed another meal.'

'I'm the brother of the Dawnbringer.'

Haxor looked surprised. Then she nodded slowly, smiling. 'So you are. So you are. Maybe you *do* have a chance.' She studied him in silence then shrugged. 'If you stay alive, of course. Don't think the whole journey is going to be as easy as the last few days. And there could be people round here who won't want to see you get above your station.'

He glanced at her sword. 'Maybe I need someone to watch my back. And I hear you're the best fighter in the regiment. Maybe we could work together?'

She laughed. Then, when she realised he was being serious, she looked him up and down. 'I suppose you do have good connections.' The steely look was back in her eye. 'Let's see how you get on. Let's see what you amount to, sellsword.'

They sat in awkward silence, watching the campsite spread across the field, then a sergeant looked up their way and noticed they were sat down.

'Get down here!' he bellowed. 'There's work to do.'

'I seem to have been adopted by your regiment,' said Niksar as they clambered down the rocks. 'And I don't even get to wear one of your fancy breastplates.'

'Well, if you're going to eat our food and sleep in our tents, the least you can do is a bit of digging.' She grabbed a pair of shovels as they reached the muddy field and threw one to him. 'Maybe you'll use this better than your sword.'

They joined the others in attempting to clear some of the dead creatures. It was hard enough trying to pitch tents in such muddy ground but hammering stakes into invertebrates was impossible. All across the field people were grunting and cursing as they cleared the rubbery corpses. Niksar looked around as he dug, thinking about his sister again. His thoughts flipped from excitement to fear every time he pictured her face. What were they saying to her? She had seemed changed last time they spoke. How much more might she have changed since? Near the centre of the encampment there was a circle of grand-looking pavilions – colourful, canvas domes, stitched with Sigmarite hammers and comets and surrounded by carts. Zagora would probably be in there somewhere, he decided, surrounded by fawning zealots who treated her like a fatted calf.

Near the priests' campsite there was a circle of equally impressive tents. From the steeds tethered outside, Niksar guessed they belonged to high-born Freeguild knights. The steeds were huge, eagle-headed lions called demigryphs. The regal-looking animals wore armour that was finer than anything worn by the men and women of the Phoenix Company, and they surveyed their surroundings with withering disdain. Further back, hazed by the smoke, he glimpsed the duardin encampment Haxor had pointed out.

'I might go over there,' he said, nodding to the tents. 'And introduce myself to Kolgrimm.'

'Don't just wade in. You need to think this through. What do you have to offer him?'

'I'm the Dawnbringer's brother.'

'So you keep saying, but what does that mean to Kolgrimm? He's got his commission. He's going to build Ardent Keep. And whatever else comes after. What does he need you for? Think like a noble. They don't make a move until they know what cards to play. We can make this work. We just have to avoid doing anything stupid. Let's bide our time.'

'*Our* time?'

She shrugged. 'You clearly need guidance if you're not going to ruin your chances with a series of social blunders. How much do you know about duardin etiquette?'

'Etiquette? Have you ever met any duardin?'

'They're proud. And they have ways of doing things. If you blunder over there and offend one of them they'll remember it for fifteen generations. And, from what I hear, Kolgrimm is even odder than most duardin. He's had his head next to too many anvils.'

Niksar was not as uncouth as Haxor seemed to think but he resisted the urge to set her in her place. There was something about her ferocious self-belief that he liked.

'So you're my tactical advisor, now?'

'You should be so lucky.'

He laughed and carried on digging. Most of the work had been done while they were sparring and it was not long before the regiment had set up a temporary bastion of canvas and trailing pennants. As the guardsmen finished their work, they gathered round one of the fires that littered the camp. Niksar sat with Haxor, taking the bowl of food he was offered and nodding to the familiar faces by the fire. In the last few days, as his sister spent her time with high priests and immortal heroes, Niksar had been getting to know her friends.

Haxor was at his left, eating hungrily, and to his right was a broad-shouldered youth called Brod who looked like he would have been more at home in a labourer's smock than his brightly coloured uniform. Brod did not look up as Niksar sat, his attention fixed on the soldier to his right.

'Women like to know who's in charge,' said Drannon, a ruddy-faced sergeant with a ginger beard tucked into his cuirass and skin like old leather.

Brod nodded eagerly, his eyes wide. 'You mean finding places and that.'

Drannon stared at the boy. 'Finding places? What?' He shook his head. 'I mean you need to be confident. If you like the girl you need to tell her. Make no bones about it. She won't want you messing about being coy.'

Haxor leant past Niksar and tugged on Drannon's beard. 'Tell the lad why you grew this.'

Drannon glared at her and returned to his meal, muttering as he ate.

Brod looked confused and turned to Haxor.

'The last time he tried to woo someone,' she said, 'she cut half his chin off.'

Drannon shrugged. 'There was a language barrier.'

'I understood you,' said Haxor. 'That was the problem.'

There was a chorus of laughter from around the fire.

Brod's eyes widened. 'It was you?'

She tapped the hilt of her sword and smirked. 'I *do* like to know who's in charge. And I like it to be me.'

There was another burst of laughter and Haxor leant over to slap Sergeant Drannon on the back.

'If I'd known you as well as I do now...' She paused. 'I'd have cut the rest of your chin off.' There was more laughter and she held up her hands. 'Joke! I love him like a brother.'

'You remind me of my brother,' said Drannon. 'Uglier, though.'

Haxor blew him a kiss and carried on eating, picking meat from her bowl and grimacing at it. 'What's the news, then?' she said to no one in particular. 'Do we march in three-day stints until we reach the tor?'

Drannon shook his head. 'Not according to the captain. He said that the bride of Sigmar...' He caught Niksar's glance and corrected himself. 'He said that Zagora has foreseen all this. She saw a vision of us reaching this spot on the third night. So we had to make sure we got here for the third night. We can thank her for the tough pace.' He ate another mouthful of food and shrugged. 'Hopefully we can expect a bit more rest from now on.'

Niksar looked around the circle of firelit faces. 'Rest?' he said. 'Out here in the wildlands? I'd rather keep marching.'

'It's amazing what the human spirit can endure when it has to,' said the man sitting opposite Niksar, looking up from the piece of paper he was drawing on.

It was an old guardsman called Taymar. Niksar had never spoken to him before, but he had noticed him on the day they left the city. He wore a strange approximation of the regimental uniform. It conformed to the basic design but it had been finessed. His breast-plate was polished, filigreed and engraved to an absurd level, and his doublet was silk-lined and trimmed with gold thread. The man spent half his time looking thoughtful and drawing in sketch pads. He seemed more like an eccentric noble than a soldier but, when Niksar had pointed that out to Haxor, she suggested Niksar watch Taymar when he was drilling with the others. Niksar had done so and understood immediately why Captain Tyndaris indulged the man's pretensions. He fought like a daemon, handling his sword with almost as much grace as Haxor did.

'You only have to look around you,' said Taymar, smiling at Niksar disarmingly. He waved his paper at the crowds shuffling past the campfire. 'Most of these people have never marched for three hours, never mind three days, but look at them – they're still eager.' Taymar's eyes flashed in the firelight as he looked around at the crusaders. His face was jowly and lined but the passion in his eyes made him look like a youth. 'It amazes me what these people are capable of. I was born and raised in Azyr, and...'

At the mention of Azyr, Niksar stopped listening to the man. He would have guessed he was an Azyrite, from his fine clothes and his affected air, but it still grated on him to have his suspicions confirmed.

'You talk about them like they're a different species,' he said, his tone harsher than he intended.

Taymar's face flushed and he shook his head. 'No, not at all. That's not what I mean.'

Haxor cast Niksar a sideways glance. 'I think Taymar just means that they're not used to travelling like this but they've kept going anyway.'

The conversation around the fire faltered and everyone looked towards Niksar. They were a close-knit group. He sensed he had annoyed them by digging at the old noble.

'I see,' he said. 'No offence meant.'

'None taken,' said Taymar, and the eager smile returned to his face. He leant towards Niksar. 'Look, I'm not here to set myself above anyone.' He waved at the soldiers who were now resuming their conversations. 'I joined this regiment because I'm fascinated by the human spirit. I left Azyr as a child. I'm not so different from anyone else here. But I am different enough to see how incredible this all is. This crusade is made up almost entirely of common, everyday folk.'

'Common?' said Niksar.

'I'm not speaking of their lineage. I mean they're perfectly normal. And perfectly incredible. They're prepared to march out here into the wilds of Ghur with only faith to gird them.' He waved his piece of paper. 'I spend hours trying to capture it, trying to delineate the spark that makes them so driven, but there's something ineffable at work.' He looked around at the crowds and spoke in hushed tones. 'They have a *higher purpose*.'

The man grew more enthusiastic with every word, repeating the phrase higher purpose like a mantra, and Niksar's attention wandered again. He seemed harmless enough, but every time he spoke about 'normal' people Niksar stiffened. Eventually, Taymar returned to his work, sketching the passers-by like they were holy icons.

Niksar looked back over at the domes of the command tents. 'I'm going for a walk,' he said, finishing his food and standing up.

Haxor eyed him suspiciously. 'You're not going to blunder into Kolgrimm's camp?'

Niksar considered deceiving her but then changed his mind. 'I have to try to see my sister.' He kept his voice low. 'I need to know what they're doing with her.'

'Feeding her grapes, I imagine.' Haxor shrugged. 'I don't think they'll let you anywhere near her, but I'm not sleepy either.' She stood and dusted crumbs from her uniform.

They nodded to the others and headed off into the growing gloom. Captain Tyndaris was busy talking to officers at the edge of the camp but he gave them a glance that made it clear they would be in trouble if they were gone for too long.

It was hard going making it across the field. Hundreds of pairs of feet dragging heavy belongings had churned up the mud so much that Niksar and Haxor had to lean on each other as they stumbled through the muck. Dead squid had been heaped in mounds between the campsites, but lots were still sunk in the mud, and every time Niksar trod in one he slipped and muttered a curse.

'She could be anywhere,' said Haxor as they approached the multi-coloured command tents with their streamers and rows of stern-faced guards. 'What makes you so sure she's here?'

He shrugged. 'It's somewhere to start.' They approached the row of guards outside the largest tent. 'I'm Niksar,' he said, addressing the officer in command. 'The brother of the Dawnbringer. She asked me to find her as soon as we made camp.'

The guard was about to say something dismissive, then he looked again at Niksar and his eyes widened. Before the crusade left Excelsis, Niksar had spent many hours talking with his sister, surrounded by crowds of onlookers. As a result, his face was now very well known, to the extent that most of the priests and their entourage treated him like a holy relic.

'Yes,' said the guard, sounding rattled. 'Niksar. Forgive me. I did not recognise you in the dark. Of course.' He beckoned another soldier over, ordered him to take his position, then he waved Niksar and Haxor towards the tent. 'This way. Come with me.'

Niksar looked at Haxor with a raised eyebrow, pleased at how well things were going. When they reached the tent, the soldier asked them to wait and headed into the long, tunnel-shaped porch. The sound of raised voices could be heard within and Niksar's name was mentioned several times. There were a few minutes of more hushed talking and then, finally, the soldier reappeared accompanied by a tall, elderly priestess of Sigmar. Her robes were heavily decorated and she had a gaunt, severe face. She was unusually tall, her head was shaved and tattooed with holy sigils, and she looked at Niksar like he was an endearing child.

'Niksar,' she said. 'I am High Priestess Chiana. Your sister has told me a lot about you.' She said this with a gleam of amusement in her eye that Niksar did not like.

'I have to speak with her.'

'Of course.' Chiana gave him such a patronising smile that he thought she might pat him on the head. 'That can be arranged. I'm sure she would be keen to see you.'

Niksar waited for her to say more, but the priestess simply continued smiling at him. 'Where can I find her?' he said.

'I will inform her that you came. We can arrange for her to find you when she is free.' She glanced at Haxor's uniform. 'You are with the Phoenix Company, is that right?'

Niksar was irritated by the woman's soft, cloying tone. 'I need to speak with her now.'

The priestess frowned theatrically. 'I'm afraid that won't be possible. The Dawnbringer has embarked on a strict regime of prayer and meditation. I'm sure you can understand. Your sister is carrying a great burden. And she is determined that she will not lead us astray. She spends almost every waking moment either studying the stone or communing with the God-King.' She closed her eyes and pressed a hand to her chest. 'She has sought solitude this evening, but often I am lucky enough to lead her in her prayers. The Dawnbringer has placed her trust in me as a spiritual guide.' She gave Niksar another exaggerated frown and then fell silent, clearly expecting Niksar to leave.

Niksar nodded and trudged away from the tent with Haxor struggling after him. 'I wouldn't expect to see her any time soon,' she said. 'Looks to me like Chiana wants to keep your sister away from bad influences. If your sister's confiding everything in her, she probably knows why you left Excelsis.'

Niksar gave her a shocked look.

'Take it easy,' she said, and laughed, holding up her hands. 'I don't mean that *I* know why you left. I'm just guessing Zagora might have shared it with her new friends.'

Niksar frowned, then looked around for the nearest sentry, deciding to try something. 'I am Niksar, brother of the Dawnbringer,' he said, using his most magisterial tones. 'I have just had an audience with High Priestess Chiana and she told me you could point me in the direction of Zagora.'

The man looked at Niksar in shock and nodded eagerly. 'Of course, my...'. He struggled to choose a form of address. 'Of course.' He glanced back at the command tent. 'Am I to escort you?'

'No need,' said Niksar, maintaining his lordly tones. 'I simply need to give her a message.'

'Of course.' The sentry pointed his pike at a small grove of twisted, pitiful-looking trees in the middle of the field. 'She said she would be there for the next hour or so.'

Niksar saluted. Then he strode off with as much dignity as he could muster in knee-high mud.

There was a pale light glinting through gaps in the trees as Niksar and Haxor approached. It could have been from a small fire but Niksar recognised the strange, bluish hue and guessed, even before he saw his sister, what she was doing. They found her sitting on a tree stump at the centre of a small clearing, hunched over the glimmering, holding the circlet in both hands and staring at it intently. Niksar felt a rush of sadness as he watched her. It had only been a few days since he last saw her, but already the change in her was more pronounced. She still looked impressive in her finely crafted armour, but her face was almost as gaunt as the high priestess' and she looked troubled. She did not notice that anyone was approaching.

Niksar was still a dozen feet away when his sellsword instincts warned him that people were watching him from the trees. His sister was guarded by a crowd of tattooed, shaven-headed zealots who were all gripping iron morning stars. They glared at Niksar as they approached him, whispering frantic prayers. He drew his sword and Haxor did the same.

'Brother!' said Zagora, waving the sentries away. She gave him a half smile but did not rise from the tree stump, looking back at the stone as soon as she was sure he was not going to be attacked.

Niksar put his sword away as he reached her but he kept a wary eye on the sentries. 'I'm not sure you've fallen in with the right crowd,' he said.

She ignored his comment and kept staring at the stone. It was less opaque than Niksar remembered, like dark glass, but with light dancing through its facets.

'We have to move camp,' she said.

Haxor laughed. 'You'd better be joking.' Unlike some of the Phoenix Company, Haxor did not speak to Zagora like she was a saint. 'It's taken hours to get the tents up. Tell people they've got to move them and you'll have a riot on your hands.'

Niksar had a suspicion the crusaders would do anything his sister asked but he refrained from mentioning that. 'People are settling down for the night,' he said. 'No one's going to want to up sticks now.'

Zagora put the circlet back on her head and looked up at him, seeming agitated. 'The visions keep changing. Until an hour ago I was sure we were meant to camp here. I've seen the same images since we left the city. But now, when I look in the augur stone, I see...' She started pacing around the clearing. 'This field is not safe. There's going to be an attack. Someone's going to attack us tonight if we don't move on.'

'Not a chance,' said Haxor. 'You saw how long it took to get these tents pitched. We're not going anywhere tonight. If you try to tell—'

Zagora stared at her. 'We're going to be attacked, tonight.'

'Then let's warn people,' said Haxor. 'We can tell Captain Tyndaris and the other officers. You can tell the priests and the Anvilhearts. If we spread word across the whole camp people can set guards and ready their defences. Surely that's better than being attacked as we're knee-deep in canvas trying to get our tents down?'

'That does make sense,' said Niksar. 'If you're right, and we're going to be attacked tonight, we'd be better setting up some defences here than being caught while we're struggling off through the mud.' He looked out through the trees, back towards the rocky slopes where he had been sparring with Haxor. 'We could put some sentries up there, maybe, so we have a better vantage point.'

Zagora was still pacing between the dead trees, shaking her head. 'We need to move.' She marched off, heading out of the grove with the others scrambling after her. 'I have to talk with Chiana,' she said, making for the circle of command tents.

A voice cried out in alarm, echoing through the gloom. People seated around nearby tents fell quiet as they tried to work out where the cry came from. The combination of smoke and fading light made it hard to be sure.

There was a second shout, coming from a different direction, and this one sounded even more panicked.

'I'm too late,' muttered Zagora, looking into the darkness.

One of her zealot guards coughed loudly. Then he staggered backwards and dropped to his knees.

Niksar and Haxor rushed to help him. He looked at them with a surprised expression, blood bubbling at his lips.

'What is it?' demanded Zagora.

'He's been shot,' said Haxor, nodding to the thin black shaft jutting from the centre of the man's chest.

'To arms!' cried someone. 'We're under attack!'

All across the campsite, arrows whistled through the air. Horns blew and people howled orders, rushing for cover, grabbing weapons and hunkering down next to carts. At the edge of the camp, the gall tusks stamped their enormous hooves, kicking up clouds of mud and straining at their leashes. The metaliths swayed, dropping clumps of earth onto the figures below.

Zagora raced off, her white armour flashing as she ran towards the command tents, but Niksar remained where he was, holding the arm of the man who had been shot. The wounded zealot slumped to the ground, lying back in the mud, his expression slack, his chest shaking.

Niksar loosed the man's arm and took a step backwards, shaking his head as he studied the shape jutting from the zealot's chest. There was something odd about it. It was not made of wood. He tapped it with the edge of his sword and it collapsed, forming a pile of worm-like limbs. The tendrils shivered and more blood sprayed from the man's skin.

Niksar looked around at the pale shapes in the mud. 'They're not arrows,' he whispered, backing away from the now dead soldier.

'What?' demanded Haxor, looking back towards him.

'They're not arrows! Look. It's the things in the mud.'

'What are you talking about?' growled Haxor but then her eyes widened as she saw what he meant. Shapes that had been motionless all day were now stirring. The tentacles were coiling and slapping as bulbous heads splashed in the mud.

One of the creatures catapulted forwards, moving with shocking speed, forming a dart that slammed into another soldier's chest. The man roared and tumbled into the mud, his body juddering.

'Get away!' cried Niksar, stumbling through the filth.

'How?' cried Haxor, looking around in horror. All across the campsite people were reeling as the ground shifted under their feet. The field looked like it was boiling. 'They're everywhere!'

Another one of the creatures sprang from the mud, taking down another soldier. Then a fourth one whistled past. The air filled with the sound of feeding and screams.

'There!' cried Niksar, pointing his sword. 'Up on the rocks!'

Haxor looked horrified but she shook her head. 'I have to warn the others.' She raced off across the field, heading back to where her regiment was camped. Niksar could not see his sister so he hurried after Haxor.

'We have to get up on the rocks,' said Haxor as they reached Captain Tyndaris and the others.

Tyndaris was firing his pistol at the shapes in the mud, kicking up clouds of smoke. He looked over at the rocks and nodded. 'Do it!' He lifted his cane into the air and raised his voice. 'To the higher ground!'

Most of the soldiers did as he ordered, hacking furiously and filling the air with chunks of blubber, but Haxor looked at Niksar and hesitated. There was a huge din as hundreds of crusaders cried out, so she had to step close to Niksar to be heard.

'They might be up on the rocks too.'

He gasped, wading through the rolling mud and making for the outcrop. 'They weren't. I'm sure of it.'

The scene descended into chaos. As the crusaders began attacking the ground, more of the creatures sprang up, punching into chests and filling the darkness with blood. Across the field, people were coming to the same realisation as Niksar, abandoning their tents and lurching towards the rocky slope. Horses screamed and flathorns lowed as people tried to steer them to safety. Soldiers howled curses as they tried to drag food-laden carts from the mud.

People were falling everywhere Niksar looked, clutching at their chests as they toppled into the mud. A shape rushed towards him. He cried out, halting and looking down at his chest. There was nothing there, but one of the creatures was piled at his feet, sliced neatly in half.

'Thank me later,' said Haxor, wiping her blade on her leg and dragging him towards the rocks.

As soon as they reached drier ground, they broke into a sprint and began scrambling up the incline, jostling with all the other people who were trying to escape the madness in the fens. Cuts opened on Niksar's shins and fingers as he struggled up the wet rocks but he ignored them, spurred on by the screams behind him. The noise was horrific – hundreds of people, all crying out in horror and pain. Once he reached the summit of the slope he finally allowed himself a look back.

'Sigmar's throne,' he breathed, shocked by what he saw. The darkness was crowded with dead and dying crusaders. Some of the torches had fallen and set tents alight and the flames revealed hundreds of screaming faces. At the centre of the field, a block of soldiers had formed, led by the towering shapes of the Stormcast Eternals. The Anvilhearts were attacking the ground with spears and hammers, killing the creatures with a silent, unhurried grace, but they were a single point of sanity in an ocean of lunacy. For as far as Niksar could see, the ground was bubbling and spitting death. In the space of seconds he watched dozens of people die. Whole swathes of the crowd were toppling, too mired in the mud to reach the rocks.

'It's a massacre,' he whispered.

Haxor was next to him; Tyndaris was leading the rest of the Phoenix Company up the slope. 'They're not following us,' said

Haxor, wiping some blood from her face and nodding at the shapes in the mud.

Niksar shook his head. 'Perhaps they need the water.'

'Why didn't they attack before?' asked Haxor. 'We've been wading through them all day.'

'Perhaps they were waiting until we were right in the middle of the field,' said Niksar.

'Perhaps they had to wait for nightfall,' grunted Tyndaris, reaching the top of the slope and looking back, his face even redder than usual as he tried to catch his breath. 'Maybe they can't move in the heat of the day.'

They watched in stunned silence as clouds of arrow-like shapes whirred through the darkness, slamming into the people trying to reach the rocks. Barely a third of the crusaders had gained safety so far and the rest were dropping in waves. Those that were still in the middle of the field had gathered around the Anvilhearts, pleading for help. None of the Anvilhearts had fallen. Either their golden armour was impervious to the creatures' attacks or they were such skilled fighters they were blocking the blows.

'Zagora!' cried Niksar, spotting his sister down in the field. She was near the Anvilhearts, surrounded by warrior priests and armour-clad nobles, but people were falling all around her. She was swinging her hammer furiously at the ground.

Niksar lurched to his feet, sword raised.

'Stay back!' cried Haxor, grabbing him by the arm. 'Look,' she said, pointing her sword at the lower reaches of the rocks. As people clambered out of the mud, creatures were hurtling after them, piercing the chests of those who climbed too slowly. 'What can you do for her that a Stormcast Eternal can't?'

Niksar strained against her grip but knew she was right. The Anvilhearts had spread out, forming a shield around Zagora and the senior priests. Light flashed at the head of the group and

Niksar saw that it was the Stormcast Eternal called Arulos. Rather than wielding a sword, he was swinging his staff from side to side, and with each lunge the staff flashed white, casting lightning through the gloom. The blasts juddered across the mud, incinerating the creatures, but it was not enough to save most of the people in the field.

'They're all going to die.' Niksar could not believe what he was seeing. Sigmar's grand crusade was being dismantled in a matter of moments by an enemy that probably had no idea of what they were eating. The creatures were mindless feeding machines, filling the air with crimson spray as they tore into chests.

Haxor stared at one of the corpses. 'They're just eating the hearts. They're leaving everything else.'

Already, the field was heaped with dead. Hundreds of people were still clambering up the rocks and others were climbing up ropes to the metaliths, trying to reach the drifting islands as slender shapes rushed through the air all around them. But as far as Niksar could tell, at least a third of the crusaders were still stuck in the field, either dead or thrashing frantically in the mud. Some soldiers near Niksar loosed arrows but it was a dangerous ploy – the combination of poor light and mud spray made it hard to see anything clearly.

'Look,' said Captain Tyndaris. 'They're bringing your sister.'

The Anvilhearts had stopped attacking the creatures and were moving through the mud towards the rocks. They were surrounded by panic and mayhem but the Stormcast Eternals looked like they were crossing a parade ground, moving at a calm, unhurried pace, their armour glinting in the light of Arulos' staff.

When they reached the rocks, Niksar scrambled down to meet them, calling out to his sister. She waved weakly back at him but the crowd of people between them was too great for Niksar to reach her. Her face was pale and her expression grim, but she did not appear to be injured. The Anvilhearts led her, along with the priests and nobles, up to the top of the slope, then they marched back down into the mud and began hauling other people to safety, lashing out with their weapons as they saved dozens of lives.

'So many dead,' said Niksar, staring in disbelief. Most of the people in the field had stopped moving but many of the bodies were still shivering as the creatures fed on them. He glanced back at the people on the rocks and shook his head. He guessed that maybe a thousand had made it to safety. Half the crusade. The rest had been slaughtered in the space of ten minutes, within sight of the city they had set off from.

'Climb higher!' shouted a noble, waving from the top of the slope. 'Keep away from the mud.'

The advice was unneeded. Everyone was already trying to put as much distance as they could between themselves and the creatures. Niksar saw Haxor and the others gathered on an outcrop and headed towards them. People cursed and jostled as he tried to make his way through the panicked crowd. Then, when he was only halfway towards his friends, the crowd grew even more panicked. A wave of howls and screams filled the air and someone shoved Niksar to the ground as they tried to get past him. Niksar felt a stab of pain in his forehead as it hit a rock. Feet trampled over him, pounding his back, grinding his ribs into the ground. Blood filled his eyes. For a moment he could not breathe, his air knocked from his lungs. A boot slammed into the side of his head but he managed to roll into a narrow crevasse and catch his breath. The clamour was growing all around him but he could not see why. Surely they were safe on the rocks? Unless the creatures were following…

He managed to stand, shoving people away as they barged into him. Then, by stepping sideways rather than climbing further up the slope, he managed to break into a space and look around.

Despite the terror of the people all around him, he could see no sign of the mud creatures on the rocks. So why was the panic growing rather than ebbing away? As he looked around at the people on the rocks, he noticed that lots of them were looking over their shoulders, staring back out into the darkness of the field. Something about their expressions filled Niksar with dread. He climbed onto a larger boulder and looked back out into the night.

At first, he could not see anything different. The field was still full of juddering corpses. Then he realised that the bodies were shaking in a different way. The creatures had ceased their feeding and were now slumped on the chests of the dead. They had changed from withered bags to bloated, red spheres. It looked like the bodies had sprouted berries the size of human heads. But the movement was no longer coming from the invertebrates. The ground itself was shaking, sending ripples across puddles and causing the bodies to slump and roll. He was about to speak when a thin, trembling scream cut through the night, causing everyone to look up in alarm. It was an eerie, inhuman sound.

'What in Sigmar's name is that?' whispered Haxor, appearing at Niksar's side.

People cried out in panic as something loomed into view. There was a deepening of the darkness on the far side of the field, not far from the gall tusks and the floating islands lashed to their backs. It looked like a hill rising from the ground, or a thunderhead boiling up from the mud. Only, rather than wisps of cloud, the shapes trailing from it looked horribly familiar. They were the same shape as the tentacles lying sprawled on the corpses below, only hundreds of times larger. The thin screaming sound rang out again and it was clearly coming from the huge shadow.

Niksar stared into the night, unable to believe his eyes. It looked larger than the walls of Excelsis, but it matched the illustrations he had seen on countless maps.

'A kraken,' he muttered.

The monster screamed again. The call was so loud it seemed to emanate from beneath Niksar's feet and resonate in his stomach.

Then, to everyone's horror, a second call boomed through the night, coming from a different direction, answering the first. This one was different, though – a slurred, feral roar, filled with brutish rage.

Everyone fell quiet as they watched the kraken approach. The ground trembled with increasing violence as the shape began to take form: a vast, heaving mass of grey flesh, hauled by serpentine limbs, each of which could have engulfed a galleon. All along the tentacles, jutting from the suckers, were rows of curved, bone-white horns. Almost as disturbing as the kraken's size was the fact that it had a single, unblinking eye. The eye was rolling wetly in its socket, taking in the carnage on the field and then fixing on a single point.

'It's going for the metaliths,' whispered Haxor.

She was right, Niksar realised. The monster's undulating limbs were dragging it towards the gall tusks and the islands floating above their heads. The people on the metaliths started screaming and shooting arrows but it was like throwing pebbles at a mountain.

As the people on the rocks watched in horror, the quivering monster lurched forwards, causing the ground to heave, lashed out with its spined tentacles and smashed a metalith to the ground. The island exploded. Rubble and flickers of light sliced from the fragmenting stone. People tumbled from the sky along with stacks of building materials and tons of grain.

The crusaders on the rocks howled in dismay. Each of the three metaliths contained essential materials for the journey and the building of Ardent Keep. Everything they had dreamt of, everything they had placed their faith in, was being torn down before their eyes.

The kraken pounced on the remains of the metalith, cramming people and equipment into its beak, tearing at the rubble and letting out another warbling shriek.

Niksar and Haxor stared at each other in horror. Without the metaliths there was no way to feed the crusaders. Even those who had made it onto the rocks would die. Unless they tried to head back to Excelsis. And the first part of that journey would mean travelling back through the muddy fields.

The roar of the second monster echoed through the night and the ground juddered as though great trees were falling.

'It's over,' muttered Niksar, as the strength went from his legs and he sat heavily on the rocks. He wiped away some of the blood that was flowing from his forehead and stared at his fingers. 'It's already over.'

CHAPTER EIGHT

Sigmar's soul was almost within reach, sparking at the boundaries of the mortal world, vaporous and tempestuous, surging from the clouds. There was a barrier but it was like a child trying to stem a river.

Fluxonium, thought Arulos. *Aeris.*

The tempest flashed. Violence flared. Thunder-bright understanding burned in his thoughts. Every moment spent in Ghur, every breath drawn in the Mortal Realms, brought him closer – closer to understanding the exhalations of the heavens. The clouds parted, giving Arulos glimpses of truth, fragments of the whole. His pulse quickened. Here, finally, was his chance to find out what he was capable of. To see what the Anvilhearts were capable of.

'What's he doing?' cried Niksar as one of the Anvilhearts broke away from the others and began climbing down the rocks.

The nobles and priests looked equally concerned, crying out to the other Stormcast Eternals and staring out into the night, their eyes wide with horror as they watched the kraken devour the metalith.

'It's the leader,' said Haxor. 'Their captain. Stormspear.'

There were more dismayed roars from the crowd on the rocks as the kraken destroyed another piece of the metalith, smashing it across the ground. The rock exploded as it rolled, detonating with tectonic force. If Niksar had not been seated, the tremor would have knocked him from his feet. The kraken engulfed the wreckage, billowing over it in a wave of blubbery flesh, as the second, even larger monster strode into view, heading for the survivors on the rocky outcrop. It was a different species entirely – humanoid, but the size of a cathedral.

'A gargant,' whispered Niksar, but it was far larger than any giants he had seen before. In a few moments it would reach them and, with every step it took, the ground shook.

All around Niksar people howled and screamed at the destruction, but Niksar kept watching Arulos Stormspear, fascinated by his assured manner. The creatures towering over him looked like outcrops of land, or the shoulders of mountains, but the Stormcast Eternal showed no sign of fear as he crossed the corpse-crowded field. There was no wind, but his cape snapped violently behind him. As he approached the humanoid monster he broke into a run – not a panicked sprint, but an easy, rolling jog and, as he ran, he raised his staff. The jewel at its head pulsed blue, the light growing quickly brighter, like a comet racing through the night towards the metaliths.

'Is he going to attack them?' asked Niksar. The kraken was lurching towards the remaining two metaliths, shaking the ground with every movement. The idea of someone fighting such titans, even a Stormcast Eternal, was absurd.

Arulos paused when he reached the command tents. The circle of domes was burning fiercely, silhouetting the Stormcast. He raised his staff higher and threw back his head. Light thrashed around his face and coruscated down his staff.

Then a new sound rumbled through the darkness and everyone paused to look up. Even the two behemoths halted. Lights flickered through the clouds, picking out silvered glimpses of the carnage below. The sound grew into a rolling, drumming din, keeping time with the light bursts. The kraken turned from the metaliths and fixed its grotesque eye on Arulos, glaring down at his tiny, glittering form. The gargant stumbled to a halt, looking round in confusion, lowering the tree trunk it was carrying. The noise grew so loud Niksar found it unbearable but he could not tear his gaze from Arulos. The Anvilheart lowered his staff and pointed it at the kraken. Niksar expected a thunderbolt or perhaps a column of flames, but the staff affected the clouds instead. They boomed and churned as Arulos jabbed and switched his staff, as though attached to it by invisible thread.

The kraken rolled forwards, leaving the metaliths and heading towards Arulos, carried on its boiling nest of limbs. Light poured down from the clouds, blinking and settling on its flesh, like rain falling on a hillside, then the monster halted and reared up, roaring as loud as the thunder. The sky flashed white as a thunderbolt kicked down from the clouds, splashing against the kraken. The monster blazed like sun-kissed water. Its tentacles snaked and coiled around its head and its vast bulk began to tremble. Then the light died and the kraken sank back into darkness.

Arulos was still blinking in and out of view, lit by the flickering clouds. He still had his staff raised and, in his other hand, he was now holding a book that was glowing as brightly as the head of his staff. He shouted something, his words lost in the storm, then he shook his head and lowered the book. He turned his back on the kraken and began moving slowly back across the field towards the rocks.

'He's made it worse,' said Haxor, pointing her sword at the kraken, the blade rattling in her trembling grip. 'Look! He's just made the damned thing angry.'

As remnants of light danced across the kraken its movements became more frenzied. It lashed out with its barbed limbs, tearing up channels of mud as it lurched back and forth, bellowing and snorting. Arulos paid no attention to the violence behind him, walking calmly away and closing his book. He seemed to have given up. As the light faded he vanished almost entirely in the darkness, only revealed by occasional flashes across his polished armour.

Niksar shook his head, horrified. Arulos had looked so sure of himself as he marched out to meet the kraken but it now looked more terrifying than ever. Even the gargant had paused to stare at it, its jaw hanging open in a shocked stupor. Over the panicked cries he heard Captain Tyndaris, ordering the Phoenix Company to ready their weapons. Other groups of soldiers followed suit, nocking arrows and drawing swords. Niksar felt like laughing. The kraken was smashing across the field, hurling carts like they were insects. How could anyone hope to fight such a thing if even Arulos Stormspear had failed to stop it?

The kraken rolled and lurched and began powering back towards the metaliths. Niksar looked at Haxor and the despair in her eyes was a mirror of his own. Without the metaliths there was no crusade. No food or supplies.

Then Niksar realised something. 'It's headed for the gargant.' The kraken had become so frenzied it was attacking everything within reach and upon reaching the other, larger monster, it lashed out, enveloping the gargant with its tentacles.

The gargant roared and hurled the kraken back. Then it hefted the tree it was carrying and slammed it into the creature's head. The ground juddered as the monsters fought, rolling and flailing and crashing through the night. Their fight was half hidden in the darkness but the sounds were all too clear – an apocalyptic mixture of howls and ground-splitting thuds that echoed across the fields.

The crowd on the rocks fell quiet, watching in shocked silence as the kraken and the gargant tore each other apart. The gargant was larger, but the kraken was so frenzied that the giant struggled to find purchase. Blood, meat and talons rained down on the fields as the creatures lumbered through the mud, crushing groves of trees and churning up the ground. As Niksar watched the two goliaths battle he felt pathetic and insignificant, crushed by the dreadful power of Ghur.

Gradually, as the monsters' bodies collapsed, their movements slowed. Finally, after several minutes of brutal violence, the kraken began hauling itself away into the darkness, trailing innards and blood. The gargant was equally ruined but it did not relent, pounding its opponent with the tree trunk as it tried to escape. The monsters were visible for a long time, lunging and rolling as they headed away. Even when they were no longer in sight, their calls could still be heard, echoing through the darkness.

When the sound of the monsters had finally faded, the survivors on the rocks turned to look at each other. Everyone was covered in blood and muck and they all wore the same expressions of blank-eyed horror. Someone called out for light and a few torches spluttered into life, revealing the dreadful state of the crusaders.

Niksar climbed down a few rocks and edged cautiously back towards the field, squinting out into the gloom. There were bodies everywhere, slumped awkwardly against muddy slopes or floating in brackish pools. All of them carried the vile, fruit-like shapes of their sated killers. The blood creatures looked to have returned to a catatonic state, but Niksar could see others still floating in the mud, grey and crumpled, ready to attack. The absurdity of the crusade had never been so obvious.

'Don't get too close,' said Haxor, looking past him at the drifting shapes. Her words were flat and disjointed, as though she could only half remember how to talk. Niksar could understand. His mind felt shattered by what he had just witnessed.

'We'll have to wait here for now,' whispered Haxor. 'Perhaps we can stay alive until morning. Then cut back across the fields while those things are sleeping.'

Niksar could still make out the lights of Excelsis in the distance. Crawl back with their tails between their legs? He thought of what was waiting for him back in the city and had to battle the urge to howl. He looked across the rocks. Some people were tending to the wounded or helping others reach higher ground, but most were simply staring into the night, looking for more behemoths.

'I need to talk to my sister.' He climbed back up the rocks and began looking for the priests.

He found them in a steep-sided hollow at the top of the slope, like a natural alcove in the rocks, broad enough to hold dozens of people. The priests' robes were torn and filthy, as were the clothes of the merchants who were with them. Chiana was there, talking urgently to Zagora, as well as the duardin lord, Kolgrimm, flanked by a group of cogsmiths whose mechanised armour was hung with pipes and obscure-looking measuring implements. There were other nobles and Freeguild officers there but none of them were displaying their usual confidence. Everyone looked dazed and unsure of themselves, gripping weapons and watching the rocks for signs of movement.

Only one person seemed untroubled by what had happened: the leader of the Anvilhearts, Arulos Stormspear. He was standing at the edge of the gathering, accompanied by some of his subordinate Stormcast Eternals. His hands were resting on the head of his staff and he looked like he had been set in gold, indifferent to the panic that was building around him. Phoenix Company guardsmen were ordering onlookers away as others fixed a couple of torches to the walls of the hollow, casting long shadows across the gathering. Desperate voices rang out as people tried to reach the priests but the soldiers were preventing most people from entering.

'It's me,' said Niksar, spotting the soldier he had spoken to earlier. 'The Dawnbringer's brother.'

The man nodded and allowed Niksar and Haxor to approach the group, causing a howl of protest from the people nearby. Niksar hurried through the group but when he tried to reach his sister, guards shoved him back. He was about to argue when Chiana held up her hands and called the meeting to order.

'Please,' she said. 'We can't all speak at once. Lower your voices.' She had lost the smug demeanour that so annoyed Niksar earlier and there was blood running from a gash in the side of her head, but she spoke clearly and with confidence. 'Let the Dawnbringer speak.'

The hubbub died down and even the crowds outside the cavern stifled their panic for a moment. The cogsmiths took longest to quieten down, grumbling loudly and barking curses in their harsh duardin tongue.

'Listen to the Dawnbringer?' said Kolgrimm once the others had fallen silent.

He was as short and powerfully built as all his race and he was encased in so much riveted metal that he resembled a piece of talking machinery. His broad boulder of a head was encased in a crested helmet that obscured most of his face, and his eyes were magnified by thick, circular goggles. There was nothing mechanical about his tone, though. He sounded like he resented having to address such an audience, dragging the words from his gravelly throat.

'The Dawnbringer told us to set our camp in this fen. Even though it would have been easy to march east instead, and join the river at Dassena Ridge. If anyone had requested my opinion, which I note they did not, my advice might have saved the crusade.' He spoke in the blunt, slightly too loud manner of someone who had spent their life working noisy machines. 'I put a lot into this venture...' He rolled his head on his shoulders, causing the pistons on his neck armour to wheeze. 'So have others. And now we'll have a tough fight even to make it back to Excelsis.' He tapped the handle of his cog-shaped axe on the ground. 'Maybe it's time to let others have their say.'

The other cogsmiths muttered into their beards, stamping and rattling their armour.

Zagora did not even look up. She was tapping the augur stone clasped at her forehead and muttering to herself. Niksar had to concede that she was not doing a great job of looking reliable, but it riled him to hear Kolgrimm implying his sister was to blame.

'How do you know this was a mistake?' he demanded, speaking before Chiana could reply.

Chiana looked over at him, clearly surprised to see him there. She smiled patronisingly and was about to speak, so Niksar continued quickly.

'How do you know the Dawnbringer hasn't saved our lives by bringing us here?'

'Saved our lives?' Kolgrimm snorted. 'Did you see what just happened? Everyone's dead.'

'Not everyone,' said Niksar, goaded by the duardin's dismissive tone. 'And these are the wildlands. We have travelled for days and hardly been attacked until now. Who's ever heard of that happening?' He looked around the group. 'Who's ever heard of anyone coming this far from Excelsis without being eaten? Is it normal to travel through these lands so quickly and easily? Of course it isn't.' He was pleased to notice that Zagora had looked up and was watching him. She nodded encouragingly. 'There has to be some reason we've made it here so easily,' he continued. 'And that reason is Zagora.' He realised he was arguing for exactly the kind of blind faith he had been worried about, but now that he had started, and everyone was staring at him, he felt unable to change tack. 'People have been killed. They have...' He wavered, remembering the scenes in the fen. 'It's terrible. But maybe this was meant to happen. Maybe the crusade was *meant* to face those creatures at this point.' He stared at Kolgrimm. 'Who are you to say what's right and what's wrong?'

The cogsmith's face darkened and he looked too angry to reply.

'Well said,' whispered Haxor.

Chiana tried to speak but Niksar had ignited an argument. There was an explosion of voices from all sides of the cave. For several minutes no one could make themselves heard, then a voice rang out with clear authority.

'I have confidence in the Dawnbringer,' said Arulos Stormspear. 'She is the truth.'

Kolgrimm looked flustered and annoyed and prepared to launch into another rant.

'Let her speak,' said Arulos.

Everyone looked at the Stormcast Eternal, unnerved by the peculiar effect of his voice. It simmered through the air, like an electric charge. Niksar tried, again, to make out Arulos' eyes, but the effort was disorienting, like staring into a whirlpool, and he looked away.

People turned from the Knight-Arcanum to Zagora. She nodded and glanced at Niksar as she walked out into the centre of the circle.

'My brother is right.' After the resonant tones of Arulos, her voice sounded small but her gaze was so intense that no one tried to interrupt her. 'I have been sure, since before we even left the city, that we must reach this particular fen by tonight.'

She touched the augur stone again. 'I did not foresee the deaths. I did not...' She faltered.

Chiana stepped to her side, compassion in her eyes as she put a hand on her shoulder, whispering something. Zagora nodded and looked up at the crowd.

'I did not foresee the deaths. But I still believe Sigmar meant for us to be here, at this point, tonight.'

'He meant for the crusade to fail?' The anger was gone from Kolgrimm's voice. He was not accusing Zagora any more. He just sounded baffled. 'Why would the God-King want his own crusade to end in failure?'

Zagora did not reply straight away. She looked at Stormspear. Niksar had the strange sense that they were communing somehow. Neither of them spoke, but it still seemed that something passed between them. Zagora nodded. Then she looked back at Kolgrimm.

'The crusade has not ended.'

There was another eruption of voices. Lots of people demanded an explanation and others sounded angry. Some even laughed.

Kolgrimm pounded his axe on the ground. 'Half of us have been killed. And that's not even the worst of it. Did you see what those things did to the metaliths? I have lost half of my equipment and stone. Even if we reached the Great Excelsis Road, how do you suggest we build Ardent Keep? It's impossible.'

'Nothing is impossible,' said Chiana, smiling at him, 'with faith.'

The smile enraged Kolgrimm even more. '*Lots* of things are impossible. And building a wall without stone is one of them. I can tell you exactly what will happen if you–'

'We will continue,' said Zagora. She did not raise her voice but the words carried. Everyone was listening. She looked at Kolgrimm. 'The glimmering has not told me who will build Ardent Keep, only that it will be built. We will proceed to the river, as planned. If your heart is no longer in the crusade, Kolgrimm

Kragsson, then perhaps one of your kinsmen can continue in your stead.'

Zagora had not spoken unkindly and there was no accusation in her words, but Kolgrimm looked like she had struck him.

'My heart? No longer...' He looked around at the other duardin but none of them spoke.

'I am not slighting you.' Zagora impressed Niksar with how calm she sounded. She looked away from Kolgrimm to the other nobles and soldiers. 'Nor am I slighting anyone else who wishes to turn back. But this crusade will go on.' Her voice grew louder, and harder. 'And it will succeed.'

Even though it was his sister speaking, Niksar felt his pulse quicken. There was a quiet power to her that he had never heard before.

'My waking dream is still there,' she continued. 'Despite everything that has just happened. I see us reaching Faithful Tor. I see the keystone being laid. I see the walls of Ardent Keep made fast against the creatures of the wildlands. We will build our strongpoint and we will hold it. And we will reclaim the Great Excelsis Road.'

Chiana and the other priests were nodding eagerly but lots of the other crusaders were looking at Kolgrimm to see how he would respond. Niksar could understand. From what Haxor had told him, the cogsmith's pedigree was one of the reasons people believed in the crusade. Haxor had described him as a genius. What would people think about trying to build a new settlement without him?

Niksar looked over at Arulos but the Stormcast Eternal had become statue-like again, staring into the middle distance.

'The Dawnbringer has spoken,' said Chiana. 'Everything that has befallen us is Sigmar's will. And it is his will that we continue until we reach the river that the Dawnbringer has seen in her augur stone.' She waved at Arulos. 'Knight-Arcanum Storm-spear sees the truth. I see the truth. We will continue together until our work is done.' She looked around the group. 'Anyone who wishes to return to Excelsis should speak up now.' She let her gaze come to rest on Kolgrimm.

No one spoke. Kolgrimm glowered and shook his head.

'How are we going to build a strongpoint? How can we follow the strictures of the Decree Sigmaris? Even if the Dawnbringer gets us to the point where the ley lines meet, how will we build a nexus syphon? We have to harness a *lot* of geomantic energy if we're going to build the defences right. We're not going all that way to sling up a half-arsed stakefort that couldn't withstand a stiff breeze. That's not why I came. This is meant to be...' His words trailed off into angry muttering and Niksar sensed that Kolgrimm had been about to say more than he intended.

Chiana nodded, frowning sympathetically. 'It will be a chal-lenge,' she said. 'And no one will think badly of you, Kolgrimm, if you wish to renege on your commission. But we will still need the help of an engineer when we reach the river.' She looked around the group. 'I am sure we can find someone who can–'

'Renege?' The cogsmith stared at her, his eyes magnified by the lenses of his goggles. '*Renege?* Kolgrimm Kragsson does not go back on his word.' He waved his cog-shaped axe at a group of human Ironweld engineers. 'And if you think anyone else in this crusade can replace me, you're wrong. I designed those rafts. And I have the plans for Ardent Keep. The real plans.' He tapped his helmet. 'In here. If anyone can do this thing it's me. I'm the only one with the experience you need. You let some halfwit beardling try and they'll blow us to kingdom come. Only I can make it work.'

'Rafts?' muttered Niksar, wondering what they were talking about.

Chiana smiled. 'Then it *is* possible?'

Kolgrimm snarled, drummed his fingers on his axe and glared at the ground. Then he looked at one of the other duardin, who shrugged and nodded back at him.

'Aye,' muttered Kolgrimm. 'I'll make it possible.'

One of his subordinates looked up in surprise and was about to speak, but Kolgrimm glared him into silence. Chiana nodded, still smiling, and whispered a prayer.

On the far side of the circle, Captain Tyndaris raised a hand, signalling that he wished to speak. His habitual grimace was even more pronounced than usual and he was covered in cuts and bruises. 'High priestess,' he said, sounding short of breath, 'I have no doubt that Kolgrimm and his cogsmiths will find a way to overcome this setback, but can the Dawnbringer now share her thoughts on how we will reach the Great Excelsis Road?' He nodded out of the cave, towards corpse-crowded fields. 'These fens continue for miles if we keep heading north. We can wait here until morning and see if the creatures sleep in daylight, as they did yesterday, but once night falls...' He shrugged. 'You have spoken of a river and rafts. It seems that you have plans I am unaware of.'

There was a murmur of questions from around the cave. High Priestess Chiana glanced at Zagora and gave her an encouraging nod.

Zagora nodded back and looked out at the crowd. People had gathered on the rocky slopes outside the cave and there were hundreds of people listening.

'I have seen Sigmar's will in the stone,' she said. 'It was never his intention that we should march any further north across these fens. There are *no* safe paths through these lands, not for so many people. But the God-King has an answer.' She looked tired and drawn, but mentioning the stone seemed to reinvigorate her. 'Before we left Excelsis, the glimmering showed me a vision of the crusade rushing north on a great river, carried past the predators that prowl these wildlands, borne on rafts until the river reaches a falls. By the time we reach the falls we will be far away from these fens. And then, at the foot of the falls, we will see our goal – the hill known as Faithful Tor.'

She had been speaking hurriedly, almost breathless with excitement, but now she caught herself and took a deep breath.

'And there, where Sigmar's blood courses through the ground, where a great junction of divine power purifies the earth, we will build Ardent Keep.'

The crowd fell quiet. Even Kolgrimm stared at Zagora. The final words of her speech had seemed to come from another body, ringing around the cave.

Chiana smiled at Zagora like a proud parent. 'Before we left Excelsis, our logisticators compared their maps with those provided by our brethren from Azyr.' She nodded gratefully at Arulos and the other Stormcast Eternals. 'And we agreed that the river seen by the Dawnbringer is the Claw-water. It springs from a place called Karth's Cauldron, just half a day's march west from where we now stand. We will sail down the Claw-water until we reach Redmane Falls and then we will be in sight of Faithful Tor.'

Captain Tyndaris frowned. 'Sail?'

Chiana was about to reply when Zagora spoke up again.

'Kolgrimm Kragsson has prepared for the river passage, captain. He and his engineers have brought all the materials we need.'

Tyndaris looked doubtful.

'Trust me,' said Zagora. 'It will work. I have seen it in the stone. We will not need rafts for everyone. Many of us can travel on the metaliths and we will fasten the gall tusks to the rafts.'

'What about while we're assembling the rafts?' asked one of the nobles, a fine-boned, elderly woman who looked at Zagora with adoration. 'Will we be safe, Dawnbringer?'

Zagora shook her head. 'No.'

There was a murmur of alarm from round the cave.

Zagora waited until everyone fell quiet again. 'We will not be safe at any point on this crusade. Danger will follow us at every turn. The stone did not show me what would happen here tonight, it only showed me that we had to reach this fen. There may be dangers along the banks of the Claw-water. But that is the route Sigmar wishes us to take. This is his will. The God-King wants us to build Ardent Keep and he believes our best chance of success is by riding the Claw-water north.' She took the circlet from her head and held it up, letting the torchlight flash in the facets of the augur stone. 'This is no normal glimmering. It does not simply show the future or a possible future. The prophesiers told me they have never seen anything like it.' She glanced at some prophesiers in the crowd, who nodded back eagerly. 'It has made me a conduit for the will of the God-King. And he wants us to keep going. He *demands* that we keep going.'

Again, people looked at Zagora like she was a spirit, risen from another age of the realm. Whispered prayers came from every direction.

'Assembling the rafts won't be a problem,' said Kolgrimm, glancing at Captain Tyndaris. 'Not with this many willing hands. I have designed them to be quickly assembled. Two, three hours at most, and we can launch them.'

Tyndaris looked at Zagora. 'When should we try to reach the river, then? First light?'

Zagora nodded. 'Yes,' she said, glancing out at the corpses in the fens. 'We can't go back in the mud while it's dark so we will need to wait until the morning.'

'Then we should make the most of the time,' said Captain Tyndaris. 'There are a lot of wounded people on these rocks. And they're going to need to march tomorrow. We can spend the night treating them and guarding them while they sleep.'

They've been marching for three days straight, thought Niksar, but he kept his thoughts to himself.

'The captain makes a good point,' said Chiana, gesturing to the cave opening. 'Let us tend to those we can. And let us ease the passing of those we can't.'

CHAPTER NINE

Niksar slipped through the mud and the rain, trying to keep pace with a group of nobles. Their demigryph steeds were so large and heavily armoured that they resembled steamtanks, and the nobles were the first people he had seen for hours who did not look awful. Their skin was clear and their eyes shone with health. Most of the crusaders had looked dreadful even before they left the city, but these lords and princelings seemed immune to the hardships of travel. As servants struggled in their wake, holding parasols over their masters' heads, the nobles were talking loudly about what they intended to do once Ardent Keep was a reality.

'It will be beholden to *us* to set the right tone,' boomed one, his chin raised as he waved at the teeming masses that surrounded him. 'There will be no Grand Conclave where we're going. And the wildlands are exactly the kind of place where men stray from the path of true faith. Idolatry and backsliding are just as real a threat as the beasts of the forest.'

The other nobles nodded sagely, sitting erect in their tasselled saddles as they sipped their wine. 'The lower orders will look to us for guidance,' said another. 'They will be unsure of their position. They will need to learn their place in the new world. It is not enough to simply watch from afar as lesser men strive to protect the city. We have to lead from the front. We need to show the way.'

Niksar edged closer, trying to follow their conversation, shoving his way through groups of people who looked like they were about to drop into the mud. The crusaders had spent the morning marching west through rain-lashed scrubland, heads bowed beneath sodden hoods and feet dragging through the puddles. The weather was growing worse by the hour. A brutal wind drove rain into Niksar's face so hard he could barely see, but he was determined to keep pace with the nobles. They might not know it yet, but he would be riding with them soon, espousing the same, elevated principles. Everyone else he'd passed had spoken like an imbecile, boasting of how they might soon have a two-roomed hut to call their own, or a cow bigger than their old cow. Niksar refused to accept his place in such a limited world. He was destined for something more. Something better. He had to be.

The nobles reined in their steeds, leaning close to each other as they shared a private joke. They whispered and laughed, waving at the storm-battered crowds. Niksar finally caught up with them and wondered if this was the right time to introduce himself. He was as filthy as everyone else and he knew he still looked ill, but he was desperate to make a connection of some kind. He tripped and stumbled through the muck, wrenching his sodden boots from the mud with a series of noisy pops. The nobles had finished their joke and were about to ride on. Niksar lurched towards them and raised his hand, wracking his brain for the right thing to say – something that would make them understand he was more like them than the fools who dreamed of pig farming.

'Haw haw!' came a nervous laugh from behind Niksar.

A wave of nausea washed through him as he recognised the hysterical tones of Ocella. He whirled around but his feet were so deep in the mud that he unbalanced himself, falling sideways into the filth.

As the nobles rode on, trembling hands latched onto Niksar's shoulders and helped him back to his feet. Ocella looked worse than the last time he saw her. Her enormous feather headdress was caked in mud and one of her teeth had been knocked out, giving her an even more deranged appearance. She still had her bone staff, however, and she leant heavily on it as she pulled Niksar from the mud.

'We're crusaders,' she laughed, shaking and grinning at his shoulder. Her ailments seemed to have grown worse and she was shivering violently. She looked too frail to survive such atrocious weather. She took in his wasted frame and filthy clothes. 'Who would have seen that coming?' she laughed. Then she embraced him in a surprisingly tight hug. 'I'm sorry for what I said. I know you wouldn't sell me out. Not you.'

Niksar shoved her away, then had to hold her to stop her falling. He looked around for the nobles but, to his annoyance, they had already ridden on. He prayed they had not seen him wrestling in the mud with Ocella.

'What are you doing here?' he demanded. 'Have you followed me? Have you come all this way just because I'm here?'

She wiped rain from her eyes and grimaced at the mud. 'I was in hot water. Thanks to that dead docker. None of my friends in Excelsis wanted to talk to me any more.' She gave him a sideways look. 'But there were plenty of other folk who *did* want a word with me. Without you there to protect me I was in danger.'

'That docker was a heretic!' whispered Niksar furiously, leaning close to her. He looked around but everyone was too busy battling on through the rain to pay them any attention. 'What were you thinking? How could you be mixed up with someone like that? How could you get *me* mixed up with someone like that?'

She looked mortified, but only for a second, then she grinned. 'How's your sister? It's her, isn't it? She's the one. The Dawnbringer. Can I meet her? If she's your sister she must be as noble a soul as you are.' She looked around at the crowds. 'Not like all the others.'

'What were you doing talking to a man with Chaos symbols tattooed on his chest?' He backed away, leaning into the rain, being careful not to fall again as he glared at her. 'Are you involved in that stuff? *Are* you one of them?'

'One of what?' She wiped more rain from her face and tried to straighten her headdress. Then she looked shocked. For a brief moment she managed to meet his eye. 'You think I'm a cultist?'

Ocella looked so incredulous that Niksar felt bad for even suggesting it. His instinct had always been that she was odd rather than in league with daemons and dark gods and her look of disbelief was too genuine for him to doubt her.

'It doesn't matter,' he muttered, looking at the backs of the quickly disappearing nobles. 'Just keep away from me.' He turned away to rejoin the tide of stumbling figures plodding through the rain.

'Keep away?' Ocella grabbed his arm. 'I need you. You're the only one I can rely on, Niksar. I need you to protect me.' Her tremors grew much worse. Then she grabbed something from her belt. 'I have it,' she said, her eyes flashing. 'I got it. The Claw Coagulate.'

'I don't need anything from you,' he snapped, wrenching his arm free. 'If it wasn't for you–'

He hesitated, looking at the medallion she was holding. It was a silver eagle's talon.

'The Claw Coagulate?' He recognised the name from their conversations in Excelsis. 'The alkahest?' He stared at it. The thing was so beautiful he forgot what he was going to say.

'It can transmute anything,' she whispered. 'Into anything. An aetheric alkahest. Do you remember what I told you about them? How rare they are? How powerful? Think what this could mean for us.' She glanced around nervously, then gripped his arm again. 'But without you, I can't...' She scratched furiously at her matted hair, causing her headdress to shed feathers. 'They'll get me, Niksar. Without you to watch my back they'll get me.'

He pulled his arm away again. 'I can't be seen with you. This crusade is my chance to–'

'Without me there would be no crusade. If it wasn't for me, your sister would never have touched that stone.'

Until that moment, Niksar had almost forgotten that the glimmering came to him from Ocella. The contrast between the pomp that launched the crusade and this scrawny woman was startling.

'What do you know about that stone?' he asked, feeling suddenly troubled by the thought that all of this began with someone who consorted with heretics.

'What do *you* know about it?' She looked away, talking to the rain. 'Nothing. You know nothing about it. This whole crusade sprang out of that stone and only I know where it came from.'

Niksar did not like her tone. What if Ocella was not just an unhinged eccentric? What if she was something subtler? Something more dangerous. 'Tell me what you know about that stone,' he snapped, grabbing the hilt of his sword.

She stared at his sword, the colour draining from her face. Then she held up the silver talon. 'We're a team, Niksar. Think how well we worked together before. Think of all the things we could do with this.'

He looked at the nobles, worried they might be watching.

She caught the direction of his gaze and shook her head. 'You could never be good enough for them. But the truth is that you're better than them. Don't you realise? We could work together to do more than they ever could.'

'Niksar!' cried a voice from in the crowd.

He peered through the rain and saw a rider approaching. For one absurd moment he thought it was a noble, come to prove Ocella wrong, but then he recognised the Phoenix Company uniform and saw that it was Haxor.

'I thought it was you,' she said, reining in her horse next to him. 'What are you doing up here on your own?'

Niksar turned back to Ocella and found that she had vanished into the rain. He looked in every direction and could see no sign of her in the crowds of sodden crusaders.

'What are you looking for?' asked Haxor.

Niksar shook his head. 'What are you doing?' he asked, struggling to be heard over the downpour. 'Why aren't you with Tyndaris?'

'Something's happening up ahead.' She nodded to the top of the slope they were all climbing. 'Word is that we've reached the river your sister spoke of. We're supposed to be at the back still, guarding the metaliths, but the captain sent me up to see what's going on.'

He nodded, looked at the group of nobles, and then had an idea.

'Can I come with you?'

She shrugged, helped him up onto the horse and then rode on through the downpour. They quickly passed most of the people who were marching on foot and, as the horse carried them up the slope, they left the bulk of the column behind and escaped the crush. Niksar looked back over his shoulder and was shocked to see how small the crusade looked. It was still around a thousand people strong and the two remaining metaliths were still drifting in the distance, hauled by the massive shapes of the gall tusks, but everything was dwarfed by the fury of the storm. Mountainous clouds boiled overhead, flickering as they loomed over the muddy plain. Beneath such majesty and surrounded by miles of sombre fields, the crusade looked horribly insignificant.

'They've halted,' said Haxor, drawing him from his reverie. 'Look, all along the ridge. The Anvilhearts have stopped to wait for everyone else.'

He looked up through the rain and saw the Stormcast Eternals spread out at the top of the slope. Most were simply looking out into the rain, but Arulos Stormspear and his standard bearer were standing with Chiana, Kolgrimm and the other crusade leaders. They were locked in a fierce debate. Haxor geed her horse up the final stretch of the slope and they had almost reached the top of the incline when Niksar saw that his sister was with Chiana and Arulos. She looked angry, slamming her greathammer in the mud as she talked.

'Looks like trouble,' muttered Haxor, slowing her steed as they neared the group.

Niksar was about to reply but the words stalled in his throat as the horse reached the top of the slope and he saw the valley that lay on the other side.

'Sigmar's Throne,' he whispered.

They were looking down into a steep-sided ravine, with craggy walls on either side and a river hurtling down its centre. The river sprang from a pool at the southern end of the crevasse, boiling up from a pale, circular basin. The basin was created from the eye socket of a fossil so vast its tail disappeared over the horizon, and the walls of the valley were formed in the cradle of an enormous ribcage, but it was not the huge bones that caused Niksar to flinch, it was the scene on the valley floor. The gully was heaped with butchered corpses, still bleeding their lives out into the muddy fields on this side of the river. They were human, and for a moment Niksar was confused. The dead were Excelsians, but the crusade was yet to reach the valley. Then he realised the truth.

'One of the other crusades.'

Haxor nodded and pointed north down to the other end of the valley to where the river turned a bend and disappeared from view. Beneath the steep walls of the ravine, a battle was taking place. The fighting was half a mile away or more and it was impossible to see the details through the banks of falling rain, but Niksar could see banners bearing the heraldry of Excelsian Freeguild regiments. There were two groups, as far as he could make out. There was a larger gathering, many hundreds strong, not far from where the river bent out of view, and there was a smaller group, perhaps no more than a couple of hundred or so, gathered at the foot of the valley wall. The smaller group was surrounded by a much larger army that was attacking with no sense of tactics or logic.

'Greenskins,' whispered Niksar, looking over at his sister. She had not noticed him yet, still locked in an argument with Chiana and the others. 'Let's get closer,' he said.

'I have to take word back to Captain Tyndaris.' Haxor's tone was bleak. 'He's going to want to know about this. We'll have a tough time reaching that river with all those orruks in the way.'

'I just need to hear what they're saying.' Niksar nodded at Storm-spear and the others near his sister. 'Surely the captain will want to know what the Anvilhearts are planning?'

'Very well. But we'll have to be quick.' Haxor steered her horse across the top of the rise, heading over towards the arguing group.

No one looked up as they approached. Arulos Stormspear was addressing the group.

'The greenskins would not present any difficulty. But we will be delayed by a day, perhaps more.' He nodded to Zagora, who was glaring at the mud. 'And the Dawnbringer told us that her prophecy does not allow for such a delay. She saw us heading downriver today, reaching the falls and arriving at the tor in time for the conjunction.' He looked at Zagora.

Zagora refused to meet his eye, looking instead at Chiana and the other priests. 'We can't leave them to die.' She pointed at the carnage in the valley. 'Look at them! Those are *people*. And once the guardsmen are dead the orruks will turn on the civilians. We have to do something.'

High Priestess Chiana looked regal and proud, her robes whipping around her as the storm battered the hill. She frowned at Zagora. 'Your prophecy showed us reaching the tor in time for Gnorl's Feast.'

Zagora nodded. 'The augur stone showed Kolgrimm and his engineers assembling the rafts. They did it incredibly fast. And we were sailing while it was still light. We reached the falls and entered the hills before dusk, with the tor up ahead.'

Kolgrimm nodded. 'It could be done as she describes. If we leave those people to their fate.' He stared at the battle. 'But what kind of monster would do that?'

All eyes turned to Stormspear and the other Anvilhearts.

The proud-looking standard bearer, Varek Skyborn, spoke up. There was an edge of emotion in his voice. It could have been anger, or at least frustration.

'We came here, to this valley, because the Dawnbringer's vision told us to. Her plan is clear – we build the rafts and sail downriver today, and we reach the tor in time for the conjunction of the two moons. If we ignore that vision, if we disregard her plan, the crusade loses its purpose.'

'Its purpose?' Niksar jumped from the horse and approached them. 'Its purpose is to save lives.' He could not bring himself to argue with Stormcast Eternals so he addressed the rest of the group, pointing at the distant battle. 'To protect people from creatures like those.'

Zagora nodded. 'What's the point of any of this if we let those people die? That *can't* be Sigmar's will.'

'Sigmar's will?' There was no mistaking Varek Skyborn's anger now. 'No one here can claim to fully know Sigmar's will, Dawnbringer, even you. Even Arulos. We can only follow the signs he sends us and pray that we do not fail him. Your crusade...' He hesitated.

'This crusade was not intended as a rescue mission,' said Arulos. 'Its purpose is clear, and very specific, as you have seen in the augur stone. We are to reach the tor by the time of the conjunction you call Gnorl's Feast. You have said that everything hinges on that.' He pointed his staff at the battle in the valley. 'We will see many such horrors as we travel though the wildlands. Will you stop at every one of them? If we do, we will arrive long after Gnorl's Feast.'

Varek nodded. He made a striking figure, framed by the vivid colours of the banner rippling behind him in the wind. His beautifully engraved golden armour was somehow free of mud, shimmering in the rain, and the two comet tails that topped his helmet glinted as he turned to Zagora.

'It is not our place to command you, Dawnbringer. But I will remind you that your prophecy made no allusion to this delay.'

Zagora looked over at Niksar. Every time he saw her she looked more like a stranger. Her gaunt face made her eyes look even larger and the dreadful weather leant her an otherworldly aspect, as the rain glistened on her ivory battleplate. She nodded at Niksar and turned to Chiana.

'We *have* to help them. The visions in the stone *do* indicate that we have to arrive by Gnorl's Feast, but the details are not clear. And I cannot believe the God-King would want us to let these people die.'

The storm swelled with such force that Niksar had to hold his hand up in front of his face. Rain pounded the figures at the top of the hill and the sky darkened as the clouds rumbled. No one spoke for a moment, then Arulos said, 'Is that your final word?'

Zagora nodded, leaning into the wind and gripping her war-hammer in both hands. 'We can't move on while those people are being killed.'

Kolgrimm nodded and muttered and Chiana looked relieved, but Arulos shook his head, looking down at the carnage below. He turned to Varek, speaking quietly. Varek nodded and Arulos turned back to the rest of the group.

'If the Dawnbringer is set on this course, then we have a solution that will limit the delay. I and my brothers will march to the north end of the valley and deal with the greenskins. But...' He looked around the group. 'The rest of you need not accompany us. You can head straight to the riverbank and assist the cogsmiths as planned. Work with all the haste you can manage. Then I and the Anvilhearts will rejoin you in time to head north.'

'My lord,' said Haxor, riding closer and calling out through the rain. 'Will the Phoenix Company join the attack on the orruks?'

Varek looked at Arulos but Arulos shook his head. 'All hands will be needed at the river, building the rafts. That is what Kolgrimm expected and that is what must happen. The help of you and your fellow soldiers will be essential if we are to build the rafts in time. We shall deal with the greenskins.'

'Sixty against hundreds?' muttered Haxor.

She had not addressed the Stormcasts but Varek caught her words and replied in strident tones.

'We are the Stormstrike.'

CHAPTER TEN

'We are outnumbered,' said Varek as the Anvilhearts gathered at the top of the slope. There was no concern in his voice; if anything, he seemed pleased.

Arulos looked around at the Anvilhearts – rows of proud Vindictors and Annihilators, clad in flawless, Thunderstrike armour, gripping gleaming spears and hammers, their shields glinting in the rain. The Annihilators were so large they even towered over their fellow Stormcast Eternals. Arulos could not help feeling a swell of pride. The Thunderstrike. Warriors whose souls were so charged with faith that Arulos could barely distinguish them from the convulsions of the storm. The bond that linked them to the tempest had been tempered and sharpened. Grungni had made them unbreakable. They were Sigmar's wrath made manifest.

'We are enough,' said Arulos. He raised his aetherstave to the storm, letting the light play across the gem clasped at its head. Arulos rarely looked directly on the renunciation crystal. It was the power that kept his past at bay. All the frailties of his mortal life. All the things that might cloud his thoughts and dim his sight. To ride the storm one had to be free of passion. But the power in the stone was dizzying and dangerous in its own right. It had to be sampled sparingly, like a strong wine. Instead, he looked through the light that surrounded the crystal, the faint corona that only he could see. The rain-swamped valley fell away and magnetic currents whirled around him, hauling the unbreakable chains that linked the cosmos. As his spirit merged with the rain clouds, he let his thoughts shower down across the valley, running in rivulets across every rock and corpse.

Behind him, a few hundred feet away, Chiana and Zagora were gathering the crusaders at the top of the slope, preparing for their race to the river. He steered his thoughts away from the Dawnbringer. She was a mystery he had no time for at the moment. His thoughts washed over the dead in the valley and reached the huddled mass of survivors near the river. There were three or four hundred desperate souls, cowering with their belongings as they watched the fight taking place at the foot of the gully wall.

Arulos turned his thoughts that way, seeing the fight with storm-bright clarity. A hundred Freeguild soldiers had gathered on a broad slab of rock. They were armed with halberds, swords and black powder weapons and they had already surrounded themselves with heaps of greenskin dead. Hate flashed through Arulos' mind as he beheld the orruks. An echo of his former frailties. He felt the violence in the valley, burning up through his limbs. They were a savage rabble – hulking, fur-clad brutes armed with primitive weapons. But they numbered nearly a thousand strong and they could easily have butchered the guardsmen. They were toying with them, killing a few then withdrawing to taunt their victims, before launching another brutal attack. The Freeguild soldiers surely knew what was happening but all they could do was fight on, firing their pistols and muskets with howls of fury and frustration.

All the rage and hunger of the land surged through Arulos. The storm responded, hurling rain and churning the thunderheads. He let himself be carried through the tumult. He saw the barbarism of the land, the savagery, rising and growing, building with the storm, trapped like water behind a dam, like lava beneath rock, always there, always ready to burst and destroy. The valley was primed to explode, whipped and charged. All he needed was a fulcrum, a point on which to hinge the power.

There was a flicker of lightning and the light spilled over a hideous creature. At the head of the greenskins there was an orruk that was larger than all the others. It was clad in crudely hammered plates of armour and gripped a broad, two-headed axe. Every time the orruks attacked, it was this leader who called them back, snorting and laughing at the agonies of the human soldiers. The warlord was mounted on a maw-krusha – a squat, reptilian steed that looked like a winged toad – and as Arulos took in its grotesque form, he felt Sigmar speaking to him through the storm, willing him to notice how tenuous the warlord's grip was on its host. For every greenskin that obeyed there was another that broke ranks and gored the humans. All across the jeering rabble, orruks were straining at the leash, filled with such hunger for violence that it would only take a small push to send them over the edge. They were imbeciles, all of them, and the warlord was their only grasp on reason.

'Draw them away from the leader,' he said, pulling his mind back from the clouds and turning to Varek. 'Take the Vindictors straight down into the valley and then turn and march north. Make a shield wall. Attack the greenskins from the south. They will rush your way as soon as they see the Dawnbringer leading the others down to the river.'

Varek nodded. 'And you?'

Arulos looked north along the cliff-edge. 'I will head along the ridge with the Annihilators. As you attack from the south, we will sweep down from the north.'

Varek hesitated, glancing at the renunciation crystal as if about to ask a question, then he simply nodded. 'As you wish, Stormspear.'

Arulos waved the Annihilators over and began jogging along the ridge, making sure to keep out of sight of the greenskins. 'Wait for my signal,' he called to Varek as the storm surged around him, a wave rushing to shore, ready to break.

'They've seen us,' said Niksar, looking down the valley towards the greenskins. He was riding at the head of the crusade on a horse given to him by the priests. Zagora had insisted he be allowed to stay at her side.

Zagora nodded but she kept her gaze locked on the river, riding faster down the slope. 'Arulos will keep us safe,' she said, speaking with absolute conviction. 'We just have to keep our half of the bargain.'

As the crusaders raced across the valley, heading for the river, Skyborn and some of the other Anvilhearts were rushing down it, heading north towards the fighting. The rain was coming down so hard that the Anvilhearts had almost vanished from view already. Niksar could barely see the greenskins. It was the sound of their howls and drums that told him they had seen the crusaders. As the storm grew louder, the orruks matched its fervour, bellowing and jeering as they realised they now had two crusades to butcher.

Lightning broke overhead, splitting the gloom to reveal the panicked faces of the crusaders stumbling and sliding down the slope. A few had steeds or carts but most were on foot and they looked like they were already under attack, lurching and shoving their way through the wind and mud. Behind them, the gall tusks were cresting the ridge, stomping into view with the meta-liths drifting majestically after them, haloed by spray as they cut through the rain.

Captain Tyndaris was in the vanguard, as were Haxor and a dozen other Freeguild soldiers, but most of the Phoenix Company was spread out through the column, tasked with guarding the flank and keeping the crusaders moving.

'Here they come!' called Haxor, pointing through the rain towards Skyborn and the Anvilhearts.

Orruks rushed at the Stormcast Eternals, barrelling through the downpour, howling and snorting. Even through the noise of the storm, Niksar heard the crunch of armour slamming into armour. As the orruks attacked, the Anvilhearts held their line, refusing to break their stride, ploughing on into the storm. Rain banked around them and light flickered across their spears as they lowered them and punched into the orruks.

'Almost there!' cried Tyndaris, dragging Niksar's attention from the fighting. He looked ahead and saw that the river was looming into view, a broad slab of silver rushing through the rain, roaring and churning as it tore down the valley.

Spurred on, the crusaders surged forwards, driving their horses to a final burst of speed. Niksar was one of the first to reach the riverbank. As he reached it, he recoiled, pulling his horse back and shaking his head, staring in horror at the torrent.

'What?' demanded Zagora as she reached his side. 'What have you–?'

She gaped at the river.

All around them, people cried out in shock and disgust. The river was devoid of water. It was not liquid that sprang from the distant eye socket, it was life. The river was formed of millions of scaled, silvery creatures – sinuous, insect-like things that snaked and writhed around each other as they roared past. Their shiny,

segmented bodies reminded Niksar of silverfish he had seen slith-
ering through old books, but they were much larger. Some were
the size of a man's forearm but others were several feet long. As
they tumbled past, they ate. The larger creatures consumed the
smaller ones in frenzied, hungry gulps, and the smaller ones
teemed over the larger ones in swarms, tearing through carapaces
and burrowing into innards. The river was a feeding frenzy, a glinting, boiling stampede thrown forwards by an inexplicable force.

A soldier howled out in pain. One of the smaller creatures
latched onto his leg, filling the rain with crimson. People rushed to
help but, before anyone could reach him, a larger creature flipped
from the tumult and clamped its jaws around his head, silencing
the man's screams as it snatched him into the river. He vanished
beneath a tide of metallic scales.

A woman started screaming, calling out the dead man's name
as her family struggled to hold her back from the river. All across
the riverbank, people cried out in alarm, struggling to register
what had just happened.

Niksar looked at his sister, shaking his head. 'Is that what you
saw? Is this the right river?'

She was staring at the deluge with obvious disgust. But then
her expression hardened.

'Yes. This is it. This is the way.'

Niksar and Haxor looked at each other and he sensed that they
were wondering the same thing: had Zagora lost her mind?

* * *

The storm carried them and cradled them, surrounding Arulos
in a whirl of wind and rain. They reached the valley floor, turned
and charged across the rocks, splitting the gloom like sunlight
through forest boughs.

An orruk turned in surprise, sensing movement, but Arulos'

aetherstave was already in his hands. As he reached the greenskin he channelled the weather, unleashing the storm. Lightning kicked from the renunciation crystal, splitting the monster to the waist, but Arulos had already bounded through the charred remains, hurling another thunderbolt, then another, blasting through the enemy ranks without pause for breath or thought. All around him, greenskins fell and Annihilators charged, slamming into the orruks with their shields before crushing them with hammer blows. The decoy had worked perfectly. The orruks had all their attention fixed on Varek and the other Anvilhearts at the far end of the valley. Arulos saw no shame in the deception. The orruks were not worthy opponents. They were not deserving of respect. They were animals. He had simply to kill them in the most efficient way possible. All of this was a delay and he would do everything he could to hasten the crusade towards its goal.

As the Anvilhearts tore on they came within sight of the beleaguered guardsmen. The mortals stared from their rocky platform as Arulos and the others raced past, punching a channel through the mob. The humans looked at the Stormcast Eternals with almost as much fear as the orruks. Arulos understood. The violence he had seen through his aetherstave was building to a crescendo. As he and the Annihilators butchered the orruks, Ghur responded. The ground juddered. Rocks fell from the cliffs and wind howled down the gully, driving Arulos and the others on as they killed.

The orruks were all turning to face them now, belatedly realising that the real danger was behind them, but it was too late. As the Anvilhearts charged, their armour burned with the might of the tempest. Lightning flickered across the Annihilators' hammers and danced between their shields, turning them into a wall of energy. The orruks tried to fight back but they were blasted aside, sent pinwheeling through the rain or trampled into the mud.

Arulos knew the storm would only carry his Annihilators so far but he had almost reached his goal – the fulcrum around which all the violence was balanced; the trigger that would unleash all the pent-up savagery he had seen in the valley.

The orruk warlord turned its steed to face Arulos. The Annihilators were already losing momentum as they reached the maw-krusha and the warlord raised its axe, howling and spraying drool through the rain.

Arulos paused a few feet from the maw-krusha and looked up at its rider. There was a brief lull in the fighting as the other orruks saw the two leaders approaching each other. With the storm shaking his limbs, Arulos brought his sword and staff together. The metal clanged and the sound reverberated in the heavens.

The ground shook again. Orruks stumbled, unable to defend themselves as the Annihilators strode into view, slower now but even more brutal, crushing skulls and chests with ember-spilling blows.

The maw-krusha staggered and flapped its useless wings, crushing orruks as it struggled to right itself. The warlord bellowed, pointing its axe at Arulos, ordering the monster to attack.

The maw-krusha pounced, leaping through the rain at Arulos, but he rolled clear, hurled by the wind. Then he bounded up the monster's scales and lunged at the warlord.

The warlord rose in its saddle and parried, swinging its axe round so hard that Arulos almost fell. He stumbled across the maw-krusha's back, steadied himself, then attacked again, bringing his aetherstave round in a dazzling arc. The warlord grinned as it blocked the staff with its axe. Then it frowned as blood rushed from its tooth-filled jaws.

As the warlord parried the aetherstave, Arulos had jammed his sword beneath its chest armour, sinking the weapon hilt-deep. The warlord swayed in its saddle, gargling curses, then slid sideways and dropped to the ground.

The dam broke. Arulos felt it surge through him. The violence of the land filled his veins like a drug, quickening his pulse and darkening his vision. As the warlord breathed its last, the leash that had restrained the orruks snapped. With no one to lead them they *all* sought to lead. Every orruk that was larger than those nearby wanted fealty and lashed out to take it. Howls came from every direction as the orruks turned on each other. Blood billowed through the storm and the lightning filled the valley, turning the carnage into a monochrome frieze. As the greenskins were consumed by kill fever, other predators rushed to join the violence. Serpents erupted from the mud, coiling and biting. Raptors dived through the spray, tearing faces and pounding their wings. Beetles swarmed across the fallen in a glinting carpet, stripping flesh in seconds as other insects whirred through the air, filling eyes and mouths with glass-sharp wings.

Arulos gripped the maw-krusha's saddle as the monster bucked and stomped through the mayhem. Then he planted his sword between its shoulder blades and yanked the blade sideways. The creature stumbled, trampling combatants. Arulos leapt clear, landing in the mud as the beast thudded into the cliff wall and sent a jagged crack racing across the rocks.

As the maw-krusha collapsed under a shower of boulders, Arulos crouched on the ground, drunk on the vigour of the storm. Then he stood, struggling to steady himself as he signalled for the Annihilators to withdraw.

With the greenskins consumed by bloodlust, the Anvilhearts had no need to retreat. Not a single one of them had fallen. But they responded to Arulos' command without question, following him as he fought his way through frenzied creatures, heading down towards the river.

As Arulos left the fighting behind, the din grew. A new sound joined itself to the roar of the storm – a low, juddering crash like the sound of an ocean. Arulos did not need to look back to know what he had unleashed. He had tipped the balance. He had knocked the fulcrum. Ghur's insatiable hunger had been given free rein. Behind Arulos, as creatures of all shapes and hues tore each other apart, the cliff wall started to collapse, adding dust and debris to the fury of the storm. He led the Annihilators a hundred feet away before finally halting and looking back at his handiwork.

The orruks were so lost in their savagery that they did not stop fighting even as their world fell down around them. Some of the Freeguild soldiers were trying to break free and follow Arulos to safety, but others had been overcome by the same madness as the greenskins, joining the orgy of violence. The storm boomed, rocks fell and the noise became so deafening that even Arulos grimaced. It was a pitiless, apocalyptic scene but he forced himself to take in every terrible detail.

'For Sigmar,' he whispered, making the sign of the hammer across his chest.

Some of the crusaders were crying out in despair, horrified as they saw the nature of the Claw-water, but Kolgrimm and his cogsmiths had taken the setback with a quiet stoicism that made Niksar ashamed to have doubted his sister. The duardin engineers studied the flood of creatures with lenses and sextants, spoke in hurried whispers and then sent their servants rushing back across the valley towards the approaching metaliths.

'This will not stop us,' bellowed Kolgrimm, addressing all those near enough to hear him. 'The rafts are duardin-made. Nothing will get through the hulls.' He pointed at branches that were hurtling past, carried by the surging torrent. 'We can sail on grubs just as well as on water.'

Kolgrimm's air of gruff calm affected everyone and in minutes, people were dusting themselves down and running to enact his orders. Tyndaris began barking commands too, arranging the Phoenix Company into lines that stood between the crusaders and the carnage Arulos had unleashed. A few of the orruks were still trying to attack but most had been speared by Varek's Vindictors or had raced back to join the fighting at the cliffs.

'What has he done?' said Zagora, steering her horse away from the river and staring at the mountain of dust and rocks rolling down the valley.

It was impossible to make out much of the battle, but the gilded forms of Arulos and his men were visible as the destruction bloomed around them. They were standing calmly, weapons lowered, as a vast section of the valley wall was torn apart by the storm. Behind Arulos, near to the river, was the huddled crowd of civilians from the other crusade, but there was no sign of the Freeguild regiment that had been trying to defend them. They had been swallowed by the storm, along with the orruks. Booms and crashes shook through the valley, almost throwing Niksar from his mount, but he stayed by his sister's side as she stared into the clouds.

'That's not a rescue,' she muttered, the colour draining from her face.

A few minutes later the noise started to die away and the clouds of dust were dissipated by rain, revealing a shocking scene. The orruks were almost all dead, ripped apart by each other and by all the other predators that were pacing through the rubble – reptilian, panther-like creatures and scurrying, over-sized rodents vied with raptors and crows for the carrion. As Niksar peered through the rain at the feeding animals he realised why his sister's tone was so bleak – along with the corpses of the greenskins there were mounds of human dead. All of the Freeguild soldiers had been ripped apart, or smashed by falling rocks, their remains left to glisten in the rain.

'This is not what I meant,' said Zagora, turning her desolate gaze on Niksar. 'Why has he done this?'

'Stormspear?' Niksar looked at the rocks and bodies scattered beneath the cliff. 'Do you think he made that landslide happen?'

Anger flashed in her eyes. 'I know he did. He said he could defeat those orruks by himself. Then he went over there and this happened.' She clutched the stone at her forehead. 'All of those soldiers. Dead. So that we might not be delayed. That's *not* what I meant.'

Niksar looked back at the river. The gall tusks had led the metaliths to the riverbank and Kolgrimm's engineers were commanding a huge workforce. Anvils were flashing and dome-shaped engines were spewing sparks. In the clouds of smoke, a raft was already taking shape, though *raft* seemed a demeaning name for the imposing vessel Kolgrimm was creating. The bulk of it was a simple platform, but the duardin engineers were already fitting thick, studded bulwarks and clockwork chain engines.

'But Arulos Stormspear was right, wasn't he? Everyone had to stay here, working on this. If he had not found a way to kill those orruks we might have spent days here, trying to hold them off.'

'And,' said Chiana, riding over to them, 'while we fought, word would have spread. The scent of blood would have been carried on the air. More orruks would have come to join their kin. I doubt we would have ever left this valley.' Her tone was sympathetic but her expression was stern. 'The Anvilhearts have bought us a chance to continue.'

Zagora looked like she might attack Chiana. Her face was grey and she gripped her greathammer with trembling hands. Niksar could understand. It was easier to defend the slaughter when it was not a result of your commands.

'Arulos *has* saved the bulk of them,' he said, pointing to the civilians stumbling back up the valley towards them. 'They would all have died if we hadn't arrived.'

Zagora stared at him in disbelief. 'I can't believe you're defending him. He killed the orruks by sacrificing the Freeguild soldiers. Men and women. People like us. And there was no need. If we'd attacked the orruks together, with the Phoenix Company fighting alongside the Anvilhearts, we could have driven those orruks back with weapons and courage. Not…' She looked at the feeding animals. 'Not whatever Arulos just did. There were hundreds of soldiers under that cliff. People we are meant to be trying to save. Arulos slaughtered them.'

Chiana frowned. 'Stormspear did not kill them, Dawnbringer. They did not die by his hand.'

Zagora was breathing heavily, her eyes straining in her sockets. Niksar had never seen her like this.

'He did something. He used the storm somehow. And whatever he did, it led to that cliff falling and crushing those soldiers. And it led to the madness that followed. He knew it would happen. He made it happen.'

'He did not kill them,' said Chiana, clearly horrified by the sug-gestion. 'But he has helped you stay true to your vision. You said we have to arrive at the tor by the night of Gnorl's Feast and Arulos has made that possible.'

'He sacrificed them.'

'Perhaps, but those soldiers may not be the only sacrifice we have to make if we're going to succeed.' She rode closer to Zagora and placed a hand on her arm. 'Remember what we're fighting for. Excelsis itself. If we fail to build strongpoints along the coast, and the attacks on our city continue as they are, Excelsis is going to fall. Think what that means – the greatest of all Sigmar's bastions in this realm, torn down and set alight. What hope would there be for any of us if we lose Excelsis?' Her voice cracked with emo-tion. 'And in your visions the God-King has shown us a way to build Ardent Keep. A way to secure the whole of the Great Excelsis Road. But only if we are ready to begin building by Gnorl's Feast.

We can't fail, Dawnbringer. We can't be delayed.' She nodded at the corpses of the Freeguild soldiers. 'At any cost.'

Zagora took a deep breath and looked on the verge of an angry retort. Then she sighed and slumped in her saddle, shaking her head. 'Those soldiers would have seen us coming and thought they were saved.'

Niksar noticed that a small crowd was gathering around them. People had noticed the argument. 'Zagora,' he said, drawing her attention to the fact that they had an audience.

She nodded and looked out at the survivors who were heading back down the valley towards them. 'Do what you can for these people,' she said. 'We can at least give them food and medicine.'

'Of course!' Chiana beamed. 'They will join us. It was Sigmar's will that we found them here. Once we have–'

There was a roar from behind them. One of the gall tusks had stumbled into the river and its foreleg was engulfed by feeding, silver shapes. The beast panicked and lurched back up the slope, jolting the metalith that was attached to it and causing a man to fall. He screamed as he dropped, surrounded by a shower of machine parts and masonry. He landed with a dreadful crunch and lay silent as objects crashed down all around him. The gall tusk's handlers cried out, grappling with its leash as it reared, raising its massive hooves into the air and slamming them down into the mud, trying to rid itself of the creatures gnawing through its hide.

Soldiers and civilians rushed to help, hacking at the silver insects with swords and cudgels. Some of the monsters leapt from the gall tusk and coiled around their attackers, savaging faces and arms.

Some Phoenix Company soldiers raced back from their lines, halberds lowered, and waded into the fight, stabbing and lunging at the creatures. The fight only lasted a matter of seconds but, by the time the insects were dead, six people lay lifeless in the mud.

People stared at the bodies, then looked out at the teeming masses in the river, eyes filled with dawning horror.

'Get on with it!' boomed Kolgrimm, kicking dead insects aside and picking up fallen equipment.

A few people headed over to the corpses with the intention of retrieving them. On the morning after the massacre in the fens, some people had managed to bury their dead kin, digging graves in the mud before the crusade marched on, but Kolgrimm was not about to let that happen here.

'Leave them!' he cried, hauling people back from the bodies. 'Or you'll be joining them. Grieve later, if you get the chance. Boats don't build themselves!' The cogsmith was hunched by his years and leant constantly on his axe, but his voice was sure. The corpses were abandoned as people hurried back to work.

It did not take long before survivors of the other crusade began to reach them. Many seemed mute with shock, accepting cups of water in dazed silence, but some cried out in relief as they saw familiar faces and realised they had been saved by their own countrymen. Whatever leaders the crusade had, they must have died beneath the cliff face, because none of the survivors had any idea where they were meant to be headed. They had been carried this far by religious fervour and, as they heard the story of the Dawnbringer and the augur stone, most of them decided that the massacre on the riverbank must have been part of Sigmar's plan for them. Once they had been fed they rushed to join the others helping the cogsmiths and, in less than an hour, a small flotilla had appeared next to the river. Since the landslide at the cliffs the storm had been easing off, but the rain still hammered down as the crusaders worked, creating clouds of spray as planks and plates of metal slammed into place.

For a long time, Arulos and the Anvilhearts stayed at the north end of the valley, battling predators that had come down from the fens. Only when there was nothing left moving did they make their way back towards the rest of the crusaders, marching in stately procession and showing no sign of mud or damage on their dazzling warplate.

'You tricked me,' said Zagora, riding out to meet Arulos. She spoke calmly but her eyes gleamed in the rain.

Niksar and Haxor were still at her side, as were Chiana and the other senior priests, but they remained silent, waiting for Arulos to respond. He came to a stop near Zagora's horse and removed his helmet to look up at her.

'Tricked?' He said the word as though he could not grasp its meaning.

'You said you could save those people.'

'I said we could defeat the orruks.' He nodded to the survivors working on the rafts. 'And we have preserved the lives of many who would now be dying.'

Zagora pointed at the remains of the landslide, and the bodies heaped in the rubble. Her voice grew louder. 'What about their lives?'

Arulos studied her in silence. Chiana opened her mouth to speak, then thought better of it and remained silent. Arulos was motionless, rain pinging off his armour.

'I cannot foresee the consequences of all my actions.' He looked up the slope behind her. 'Any more than you could have foreseen what happened when we reached the fens.'

'But you planned this. Whatever you did to make those things turn on each other, you meant it to happen. There could have been other ways to help. You could have taken the Phoenix Company with you.'

Arulos shook his head. 'Too slow. We would not have reached the tor by Gnorl's Feast. So I made a decision to save only those that could be saved quickly.'

Zagora swayed in her saddle as though she had been struck. 'And you made a decision to let the others die?'

'I made a decision to follow your vision.'

She shook her head. 'You sacrificed them. You decided they didn't matter.'

Arulos said nothing.

'And there's a reason,' she continued. 'Isn't there? Something you're not sharing. I see it in the augur stone. I see it in you. There's a reason you're so keen to keep moving.'

Niksar could not quite believe what Zagora was doing. She was accusing a Stormcast Eternal of duplicity, arguing with him as if he were a normal, mortal man.

'Your prophecy states that we have to reach the tor before nightfall,' said Arulos calmly.

Zagora's horse bucked beneath her, sensing her anger. 'You're holding something back, I know it. I've seen it. You're impatient. You wanted us to reach the tor quickly before I even told you we had to be there by Gnorl's Feast. Why? What's the real reason you wouldn't let us save those Freeguild soldiers?'

Arulos looked off into the distance, as if he were talking to the rain. 'There are many things we do not share with mortals.' There was still no anger in his voice. Rather, he sounded sad. 'We explain as much as is needed. As much as we can. As much as we think you will understand.'

Zagora glared at him.

The standard bearer, Varek, stepped forward. 'There is much that happens in the forging of a Stormcast Eternal that would be alien to a mortal mind.'

Arulos nodded. 'We hold true to things that would seem senseless to anyone not of our order. Our reasoning may seem obscure but everything we do is by the will of the God-King.'

His calm, kind tone only made Zagora angrier. 'I have been

given leadership of this crusade. I am the will of the God-King. And I say we should preserve lives, not end them. However urgent our mission is.'

Arulos and Varek glanced at each other but seemed unwilling or unable to say more. There was a tense silence as Zagora stared at them.

'Are you done?' said Kolgrimm.

Niksar turned and saw that the cogsmith and a few of his engineers had gathered a few feet away, waiting for Zagora and Arulos to finish.

Zagora said nothing, staring over at the dead bodies under the cliff. Arulos did not seem to hear the duardin, keeping his gaze locked on Zagora, but Chiana nodded and smiled at Kolgrimm.

'Do you need the Dawnbringer?'

He shrugged. 'I've built 'em.'

He waved his cog hammer at the iron hulls hulking in the mud behind him – hammered bowls of metal big enough to hold several dozen people each. Each one was surrounded by a skirt of clacking, steam-shrouded pistons and they had metal domes at the centre, topped with smokestacks. Behind them, there were some even larger, rectangular platforms that people were already lashing the gall tusks to.

'We can stand here talking all day. Or we can get a bloody move on.'

CHAPTER ELEVEN

Once his counsellors and advisors had left him alone, High Arbiter Byzac took out the scrolls he had brought and spread them across his desk. He sat there in silence, studying the wax seals as the sounds of Excelsis drifted into his state chambers. It was early morning and the light was still weak, struggling to reach the corners of his grandiose room. It was all part of his mask; everything from the great pillars of his palace to his intricately stitched robes of office, all designed to convey a facade of stability and permanence. But now, as he opened the reports, he let his mask slip, whispering a prayer to the God-King as he saw the contents. The signatures were all different, as were the places they described, but the meaning was the same: we are lost. The land has risen against us. The beasts are in the citadel. Every outpost and strongpoint in Thondia was under attack. Forts that had been safe for years were now ash. Entire regiments had vanished without a trace, swallowed by Ghur. And as the creatures of the wilds grew ever bolder, other threats followed in their wake: armies of Chaos warriors and greenskin tribes that revelled in the mayhem, seizing a chance to regain lands they had lost.

But behind the masks of his high office Aurun Byzac wore a more profound armour, the armour of his faith. He looked at the portraits hung in the alcoves that lined his chamber: images of Sigmar's Stormhosts descending from the heavens on chariots of lightning, taming the wildlands with blazing, pitiless hammers. Their bravery was the mortar that bound Excelsis. And Byzac would not fail them. His gaze fell back to the reports. There was still hope. Sigmar had shown them the way.

Byzac spent the next hour writing replies, explaining that he had personally sanctioned every one of the crusades that had left for the coast. Once the new frontier has been established, he said, the attacks on your homes will cease. The Great Excelsis Road will be passable once more. The crusaders will forge a shield of faith, a divine bulwark that will preserve the territories Sigmar claimed in the name of Order and justice. The more he wrote, the surer Byzac felt. So many brave souls had abandoned the safety of the city to fight for the God-King. What a glorious exodus. Faith and reason pitted against the mindless hunger of the wilds. Byzac was no fool. Many of the crusaders would die, but many would live. Live to build strongpoints at the same sacred conjunctions of power that Sigmar himself used when he tamed the lands.

A door slammed, dragging him from his thoughts as slippered feet hurried down the length of the chamber. The servant looked distracted as he approached the desk.

'Forgive the interruption, High Arbiter, but the Lord Celestant is here to see you.'

Byzac struggled to hide his unease. 'He is not due for another hour.'

'He arrived early, my lord. I asked him to wait but…' The servant shook his head. 'He wished to come straight up.'

Byzac swept the scrolls from his desk and placed them back in the drawers, then he dusted down his robes and nodded. 'Have him brought up.'

The servant licked his lips. 'He's… He's already here, my lord. At the door.'

Byzac bit back a curse. 'Very well. Send him in.'

As the servant hurried back towards the door, Byzac glanced around the room, checking that everything was as it should be. He was a devout man. He had never knowingly betrayed his god or the people of Excelsis. But when a White Angel came to call, he was always gripped by the uncomfortable feeling that he had something to hide.

'Lord-Celestant Volk,' he said as the towering warrior strode towards him, his boots thudding on the thick rugs. Volk wore pristine, white armour that hid every inch of him. From a distance, it had the flawless lustre of a polished tooth, but as Volk reached the desk, and light spilled over him, Byzac saw the intricate engravings that covered every inch of the battleplate. Thousands of beautiful inscriptions had been carved into the sigmarite. Some were in Azyrite tongues that Byzac could not read, but there were also words he could understand: vows of fealty and honour, evocations of holy power and, most numerous, renunciations of weakness.

Byzac rose to greet his guest but the Lord-Celestant still towered over him, making him feel childish and ridiculous.

'I have sent them east,' said Volk, forgoing the pleasantries. His voice chimed through the metal of his expressionless faceplate, doom-laden and terrible.

'You have sent *who* east, Lord-Celestant?'

'The Ironshields.' With that, Volk nodded and turned to leave.

Byzac nodded, smiling weakly, then he shook his head. 'East? What? You've sent your men east? Then who have you sent to the Great Excelsis Road? Didn't you say it would be the Ironshields who would join the crusaders?'

Volk paused and turned to look back at Byzac. 'I have sent them to the muster called by Yndrasta. They are going to Delium. So my chambers are all accounted for.'

Byzac had to be careful. If Volk doubted him, he would have him executed. It was as terrifyingly simple as that. Embroidered robes and grand palaces meant nothing to the Knights Excelsior. If Byzac said anything that troubled the Lord-Celestant he would be dangling in a cage over the harbour that very morning. But still, afraid as he was, Byzac could not suppress his shock.

'What do you mean?' he asked. 'Accounted for?'

Volk studied him in silence.

Byzac's pulse quickened but he continued staring at the Lord-Celestant's brutal, beautiful mask.

'I mean,' said Volk, 'that I have deployed my chambers in the locations I deem most appropriate. The Ironshields will no longer be heading inland, so they will not cross the Great Excelsis Road and they will not join your crusaders. They are joining the Angel Yndrasta at the Siege of Delium. Her need was greater.'

'Her need was greater?' Byzac's shock was quickly being replaced by anger. He forgot, for a moment, the cage that might be waiting for him outside the Consecralium and marched out from behind his desk, glaring up at the Stormcast Eternal. 'We have sent hundreds, no, *thousands* of brave people to that road, Lord-Celestant. They went because they knew they would only have to hold out until your Ironshields came. You agreed to the plan.'

Volk nodded. 'That was the best strategy at the time.'

'At the time? And what about now? Now that we have sent those people out into the wilds with the promise that your men will be coming to keep them alive?'

Volk's stern gaze was just visible through the eyeholes of his mask.

'They will all die,' said Byzac, his voice trembling with rage. 'Any crusaders who make it to the road will have made the journey for nothing. Without the Ironshields they have no hope. No way of surviving.'

'Perhaps. But the situation has changed. The siege at Delium *must* be broken. And, at the same time, greenskins have been flooding down from the Shattered Hills. So we are pressed on two fronts. My chambers are all accounted for.'

Volk turned to leave again but Byzac grabbed his arm. 'How dare you?' All thoughts of his own safety were gone. All he could think of was the devout souls he had sent from the city, promising them they would not be left to stand alone. 'How can you leave all those people out there to die? What kind of monster are you?'

Volk looked down at Byzac's hand. It looked small and grubby, latched onto his gleaming armour. Byzac removed it.

'Monster?' Volk stooped, moving the faceplate of his helmet close to Byzac. 'Tell me what you know about monsters, High Arbiter.'

Byzac felt suddenly cold. His righteous fury was crushed, in an instant, by terror.

Volk nodded at the desk. 'Do you think your reports tell you everything that happens in this realm? Do you think you understand even a fraction of what we are facing? High Arbiter, the enemy is amongst us.' He looked around, taking in the grand colonnade that ran down the room and the distant, domed ceiling. 'All of this could fall. Everything we have built. The old gods of this land are waking. And the beasts of Ghur are rising from the pit, hungry for blood.' He looked back at Byzac. 'I have sent my men to block the cracks in the dam, High Arbiter. Pray, with all your heart, that they do not fail. This city hangs in the balance. Excelsis.' Anger crept into his voice, making it even more dreadful. 'The God-King's city. Do you understand what it would mean if we let it fall? We would damn every pure soul in the realm but, even worse than that, we would have failed him. We would have failed the God-King. Through our indolence and cowardice we would have committed the ultimate betrayal. I will not allow that to happen. The crusades were a costly error. The resources we sent out on those metaliths should have been deployed here, bolstering our defences against the coming storm, but there is no time to grieve for past mistakes. We must play the cards we have. This is our great test. This is the moment in which we will claim glory or fail. And I will not let us fail.' He stared at Byzac and spoke with quiet menace. 'Are you with me, High Arbiter? Or against me?'

Byzac suddenly found it hard to catch his breath. He stumbled across the carpets back to his desk and sat down heavily, gripping his head in his hands. He finally managed to draw a breath and slowly let it out. When he looked up to make one last plea, the Lord-Celestant was already marching out the door, vanishing into the morning light.

'If Sigmar means for those crusaders to live,' called Volk over his shoulder, 'they will live.'

Byzac stared at the ceiling, his mind filled with images of marching crusaders, their faces bathed in the blue and red that spilled through their canopy of banners.

'Sigmar forgive me,' he whispered.

CHAPTER TWELVE

Arulos steadied himself as the boat rocked beneath him. The din was almost as deafening as the battle had been. Thousands of the silver insects were thudding against the hull. It sounded like rocks hitting a gong. Most of them bounced harmlessly away, but occasionally one of them would flap onto the deck and attack. Every time that happened, the Freeguild soldiers arrayed around the railings rushed forwards and skewered the beast with a row of halberds.

The journey was going exactly as Zagora had predicted. The torrent of creatures had taken the rafts and hurled them forwards. The power of the river was incredible. Even now, half an hour after they launched from the shore, people were still reeling and clinging to the railings. It was like being caught in a landslide. Kolgrimm was at the prow, bellowing orders as his underlings stoked the engines – roaring, metal-shod wheels, churning through the insects at a furious speed, hurling the raft on.

They were travelling so fast that the lands either side of the river were a blur. Even so, it was clear that the crusade would never have survived travelling through them. Gargantuan shapes burst from the rocks as they passed, howling and clawing, drawn by the movement of the rafts. And every time a colossal shape rose, a larger one tore it down. The crusade had triggered a feeding frenzy. Unable to catch the rafts, and driven mad by hunger, monsters turned on each other. The land groaned and heaved. Rocks spewed serpents. Lakes spawned gargants. Geysers spat griffons. Feathered apes burst from trees, scrambling towards the riverbank before being savaged by reptilian hounds. Hills shed coats of soil to reveal pitted, lumbering crustaceans like walking burial mounds. Every new creature that appeared summoned a host more but, as the stampede grew more frenzied, the rafts rushed by unharmed, catapulted by Kolgrimm's thundering engines.

Despite the success of their launch, Arulos felt distracted, drumming his fingers on the railings and muttering to himself.

Varek was standing at Arulos' side and noticed that Arulos was looking at Zagora.

'Delium, remember. That's why we came. Don't let that woman muddy your thoughts.'

Arulos nodded. 'It is worrying how well you read my mind, Varek.'

Varek laughed. 'You can hide your emotions from the others, Arulos, but not from me. I saw how she rattled you. But there is no need. You have spent too long in your own mind. You're forgetting how erratic mortals can be. She was not thinking clearly, that is all. Her words are no reflection on your judgement. They are a reflection on her. She failed to grasp the logic of your decision. Imagine what would have happened if you had agreed to her plan. If you had let the mortals join us in fighting the orruks, these rafts would still not be made, might never get made. Your judgement is sound.'

'That is not what troubles me.'

'What then? Do you doubt her?'

'No, not that. She is just not what I expected. I see our purpose in Ghur clearly and she is not part of it. But when I speak with her, I have the troubling feeling that I have overlooked something. She does not seem like any other mortal.'

They both had to steady themselves as the boat shook with even more violence. Kolgrimm's engines were driving it ever faster and, as the vessel accelerated, the creatures beneath attacked with more fury, straining to puncture the hull.

'She isn't a normal mortal,' said Varek, gripping a railing. 'She is their prophet. Their chosen one. Are you surprised that she seems different?'

Arulos lowered his voice, despite the cacophony that surrounded them. 'Grand Conclaves anoint prophets at the drop of a hat. They need religious figureheads or no one would join these crusades. You know that as well as I do. But she is… She actually does seem to possess a presence. A power.'

'So we have a prophet who can prophesise. And a leader who can lead.' Varek patted his shoulder. 'These are good things, Arulos. Don't overthink them.'

'*Under*thinking is usually the problem.' Arulos shook his head. 'Until now, everything has happened as I would expect. Even this detour with the crusaders does not really change anything. We will still answer Yndrasta's call and we will crush the greenskins at Delium. It is hard to explain, Varek, even to you, but I see the land, through the lens of the Eternal Storm. I feel its currents, leading us on. I understand what is happening to us and that is how I can be so sure of victory. But she is different.'

Varek shook his head. 'How? Is she separate from all that? Does she stand apart from the things you have seen in the storm?'

'No, quite the opposite – she *is* the storm. Or, rather, she is the centre of the storm. In the place where I should see the God-King, I see her, clearer than I see you, looking back at me as though she has more right to be there than I do. It makes me wonder if I might have misunderstood something.'

Varek frowned. 'You do not have to solve *every* mystery, Arulos. Leave a few for others to untangle.'

Arulos turned his attention back to the brutality on the shore. As the hills and forests rushed by, he caught glimpses of more horrors striving to reach them – towering, slavering things that looked like they had been dredged from a child's nightmare. There was a rhythm to the bloodshed: larger creatures devoured smaller ones, smaller ones swarmed over the larger ones, then the whole cycle began again. Varek knew better than to keep interrupting his thoughts so the two of them remained silent as the rafts ploughed on down the river, crashing through living waves of violence. He cast his mind into the Eternal Storm, searching for answers, leaving the mortal world behind as the clouds snatched him away.

He saw something he had not noticed before: a dome of light in the sky. He tried to reach it but it kept moving away, always just out of reach. He sensed that the dome was linked to Zagora in some way – that it contained the answer he was looking for. Time became abstract as he pursued the dome and, when shouting drew him back to the raft, Arulos could not have said how long had passed.

'The falls are up ahead,' said Varek, gripping his arm. Arulos had the sense that his friend had been calling him for quite a while. The crusade's leaders were gathered around him: Zagora, Chiana and the other prelates, various knights and princelings and the cogsmith, Kolgrimm.

The raft slammed into another swell and they all staggered. Arulos looked around and saw that several soldiers had been killed while his mind was elsewhere and there were dozens of the silver-scaled monsters heaped on the deck. The noise beneath the hull had grown too, becoming a feverish, rolling beat that sounded like it was about to tear the vessel in two. But when Arulos looked beyond the riverbanks, he saw that the carnage in the fields was gone. They had entered a region of blasted, dusty rocks littered with fossils the size of galleons. Beyond the river, nothing was moving. They had come through the danger. When they were able to speak again he nodded at the duardin engineer.

'You have done well, Kolgrimm Kragsson.'

Pride flashed in the cogsmith's eyes and he muttered something. Arulos knew Varek would approve.

'We have to be careful, though,' bellowed Kolgrimm, staggering in the wind and struggling to be heard. He gestured to an enormous harpoon mounted at the prow. 'We need to haul ourselves to shore before we reach those falls. We don't want to overshoot and end up in the rapids. Even these rafts wouldn't survive a drop like that.'

Arulos looked downriver. They were riding in the rearmost vessel and he could see that the others were already doing what Kolgrimm had described. A few rafts were already attached to the rocks by thick, metal cables that had halted them and were now hauling them to the riverbank. Some of the other rafts were still firing harpoons, trying to find purchase on the rocks. Arulos watched the last few as they halted and began battling sideways across the river, pumping great clouds of smoke as the duardin engines battled with the tide of insects slamming into their hulls.

'Our turn next,' said Kolgrimm. He extended a concertinaed spyglass and held it to his goggles, peering downriver. 'I can already see the spray from the falls. We need to get out of the currents.'

Arulos nodded and was about to reply when screams broke out behind them. Another one of the insects had slammed down onto the deck. It was much larger than any of the others, bigger than the flathorns that strained against their leashes as it approached, but it scuttled across the metal plates with surprising speed, its six legs clanging against the iron as it reached the nearest group of crusaders and tore into them, filling the air with blood and panicked howls.

Phoenix Company guards ran towards it, halberds lowered. It turned and hurled itself at them, ripping weapons aside with its mandibles and tearing through their armour.

Arulos drew his sword and marched across the deck. The monster sensed his approach, looking up from the gory pool it had created. Arulos felt a wave of distaste as he saw its face. This was the first time he had seen one of the creatures close up. Its face was formed of the same metallic carapace as the rest of the beast, but it looked distinctly human, grinning maniacally as it leaped through the air and hurtled towards Arulos.

He brought his sword round in a quick, backhanded slash. The monster tried to sidestep but, airborne as it was, the best it could manage was to twist its abdomen, trying to avoid the blade. Arulos sliced easily through its carapace and the insect landed behind him in a crumpled heap.

Varek raced past him, sword raised. More of the insects had thrashed down onto the deck. Varek beheaded the first and strode on to impale a second but, as the river heaved beneath the raft, it hurled several more monsters over the bulwarks.

Arulos dashed across the deck and brought his aetherstave down, hammer-like, onto a monster's head. It snaked towards him and locked its mouth on his leg armour. Again, its face was horribly human, but its teeth were the cruel, long tools of a predator and, to Arulos' shock, sparks tumbled from his shin armour as the monster thrashed and heaved around him, its jaws tightening. He brought his sword down, beheading the thing then kicking it aside and raising his blade to meet another.

In the space of a few moments the deck was crowded with glittering monsters and people gathered in groups, backs together and weapons raised as they struggled to drive the beasts away. The drumming sound underneath the hull swelled, growing more frenzied.

More of the creatures flipped and scuttled across the deck and, as he fought, Arulos was taken by how vulnerable the mortals were. Nearly a dozen had already fallen to the insects, their blood pooling around them on the deck. If he did not move fast, they would all be butchered.

He cried out commands to his men, ordering them to drive the monsters back the way they had come. The Annihilators were scattered across the other rafts, but his Vindictors leapt to obey, breaking away from the railings and slamming into the insects, spears raised in perfect unison as they sliced through carapaces and claws. Kolgrimm was shouting something about the harpoon, but Arulos kept his thoughts on the battle. Chitin thudded into sigmarite and stormspears flashed with elemental charge as they punched through barbed tails.

Then the scene changed. Rather than attacking in ones or twos, the insects began pouring onto the deck in their dozens. The air was filled with the clicking, tapping sound of their segmented limbs and snapping mandibles and Arulos found himself submerged in a sea of silver scales.

'Look at the deck!' cried Varek, pointing his sword back towards the stern of the raft.

Arulos was suddenly finding himself hard-pressed. A wall of the creatures was crashing into him, some larger than he was, and all with the same leering, grotesquely human faces. Chitin and ichor washed over him as he hacked and lunged, cutting through the morass with less grace than he would like. This was more like butchery than a battle.

He snatched a look back down the deck to where Varek had pointed. The deck had split in several places, the metal torn by the forest of claws scratching into view. The mortals were doing their best to drive the monsters back but, to Arulos' alarm, the raft was starting to come apart. All of the other rafts had now reached the riverbank and were unloading. Only this one had been attacked with such ferocity.

Arulos whispered a prayer and lightning glimmered down the blade of his sword. He lunged forwards, head down, shoving through the heaving mass. As he lost himself to the fury of fighting, his mind was snatched up by the Eternal Storm. His thoughts howled in a hundred directions at once, letting him observe the battle from his vantage point in the tempest. It was then that he saw the truth: Ghur had fixed its savage gaze on Zagora; she had become its most eagerly sought prey. The rocks and fossils were a gaping jaw, straining to devour her. This was why the other vessels had landed on the riverbanks unharmed. The fury of the river was directed solely at the Dawnbringer. She was a beacon in the dark, drawing clouds of light-hungry predators. Such violence was unstoppable. As Arulos watched from on high, the raft started to fragment, crushed by the incredible weight of the creatures attacking it.

'The harpoon!' cried Kolgrimm, dragging Arulos back to the fight. Arulos punched an insect to the deck, beheaded another and then stepped back to look at the cogsmith. Kolgrimm was still at the prow but several of his engineers had been torn apart, their body parts scattered amongst shards of broken armour. Behind Kolgrimm, the harpoon was also broken, its barrel snapped in two.

'Stormspear!' cried High Priestess Chiana. She was near Kolgrimm, surrounded by guards who were battling furiously to defend her and Zagora.

'The rapids!' cried Kolgrimm, breaking from the fight to point his axe at the river. Up ahead of the prow there was a great cloud of thrashing insects. They were moments away from the edge.

'Hold the line!' cried Arulos to Varek and the other Anvil-hearts, then he stepped back from the fighting, finding a space in the crowds. He sheathed his sword, gripped his aetherstave in his hands and stared through the crystal's corona, letting sacred light pierce his thoughts and focus his sight, blocking out all the distracting noise and movement so he could discern the truth.

He immediately saw how to proceed. He could feel Sigmar's presence coursing through the fibres of his being, in the blessed joints of his armour. He whispered, reaching out into the squalls of astral magnetis, turning them towards the raft, willing it to move towards the riverbank, harnessing true power.

Torrents of energy rushed through him. The land was so infused with savagery that it almost overpowered him. It took all of his training and strength to stay on his feet and drive the tempest through his aetherstave, hurling it into the hull of the ship. The storm collided with the incredible force of the river. The air shim-mered. Sparks leapt from Arulos' armour as he struggled not to collapse.

'Arulos!' cried Zagora. She crushed one of the insects with her hammer and then pounded another, shattering its carapace. Then she pointed the bloody weapon at the people on the deck, fighting for their lives. Her face was drawn with pain. 'What do we do?'

Arulos pitied her. Zagora thought the frail, terrified wretches from Excelsis could somehow turn the storm back; that they could stand against all the hunger of Ghur and fight their way back to the land. She was so vivid, so laden with weight and significance, but at the same time she was like a child, confronted by the complexi-ties of the world and thinking she could simply shout them down.

He turned his back on Zagora and the others and kept his thoughts on the tempest. In a moment of unexpected clarity, he saw that all the power of the tempest had become a serpent, always hungry, always waiting, always hunting – the ground, the air, the river, the distant whitecaps of the Thunderscorn Peaks; all of it was just a fragment of the serpent that circled endlessly in the deeps. And it was this serpent that had locked its thoughts on the Dawnbringer. As mortals and Anvilhearts reeled around him, howling and lashing out at the monsters, Arulos met the gaze of the serpent, locking wills. As the mortals fought desperately for their lives, he would use the power of the thunderstrike to drive the serpent down.

'The falls!' cried Kolgrimm.

'Arulos!' shouted Chiana, but her voice seemed like a distant memory, or an echo, as Arulos held the gaze of the serpent. It slipped away from him, snatched on the breeze, dissolving into the marshes and swamps. Time was running out. With his waking mind, he could see the falls, rushing towards them. Kolgrimm was working desperately at the harpoon with his engineers, pounding it with hammers and lashing cables around it, but to no avail. The Phoenix Company battled to give them space, driving swords and halberds into the creatures or firing their black powder pistols. Zagora had moved away but Chiana was still there and she had dropped to her knees, praying as guards toppled all around her, butchered by scurrying, silver shapes. Even the Anvilhearts were being driven back, overwhelmed by the sheer volume of life that was crashing down onto the raft. The vessel was sinking, buried under a glittering tide of scales and mandibles.

The ship was turning, but it was too slow. They were not going to reach the shore in time. Arulos dragged even more power from the clouds and the winds, his whole body juddering. The raft lurched towards the land but then the deck shook beneath him and started to split. The collision of energy streams was too much for Kolgrimm's vessel. People howled and wailed, praying and cursing as the insects crashed over them.

No. It could not be. Arulos would not believe that he might die in this river. He had to reach Delium. He was fated to lead the Anvilhearts and turn the tide of the campaign. Nothing could prevent that from happening.

As people died all around him, he remembered the dome of light he had glimpsed in the storm. It appeared to him again, more vivid than ever before. He saw now that it was the moment of his glorious victory. Saint Yndrasta was there with him, her angelic wings spread, her mighty body clad in god-forged armour. She was the Celestial Spear, a divine being, forged by Sigmar to save the realm. Arulos knew it was his destiny to fight at her side. He had known it since he sparred with her in Azyr and had been humbled by her wisdom and strength.

Inspired by the memory of Yndrasta, Arulos hurled more of the storm into the raft, determined to reach the shore, but the river surged against him, refusing to give, causing more of the raft to collapse.

Then he heard a chorus of voices, raised in song. The sound was so powerful, so full of majesty that it took him a moment to realise it was not coming from the heavens, but from the sinking raft.

'Stooping from celestial spires he rides the storm to conquer,' roared the crusaders.

As Arulos looked back out at the bloodshed on the raft, he saw that most of the crusaders had moved away from the prow and had gathered along the starboard railing. Zagora was in the middle, raised up on someone's shoulders, and she was leading them in the song.

'He rides the storm to conquer!' she howled, her hammer raised into the tumult. Wind and rain spiralled around her weapon and light flashed across its surface, as if she were commanding the weather.

The silver monsters tore into the crusaders, leaping up over the railings and slaughtering them. It was horrific. But the crusaders, incredibly, ignored them, singing along with Zagora with such passion that they even drowned out the noise of the river. One by one, they were ripped apart by the insects, but they sang on. There was something so incredible about the sight that it took Arulos a moment to realise something else was happening – the raft was lurching towards the riverbank, battling against the current. The hymn was so glorious that Arulos thought, for a moment, that the power of the crusaders' song was steering the raft. Then he realised that, as they sang, the crusaders were leant over the railings, paddling furiously with whatever they could find – broken pieces of deck, weapons and engine pieces. They could not defend themselves but they seemed oblivious to the bloodshed, heaving at the current with every verse, their eyes locked on Zagora who, in turn, was staring up into the banking rain.

Arulos stumbled across the deck, fending off insects, staring at the crusaders. Those around the edges of the group had no chance of survival, monsters were devouring them in a series of frenzied attacks, but they carried on all the same, paddling with all the strength they could muster until they died and someone else replaced them.

Arulos had seen the wonders of Azyr. He had seen entire Stormhosts muster. But this was somehow more incredible: people he had dismissed as frail and pitiable were driving the raft to the shore, dying in droves but still raising their voices in tribute to the God-King, elevated by Zagora's passion into something more than human. Or perhaps this was what humanity truly meant – this incredible, collective will to overcome.

'He rides the storm to conquer,' muttered Arulos, dazed. Then he raced forwards, crying out to Varek and the other Anvilhearts. 'Keep them alive!'

The Anvilhearts were already racing to protect the crusaders and, with a wall of blazing spears, they managed to drive some of the monsters back, stemming the bloodshed. Moments later the raft crashed into the riverbank, hitting the rocks with such force that everyone was thrown from their feet. Those who were still able stood up and ran to the railing, leaping to the ground and racing from the river.

Arulos staggered across the deck, watching the crusaders pour onto the land, dragging the wounded with them. The words of their song circled his head, growing so loud he thought it might split his skull. At the head of the group, hauling people over the railings to safety, was Zagora, her white armour splashed with crimson, her face resolute as she yelled orders and threw people onto the rocks. Arulos fought his way across the deck, cutting down monsters before leaping onto the land. The raft was splitting and shearing behind him, but most people were clear. He and Varek helped those that were struggling and then clambered further up onto the rocks.

The crusaders watched in silence as the vessel finally broke apart, splitting in two and vanishing beneath waves of insects. Kolgrimm shook his head, muttering something to one of his engineers, but most people looked incredulous that they had survived. People were sprawled on the rocks or huddled over the fallen, tending wounds. None of the insects attempted to follow them and once the raft had finally sunk, an eerie quiet descended. Chiana and the other priests bustled through the crowd, praying over the bodies of people who had died within moments of escaping the river. Captain Tyndaris and some of the Phoenix Company were already spreading out across the craggy terrain, looking for signs of predators. And the cogsmiths were hunched over the pieces of engine they had managed to drag from the raft. For a moment, Arulos could not see Zagora, but then he spotted her clambering up some rocks with another mortal. It was her brother, Niksar.

Arulos cleaned his sword and slid it back into its scabbard as Varek approached.

Varek gripped his shoulder. 'That was impressive,' he said. 'I have never seen you harness the aether-storm in that way, channelling it through a huge crowd.'

'I did nothing,' said Arulos.

'What do you mean? I saw it. I saw what you did. You summoned lightning from the sky and those people rallied. They turned that raft to shore.'

Arulos shook his head. 'I did call on the storm, but it was too wild, and the river was too strong. All that I achieved was to split the raft.'

'Then how did we get here?'

'It was her.' Arulos nodded to Zagora, climbing up the rocks with her brother. 'She rallied them. She gave them the power to fight.'

'How? Is she a sorcerer? Because if she is, we need to know–'

'No, it was not the power of the astral magnetis that gave those people strength. It was her.'

Varek stared at him, then shook his head. 'It makes no difference. We made it down the river, now we can get these people to their tower and move on to the work we were sent to do.'

Arulos did not reply, watching the Dawnbringer head away from them. Then he wiped some of the blood from his armour and headed after her.

The two mortals looked around in alarm as they heard armoured boots clanking behind them. Zagora nodded at Arulos and Varek and carried on climbing, but her brother looked unnerved by their presence and kept glancing back. They came to the top of an outcrop and saw a broad valley spread out before them in the sun.

The Claw-water tumbled away to the east, crashing down a mile-high drop before carrying on across a land of muddy plains. Up ahead, in the centre of the valley, was a cluster of bowl-shaped hills, similar in size and spaced about half a mile from each other. Two of them were topped by what looked, at first glance, to be white towers but on closer inspection turned out to be spurs of bone. Beyond the valley, a few miles to the north, a row of sil-houetted figures was just visible – the lines of ancient statues that bordered the Great Excelsis Road.

'We made it,' said Zagora, staring at one of the hills. Her voice was faint and hoarse and, looking at the side of her face, Arulos saw how exhausted she was. On the raft, with the hymn rising around her, she had looked invincible, but now, with the rain lashing into her, even her armour could not hide the fact that she was a frail mortal.

Her brother noticed it too. He put his arm around her. Niksar was as gaunt as she was, and his dark, straggly beard made him look more of a prophet than his sister.

'You need to rest,' he said. 'And eat.'

She nodded vaguely but she was looking at the hills with an intense expression, her gaze passing between the two that had a spur of bone rising from their centre. Then she nodded, gesturing to the easternmost hill.

'It's that one. That's Faithful Tor. Kolgrimm needs to lay his keystone near that spire of bone. And he has to do it quickly.' She glanced up at the clouds. 'Tonight is Gnorl's Feast. We have to make sure it's in place before nightfall. That's when the great conjunction will occur. As Gnorl consumes Koptus, aether will flow beneath this valley in great tides. Kolgrimm has to be ready to tap into it.'

Niksar looked down at the hills and frowned. 'We're going to build our new home at the bottom of a valley? Wouldn't it make more sense to build it at the top of the slope?'

Zagora shook her head. 'Sense has nothing to do with it. The stone showed me the tor. Kolgrimm needs to build the walls around the top of that hill.' She waved from one end of the valley to the other. 'Sacred power runs beneath these hills.' She thudded her warhammer on the ground. 'Through ley lines. It's the same magical current that Sigmar tapped into after the Realmgate Wars, when he ordered the construction of his first Stormkeeps.'

'Did the glimmering show you everything that will happen?' asked Arulos. 'Did it show you what would happen on the raft? Did you know it would be you who led us to safety?'

'It was everyone else who did the work,' she said. 'Everyone else who risked their lives. I just told them what to do.' She kept her gaze fixed on the hills. She looked like she would have fallen if her brother hadn't been holding her. Arulos had expected the same, angry tones she used after the landslide, but she just sounded weary. 'The stone only shows me glimpses. And they are confusing.'

'What made you choose that particular hymn?'

'Hymn?'

'The hymn. The one you sang when you rallied everyone, the one you sang when they were all trying to turn the boat.'

Zagora gave Niksar a puzzled look and they both shook their heads.

'I wasn't singing,' she said. 'I don't think anyone was singing.' She shrugged. 'I told them to row or die. They would have done the same for you if you'd asked them to.'

'No song?' muttered Arulos but as soon as he said it, he felt the truth of it. The hymn was from his own, hidden past. He knew every word. That was why it had summoned such powerful emotions in him. He glanced at the renunciation crystal in his aetherstave. Was it failing? Was it allowing memories of mortal life to pollute his mind? That could be fatal for a tempestarii like him. If he could see what he once was, and how much he had been changed in the years since, it could drive him to madness.

He tried to focus on the present, thinking of the orders he had been given. Then a troubling thought occurred to him.

'The White Angels,' he said, looking up and down the valley.

'What?' said Niksar.

'The Knights Excelsior. They are meant to be here, waiting for you.'

Niksar shrugged. 'These are the wildlands. Maybe they got delayed.'

Arulos shook his head. 'The White Angels should be here.' In all the dealings he had had with them, he had never known them to be late. 'Something is wrong.'

'Actually,' said Niksar. 'There doesn't seem to be *anything* in this valley. That's odd too, if you think about it. Who ever heard of a place in the wilds that isn't crawling with beasts?'

Arulos scoured the valley for signs of movement but there was nothing. After the endless carnage of the last few days the quiet was jarring. Then he held up his hand to silence the others.

'Listen. There is something there.' There was a breeze whipping down the valley, and carried with it he heard voices. They were faint and distant, but they sounded like screams.

'I hear nothing,' said Niksar.

'Neither do I,' said his sister.

'You're right,' said Varek, 'there is something out there. I hear it too.' He glanced at Arulos. 'I hear hunger. It sounds like people pleading for food.'

'The land is always hungry,' muttered Niksar.

'What did you say?' asked Arulos.

'Nothing. Just an old song.'

Arulos studied Niksar. He looked more like a criminal than a crusading hero, with a gaunt, grubby face, a scrappy mess of a beard and a wary look in his eyes. There was a family resemblance, but the features that looked proud and sincere on Zagora looked cagey and cynical on Niksar. And yet, there was some-thing about him, a presence, that reminded Arulos of how he saw Zagora in the Eternal Storm. He wondered what part Niksar had to play in his sister's story.

Niksar looked distinctly uncomfortable under Arulos' gaze and turned away. Zagora looked at him with a troubled expression, but then Niksar cried out.

'There *is* something down there,' he said, peering down into the valley. 'Look at the rocks.'

The land was blurring and flowing, like a painting left out in the rain. The rocks around the hills were scattered with muddy pools and patches of scrubland, and as Arulos studied them they shimmered. He stepped closer to the edge of the cliff and squinted out into the distance. Whatever the phenomenon was, it spread quickly, transforming the whole valley, making everything quiver and dance.

One of the Vindictors appeared behind him. 'There's nothing out there, Knight-Arcanum,' he said. 'It's very odd. We've searched all the surrounding slopes and there's no sign of wildlife. It's like a burial ground. But there is a sound, like voices on the wind – howling noises.'

Arulos nodded, his attention still fixed on the movement that had filled the valley. 'And there is this,' he said. The peculiar blur-ring of the landscape was rushing up the side of the valley towards them, creating a haze of colour. He looked at Zagora and her brother, considering how tired and battered they looked. 'We should find shelter until we know what it is.'

The siblings nodded and the Anvilhearts began leading the way back down the slope towards where all the other crusaders were gathered. They had only taken a few steps when they paused again, hearing a rushing sound behind them.

'What is that?' muttered Niksar, gripping the hilt of his sword.

Arulos looked around but there was nowhere they could take shelter and the sound was approaching at such speed that they would not reach the bottom of the slope in time.

'Form a circle around them,' he said, waving Varek and the others into place.

The Anvilhearts barely had the chance to huddle around Zagora and Niksar when they saw the cause of the noise. A storm of tiny, colourful shapes billowed around them. At first, Arulos thought they were leaves, or petals, they were so colourful, but as they began pinging against his armour he saw that they were tiny songbirds, no bigger than a thumbnail, massed in such incredible numbers that they made it look as though the land itself had fragmented. After everything he had seen in Ghur, Arulos assumed the birds would be a threat, but after a few seconds he realised that they were simply feeding from his armour, hovering around him in a cloud and pecking at the scraps of muck, skin and blood that covered him.

Zagora and Niksar cursed in surprise, trying to bat the creatures away. Then, when they realised the birds were only cleaning their armour they smiled in relief.

'The stone didn't show me this,' said Zagora, holding her hand up to study the cloud of wings burring around her fingers.

Niksar watched as the birds swarmed over the rest of the crusade and then he laughed.

'I'm taking it as a good omen.'

Arulos thought again of the desolate valley and shook his head. 'We'll see.'

CHAPTER THIRTEEN

'It truly is an age of miracles,' said someone from further down the ditch, their voice full of awe.

'An age of shovels,' muttered Sergeant Drannon, who was digging next to Niksar.

Night had fallen and as others were given more elevated tasks the Phoenix Company had been set to work, digging a trench around the foot of the tor. All across the hill, crusaders were pitching tents, unloading carts and tending to the wounded, while at the summit, the crusade leaders were watching Kolgrimm and his engineers work furiously to assemble a circular shrine around the keystone he had brought from Excelsis.

The awestruck voice belonged to the old, aristocratic soldier called Taymar. He was working further down the ditch and had paused to look up at the circle of pillars that the engineers had already moved into position. The two metaliths were drifting on the far side of the hill, still fixed to the gall tusks, and hundreds of people were clambering up and down ropes, passing building materials as Kolgrimm and the other cogsmiths howled commands.

The word 'miracle' grated on Niksar, reminding him of the dangerous role he had landed his sister in. If he had never suggested taking the glimmering to the prophesiers, Zagora would still be safe in Excelsis.

'If Kolgrimm's such an incredible engineer,' sneered Sergeant Drannon, 'why doesn't he come down here and help dig these bloody earthworks? He could build a mechanical wall instead of a... What even is that thing? A temple?'

Taymar's eyes shone in the dark. 'He calls it a nexus syphon. Do you see the document Kolgrimm's holding? That's the Decree Sigmaris. Every detail of the construction work is outlined on that scroll. Kolgrimm needs to follow it to the letter, at least in these early stages.'

'Are you an engineer now, then?' muttered Haxor.

She was digging on the other side of Niksar, her sweaty face blinking in and out of view as flames danced in the breeze. Before the darkness had set in, Captain Tyndaris had ordered the regiment to plant brands all around the circumference of the tor, but since then the wind had picked up, howling through the distant, unseen trees, and as it buffeted against the hillside the light became more erratic.

'You seem to know a lot about Kolgrimm's job.'

'I know nothing about engineering,' said Taymar. 'But I know a lot about these crusades. They mean everything. I don't think you realise how much hinges on our success. It is these courageous souls who will determine the future of Excelsis. And the future of all Thondia. That's why the manner of the strongpoints has been determined in Holy Azyr. The details are a matter of public record. Each crusade must build its stronghold according to the precepts of the Decree Sigmaris. And the nexus syphon is probably the most important part. These outposts will be far more than just bricks and mortar. The Dawnbringer has led us to this hill because there is untapped power here.'

He waved his spade at the two moons hanging over their heads. Gnorl's crescent was so close to the other moon that it seemed about to devour it.

'Once Gnorl and Koptus align, the lifeblood of the land will pulse through this site. It will pass under our feet and the confluence will be caught by the syphon that Kolgrimm's building.'

'No one's building anything if we can't protect this hill,' snapped Captain Tyndaris, limping from the shadows. 'Don't worry yourself about magic syphons.' He waved his cane at the ink-dark valley. 'Worry yourself about what's out there. Greenskins have held these hills for years. I've no idea why they're not currently pulling our limbs off, but rest assured it's only a matter of time. Kolgrimm's instructions were to get these earthworks up before dawn. If you keep gassing we'll still be knee-deep in mud when the first orruks arrive.'

They all saluted and continued digging, and Tyndaris marched on, barking orders as he moved down the line. Most of the regiment were hunched over spades and a large proportion of the civilian crusaders had been roped in to help. Everyone looked exhausted, but the idea of assembling walls and defences had spurred people on. After all they had faced since leaving Excelsis, and so many nights sleeping in the open, the idea of creating something approaching civilisation was a thrill. As Niksar watched people working he felt a sinking sensation. The nobles and highborn were all at the top of the hill, gathered around tents, eating and talking as their servants fussed around them.

'You were right,' said Niksar, looking at Haxor.

She had paused to drink from her flask. 'About what?' she said, wiping her mouth and frowning.

'They're not up to their bloody knees in mud,' he said. 'Look at them. It's business as usual. The princes play while the idiots work.'

'Would you rather swan about until the greenskins turn up and mount your head on a stick?' laughed Sergeant Drannon.

'I don't mind the damned work. It needs doing. It's just that, while we're down here, and they're up there...' He shrugged. 'They'll be making deals. They'll be feathering nests. By the time this place is built they will have hoarded all the chances to themselves. They'll make it so that people like us won't get a look in.' He slammed his spade into the mud. 'I might as well have taken my chances in Excelsis. At least everything wasn't trying to eat me there.'

Haxor gave him a sympathetic look. 'It's still early days. You'll get your chance.'

Niksar grunted.

'Why don't you go up there?' she said, nodding at the half-assembled building. 'You have an excuse. You can mention your sister. Say you've come to check on her or something. Or say you've come to watch over her.'

Niksar paused, looking up at the figures on the hill. Even after everything they had been through on the river, the nobles and merchants somehow managed to look resplendent. Their servants had found them new clothes so while everyone else looked filthy and half drowned, they looked like they had only just left their palaces and townhouses.

'I suppose I could. Tyndaris treats me like I'm one of his men, but I'm not.'

'Do it. If Tyndaris asks where you are I'll tell him your sister required your presence.'

Niksar looked at her. Since the battle on the river she seemed to have abandoned the cynical tones she had used when he was first getting to know her.

'Thank you,' he said.

She nodded. Then smiled. 'Just remember me when you're the one who's swanning around in fancy robes drinking wine while the rest of us do actual work.'

Drannon patted her on the back and laughed. 'He won't.'

The lights grew brighter as he climbed the tor. Hundreds of torches had been placed across the campsite so that the people working on the syphon could see what they were doing. Niksar made his way beneath one of the gall tusks, dodging the cases and sacks that were being hurled from the metalith drifting overhead. He made straight for the building Kolgrimm was erecting, guessing that his sister would be there with the rest of the crusade leaders.

It was only as he neared the structure that he realised how large it was. The design was simple – a circular plinth supporting a circle of columns that looked like they were going to hold up a roof of some kind – but the thing was as tall as one of the grand palaces back in Excelsis. He stopped to admire it. Even half completed it was beautiful, built in the classical Azyrite style. More blocks of masonry were being carried across the hilltop, great, curved slabs that had to be hauled on carts pulled by flathorns. From the shapes, Niksar guessed that the columns were going to be topped by a large dome, similar to many of the shrines in Excelsis. The stones had been painted a deep blue colour and there were intricate astrological markings scored into the surface, edged with gold paint.

Kolgrimm was unmissable. Despite his advanced years and bulky armour, he was rushing around the construction site, clutching the Decree Sigmaris and yelling orders at the people climbing on the stonework. He looked possessed. He had removed his helmet, and his eyes were wide and unblinking as he stomped back and forth, measuring angles by looking through a handheld device. Every now and then he would glance up at the moons, mutter a curse and continue howling orders with even more vigour.

Arulos and the Anvilhearts were nowhere to be seen, but Chiana and the other priests were there. They were gathered in a circle around the nexus and they were all on one knee, hands clasped and heads bowed. As Niksar approached them, he heard their fervently whispered prayers. He did not see Zagora at first, but then he realised she was kneeling next to Chiana, her head bowed like the others.

The sound of the prayers washed through Niksar, seeming to reach him through his mind as much as his ears. There was a charge in the air. At first he thought it was just the dramatic nature of the scene: the nexus rising up into the darkness, bathed in torchlight; Kolgrimm whirling through the crowd, eyes blazing as he howled commands; the priests' prayers. But then he realised it was more than that. The air was alive with power. He could feel it tingling across his skin and crackling in his beard. The closer he came to the building, the stronger the feeling grew. The power was radiating up through the ground. He dropped to one knee and placed his palm on the soil. It was trembling. The movement was barely perceptible but it was there, like the echo of a distant earthquake.

Niksar's tiredness fell away and he felt suddenly invigorated. Ideas tumbled through his mind: plans and schemes for how he could make his new life different from his old one. The fears that had plagued him at the bottom of the hill now seemed absurd. The nobles had some advantages, but they also had flaws and needs. And Niksar was clever. He had always been clever. Out here, in the wildlands, he would make himself invaluable. He recalled Haxor's words about Kolgrimm, about how he would be the architect of more than just the new buildings.

He joined the group following Kolgrimm, breaking into a jog so he could keep up as they rushed from rattling pulleys to chiselling masons.

'Master Kolgrimm!' cried Niksar, but the duardin was too busy berating one of the masons to hear. 'Master Kolgrimm,' repeated Niksar, stepping in front of the cogsmith as he tried to move on.

'Out of my way!' snarled Kolgrimm, marching around towers of scaffolding to where some of the crusaders were heaving another slab into place. The stone was twelve foot tall and several foot deep and they were groaning as they struggled under the weight.

'Don't just stand there!' cried Kolgrimm, shoving Niksar towards them just as the slab started to topple backwards. Niksar rushed to obey and his momentum managed to stop the stone from crushing everyone. Niksar's arms screamed under the weight and he joined the others in a howl of protest as they slowly shoved the thing upright again.

There was a thunder of mechanised hammers as duardin fixed the stone into place and, once it was secure, Niksar and the other crusaders tumbled back onto the soft turf. Most of them lay there for a moment, catching their breath, but as Kolgrimm and his cogsmiths marched on Niksar staggered after them.

'Master Kolgrimm,' he said again. 'I'm the Dawnbringer's brother.'

Kolgrimm halted and finally looked at Niksar. His scowl deepened. 'You?'

It was only then that Niksar remembered their argument after the battle in the fens, when Kolgrimm had argued against listening to Zagora. 'Yes,' he said weakly.

Kolgrimm glanced over at where Zagora was knelt in prayer, then looked back at Niksar. 'I can't get a word out of any of them. Apparently they are *not to be interrupted*. Has your sister told you anything useful? Do you know her plans for this place?'

'Yes,' lied Niksar with practised ease. 'The augur stone was actually mine, originally. Zagora and I worked together to clarify the details of the prophecy. It could quite easily have been me who took on the mantle of Dawnbringer but we decided it would make more sense if I–'

'What about the transference chamber?' Kolgrimm jabbed one of his blocky fingers at the Decree Sigmaris. 'Which way should it face?'

Niksar stared at the scroll. It was covered in arcane diagrams and lines of tightly packed writing. None of it meant anything to him.

'I thought that document told you how to build everything.'

'Tells me how to build everything?' Kolgrimm's face flushed an unpleasant shade of purple.

'Well, I don't mean that exactly. But someone told me it tells you what order to build things.'

Kolgrimm looked around at the other cogsmiths in disbelief and they shook their heads. 'This document,' he said, waving it in Niksar's face, 'gives me the prescribed order of construction. But it's not a bloody recipe. Those high and mighty lords in Azyr have as many grand ideals as they have gilded towers, but they don't have to deal with the actuality of trying to make things work. That falls to mere mortals like me. If they'd asked me, I could have given them a dozen better ways to build a strongpoint, but our noble guardians in High Azyr neglected to consult with people that have actually built things in the Mortal Realms. Besides, there are environmental factors to consider. The direction of the transference chamber will be dictated by the direction of the aetheric currents flowing through the valley.' He waved at the surrounding darkness. 'It's either coming in from the east or the west.'

He looked at the diagrams again, muttering to himself.

'Perhaps it doesn't matter.'

At the words 'doesn't matter,' Niksar decided to lie again.

'The current enters the valley from the east,' he said confidently. 'The glimmering was clear on that.'

Kolgrimm squinted at him. 'You're sure?'

'I am. But you have to wait until the great union in the sky.'

'You mean the conjunction?' Kolgrimm looked up at the moons. 'When Gnorl swallows Koptus.'

'Yes. Exactly.'

Kolgrimm looked at Niksar with interest. 'You'd better stay with me, lad. Your sister's neither use nor ornament, as far as I can see, but you seem to have a bit more nous.'

Niksar felt drunk with excitement. The person Haxor described as the architect of the new kingdom was not only talking to him, but had also decided he was important.

'I'm happy to assist you, Master Kolgrimm,' he said.

Kolgrimm slapped him on the back and marched on, yelling orders and clouting people who paused for breath. Between bellowing instructions he pointed out parts of the Decree Sigmaris to Niksar, explaining their purpose, the difficulties of their construction and the wrong-headedness of its Azyrite authors. There was a string of incomprehensible jargon: aetheric transference, apogee fulcrums and apotheosis lenses. Niksar nodded sagely, pretending to understand as, all the while, his head was filling with grand visions of the wealth that would flow his way now that he was Kolgrimm's advisor. Initially, Ardent Keep might be a simple affair, but perhaps, in time, there would be room for the kind of gilded palaces and townhouses he had spent his whole life unable to enter.

'Do you have plans beyond Ardent Keep?' asked Niksar when Kolgrimm was between yells.

Kolgrimm's nostrils flared and, for a moment, Niksar thought he had angered him again. But then he realised that the cogsmith was excited.

'I have plans you could not imagine, boy.' He waved the Decree Sigmaris. 'Forget about this. Ardent Keep is just the beginning. Once I have–'

One of the other cogsmiths glanced at Kolgrimm and he paused. 'This is not the time,' he said, marching on. 'We can talk tomorrow.'

As the work proceeded, Niksar was pleased to see that Kolgrimm knew exactly how to assemble most of the building. Despite his roughhewn, surly manner, he was clearly the right person for the job. The questions he asked Niksar seemed of a very minor, cosmetic nature, and Niksar felt little compunction in claiming to know the answers. Kolgrimm looked like he was conducting an orchestra, directing hands and chisels with dramatic waves of his axe. Every time he ordered someone to adjust a stone or replace a lintel, the current in the air grew more powerful. Niksar lost track of how long he had been following the cogsmith around the site but he felt more energised as the night wore on. The chorus of prayers was washing through the darkness in waves and the ground was humming with aetheric charge that resonated through his whole skeleton. Around the edges of the hilltop, other teams used winches to haul statues onto their feet – towering, spear-holding likenesses of Stormcast Eternals. Finally, after what must have been hours, the dome-shaped roof of the nexus was in place and people started dismantling scaffolds, revealing the full, glorious design of the building.

Kolgrimm backed away, nodding and muttering as he studied his handiwork. Then he took out a notched circle of brass with a lens in the middle and held it up to study the two moons. 'It's time.' He waved his subordinates to different positions all around the building and they each grabbed one of the levers that were fixed to the base of the columns.

Kolgrimm glanced at the circle of priests. They were still deeply absorbed in their prayers. If anything, their whispered entreaties were even more urgent. Niksar realised that the strange power he could feel was not just thrumming under his feet, it was also emanating from Zagora and the priests. Kolgrimm grunted in annoyance then looked around the hillside. A few people were standing around the nexus syphon, staring up at it in amazement, but most were performing tasks they had been allocated by Captain Tyndaris or Kolgrimm. The earthworks were progressing at an impressive pace and it occurred to Niksar that the vigour he was feeling must have infected everyone else. It was the only way to explain the fact that they were still standing. Just inside the circle of earthworks, people were cutting guy ropes and wheeling winches clear of the statues, letting the structures bathe majestically in the torchlight.

Niksar was filled with a sense of momentousness. Something incredible was about to happen.

'Where are the bloody Stormcasts?' Kolgrimm looked at Niksar as though he would have the answer.

Niksar shook his head. The vitality that was rushing through him made him hesitate to speak. He felt as though, if he opened his mouth, he might howl or launch into song.

'They should be here,' muttered Kolgrimm. 'They should see this.'

There was a peevish quality to his voice and Niksar realised Kolgrimm wanted Arulos and the others to be impressed by him. However derisive he was about Azyrites, the duardin clearly wanted their approval.

'No matter,' he said, trudging back over to the building and waving for Niksar to follow. 'The whole valley will see this thing when it goes up.'

'Goes up?' said Niksar, but Kolgrimm ignored him, heading for the one lever that was unattended. As his hands latched onto the metal, the sound of prayer rose in pitch. Even though the priests all had their heads bowed they seemed to know that the moment had come.

'May Grungni guide me,' said Kolgrimm in reverential tones. Then he cried out, 'Now!' and yanked the lever down.

Niksar laughed in delight as the whole structure blazed with light. Cords of energy lashed across the spherical roof, like liquid lightning. Gouts of electricity erupted from a hole in the centre of the plinth and, as the rising power collided with the falling currents, they created a blinding, miniature sun; a ball of energy that hovered in the air, rolling and spitting fingers of electricity into the darkness.

'Wait!' cried Kolgrimm, his voice almost lost beneath the crackling of thunderbolts. His arms were shaking violently as he fought to hold the lever and the other cogsmiths were having the same problem, their whole bodies juddering as they struggled not to tumble back into the grass.

Kolgrimm looked up at the moons again. Koptus' disc had fitted perfectly inside Gnorl's crescent.

'Let go!' he cried, staggering back and slamming into Niksar, who just managed to keep the duardin upright.

The other cogsmiths followed suit, falling away from the columns and, as they did so, the miniature sun hurled limbs of energy across the hillside. Each beam crashed into one of the statues around the perimeter, then died.

Niksar realised he had been holding his breath for several seconds and took a juddering gasp. As the light died away, he saw that the miniature sun remained, spinning and flashing at the centre of the nexus syphon. Meanwhile, all around the perimeter of the campsite, the statues were now burning with the same fire, lit up by balls of energy buried in their chests.

The light was so fierce that it lifted the whole hillside from the darkness. Unlike the torchlight, this was cold and steady. It made the tor look like an island of sunlight set adrift in the night. Niksar gasped as Kolgrimm enveloped him in a hug so fierce it left him winded.

'We did it,' cried the cogsmith, clapping Niksar on the back repeatedly and laughing. 'You did actually know what you were talking about.'

'Of course,' Niksar laughed, staring at the lightning ball in disbelief.

'We've captured the power of the land,' said Kolgrimm, waving at the rolling ball of light. 'This beauty will power the guardian statues. Just the look of them, lit up like that, will ward off any smaller predators, and the aether currents will temper our defences so that they can stand against pretty much anything else. Ale!' he cried, slapping the back of everyone nearby. 'The hardest part is done! We have power!'

Niksar was grinning as he stumbled after Kolgrimm, but then he paused, turning down the cup of ale that was thrust in his direction. 'That's odd,' he muttered, walking away from the crowd at the nexus syphon. He had heard the wind howling earlier, when he was digging the earthworks, but it had suddenly grown much louder, even rising over the din of Kolgrimm's lightning engines. The strange part was that there did not seem to be any wind. The noise was increasing but Niksar could not feel even the slightest breeze on his face.

Lower down the hill he heard some of the Phoenix Company crying out in alarm. The light from the statues was so bright that he could see the rows of soldiers in stark clarity. Many of them had dropped their spades and grabbed weapons, pointing pistols and swords at the wall of darkness that surrounded the tor.

Zagora and the priests had risen from their prayers and Chiana rushed to Kolgrimm to congratulate him, but Zagora saw Niksar's troubled expression and hurried over to him.

'What is that?'

He shook his head, jogging across the hillside with his sister following. Captain Tyndaris was striding up and down the lines of soldiers, crying out commands, and Niksar and Zagora drew their weapons as they reached him.

'What is it?' demanded Zagora.

Tyndaris looked even fiercer than usual, his huge moustache bristling as he turned to face them. 'That's not a storm,' he said, pointing his sword out into the night.

Niksar looked over the heads of the soldiers, beyond the light of the statues, and saw movement in the darkness. There were faint glimmers of light drifting towards the tor. At first he thought they might be embers, or perhaps some kind of firefly – pale, insubstantial lights that billowed as they came nearer, like cold fire caught in a draught. Then, as the lights came closer, Niksar muttered a curse. They were people. The shapes were drifting dozens of feet up in the air, but they had limbs, bodies and shrouded heads.

'Ghosts?' whispered Zagora.

It was a reasonable suggestion. The pale figures had a wispy, diaphanous quality, as though formed of moonlit smoke. There was nothing faint about their voices, however. The howling Niksar had heard in the distance, hours earlier, was not the wind at all – it was the voices of these floating spirits. Every one of them was screaming. It was a dreadful sound. Even though it was wordless, its meaning was unmistakeable: the spirits were hungry. And it was a terrible, maddening hunger that was awful to hear. Whips of aethereal cloth trailed behind them and their faces were contorted by wild mania. Each of them was holding a blade – a long, colourless knife that glinted, looking far more substantial than the hands that gripped them.

'Banshees,' he said, summoning the name from tales he had heard as a child. 'The souls of dead women, robbed of their immortal rest and forced to roam the Mortal Realms.

'Form a line!' cried Tyndaris, limping around the hillside. 'Ready your weapons!'

His warning was not needed. The banshees were rushing at the tor from every direction, their spectral faces shaking and twitching as they screamed.

Zagora pointed at the lights in the statues' chests. 'The barrier is up!' she cried. 'This tor is sanctified. It is Sigmar's domain. He will be with us as we fight.'

All across the tor, people grabbed weapons and rushed to bolster the lines of Freeguild soldiers. The shapes rushing towards them were hideous, but Niksar noticed how resolute everyone looked, buoyed by Zagora's words. The crusaders had changed since he first saw them gathered in the square in Excelsis. The people they saved on the banks of the Claw-water had merged seamlessly with the original crusaders to form a steadfast host. As the banshees approached, the crusaders faced them down, stern and unyielding.

It was only when the screaming spirits were almost at the tor that Niksar realised his mistake. They were not coming to attack the people gathering behind the earthworks, they were too high.

'They're going to fly over us,' he said.

Zagora shook her head. 'Why would they rush at us and then fly past?'

'Hold your fire until they're closer!' cried Tyndaris from further down the line. 'Make every shot count!'

The banshees picked up speed, hurtling towards the tor with another chorus of screams.

'Fire!' cried Tyndaris.

To Niksar's dismay, the gunshots and arrows had little effect. Some of the spirits jolted and faltered as the barrage ripped into them but many rushed on, passing over the heads of the crusaders.

'What are they doing?' said Zagora, but the words had barely left her mouth before she had her answer. The banshees rushed towards the statues and dived at the balls of light in their chests. Their screams shifted up a key as they grabbed the lightning and began stuffing the energy into mouths that opened horribly wide, like the dislocated jaws of snakes. The sound shifted from desperate hunger to a kind of deranged ecstasy.

The soldiers continued firing up at the spirits, but none of them paused to fight back, rushing on to the lightning spheres, wailing with pleasure as they consumed the energy. Others glided quickly across the hilltop, heading for the light that was burning in the nexus syphon.

'They're eating it,' gasped Niksar, as banshees hurtled towards the statues. 'You said it would repel them. But they *want* the power. They're hungry for it.'

CHAPTER FOURTEEN

'So quiet,' said Arulos as he looked down across the Great Excelsis Road.

He had led the Anvilhearts in a sprint across the valley then climbed the opposite slope, hoping to gain a better view of the surrounding lands, but the weather had conspired against them. The landscape was bathed in low, rolling mists that deadened sounds and made it impossible to see far with any clarity. Arulos could just make out the statues that lined the Great Excelsis Road, but they were disembodied body parts, adrift in a sea of murk. There was still no sign of the Knights Excelsior. Or anything else, for that matter. Like the valley behind them, the marshlands bordering the road were oddly peaceful. Rather than calm, however, the mist radiated a sense of foreboding, as though biding its time, waiting to reveal something dreadful.

'That fog could be hiding anything,' said Varek, planting his standard in the ground. Steam belched from the mud, coiling around his staff and releasing a brackish stink.

Arulos gave a vague nod as the rest of the Anvilhearts reached the top of the ridge and took in the dreary view. 'Where are the Knights Excelsior?' he said. 'We have to keep marching. We have to reach the coast.' He looked south, recalling his vision of a dome blazing in the heat of battle, the moment of his glory. 'We can't wait here.'

Varek removed his helmet to massage his temples, revealing a stern, weathered face with heavy brows and a short, black beard. The fog did not reach down into the valley and, behind him, the tor was lit up like a beacon as Kolgrimm's engines blazed. Varek stared at the distant statues that marked the route of the road.

'We need not skulk through the shadows any more. Once we have taken our leave of the mortals we can march straight across that road and head to the coast.' He raised his standard a little higher, letting the moonlight play across the metal. 'We can march to Delium in a manner that is more befitting of the Anvilhearts' proud history.'

Arulos was looking back down towards the tor. 'We cannot leave them yet. The Knights Excelsior are not here. And if the crusaders are not under the aegis of a Stormhost, they have no chance of building that fortress. Tapping into the aether streams is just the beginning. It will take them months to build something that can withstand sustained attacks.'

Varek shook his head. 'Our orders are clear, Arulos. We must not be delayed any further. The siege at Delium has to be lifted. Saint Yndrasta herself has sent out the call. We must move on and trust that the Knights Excelsior will arrive soon.'

'Varek, I understand. I know how it galls you to think of others striking the blow that is rightfully ours to land, but–'

'You think I am vainglorious? You think I am glory hunting?'

'No. You are proud of the Anvilhearts and you know that we could turn the tide of that battle. I feel exactly the same, and a week ago I would have agreed that we should move on. Crossing that road and striking out for the coast *is* the logical thing to do. The right thing. But I saw something on that raft, Varek. Zagora has a great destiny here, I can feel it. And if we do not help her fulfil it, we will fail the God-King just as surely as if we do not reach Delium.' He drummed his fingers against his sword hilt. 'We can't just leave those people to die. We must find the Knights Excelsior or, failing that, we must at least ensure that Zagora and the others join up with the other crusaders that have come out this way. We will have to try to find one of the other settlements.'

Varek's cheeks flushed with anger. 'I know where this has come from. You have been ruminating ever since Zagora criticised you for letting those Freeguild soldiers die when we rescued the other crusade. And now you want to avoid having the blood of more mortals on your hands. Isn't that right?'

'Do *you* want their blood on your hands?'

'We are not here to safeguard their future. The decision to send them out here was made in Excelsis. We have made sure they reached their destination and we have kept them alive. No one ever suggested we form a permanent garrison.'

'So you would be happy to leave them, with no idea what's out here and no idea if they have any nearby allies?'

Varek made a strangled groaning sound. 'No. No, of course I wouldn't. But what do you suggest? Shouting for help?'

'Let me see the map that High Arbiter Byzac gave us.'

Varek shook his head, unclasped a metal cylinder from his belt and took out a scroll. 'I didn't think you even noticed him handing it over. You thanked Byzac in such a peculiar tone that I assumed your mind was elsewhere.'

They both leant over the paper and Varek traced a finger along the drawing of a road that snaked across it.

'We are here,' he said, then his finger came to rest on a marking further up the road. 'What are these markings?'

'Byzac guessed the locations of the other settlements. They had specific sites in mind when they left Excelsis, just as Zagora did. If they survived, and if they stuck to their plans, these markings show where they should have built their strongpoints. That tall one would be the Shining Tower.' He looked further up the scroll to another settlement that had been marked to the north-west of the tower. 'And that second one must be Fort Amul. Beyond that lie all the other strongpoints built by earlier crusades.'

They both looked north into the sea of fog, but apart from the fragments of statuary around the road there was nothing to break the monotony of the view, just banks of endless grey, coiling through the night.

'The leaders of the other crusades will know the whereabouts of the Knights Excelsior,' said Arulos.

'Possibly.'

'Then we should head north to the Shining Tower. It would only take us a couple of hours to get there. If the Knights Excelsior are there we can inform them that the Dawnbringer has arrived. And if the Knights Excelsior are not there, we can find out how the settlers have managed to survive. And we can ensure they send aid to the crusaders at Ardent Keep. They need to share resources and soldiers. It would be a delay, but only a small one. We will have aided the Dawnbringer immeasurably and then we can play our part at the siege with a clear conscience.'

Arulos waved at the row of Vindictors lined up along the ridge. They were standing proudly to attention, shoulders thrown back, shields and spears glinting in the moonlight. Even the murky air could not dampen the lustre of their armour. Beside them stood the hulking Annihilators, armour-clad goliaths, their meteoric hammers glowing in the mist, charged with aetherfire.

'We are the Hammers of Sigmar, Varek. We have a proud history, but it does not just concern strength in arms. We do what is right. And we are *seen* to do what is right. Do you understand? The people in these lands lived under the boot of Chaos for years beyond counting. Their grandparents told tales of how Sigmar abandoned the realms and left their ancestors to die. The coming of the Stormhosts has shown them that they have not been forgotten, but we must also show them what the God-King is. We must show them how he is the antithesis of the Chaos legions. We are not just fighting for territory, Varek, for Stormkeeps and cities, we are fighting for minds. We are fighting for souls.'

'We won't be fighting for anything if Delium falls.'

Arulos shook his head and was about to say more but Varek held up his hand.

'No more lectures. I understand. We can't leave them until we know they have a fighting chance.'

Arulos nodded. 'Exactly. There's no need for all of us to go though. I told Chiana we were just scouting the valley. We can't simply vanish without explanation.' He singled out a Vindictor. 'Turris, pick nine men and return to the tor. Take word to Zagora and Chiana. Tell them that the rest of us are heading north up the road. We will find the Shining Tower or one of the other crusader settlements. I will announce the Dawnbringer's arrival and discern the whereabouts of the Knights Excelsior. We will return before dawn.'

The warriors slammed the hafts of their spears against their chests, then turned and ran into the darkness, heading back down into the valley. As Arulos watched them go, he cast his stormsight over their heads, letting the wind carry his thoughts to the tor. Kolgrimm's engines were blazing. He had tapped into the aetheric ley lines in exactly the manner Zagora predicted. He could not see the crusaders in detail, but they looked to be busying themselves around the statues and continuing with the construction work. There was a fierce wind howling around the hill, but nothing else. Arulos could not sense any predators in the valley. The whole region was still strangely peaceful.

'We must be quick,' he said, turning back towards the swamps and marching out into the fog.

The Anvilhearts had not gone far before they realised the mists were even thicker than they had thought. Arulos could only see a couple of feet ahead as he descended the muddy slope. He did his best to maintain a proud, dignified air, but it was hard to keep his footing as the ground grew marshier. Flies buzzed around his helmet, clogging the eyeholes of his faceplate so that he had to stop every few paces to scoop them out. The ground was peculiar – a gluey tar that was as black as ink and hot, bubbling like a broth over a stove, belching clouds of reeking steam. None of his men uttered a word of complaint but he could hear them slipping and stumbling, battling to drag their heavy armour through treacly pools. The lower they climbed, the wetter things became, until the tar was knee deep and their pace became interminably slow.

Varek was at his side, using his standard to lever himself through the mire. 'We should move quicker once we reach higher ground,' he said.

Arulos nodded. 'The road is somewhere up ahead. We can travel on that for a while.' He could not actually see the road, or even the statues that lined it, but he could recall the location from when they had looked down into the swamps and he was sure they had not deviated.

After a few minutes of trudging on, however, batting away flies and wrenching their boots from squelching pools, Arulos started to doubt himself.

'We should have reached it by now.' He held up a hand and the others stumbled to a halt around him. Then he gripped his aether-stave, whispered an incantation and peered through the corona of the renunciation stone. Sigmar's storm was there, as always, but it was oddly opaque. He could see the swamps around the road, but his stormsight saw them no more clearly than his physical sight.

Arulos was just wondering if they should head back the way they came, when one of the Vindictors broke away from the others and pointed at something. It was Maratha, the Prime in charge of the other Vindictors.

'There!' she snapped, pointing her spear. 'My lords! There's someone out there. Do you see?'

A slight, stooped figure was moving quickly through the fog to the north of them. Arulos could only see a vague silhouette, but it was humanoid rather than bestial.

'Halt!' cried Arulos, lending his voice all the power of the storm.

The figure stopped and glanced back. Then it rushed on, racing away from them.

Arulos waved his men on and chased after the distant shape. Wading through the tar pits was infuriating but he was determined not to let the stranger escape.

'This could be our link to the other crusader settlements,' he said, turning to Varek. 'There may be no need to go to the Shining Tower at all if we can catch that person.'

He powered on, battling through the mud with such force that Varek and the others struggled to match his pace, trailing behind him in the fog.

'Damn it,' he muttered as the figure faded from sight.

The others gathered around him, plucking flies from their faceplates and wiping mud from their armour.

Maratha pointed her spear again. 'Look. He's still there.'

Arulos leapt into motion but it was only as he ran on that he realised the figure could not have doubled back so quickly. 'There must be two of them,' he said but, as he peered through the miasma he was not sure; the figure looked identical to the one he had been following a moment earlier – frail and stooped, but moving very quickly.

After a few minutes the figure vanished again before being spotted heading in another direction. This happened several times and Arulos had the peculiar sense that the land was playing a trick on him; having a joke at his expense. He was about to say they should head back towards the tor when he realised he had no idea which direction that would be. The fog was not just in the air but in his mind, clouding his stormsight, making him unable to see anything but the gloopy puddles he was wading through. Then, finally, they saw something different.

'Is that a group of them?' asked Varek, as everyone paused, studying a line of shapes up ahead.

Arulos shook his head. The shapes were too wide and blocky to be people. He staggered on through another puddle and stared through the mist. 'They're buildings.' The closer he got the surer he was. He started to discern recognisable shapes: roofs and walls. 'And they are intact.'

It was not strange to find abandoned outposts in the Ghurish wildlands. Few structures survived the predations of the beasts that hunted constantly for food, but it was odd to find an empty settlement that was not ruined. The denizens of Ghur delighted in destruction and violence. They could not understand concepts such as beauty or civilisation. All they knew was how to tear down and deface.

Arulos gripped his aetherstave in both hands as he advanced. 'Anvilhearts, ready your weapons.' There was a clattering sound behind him as Maratha and the other Vindictors closed ranks, raising their shields and locking into a seamless wall of sigmarite, bristling with stormspears. The Annihilators were further behind, weighed down by their bulky armour, but he could hear the rattle of their hammers and shields.

Arulos held his staff before him, whispering phrases that made it simmer quietly with aetheric power. There were twelve huts, protected by a watchtower and stockade, but no sign of any inhabitants.

Varek looked back at the stockade they had just passed through. 'The place does not seem to have been attacked.'

Arulos marched through an opening in the stockade and approached one of the huts. The door was open but it was too dark inside to see if the place was empty. He approached the door, then halted a few feet away.

'Do you hear that?' He had heard a distant, unfamiliar sound – a thin, rippling noise that could equally have been gurgling water or someone laughing.

'I hear it,' said Varek, as the sound was repeated, echoing oddly through the mist. 'An animal, perhaps?'

Arulos looked around at the dark windows. 'There's a morbid chill to this place that I do not trust.' He raised his aetherstave. It burned cool, leaking blue light, throwing back the shadows as he stepped into the hut.

The dwelling consisted of two small rooms. In the first there was a wooden table, covered in discarded dishes, as though a meal had been interrupted. In the second room there were a few crates, some carefully folded clothes and a mattress on the floor. There was no sign of the occupants and still no signs of any fighting.

As Arulos passed his light over the walls a face leapt from the darkness. It was cruel and sneering, its mouth crowded with dagger-shaped teeth. He backed away and almost hurled aetherfire from his staff. Then he realised it was just a painting. Someone had daubed a grinning, circular face on the wall. As he stared at the repulsive image, Arulos heard the distant sound again. This time he was sure it was no animal. It was definitely laughter.

'Someone is playing games with us,' he said, waving Varek back out of the hut.

'Greenskins?'

Arulos shrugged. 'Orruks are not known for their patience. If there were greenskins here they would be attacking rather than hiding.' But the face on the wall did remind him of markings he had seen on greenskin shields. He marched over to one of the other huts and stepped carefully inside, signalling for the others to spread out and search the rest. There was no face on the wall this time, but it was otherwise the same as the other hut. Devoid of life but full of its signs, as though it had been abandoned in a hurry.

They searched all the buildings and found no trace of any people. Then, as they reached the far side of the settlement, they saw more buildings in the distance. Arulos waded through the mud towards the next set of buildings and found an almost identical scene – buildings that had been abandoned with no sign of a struggle. This happened several times. Each time they reached another group of buildings, the rippling laughter rang out again.

Arulos had lost track of how long they had been exploring the tar pits when they spotted a much larger building up ahead in the fog. It was a stone redoubt, built in similar style to the older parts of Excelsis – an attempt to echo the majesty of Azyr, with domes, cupolas and arches made to resemble celestial halos, all built around a single, slender tower. But the dreary weather had drained the colours of life and the place seemed to be wilting in the mire. And where Excelsis would have been teeming with traders and soldiers, the fort was as silent as a corpse. The only movement came from the fog, coiling and rolling over the walls.

'This must be the Shining Tower,' said Arulos. 'But it does not seem we will find any crusaders here.'

'Could they be hiding?' asked Varek.

Arulos shook his head and pointed his aetherstave. 'With the gates left open?'

'There!' said Varek.

The figure had returned and it was closer this time, just ahead of them, dashing towards the gates. It was dressed in rags, and as it raced into the fortress Arulos saw it clearly for the first time.

'That's not a man,' he said, as the thing vanished from sight. He had only caught a brief glimpse, but he had seen weirdly elongated limbs and an oversized head hung low between stooped shoulders. Whatever it was, it had been carrying a spear and a round shield that bore a face – the same grinning face he had seen painted on the walls.

Varek made to run after it but Arulos held him back. He looked warily at the tides of mist. The silence was ominous and unnatural. They were still thirty feet from the gates and Arulos could not see far into the square that lay beyond them. The creature had vanished, disappearing into the fog.

'Advance slowly,' he said, waving his troops on. 'There is something odd happening here.'

When they reached the gates, he stopped and squinted into the mist. They had entered a small square, surrounded by barracks and warehouses. Roads led to the left and right, tracing the inside of the walls, and a third led straight on, towards the base of the tower.

'Circle round,' said Arulos, glancing at the Annihilators, waving them to the left. He sent half the Vindictors in the opposite direction and headed straight on with Maratha and the rest, Varek at his side. 'Meet at the rear gate.'

They passed a few more empty buildings and then Arulos heard the sound again. He was sure now that it was laughter. It drifted through the darkness, coming from every direction.

Arulos felt a rush of unexpected anger. He halted, gripped his staff and stared into the crystal at its head. Then, when he was calmer, he marched on, his sword and armour dripping in the mire and his boots squelching in the flooded street.

They inspected a few buildings and found no sign of anyone, but as they passed the tower he halted and held up a hand.

'Do you hear that?'

'The laughter?' said Varek. From his tone, Arulos realised that Varek found the sound just as annoying as he did.

'No, something else. Listen.'

They all stood in silence for a moment, then Arulos looked up at the tower.

'It's coming from in there.' It was not laughter, this time, but a murmuring sound, like wind through leaves. 'Fetch the others,' said Arulos, sending Maratha on ahead. 'Tell them to join us back here at the tower.'

As Maratha saluted and rushed off, Arulos tried again to use his stormsight, peering through the corona around his stone. The fog was thicker than ever. He could not even find Sigmar's tempest, let alone ride the currents. He was anchored in the corporeal world.

'Someone's here,' he said. 'Perhaps you were right, Varek. Perhaps they are holed up in this tower.' He looked around for the door and entered the tower, holding his aetherstave before him, driving back the darkness.

His boots crunched across broken timbers and rubble. The tower had been gutted. All the floors had been ripped out and sent crashing to the ground. It was a hollow, stone tube with shafts of moonlight hanging from its broken windows. The noise was louder in here though – a strange, muffled murmuring that echoed around the empty structure.

'Is it an insect nest?' asked Varek, pointing his sword to the top of the tower. Hundreds of feet up, swaying in the darkness, there was a dark, misshapen ball. It was hard to say how large it was from so far away, but it seemed to be suspended from the ceiling. It was the source of the droning sound.

Arulos looked at Varek. 'Do you feel it? Someone is mocking us. Someone is playing games.' Then he noticed that there was still an intact staircase – stone slabs that spiralled up the walls, circling the inside of the tower. 'Stay close,' he snapped, striding over to the stairs and starting to climb.

The staircase was so narrow that they had to proceed in single file. Arulos was halfway up the tower when he realised that the shape swaying above his head was not a nest but an enormous net – a sagging bag made of thick ropes that had been knotted together and hung from the ceiling. It was huge, and as he came closer Arulos saw that it was full of animals that had been tied together – hundreds of them, struggling and writhing. These pitiful beasts were the cause of the murmuring sound he had heard. He was now even more certain that this was all some kind of strange prank. It was as though someone were trying to deliberately delay him. He debated heading back down the steps but curiosity got the better of him. Why would anyone suspend animals at the top of a tower? He clambered over a broken rafter and continued up the steps with Varek and the others hurrying after him.

When Arulos was about thirty feet from the slowly spinning net, he stopped and whispered a curse.

'They're not animals.'

'By the Anvil,' gasped Varek.

The net was crowded with hundreds of men and women, all tightly bound and gagged, trussed like animals and heaped on top of each other. Their eyes were wide with terror and they were all howling behind their gags, producing the strange sound that had drawn Arulos into the tower.

Arulos had seen many horrors. He had fought in the Realmgate

Wars, Sigmar's first strike into kingdoms that had been oppressed by Chaos for centuries. He had battled monsters dragged from the minds of sorcerers and necromancers. But the sight of these people, bound like cattle, screaming in mute terror, was one of the most appalling things he had seen.

'Who would do this?' he whispered.

'There are so many of them,' said Varek, shaking his head. 'This must be the people from the surrounding settlements too. Why would someone leave them like this? Why not just kill them?'

Arulos shook his head. 'I have the strangest feeling. As though this has been done for our benefit.'

'That makes no sense,' said Varek, still looking up at the terri-fied prisoners. 'How could anyone know we were going to arrive now? And why would they be interested in us?'

'We matter, Varek. When we help Yndrasta break that siege we will secure this whole stretch of coast. We will safeguard Excelsis. And in their own, crude way, the creatures of Ghur might have sensed that. I think they are hunting us, trying to tear us down.'

Arulos looked up the steps and saw that at the top there was a wooden gantry leading to the side of the net.

'Come, let us at least free these poor souls and lead them back to Zagora and the others.' He marched up the final stretch of steps. 'And perhaps one of these people will tell me where the Knights Excelsior are.'

They circled the tower one last time and reached the gantry. It was broad enough for the Anvilhearts to advance in a group, weapons raised, but there was no sign of whoever had created the huge net. The prisoners struggled even more desperately as Arulos approached them, desperate to escape their bonds. The sight of Sigmar's people treated in such a way appalled Arulos. It was so degrading. It seemed somehow worse than if they had been killed in battle.

The gantry was crudely built but showed the rude ingenuity Arulos had seen before in greenskin structures. Buildings and vehicles had been dismantled and repurposed, creating a forest of levers and pulleys that held the net in place. The gantry reached right up to the side of the net and Arulos could see a place where he could cut a hole in the ropes and start hauling people out.

He walked towards it.

There was a click and a rush of sliding ropes as the sack was released. Arulos caught one last glimpse of terrified faces, then the whole thing plummeted down the length of the tower, trailing ropes and muffled screams.

A few seconds later it slammed onto the distant floor and the murmuring stopped.

For a moment, Arulos could not understand what had happened. Then he looked beneath his boot and saw the hidden lever he had trodden on.

He had killed them.

The laughter returned, drifting in through the windows of the tower, much louder than before.

CHAPTER FIFTEEN

Niksar lashed out with his sword as a banshee screamed towards him. It was a storm of gossamer, ghostly tendrils raging around a howling skull. But its knife was not so insubstantial. It clanged against Niksar's sword so hard his arm juddered.

He was clinging to the side of a statue, gripping its stone spear and, as he parried blows, he struggled to hold on. All across the hilltop, people were flinging scaffolding back into place, propping ladders and platforms against the statues in an attempt to defend them. Kolgrimm was bellowing orders, demanding that the statues be protected, and his cogsmiths were wheeling heavy weapons across the muddy turf, turning winches and grabbing sacks of black powder.

'We made this happen!' yelled Niksar, turning to Haxor, who was a few feet lower down the statue. 'The lights drew them to us.'

'Great start!' she cried back, hacking furiously at one of the spirits, trying uselessly to land a blow as it whirled back and forth, wailing and screeching as it tried to get past her. 'We've summoned an unkillable foe. Maybe Kolgrimm isn't quite the genius he thinks he is.'

The banshee attacking Niksar was trying desperately to reach the light in the statue. Every time it neared the blaze, Niksar lashed out with his sword, striking at its weapon and knocking the revenant back into the darkness, but the thing simply dissipated and reformed, rushing at him over and over again, shrieking and hissing.

'How do you kill something that's already dead?' he gasped.

Blades clanged all around him but everyone was struggling in the same way. Panicked cries echoed across the hillside. The banshees seemed to thrive on the fear, attacking with even greater fervour, cutting people down with rusty, pitted blades.

Niksar parried another slash. The phantom stared at him with empty, bleached sockets, screaming in his face, enveloping him in spectral robes that crawled across his skin, clammy and burning at the same time. It was like being engulfed by a toxic mist.

Niksar howled in pain and fear. He had fought countless predators in his life but never anything that his blade could not touch. And it was getting worse. His first few blows had had *some* effect on the spirits, knocking them off course even if they did not actually do any harm. But as he grew more afraid, his sword grew even less effective, slicing through the ghosts with only the faintest ripple. He was surrounded by screeching, tormented souls. They were packed so tightly around him that he lost sight of the other people who were fighting with him on the hilltop. All he could see was nightmarish apparitions. He parried another blow but more of the banshees flowed towards him, all lashing out with the same frenzied screams.

He clambered higher up the statue, trying desperately to fend them off. To Niksar's dismay, he saw that several of the lights were flickering and guttering. Even the light in the nexus syphon was dimming.

'Look!' he cried. 'The power is dying!'

'Is that bad?' gasped Haxor as she fought. 'If the lights fail, these things might…' She paused to hack at one of the banshees, hammering furiously at its sword in an attempt to drive the ghost back. 'If the lights die,' she said, clambering up to Niksar, 'the spirits might go.'

Niksar gasped, parrying several blows at once. But he was unable to stop others from cutting into his arm and chest. Blood flew through the darkness, making it even harder to see.

'Kolgrimm said we need the lights! They are the power that will protect the keep.' He looked around at the battle and saw the cogsmith not far away. The duardin engineers were now firing their weapons, a kind of black powder ballistae that launched several arrows in a single shot. They boomed like thunder every time they fired, but the arrows simply whistled through the banshees without doing any harm. Kolgrimm howled at his engineers as if it was their fault, but there was nothing they could do.

'Look at that!' said Haxor, grabbing him so suddenly he nearly fell from his perch.

'Sigmar's throne!' gasped Niksar as he saw Chiana striding purposefully across the hillside. She was flanked by crowds of the shaven-headed zealots armed with morning stars and flails. 'They're killing them.'

Unlike everyone else on the tor, Chiana's fanatics were cutting the gheists down, clubbing them to the ground as if they were living, breathing foes. As the zealots fought, they howled prayers, calling out to Sigmar as they destroyed the banshees with a storm of brutal blows. Chiana walked calmly in their midst, hands clasped together and eyes closed.

'It's the prayers,' said Haxor. 'The prayers are making their weapons work.' She whispered a prayer and lunged again, but nothing changed – her sword passed through the banshees just as uselessly as before.

As Chiana and the zealots came closer, Niksar saw his sister following in their wake. She was pounding the banshees with her huge, two-handed hammer, shattering skulls and obliterating bodies. She had the same look of furious conviction as the priests, but her mouth was clamped tightly shut.

'No,' gasped Niksar. 'It's not the words. The words don't matter.' He looked at the banshee that was drifting in front of him, squealing and preparing to attack again. 'It's faith.' He thought of how his blows had been growing less effective as his dread grew. 'It's belief.'

He crushed his fear and replaced it with furious conviction, determined that, this time, he would land a blow. He attacked with a wild, backhanded swipe and his blade thudded into a banshee's chest. The gheist fell apart, tumbling away from him, collapsing into a torrent of pale tendrils.

'What?' cried Haxor. 'How in Sigmar's name did you do that?'

'In Sigmar's name!' cried Niksar, cutting another banshee down, his pulse racing as he saw a chance to finally do some damage. 'That's exactly it. Call on your faith, Haxor! Believe in Sigmar! Believe he is with you! Believe you can hurt them!'

Haxor stared at him, looked down at the zealots, then grinned. 'Believe! I understand!' She stood on the statue's shoulder, planted her boot against its chin and lashed out with her sword, howling an oath to Sigmar. Her sword cut one of the ghosts in two and sent another rolling back into the darkness. The spirits nearby all faltered, sensing that Haxor and Niksar were no longer defenceless prey.

A tide of belief washed through the crusaders. People called out to each other, explaining that faith would temper their weapons, and soon the hillside rang to the sound of howled prayers. Niksar and Haxor had cleared a space around the top of the statue, but as Niksar paused for breath, he saw that waves of banshees were still flooding over the walls. For every one that was hacked down, ten more rushed to attack. Crusaders were forming a crowd around Chiana and the priests, howling triumphantly as they fought, but it was not enough. People were dying all across the hillside and there were still hundreds of spirits rushing towards the statues.

Niksar watched the duardin reload their weapons and pointed them out to Haxor. 'Those guns are the answer. But there's no way they can protect all the statues at once. We have to drive the banshees to one place. We need to round them up.' He started to climb down the statue, still fighting off spirits as he went. 'Let's find Captain Tyndaris. He could order the Phoenix Company to drive them in one direction.'

Niksar had only climbed as far as the statue's knee when a roar boomed over the sound of the fighting. For a dreadful moment, Niksar thought it was another gargant, like the one they had seen in the fens, but then he saw the real cause. One of the gall tusks was rearing up, assailed by banshees. They were trying to reach the metalith drifting above the huge beast. The spirits were whirling over the poor creature as they raced up to the drifting island. The gall tusk's handlers called for aid, trying to calm the animal, but as more of the banshees rushed towards it the gall tusk rose on its hind legs, shaking its enormous head, and let out another terrified roar.

People tumbled from the metalith as it shook and others fell from the howdah on the gall tusk's back. Some of the Freeguild soldiers broke away from the fighting at the statues, rushing across the tor towards the panicked gall tusk. Before they reached it, the beast gave such a wild shake that the chains connecting it to the metalith started to snap. The metalith slumped at an even more disastrous angle, hurling people and supplies onto the hillside, then, as the gall tusk thrashed its head furiously, trying to rid itself of banshees, the rest of the chains snapped and the whole metalith came loose. The momentum of the panicked beast sent it hurling off into the darkness.

'Follow it!' howled Kolgrimm, barging through the crowds, waving his axe at the disappearing metalith. 'Stop it!'

Some people did as he ordered, stumbling away from the fighting, leaping over the earthworks and racing down the hillside. But others stayed where they were as Captain Tyndaris waved his cane at them, shouting with just as much fervour as Kolgrimm.

'Protect the statues!'

Now that Niksar had spotted the captain, he jumped down onto the sodden turf and raced across the hillside, dodging people, jumping over discarded scaffolding and half-assembled tents with Haxor running after him.

'We have to trap the spirits in one place!' he cried, shoving his way through Freeguild soldiers to reach Captain Tyndaris. 'We need to round them up!'

Captain Tyndaris glanced at him but did not register his words, still howling at people to get back to the statues.

'We can't lose that metalith!' roared Kolgrimm, marching into view and yelling at Captain Tyndaris. 'We've already lost a third of our building materials. If we lose even more we might as well have stayed in Excelsis. I can't build if I have nothing to build with.' He paused to swing his axe, beheading a banshee in a flash of spectral fire. 'And we can't dig a bloody mine. We need those blocks.'

All around Kolgrimm and Tyndaris an argument broke out.

'We just need to round them up!' yelled Niksar.

Tyndaris was about to ignore him again but Kolgrimm held up a hand, recognising Niksar.

'Eh? What's that?'

The arguments faltered as people looked his way.

'If we drive the spirits to one place, you could use your...' He looked around and pointed his sword at the ballistae. 'You could turn those things on them.'

Tyndaris glared at him. 'So we ask the ghosts to line up?'

Haxor held up her sword. 'Wait, there could be a way.' She looked at Kolgrimm. 'If they're feeding on the aetherfire, maybe we could use that against them. Is there any way of focusing the power in one place, so it draws them all together?'

Everyone stared at her. Then Kolgrimm laughed.

'Yes. Yes, there might be a way.' He nodded at one of his cogsmiths. 'Target all the ballistae on one statue. Quickly.' Then he waved at some of the other duardin, signalling for them to follow as he stomped off across the hill, heading towards the nexus syphon. He nodded for Niksar and Haxor to follow.

By the time they reached the nexus syphon, several of the statues were so shrouded in banshees that the lights were barely visible, failing fast. The tor that had seemed so brightly lit just ten minutes ago had now fallen almost into darkness.

Kolgrimm ordered his engineers back into position, gripping the levers at the base of the syphon's pillars. Then he spent what seemed like an age adjusting engine parts beneath the plinth. Then, after a muttered curse and a shake of his head, he grabbed a handle and turned a crank shaft with a few quick jolts.

The lights all died apart from one, burning brightly from the chest of a statue on the far side of the hill.

The banshees howled, causing people to clutch their heads and gasp, tormented by the sound. Then the spirits rushed through the dark towards the statue, which was now so bathed in light it looked like something that had fallen from the heavens.

'Wait!' cried Kolgrimm, rushing over to the ballistae. 'Give 'em a chance. Let 'em get in one place!'

Just as Haxor had predicted, the banshees congregated on the light. Gathered together in a single group, they looked even more nightmarish, rolling and turning around each other in a frenzy.

Once all of them were swarming over the statue Kolgrimm gave the order to fire and his engineers launched a deafening barrage, bellowing prayers to duardin gods as they worked. The banshees screamed as arrows ripped through them, shattering skulls and buckling knives. The spirits grew even more frenzied. They seemed to realise their danger, but their hunger for the aetherfire would not let them flee, trapping them at the statue.

The duardin reloaded their weapons and fired another volley, ripping more of the banshees from the air. Still the spirits could not tear themselves away from their feast, glutting themselves on the light as the cogsmiths reloaded and fired again. Wave after wave of shots cut through the spirits until, a few minutes later, it was all over. The statue was badly damaged, with scores of holes punched from its chest and shoulders, but it was still standing, and as the last of the banshees fell away the aether light burned fiercely.

Kolgrimm hurried back to the nexus syphon and adjusted the engines again, redirecting power to the other statues and back into the syphon itself, surrounding the hilltop with a blazing halo.

Cheers broke out across the tor. Haxor swaggered over towards Niksar and gave him an elaborate, only partially sarcastic bow.

'Turning the lights off was your idea,' he said, grinning back at her and returning the bow. Then Niksar saw Kolgrimm and his good humour faded. The old cogsmith looked even grimmer than usual as he shoved his way through the celebrations.

'Find the sodding metalith!' He waved his axe at the darkness. 'We need that stone. And the metal. And the tools.'

Captain Tyndaris was nearby and he sent men out into the night after the floating island. 'Take the gall tusk!' he cried. The beast was still agitated, but the handlers had managed to hurl ropes back over its neck and it looked less likely to bolt. 'The rest of you,' said Tyndaris, looking around at everyone else, 'get back in those trenches. The night isn't over yet.'

CHAPTER SIXTEEN

For several minutes, Arulos could neither move nor speak. The anger that had been simmering since he first heard the laughter had now become a torrent. And mingled with the anger was shock. He had just sent hundreds of people to their deaths. His flesh and spirit had been forged to be superior but here, in a land of brutes and animals, he had been tricked into murdering the very people he was created to protect.

'Knight-Arcanum,' said Varek, sounding dazed. 'What…?' He could not finish his sentence, looking at the tragic shapes piled at the bottom of the tower.

'By the anvil,' muttered Arulos, peering into the darkness. 'Some of them are moving.' He waved his men back towards the steps, trying to ignore the laughter that was still drifting through the windows. 'Quickly. There may be time to save some of them.'

The Anvilhearts rushed down the narrow steps as fast as they could and raced over to the mound of bodies. It was a horrific sight but he steeled himself and began cutting ropes, looking for survivors. The movement he had seen from the top of the tower turned out to be no more than death throes and bodies tumbling to the ground, but after several minutes of fruitless searching one of the Vindictors cried out.

'Here, Knight-Arcanum. I've found one. She's alive.'

Arulos hurried around the edge of the mound and reached out as the Vindictor gently handed him a blood-drenched woman. She was raving, blood frothing at her lips, her eyes rolling and her legs dragging beneath her as he laid her carefully on the flagstones. He took a vial from his belt, removed his gauntlets and poured the contents onto his palm. Then he clasped his hands together and prayed furiously. The laughter was still there, mocking him and stoking his rage, but he battled to block it out, searching his thoughts for a glimpse of the tempest. It was faint, but it was there, summoned back into view by his determination to save the woman's life. Aetherfire crackled across his hands, sparking between the gaps in his fingers. He whispered another prayer, calling on the power of the anvil, then he pressed his palms against the woman's head, directing the storm into her broken body.

'My lord,' said Varek, appearing at his side, a warning in his voice.

Arulos ignored him, coaxing what little of the storm he could snatch and guiding it into the woman. 'She's not dead,' he said. 'This is healing, not necromancy.'

She coughed and stiffened in his grip, her eyes opening wide. At the sight of her surroundings, she began to scream, thrashing against Arulos with her fists. He tried to steady her, gripping her arms as gently as he could, but holding her seemed to increase her agitation so after a while he let her go. She dragged herself away from the pile of bodies and pressed her face against the wall, gasping and muttering gibberish.

No, thought Arulos, it was not all gibberish, there were intelligible words mixed in with her babble. He looked at Varek.

'What does that sound like to you?'

'The end of empires?' replied Varek.

Arulos nodded. 'I thought the same.' The words meant nothing to him, but the woman gasped them in such fearful tones that they seemed horribly significant. 'Who did this to you?' he asked, crouching at her side.

'The end of empires,' she repeated, then her body was rocked by such a dreadful cough that Arulos realised he had not saved her. Even the power of the tempest could not preserve a body that had been so traumatised. Despite his eagerness to move on, Arulos could not leave the woman's side, waiting with her as she died. Near the end, she regained some clarity, turning her face from the wall and looking at Arulos and the others in surprise.

'You came too late,' she said, the terror leaving her eyes, replaced by a grief that was hard to witness.

Arulos handed her a flask of water, holding it to her lips as she drank. 'Who did this to you?'

'Greenskins,' she said. Pride flashed in her eyes. 'We held this place. We held it for a year. Do you understand? We fought off everything the land threw at us. We reclaimed miles of this damned road. But they tricked us. In the end they...' She paused to draw a painful breath, keeping her gaze locked on Arulos. 'In the end they tricked us. Hiding and laying traps.' She frowned, looking confused again. 'They're different. Not like... They're almost like men.'

'Orruks are dim-witted,' said Arulos. 'Perhaps they *were* men? Men corrupted by Chaos? I have seen cannibal savages who are so perverted by Chaos that they barely look human any more. Transformed by their dark worship.'

She shook her head. 'They weren't men. You'll see. When you see them, you'll understand. They're different. They're greenskins, but they don't just attack, they wait, plotting and biding their time.' Her eyes widened and she reached up, trying to grab Arulos' pauldron.

'You might still be in time… You could… For the others… You might still be able to save them.' She looked past Arulos, struggling to focus on the rest of the Anvilhearts. 'Are there many of you?'

'There are enough. What do you mean, the others? People from the Shining Tower?'

'No…' She closed her eyes, battling waves of pain. Her voice grew weaker with every word. 'No. I mean the other strongpoints. Fort Amul. Ulfarsson Keep. The Saros Bastion. The greenskins will reach them next. They mean to ruin all the strongpoints. All the crusades will have been in vain. You have to…'

'Rest,' said Varek, kneeling next to her. 'Save your strength.'

She tried to haul Arulos closer. 'You *have* to help those people.' She glanced at the grotesque mound a few feet away, tears of rage in her eyes. 'Don't let them end up like this. You could…' She coughed. And then she could not stop coughing until Arulos gave her more water and she fell silent, leaning back against the wall. When she finally exhaled her last breath, her eyes remained fixed on Arulos, filled with a silent plea.

Arulos rocked back on his heels and sat next to her, his back to the wall, struggling to think clearly.

'Scout the buildings again,' said Varek, waving the other Anvil-hearts away. 'Make sure there is no one else out there.'

Once they were alone, he sat next to Arulos and the dead woman.

'It was a trap. You did not hang those people up there. Their deaths are not on your head.'

'It was a trap that I walked into. But greenskins do not usually behave like this.' Arulos took a deep breath and stood up, fastening his gauntlets and grabbing his staff. He gestured for Varek to follow as he headed past the corpses and back towards the door. 'We have to move.'

'We cannot do as she asked,' said Varek as they headed back

out into the foggy streets. 'Not if we are going to reach Delium in time.'

Arulos stared at the fog. Varek was right. Delaying here meant neglecting his duty and disobeying orders. But the woman's gaze haunted him. Then he thought of Zagora and her presence in the storm. The two things were linked somehow. He paced in a circle, battling to clear his thoughts.

And then, from somewhere to the north of the buildings, came more laughter.

'Sigmar!' said Varek. 'What *is* that sound?'

Arulos marched down the main street and headed for the north gate. It was open, like the one they had entered through, and Arulos found himself facing a wall of moonlit fog. 'It's that way,' he said. 'And it is clearly another trap.'

'Then we should return the way we came,' said Varek. 'We can head to the coast and still be in time to join Yndrasta.'

Arulos shook his head. 'What do you think will happen to Zagora and the others if we head on to Delium?'

'Are we abandoning our mission then? We *swore* to join Yndrasta at Delium. She is counting on our aid. You were just saying how crucial it is that we secure the coast.'

'It is, old friend, it is crucial. But there is something else happening here. I have seen something in the storm. When the Lord-Imperatant ordered us to march with the crusaders, I thought it was just a frustrating delay, but now I am not so sure.'

Varek shook his head. 'What do you mean?'

'I mean that Zagora is the eye of the storm. She is the point around which we revolve.'

'You're talking in riddles.'

'All I mean is this – we cannot abandon the crusaders to these greenskins. If these other settlements have fallen, then Ardent Keep will be next. We cannot move on with no idea of what's out here. And no idea where the Knights Excelsior are. And it is not merely pity that makes me say that. When I look into the tempest, it shows me Zagora. That means she is *central* to our purpose. Not merely a distraction. I have yet to understand completely, but I believe the God-King wants us to do more here.'

'Very well, then we should return to the keep. We won't help Zagora by wandering lost through this fog.'

'And how would we do that, Varek?' Arulos waved at the miasma that surrounded them. 'How will you use your map now?'

Varek looked around and waved vaguely at the fog. 'We came from that direction.'

Arulos shook his head. 'Do you recall that crooked tree stump?'

'Perhaps we missed it.'

'It was not there. The land has been changing every step of the way. There is something in this fog. It is not just blinding us, it is deceiving us. It is moving the ground from under our feet. We are lost out here, Varek. And if we march back that way we will remain lost.'

'And how will it help if we keep going? If we march deeper into this fog we shall only become more lost.'

'I mean to find our tormentors, Varek. Someone has led us out here and I mean to hunt them down. Let them play their games and ready their traps. We are the Hammers of Sigmar. We are the Thunderstrike. They have no idea what they are playing with.'

Varek shook his head and seemed on the verge of arguing, but then he nodded. 'You have not led us wrong before, Arulos.'

'We are led by the Eternal Storm, Varek.' Arulos patted him on the shoulder. 'And we will avenge those people in the tower. Every one of them.' He turned and marched on into the fog. 'Spread out,' he said, waving to his left and right. 'Form a broken line. There will be something waiting for us out here.'

The land rose to the north of the Shining Tower and for a while it was drier than the ground to the south. It was muddy, spongy turf rather than pools of black tar but Arulos resisted the urge to break into a run. He did not fear the creatures of Ghur, but he was determined to be ready when they sprang their next trap. They passed leafless, stunted trees and reached a narrow, high-walled gully littered with fallen rocks. As they picked their way through, Arulos saw something moving at the far end, shapes that were bobbing from side to side in the murk.

He tried again to harness the power of the unseen storm. It was no use. He held up his aetherstave and whispered, drawing some light from the renunciation crystal. For a brief moment, he saw a surreal sight. At the far end of the gully his light revealed a row of faces, about twenty or so. The faces were perfectly circular, with mouths that stretched from ear to ear with lunatic grins. The heads were each as large as a cartwheel and their eyes glowed in the darkness. As the faces jiggled and lurched, there could be no doubt that they were the source of the laughter.

Arulos cried a command and jabbed his aetherstave at them. Thunderbolts leapt from the crystal and ruptured the darkness, crashing into one of the laughing faces.

The laughter increased but the faces vanished from view, rushing back into the fog. Arulos ran down the gully, vaulting rocks and racing to the place where his bolt had hit its mark.

Most of the Anvilhearts maintained their position, spread out through the fog in a long line, but Varek rushed over to Arulos as he stooped to examine his kill. The grinning face turned out to be no more than a shield with a face painted on its surface. But lying underneath it, still smouldering, was a peculiar corpse. Arulos ripped the shield away and stared at the body. It looked like a distant relative of an orruk, with the same grubby green skin and bestial features. But where a normal orruk was built like a battering ram, with rounded shoulders and mounds of scarred muscle, this creature was wiry and lean. The head was elongated and the face wore an expression of sly cunning.

It was only when the creature giggled that Arulos realised it was still alive.

'What are you?' demanded Arulos, drawing his sword and pressing it to the monster's throat.

'Kragnos,' said the creature in a ragged whisper, struggling to wrap its tongue around human speech.

'Kragnos? What is Kragnos?' said Arulos.

But the monster's eyes glazed over and it slumped back into the muck, grinning even in death.

'Do you know that name?' he asked, looking at Varek. 'It sounds familiar.'

'Aye. I think I heard it mentioned in Excelsis, by the High Arbiter perhaps? In connection to an attack on the city. Or perhaps the attacks on the other settlements? The details elude me. Perhaps Kragnos is the warlord who leads these...' He looked at the corpse. 'Whatever these things are.'

'They're greenskins.' Arulos resisted the urge to kick the corpse. 'Just a different breed. Native to these swamps and tar pits, I imagine. These are the wretches that strung those people up in the tower.' He stared at the leering face on the shield. 'They have to pay. Before we leave I will make them pay.'

'Knight-Arcanum!' called one of the Anvilhearts, pointing her spear at something in the mist.

Arulos ran to the end of the gully and looked out at more banks of fog. A hundred feet to the north-west he saw grinning shields rushing away from him, presumably slung over the backs of fleeing greenskins.

Some of the Anvilhearts moved to pursue them but Arulos held up his hand.

'Wait! Hold your positions.' He howled an oath and thrust his staff forwards. Lightning shivered through the gloom, hitting the shields with a crack. Shapes tumbled through the fog. Pained cries echoed towards them.

'Now!' cried Arulos, racing towards the site of the blast.

As soon as he left the gully, he found himself wading through black water. It was only knee high but it hissed angrily as he splashed through it and it stretched as far as the eye could see. After a few minutes he reached a smouldering, blackened shield bearing the same absurd face as the last one. He wrenched it from the water, dragging its dead owner into view. The greenskin was even more grotesque than the last one. It seemed to be dissolving, the flesh sliding from its bones. Arulos threw it back in disgust then, catching sight of movement up ahead, he raced on.

One of the Anvilhearts cried out and hurled a spear past Arulos. It hit something with a resounding *thunk* and there was a splash as another greenskin fell. When Arulos found the monster it was surrounded by plumes of smoke, as though it were being cooked.

'What is the matter with these things?' cried Varek. 'Are they diseased?'

Another chorus of laughs rang out, trying to draw Arulos on but, as he waded through the black liquid, he knew he was being manipulated. 'Do not follow them!' he said, looking around at the steaming pools. Then he peered at the greaves of his armour. There was a dark patina forming on the metal. He tried to wipe it away. 'I see what they're doing,' he muttered. 'It's not water.'

Varek shook his head. 'What do you mean?'

'It's some kind of tar,' said Arulos, pointing at the dark patches on Varek's armour. 'Or acid. It's corroding the metal. Burning through it.'

'Impossible!' Varek stared at the palms of his gauntlets, studying the intricately worked metal. 'This is sigmarite.' But even as he said the words, the details blurred and ran into each other. He lifted one of his thighs from the liquid and it was even worse. The Azyrite runes had almost entirely vanished.

Arulos looked back at the others and saw that they were all the same. Large patches of their armour had been turned from gold to a blackened mess.

Again, the laughter billowed around them in the fog and Varek moved to chase the sound.

'No,' snapped Arulos. 'That's what they want. We have to reach them by another route. If this liquid can eat through sigmarite, it will make short work of flesh and bone.'

Varek looked around at the walls of fog. 'Then which way?'

'Give me a moment,' said Arulos, looking at the renunciation crystal, thinking of all the secrets it hid from him.

The art of the Knight-Arcanum required only a fleeting glance at the stone, always looking through its halo rather than its heart. This had been written across his soul by countless years of instruction in Azyr. The heart of the crystal was the most powerful part and the brightest point, and to look through it was to risk madness. But Arulos could think of no other way to pierce the gloom that had engulfed his mind. The heat grew as the tar ate into his armour. Standing still seemed to make it worse. Clouds of steam were pluming around all of them as the golden plate warped and blackened. He had to act quickly.

Arulos, who had faced countless enemies without hesitation, felt fear as he looked into the very centre of the stone, seeking a route back to the heavens.

'We will die,' said a young woman, her eyes brimming with furious tears. She pointed a trembling finger at him. 'You are a coward, Arul. You're running away because your brother told you to.'

There were children behind her, dressed in luxurious robes, their eyes filled with tears. The woman and her children were standing in the courtyard of a great keep, surrounded by servants and soldiers wearing domed bronze helmets. The woman was his wife. The children were his family.

'Melfa has spoken to the storm warriors,' he said, filled with anger. 'They demanded that he and I present ourselves to their general. The God-King himself has summoned us.'

'Gods!' spat the woman. 'You'll fight for them, but you won't fight for your own kin!' Her words were strangled with rage. 'It's glory you're after. You're going to leave us to die so that you can see your name on a banner. You want people to tell stories about you.'

'Would you have me deny the God-King?' He looked at the soldiers, wondering if they could hear how badly he was being wronged. 'Would any of you? If Sigmar summoned you, by name, would you refuse to go? If he said he needed you, would you turn away? Would anyone?'

'To save their families? Of course they would.' Her eyes strained as she backed away from the children, muttering to herself. 'Then I will leave too!' she cried.

The children howled in protest and hugged each other.

The woman was white with anguish. 'If you go, I will leave them. I swear it, Arul. If you abandon these children, so will I. I will leave here and find my way to the city. Your children will have to face the world alone.'

'You would not,' he said, turning and walking away. His rage had faded, replaced by the horror of what he was doing. The keep was under constant attack. It was no longer safe. Without him to lead its people, he was not sure if it would survive. Perhaps she was right. Perhaps he was leaving them to their deaths. Melfa's words drove him on through the agony, keeping him going across the courtyard. '...He asked for us by name, Arul. Can you understand that? He said we are to go to High Azyr. He said we are to become storm warriors...'

He reached the gates and crossed the threshold. He could still hear *his children howling as he mounted his horse and headed out into the fields, but he also heard them cry out in relief as their mother returned to them. As he rode towards the forest, the cries of his family seemed to grow louder rather than more distant, echoing round his head. Then, they began to change, twisting into a rippling, hiccupping laugh.*

The greenskins, remembered Arulos, jolted back into the swamps by the memory of his prey. For a moment, all he could think of was the horror of what he had just seen. The memory of leaving his family had been hidden so entirely by the renunciation crystal that seeing it now, so vividly, had felt like a hammer blow. All these years, and he had not even thought of them. They were the people he had loved more than anything in the realms and he had not spared them a thought for decades. Even if they had survived the attacks on their home, they would almost certainly be dead by now. What had they thought of him? What must his children have thought as they grew up and grew old? Even now, after seeing them so clearly, he could not remember their names. Pain and guilt tightened his stomach.

Then he forced himself to look past the memory, using the full might of the crystal. Finally, he caught a glimpse of the numinous storm. It was nothing compared to his usual union with the tempest. He did not rise up into the thunderheads, but he did see enough to grasp a fragment of the infinite, snatching it from the clouds and hauling it down to the Ghurian tar pit. The thunderstorm filled his chest and arms then rose around him in howling squalls, radiating from the staff. The Anvilhearts staggered away from him, battered by the powerful blasts and battling to stay on their feet. Arulos chanted the invocations he learned in Azyr, goading and directing the wind, sending it ahead in a roiling wave.

Ahead of Arulos and the other Anvilhearts, the tar rolled away, revealing a path of charred earth, forming a shimmering, rolling passageway through the pools. The earth howled beneath their feet, furious at being manipulated in such a way, and the air creaked with aetheric currents, flickering and sparking.

'Run,' gasped Arulos, struggling to breathe. It was not the act of forming a safe passage that was exhausting him, he was battling something far more dangerous than tar. The memory he had unleashed was circling his mind, trying to find a way back in, desperate to torment him.

Varek and the others did as he had ordered, racing down the shimmering avenue, glancing warily at its dark, liquid walls. Arulos stumbled after them. He could feel all the weight of the tar pressing in against his mind, but the splinter of storm he had borrowed could easily take the strain and, with a rush of pleasure, he realised that the laughter in the fog had ceased. He had turned the tables on the greenskins. They had not expected this. They had not expected the stormstrike.

The Anvilhearts ran for several minutes, but then the memory of Arulos' wife broke through his defences and he saw her face, white with anger as he left her behind. Instantly, his grip on the tempest slipped. A wave of hissing tar slammed into them, knocking some of the Vindictors over and submerging them. The Annihilators braced themselves against the tide, given ballast by their massive suits of armour as they hauled the Vindictors back to their feet. Varek leant against his standard, managing to stand until Arulos banished the memory and hurled the tar back once more.

They ran on again, even faster this time as the pool churned and hissed around them. This time, Arulos managed to wield the storm for longer and the Anvilhearts eventually started to climb a slope that led them up, out of the tar and onto a shelf of rock that looked down over another mist-filled valley. Once they were clear of the tar, they paused to catch their breath. Arulos had clung to the storm for as long as he was able, and once he was sure they were safe he let it go, taking his gaze from the staff.

It was only then that he saw how the Anvilhearts had been damaged. They were unrecognisable. Most of their armour had been blackened by the tar, leaving just a few patches of golden sigmarite. They barely looked like Stormcast Eternals. They looked more like hulks dredged from an ocean bed, pitted and tarnished. He looked down at his own armour and saw that it was the same.

'We cannot arrive at Delium looking like this.' He tried to pick at the damage, but that only made it worse, causing brittle, burnt flakes to fall away.

Varek shook his head, sounding grim. 'I would say our appearance is the least of our problems.' He hurried over to where some of the Vindictors had gathered round a comrade who was lying near the edge of the rocky outcrop. Arulos followed Varek and saw that it was the senior-most Vindictor, Maratha. She was convulsing, gasping and jolting on the ground.

'What is it?' demanded Arulos, barging his way through the group.

'It's the tar, Lord Stormspear,' replied one of the other Vindictors. 'It's eaten through Maratha's armour.'

Arulos knelt and grabbed the fallen warrior. Her neck armour was so tarnished it was crumbling. Arulos had seen Anvilhearts cut down on the battlefield, but he had never seen their armour fall apart like this. Sigmarite was no ordinary metal. It was mined in the heavens and crafted by gods. The loremasters in Azyr claimed it was cut from Mallus, a shard of the realm that spawned Sigmar. It did not corrode.

The downed Vindictor howled, grasping at her throat. Blood and embers tumbled from her neck brace.

Arulos tried to breach the celestial storm, striving to steal another portion of Sigmar's divine might. It was useless. Without looking directly through the crystal he could not pierce the mists that surrounded him. And he would not risk seeing his past again. Just the idea summoned the faces of his children, begging him to stay. With a great effort, he crushed the memory, but it was growing harder to hold it back. When he focused back on the wounded Vindictor, he saw that the warrior was growing limp, her coughs quieter and her movements less violent.

'Stand back!' said Arulos. 'This is Thunderstrike armour. And her body is about to fail.'

Arulos led his troops further along the shelf of rock until they were a dozen feet away from Maratha.

Finally, the storm pierced the fog. As Maratha exhaled her final breath, lightning knifed from the clouds, hitting her with a thunderclap.

Arulos and the others staggered as dust and fog whirled around them, thrown by the blast. Varek gripped his standard and intoned a prayer for the warrior's safe passage to Azyr and some of the other Anvilhearts muttered a response, making the sign of the hammer across their chests.

Arulos was furious at himself for losing Maratha but he kept his voice level. 'Move away from the tar pits.' He spotted a narrow path cut into the cliff wall and hurried towards it. 'This way. Down into the valley.'

He turned and marched down the path, trailing fragments of blackened armour and battling to rid himself of memories.

'The greenskins won't be far,' he said, forcing his mind to stay in the present. 'And they won't have expected us to make it through those pools. Ready yourselves for battle.'

CHAPTER SEVENTEEN

The crusaders had gone another night without sleep, working tirelessly on the trenches and fortifications, but as dawn washed over the tor hundreds of people were finally resting, lying in tents and the back of carts or just sprawled across the muddy ground, piled against each other like corpses.

Niksar was sitting with Zagora on a half-assembled wall, watching the sunrise and eating bread. They were leant against each other as they looked across the hilltop into the golden light. It seemed as though a gilded town had been born in a night. Kolgrimm's plans had been so meticulously laid that months of work had been achieved in hours. A tall, wooden palisade surrounded the top of the tor, and in many places it was already being superseded by prefabricated stone walls that had been lowered down from the one remaining metalith and slotted together like a giant puzzle.

Near the nexus syphon, several other, equally impressive buildings were taking shape: a large Sigmarite temple, complete with a colonnade of fluted pillars; some stone-built, thatched longhouses; and a sturdy-looking gatehouse that loomed over the main entrance. The buildings had been built weeks earlier, in Excelsis, and under Kolgrimm's expert guidance they had been lowered into place with incredible speed. Work had finally slowed now, as half the crusaders took a chance to rest, but Kolgrimm had not stopped and he was bellowing orders at the people who were still at work.

One of the first buildings Kolgrimm completed, lifted intact from the metalith, was a hulking bronze forge, built in the shape of a duardin head. Its gaping metal mouth had roared all night, spewing fumes and embers as the cogsmiths worked its bellows and hammered at anvils. Even now, as the morning light washed over its sooty brow, the thing had a fierce, almost monstrous aspect.

'You did it,' said Niksar. 'You got them here. You made this happen.' He could not quite believe it even as he said it. It was incredible to think that all this was born out of his panicked attempt to ditch the things he acquired from Ocella. The memory of Ocella reminded him that she was here, somewhere, with the crusaders. He grimaced at the thought that she might find him.

'*They* did it,' said Zagora. 'They got themselves here.' She nodded at the ten Stormcast Eternals who were scattered around the stakewall, watching the surrounding hills. 'And the Anvilhearts got them here.'

Niksar shook his head. 'We would all have died in that river if it was down to the Anvilhearts. Arulos might be powerful but he had no idea what to do on that boat. You were the one with a plan. You were the one who drove people on. We were all ready to give up and die until you told us there was hope.' He hugged her. 'You've done it. You've achieved something with your life. You've become someone. Imagine if our parents could see you now.' He laughed and nodded to the foot of the wall. There was a group of crusaders kneeling a few feet away, praying to Zagora.

'Imagine if they could see this. Isn't it funny though? They sent us to Excelsis for a chance of becoming something, but it's only by coming out here, back out into the wilds, that one of us actually managed it.'

Zagora looked at him. '*Both* of us have managed it. What more could they have wished for, Niksar? We've survived to adulthood, against all the odds, and we've joined a great crusade. Our names have been recorded in the Tomes Valoris. We are doing Sigmar's great work.' She shoved him. 'So why do you look so grim?'

He laughed and shook his head. 'I'm proud to be your brother, Zagora. I just wish…' He shrugged.

Zagora continued studying him. Then she nodded at a grand-looking marquee not far from where they were seated. It belonged to a family of nobles and their servants were already bustling around a campfire, preparing an impressive-looking breakfast. 'Are you still comparing yourself to them? Still jealous?'

Zagora knew Niksar too well for him to bother lying. 'They have power. While I'm crawling around in a ditch they're planning dynasties – dynasties that will ensure I never rise above my place. They hold the reins, Zagora. They make the decisions. They've won the great game.' Bitterness filled his mouth with bile. 'And I have not.'

'They've won nothing! They were born into that life. They never earned it, it was handed to them. So it's meaningless.'

'Meaningless? It means everything.'

This was the old argument that always left them both exasperated. Zagora waved her bread at the buildings springing up around them.

'This is what matters – reclaiming lands that were lost, making people safe. Or, if not safe, at least able to hold on to what they have, able to chart their own course in life. And between us, we're doing that. Who cares what kind of tent you sleep in? Who cares what you have for breakfast? What matters is that you make a difference. What matters is helping those who need help.'

Niksar shook his head, noticing Chiana and a group of priests rushing across the tor towards them. 'They'll bleed you dry. They don't care what all this does to you.' He leant close to his sister. 'And tell me this, have you ever noticed how fine Chiana's robes are? Have you ever noticed how soft her hands are? She's one of them. She's never done a day's work in her life and she's never slept on anything that wasn't covered in silk. You're like her pet. She'll use you but she'll never think of you as one of her kind.'

'Dawnbringer!' grinned Chiana, holding out her arms. 'We are beginning our rounds. We are going to pray for the souls of those who did not make it through the night.' She waved at the new temple where a small crowd was gathering. 'Will you join us?'

Zagora looked at Niksar with a troubled expression, then she nodded. 'Of course, high priestess.' She finished her bread, squeezed Niksar's arm and dropped from the wall. 'You already are someone,' she said, before heading off across the hillside with the priests. She pointed at him as she walked away. 'Stop trying to be someone else.'

Niksar watched as people scrambled after Zagora, whispering prayers and making the sign of the hammer as they followed her towards the temple. Then, as she and the priests passed the cogsmith's forge, he caught sight of Kolgrimm, talking to some of his apprentices near the furnace, his bulky armour glinting in the firelight. He looked even more agitated than usual, waving his axe around with such fervour that no one dared to stand anywhere near him. Niksar jumped from the wall and marched over to the furnace.

'I'm surrounded by idiots,' snarled Kolgrimm as Niksar approached.

'The wooden palisade is all that's required by the Decree Sigmaris,' rumbled one of the other duardin, a cogsmith who looked almost as ancient as Kolgrimm. 'The nexus syphon is fuelling the guardian statues. The watchtowers are almost up.' He waved to the scroll at Kolgrimm's belt. 'You've already achieved miracles. The materials on the other metalith were only there in reserve. Bringing three was just a precaution.'

'Precaution my arse.' Kolgrimm pointed his axe at the palisade. 'Do you think a row of sticks would hold back that gargant we saw in the fens? Or the kraken? Are you really so dim-witted you think nothing big ever comes into this valley?' He caught sight of Niksar. 'Tell them, will you? Should we build a scrappy little stakefort that will blow over in a stiff breeze, or make something that will last?'

Niksar positioned himself at Kolgrimm's side and nodded studiously. 'In the visions I discussed with my sister, Ardent Keep was surrounded by sturdy walls.' He nodded to the sections of the fence that were being replaced with stone blocks. 'Just as you are building there.'

Kolgrimm's eyes lit up and he jabbed Niksar with his stubby finger as he bawled at the cogsmiths. 'The lad knows. He saw it. He's the Dawnbringer's brother, do you know that? He saw the same visions she did. And he says we need stone walls.'

The cogsmiths glanced nervously at each other. 'We've had people out all night, Master Kolgrimm. No one has seen any sign of the metalith. And there are hounds to the south of here that are bigger than horses. Iogar was mauled and Jorun's team haven't even returned. All twelve of them are missing. Is it wise to keep roaming the hills when there is so much work to do here?'

'Roaming?' said Kolgrimm. 'I'm not saying you should go for a damned stroll. Get one of the ornithopters assembled and get it up in the air. Then keep your spyglasses fixed to your eye until you find my bloody stone. That metalith is as big as a house. And it's floating. In the sky. How hard can it be to spot?'

The other cogsmith shook his head. 'Beyond the valley every-thing is covered in a fog that–'

'Fog?' Kolgrimm's eyes strained behind his goggles. 'We've survived monsters that could crush a city and you're scared of fog?' He grabbed the cogsmith by the shoulders, turned him to face the remaining metalith and shoved him towards it. 'Get the ornithopter working. And don't come anywhere near me until you've got something useful to say.'

The cogsmith stumbled away, muttering into his beard. Kolgrimm waved the others back to the furnace and then stomped around to the back of the structure, gesturing for Niksar to follow him. There was an imposing arched door at the back of the forge and Kolgrimm led Niksar inside, slamming the door behind them.

They had entered a swelteringly hot room. It was heaped with so many crates and pieces of machinery that it looked like a storeroom but there was a desk shoved against the far wall, covered with books and schematics. Kolgrimm poured cups of ale, then grabbed a sketch from the desk and held it up to Niksar.

'Did you see the walls looking like this?'

The parchment was covered in so many scribbles, notes and crossings-out that Niksar could not recognise anything that might be described as a wall. 'Yes,' he said, after sipping the ale, hoping that was what Kolgrimm wanted to hear.

'Exactly!' Kolgrimm waved the paper in Niksar's face. 'They're all idiots. Calling me a gloryhound for wanting to build something worthy of Grungni.'

Niksar did not know much about duardin religion, but Grungni was the most widely known of all duardin gods, so well-respected that even some humans worshipped him. He was the god of smithies and forges and, if the legends were true, he was Sigmar's armourer, cladding the Stormhosts in their heaven-forged battleplate.

'Who called you a gloryhound?' asked Niksar, surprised that anyone would dare say anything derogatory to the ferocious cogsmith.

'No one's actually said it. But they're thinking it.' He grabbed another scrap of paper, covered in more indecipherable scribbles. 'This is what they wanted. A stakefort so small it could barely hold us, made of materials that would rot in a year, even if we weren't attacked.' He slammed his fist on the desk, rattling some tools. 'They want *that* to be my memorial. Well I won't have it, lad, do you hear me? Ardent Keep is what I will be remembered for. I won't be building anything else. I struggled to drag my bones this far. This will be my swansong. It has to be my masterpiece, not something that looks like it was built by drunks.'

'From what I've seen so far, it looks like it will be an impressive sight.' As Niksar spoke he was trying to decipher some of the other documents on Kolgrimm's desk. Some looked like maps, covered in demarcation lines, and there were names scribbled on them in locations on either side of the Great Excelsis Road. *They're already dividing the spoils,* thought Niksar, his pulse quickening.

'It's not going to be impressive if they don't find that metalith,' muttered Kolgrimm. He dropped heavily into a chair that groaned under the weight of his armour. 'I needed that extra stone. That was the only way I could build this place into something worthy of the name Kolgrimm Kragsson.' He removed his helmet and massaged his rocky outcrop of a face. His eyes were red from lack of sleep and one of his eyelids was twitching. 'But I don't have much time left.'

He pulled a drawer open, rummaged through the contents and took out a glass vial. He popped the cork and a chemical reek filled the air, causing Niksar to back away and hold his breath. Kolgrimm lifted the bottle to his huge, pockmarked nose and sniffed hard, before closing the bottle and placing it back in the drawer. His eyes grew wider and he started pacing around the room, reenergised, speaking much faster.

'Did you see what Ulfarsson had planned for his strongpoint?

It was far more than the Decree Sigmaris specified. And he was only doing it to outdo me. He even got them to name it after him. Ulfarsson bloody Keep. Whose back was he scratching when they called it that? The old goat has always hated the fact that High Arbiter Byzac asked me to build the south gate and he knows I'm on my last legs. And did you see what Khrugsson designed for the Saros Bastion? Was that a bloody stakefort? No, it was not.'

As Kolgrimm paced around the room his words ran together into a stream of gripes and accusations, making it impossible for Niksar to follow the details. The general gist was clear enough, though: he was tired, old and obsessed with the notion that his peers were going to surpass him. He seemed horrified by the idea that the bridgehead around the Great Excelsis Road was going to prove him inferior to all the other cogsmiths who were building along the coast.

'You sent your engineers to get an ornithopter,' said Niksar when he managed to get a word in. 'I'm sure they'll find the metalith.'

'Of course they won't find the bloody metalith. Those things don't stop once they've got moving. It wasn't tethered to anything. It's probably at the coast by now. If anyone was going to spot it, they would have seen it last night. We haven't even got an ornithopter.'

Niksar shook his head, baffled. 'But you just sent your engineers out to look for it.'

'I just couldn't bear to look at Vifilsson for another minute.' He laughed. 'And I feel better knowing he'll be in a panic for the next hour.'

The chemical smell was still filling the small room and Niksar's head was spinning. He later wondered if that was why he said what he did.

'Would it help if you had an aetheric alkahest? Would this

furnace be able to use it in some way? Could you use it to make the walls tougher? I once heard someone say that an aetheric alkahest could change things into–'

Kolgrimm grabbed him by the shoulder. 'What do you know about the aether-ignis?'

Niksar was transfixed by the intensity of Kolgrimm's stare. 'I... Er... When I acquired the augur stone, I also acquired an alkahest.'

'And you have it here? On the tor?'

'I... An acquaintance of mine is keeping it safe.'

Kolgrimm looked stunned as he paused to drink from his tankard. Niksar could not be sure if he was ecstatic or horrified. Perhaps he was about to alert the Order and announce that the Dawnbringer's brother was a deranged heretic who peddled forbidden magics. Kolgrimm leant close to Niksar, filling his nose with the harsh, chemical aroma.

'If I had an aether-ignis I wouldn't need to worry about making the stakes stronger. I could make *stone*. And not just any stone.'

He rushed over to a chest and began hurling books across the room. When he found the tome he was looking for he blew the dust off it and brought it over to Niksar, prodding the cover and releasing more dust from the leatherbound pages.

'*Secrets of the Aetheric Alkhahest*.' He was breathless with excitement. 'Hausson's masterwork. If I had an aether-ignis I could turn mud into stone.' He closed his eyes, gripping the book to his chest like a prize. 'Ulfarsson can build what he likes but it wouldn't hold a candle to what I could make with *limitless* amounts of stone. Ardent Keep. I always knew it was destined to be my masterpiece.' He gripped Niksar's shoulders. 'Don't you see? That's why Grungni brought us together, you and I. This is fate. I was fated to build something magnificent out here.'

Then he held Niksar at arm's length and gave him a suspicious look.

'You're sure? You're sure it is an aetheric alkahest? How do you know?'

'I know,' said Niksar. 'I'm sure of it.'

For a moment he thought Kolgrimm might kiss him, but he embraced him instead. 'Take me to it, lad!' He grabbed the door and threw it open, flooding the room with morning light.

Niksar held back, shaking his head.

Kolgrimm frowned. 'What?'

'My acquaintance… She… She's a very nervous person. And I've warned her to keep the alkahest hidden. I must fetch it myself.'

'What are you talking about, lad?' Kolgrimm marched out into the light. 'Let's just get the thing. I promise not to shout.'

'No!' Niksar was horrified by the idea that Kolgrimm might encounter Ocella. He did not want to start his new life by being associated with the most deranged part of his old one. 'I have to go alone, but I can have it back here soon. It will take me ten minutes at most. But I must go alone.' He felt a rising sense of panic as he wondered what could have possessed him to mention something that belonged to Ocella. It was bad enough that the whole crusade was built on one of her acquisitions, was he really going to make it so that the walls were built with the help of another one?

'Ten minutes?'

'At most.' Niksar tried to smile. 'It will be better this way.'

Kolgrimm looked annoyed. Then he muttered 'aether-ignis' to himself and his eyes lit up again. 'That would do it. That would sodding do it. That would show them all.' He looked around at the building works with a rapt expression on his face, as though he were picturing the wonders he could create with limitless stone.

Niksar grinned and dashed off across the muddy hillside, heading for the crowds that were milling around the longhouses. That was the largest gathering of people on the hill so it seemed his best chance of finding Ocella.

'Niksar!' cried someone as he reached the crowd, but it was not the nervous, faltering voice of Ocella. It was a rich, theatrical voice that perfectly enunciated each word. 'Over here!'

It was Taymar, the elderly noble who had attached himself to the Phoenix Company. He was sat on the back of a cart, sketch-book in hand, drawing one of the guardian statues. At the sight of Niksar he dropped from the cart and pocketed his book, strid-ing over with a grin on his face.

'Shouldn't you be guarding the perimeter with the others?' said Niksar, keen to avoid being drawn into a conversation.

Taymar smoothed down his elegant uniform and shook his head. 'I'm meant to be sleeping. But who could sleep at a moment like this? The rebirth of civilisation. The moment that Sigmar's people *defy* the wildness in Ghur's heart. What a time to be alive, Niksar.'

'I can't stop,' said Niksar, holding his hands up and heading on towards the crowd. To his frustration, Taymar kept pace with him.

'I've decided to write a history of the crusades,' he said. He was wearing the same expression of dazed wonder he always wore. 'Someone has to record this. In later generations, people will want to know every detail of how these lands were tamed. And you could tell me what you know. You're the Dawnbringer's brother. You were with her at the very start. I'm sure you could tell me the most amazing stories of how the crusade was conceived.'

Niksar was about to wave the man away when it occurred to him that there might be opportunity here. If the history of the new frontier was going to be chronicled by this starstruck noble, he could ensure that his own role was not overlooked.

'Zagora and I were born out here in the wilds,' he said, pausing to talk. 'I think we were always destined to reclaim the lands that are rightfully ours. These wilds are our birthright.'

Taymar nodded eagerly and took his book out. 'Let me make some notes. This could be the opening of my book. I could–'

'No,' interrupted Niksar. 'I have no time at the moment. I'm helping Kolgrimm Kragsson.'

Taymar looked even more excited. 'Then, through you, I might be able to talk to him about how he designed Ardent Keep.'

Niksar nodded. 'The basic design is set by the Decree Sigmaris, issued by the lords of High Azyr, but Kolgrimm and I are currently working on making some improvements. I have to go now, but perhaps we can talk later after I report back to Captain Tyndaris.'

Taymar seemed too pleased to speak. He just nodded and grinned, squeezing Niksar's shoulder.

Niksar hurried on into the crowd, looking everywhere for a scrawny face and a feather headdress. Ocella was nowhere to be seen, and Niksar was not altogether surprised. She was terrified of crowds at the best of times. He was still amazed she had plucked up the courage to join the crusade and leave her junk-crowded loft in Excelsis. As he thought about her, Niksar felt a chill of realisation. He was about to do the very thing he had promised his sister he would not do: he was going to start dealing with a woman that the White Angels would execute for heresy. What had possessed him to mention the alkahest?

Then he saw her, hidden in the shadows, hunkered down under an awning attached to one of the longhouses. She was not far from a mound of dead bodies, piled in a heap during the night but yet to be buried. She was talking urgently to someone who looked even more disreputable than she was – a grubby, ragged-looking man wearing mud-splattered robes. He was showing her something in the palm of his hands and she was nodding eagerly, twitching and flinching as she touched it with the beak on the end of her wing-bone staff. They both kept glancing over at the corpses and nodding.

Niksar strode towards her. When he was still a dozen feet away, Ocella and the man sensed his approach, looking out at him with wary expressions. The man immediately hobbled off into the drizzle, vanishing from sight, but Ocella stayed where she was, cowering under the awning, trembling and fidgeting as she watched him approach. As he had done many times before, Niksar wondered how old she was. Her face was so filthy and her hair was so matted that it was almost impossible to pinpoint her age. She could have been anywhere between eighteen and forty.

She gave him a nervous grin as he reached her. 'How are you?' she said, struggling, as usual, to meet his eye.

He nodded at the corpses. 'Better than some.'

She kept her grin on her face but he could sense her unease. She was no doubt wondering why he would seek her out after being so reluctant to speak with her before.

'I...' He hesitated, unsure how to explain the situation.

Her smile became more relaxed as she saw he needed something from her. 'You are my friend,' she said. 'If you need help with something, just tell me what it is.'

Niksar remembered all the things his sister had said to him on the day she shot the docker. He remembered the sound of the Order, hammering at his door. Was he really going to start all this again? It felt like his life was starting back down the very path he had come here to escape.

'Who was that?' he said, looking around for the old man in the dirty robes.

She scratched furiously at her mass of hair, staring at the mud. 'You did not used to be so suspicious of me.'

'Because I didn't know you were dealing with Chaos cultists,' he hissed, leaning closer to her. 'We're lucky to be alive.'

'I didn't know what that man was,' she said. 'He lied to me.'

Niksar paced around in the mud, furious that he had put himself in the ridiculous position of needing her help. He had to drag the words from his throat. 'Do you still have the aetheric alkahest?'

She did not seem surprised by the question, taking the small, silver claw out of a pouch in her animal skins. It gleamed against the grubby hides, beautiful and delicate.

'Where does it come from?' demanded Niksar. 'The cultist?'

She shook her head.

'Can I trust it?' he said, looking closer at the thing, trying to see if it bore any heretical markings. 'Is it evil?'

'It's an alkahest,' she said. 'Forged by metallurgists in Chamon. It's neither good nor evil. It simply is. It's a tool. It can be used to change matter. How it's used depends on the wielder.'

'Can I hold it?'

She nodded without hesitation and placed it in his palm. It felt oddly cold, as though it were made of ice rather than metal. The thing had a cruel look to it, thought Niksar, but that was just because it was an eagle's claw, a thing designed for rending and tearing.

'It's a catalyst,' she said. 'But it can't transmute anything alone. There are various procedures that we would need to follow. And we would need an athanor.'

Niksar felt a moment of panic. 'A what?'

'A furnace. One that's capable of sustaining steady, high temperatures.'

Niksar relaxed. 'He has that.'

Ocella frowned. 'Who?'

Niksar considered keeping the truth from her. But the trust in her eyes disarmed him. 'Kolgrimm Kragsson.'

'Who?'

'How can you not know who Kolgrimm is? He's the cogsmith in charge of building this whole place.'

Ocella picked at a scab on her cheek, looking none the wiser.

'Do you know anything about the crusade?' he asked. 'Do you know anything about the people who have led you out into the wilds?'

She pursed her lips. 'Priests. And White Angels. And–'

'White Angels? The Knights Excelsior are not here. They never were. They never arrived.' He pointed out the Anvilhearts watching over the palisade. 'Didn't you notice that the Stormcast Eternals are wearing gold, not white? They're called the Anvilhearts. They belong to the Hammers of Sigmar. It's a completely different Stormhost.'

She smiled vaguely and let out one of her 'haw haw' laughs. 'That's fine. No matter.' Then she looked near Niksar's feet. 'Will your Kolgrimm friend be happy for us to use his furnace?'

'You don't understand. It's Kolgrimm that wants the alkahest. He needs more stone to finish Ardent Keep. With two metaliths lost he can't build everything he was planning to build.'

Ocella looked puzzled as she waved at all the buildings being assembled around them. 'He seems to be managing well enough.'

'He needs more stone. The walls need to all be made of stone too. Or this place isn't going to last. Wooden stockades aren't good enough, but he's had to use lots of the stone on all these extra buildings he's designed.'

She frowned. 'Perhaps he should have finished the walls first then, eh?' She shrugged. 'Take it to him.'

Niksar hesitated, confused. 'You're just going to give it to me?'

She gave him a sideways glance. 'We work together.'

He could not think how to answer. Ocella was everything he wanted to leave behind. She signified his old life as much as the nobles signified his new life.

'*Are* we going to work together again?' she asked.

'You trust me with this?' he said.

She looked genuinely baffled. 'Why shouldn't I trust you?'

Niksar felt irritated by her lack of guile. If she had been more devious it would have been easier to deceive her. 'We'll work together,' he lied. 'But it's better if Kolgrimm doesn't know where this came from. He only trusts me because I'm the Dawnbringer's brother. I told him this thing is mine and I simply had to collect it. It would be better if… I think you should stay here and let me take the alkahest to him. It might unnerve him if he knew it was not mine.'

She frowned, still picking at the scab. The scab came free and she peered at it, before popping it in her mouth and nodding. 'I understand.' She grinned. 'I shall be a silent partner.'

'Exactly. A silent partner. Once I've given Kolgrimm the alkahest he will be completely in my debt. He'll be happy to do anything for me. When he's deciding who has what, I will be able to ask for anything. I'll be wealthier than anyone in Ardent Keep.'

'*We* will be wealthy,' said Ocella with a half-smile.

'Yes, we, of course. Once I have made myself invaluable to Kolgrimm, I'll be able to ask him for anything. Whatever it is that you want, I'll be able to get it. Is it wealth?'

She shrugged, looking at the mud. 'Something like that.'

Niksar nodded, his heart racing as he gripped the silver talon, feeling the metal pressing into his palm. 'This is the key to everything. Once the keep is finished, Kolgrimm will remember who helped him achieve everything he wanted to do. He'll consider me his most trusted advisor.'

If Ocella had looked a little cleaner, he might have hugged her. 'This will be the making of me.'

CHAPTER EIGHTEEN

Arulos raised his hand and the Anvilhearts came to a halt. He was walking through a field of wet, waist-high grass, surrounded by walls of fog. The fumes were thicker with each step he took. Every lungful deadened his limbs and jumbled his thoughts. Memories of his wife merged into visions of Zagora on the raft, leading the crusaders in a hymn, and behind it all he caught glimpses of his triumph at Delium. It was such a dizzying, beguiling mixture of scenes that it had taken him a long time to understand what was happening, but finally the pieces were falling into place.

'They're hiding something specific,' he said.

He was only thinking aloud, but Varek was nearby. 'What do you mean? The greenskins?'

'Yes. This fog. It has a purpose. It's contrived. They're using it to muddle our thoughts. They want us out here for a reason.' He shook his head. 'How long do you think we have been wandering through these swamps?'

Varek hesitated. 'I… It's hard to say. Strange… My first thought was that it has been a matter of hours but, now that I consider it, perhaps it has been days.'

'Or weeks?'

Varek studied him. 'Perhaps. Is that possible?'

'This fog is in my head, Varek, and I'm sure it is the same for you. It has been laced with something. Can you taste it? Can you feel it in your veins? It's not natural. It has been engineered. It's a kind of mind-poison.' He looked back the way they had come. It was indistinguishable from any other direction. 'I thought these creatures were just deranged. I thought they were toying with us because it amused them. But now I think otherwise. I think there is a purpose to all this. Something cunning. They want us in this mist so that we are not somewhere else.'

Varek nodded. 'Perhaps they are just too cowardly to face us?'

'Have you ever known orruks to run from a fight? But I do not think they are leading us anywhere. I think they are leading us in circles to keep us *away* from somewhere. Or something. My stormsight is so faint, Varek. I cannot be sure of what exactly is happening, but that is what I sense Sigmar is trying to tell me – that we are being kept away from something. That is why they are confusing our sense of distance and time.'

'Well,' said Varek, lowering his voice, 'whatever the reason, they're doing a good job of confusing us. With no stars to guide us, and no landmarks to compare to our map, it won't be easy to escape their snares and traps.'

Arulos held up his hand for silence. 'Listen to that laughter. Our only sense of direction comes from that sound. It's our only guide. And my guilt over the deaths in the Shining Tower has kept me chasing it. But what if I stop hunting them? What if I relinquish my guilt? What then would I see?'

'Knight-Arcanum, I do not understand. What else can we do but follow them? As you say, their laughter is our only guide.'

'Tell me this, Varek, where do you *not* hear their laughter?'

Varek looked around. 'It comes from everywhere. I can hear it whatever direction I face. Even if I…' His words trailed off and he stared into the distance. 'No. Perhaps not that way. I am not sure the laughter is coming from that direction.'

Arulos nodded. 'And that is the *only* place where there is no laughter, do you agree?'

Varek looked around again. 'Yes. I can hear them everywhere else.'

'So I wonder what we would find in that direction. Quickly,' he said, striding in the direction Varek had indicted and gesturing for the others to follow. 'Let us see what our laughing friends are trying to hide.'

They had not gone far before Arulos grew certain that he was right. After just a few minutes of heading in the new direction, the laughter started to falter and fade. This made it harder to be sure of their route but Arulos had spent years navigating the Eternal Storm. He knew how to plot a true line. He picked up his pace, exhilarated by the thought that he had surprised his tormenters again. Finally, he was turning the tables.

The ground started to rise ahead of them and Arulos saw the shoulder of a large hill, perhaps even a mountain. The ground had been uniformly flat for as long as he could remember, so this was another sign that they were breaking out of their trap. As they climbed the slope, the fog cleared a little, and he made out a scrubby expanse of mud and shrubs punctuated by the odd dead tree. It was not the landscape that interested him, however.

'Here we go,' he said, spotting a row of large, perfectly round faces gathering at the top of the hill. It was more of the shields that they saw earlier. 'Finally,' he said, 'we've forced their hand. They have been trying, all this time, to lead us away from this hill. And now that we're here, they will finally have to face us in open combat.'

There was no laughter as the line of grinning shields grew larger and Arulos was no longer in any doubt that the greenskins had been trying to keep him from this hillside.

'What are you hiding?' he muttered, signalling for the Anvil-hearts to pause. Sigmar's tempest was still beyond his reach, so he fixed his aetherstave to his back and drew his sword instead. Its name was Arphax, and runes shimmered along its blade as he tapped the sanctified metal against his faceplate and whispered an oath. He turned to the others. 'I will lead the charge with the Annihilators. I am sure these worms still have a few tricks left to play, but they have no idea what we are. They may have encountered Stormcast Eternals before, but they have never felt the power of the Thunderstrike.'

He saw his words lift his warriors' hearts. Their armour was scorched and torn and their weapons blunted by the tar pits but as Arulos said the word Thunderstrike, the tiredness fell from their limbs and they stood tall, throwing back their shoulders and raising their chins.

'Varek will follow behind with the rest of you in a shield wall. Do not cleave too tightly to us. Leave a clear gap. I think we have caught them unawares, but they may still have traps prepared. Wait to see what we trigger before you follow.'

'Anvil born!' they cried, hammering their weapons against their chest armour.

Behind the faceplate of his helmet, Arulos smiled. Finally, he was going to lock horns with his foe.

More of the leering shields rattled into place up ahead and the greenskins whined as they jostled into place. It sounded like wolves, howling at the moons. There was no trace of amusement there now.

Arulos made a quick head count. Even in the front ranks, he guessed there were a couple of hundred greenskins. Probably not enough to *really* test the Anvilhearts but he would reserve judgement until he saw what else they had in store. The deaths in the tower had shown him that he was facing a new kind of greenskin – one that liked to spring surprises.

'Anvil born!' he cried and charged up the slope, Arphax lighting the way.

The Annihilators trailed behind him at first, slowed by their massive suits of armour but, as they gained momentum, the ingenious workmanship of the battleplate came into play. The thick, reinforced sigmarite started to blaze with aetherfire, sparking at the joints and crackling with fingers of light. Lightning danced across their shields and hammers, growing brighter as the Annihilators picked up speed, flooding their legs with divine vitality. Arulos' smile broadened as a storm rose behind him, rumbling in the Annihilators' greaves and pauldrons.

Arulos and the Annihilators were still thirty feet from the line of round shields when they reached the trap. Slender ropes had been stretched across the hillside and, as the Anvilhearts ran through them, they triggered a wall of spiked planks that flew up from the rocks, slamming into Arulos and the others.

The tempest that had been building in the Annihilators' armour erupted, booming across the hillside, filling the fog with light. As they hit the Annihilators the planks exploded and, rather than slowing their advance, the blast lent the Stormcast Eternals even more force, catapulting the Anvilhearts up the slope. Rather than lagging behind Arulos, the Annihilators now barrelled past him, smashing into the ranks of greenskins so hard they could not halt, ripping through the grinning shields like a wave through pebbles. Spears, shields and bodies were cast into the air.

By the time Arulos reached the sight of the impact, the Annihilators were finally slowing, the light fading from their armour as they laid about themselves, pummelling the greenskins with hammer blows. As the Eternal Storm faded from their armour, the Annihilators changed from a thunderhead to an impregnable bastion, their hulking armour making a mockery of the greenskins' desperate spear lunges. The monsters' weapons splintered and broke against the sigmarite. It was like watching children assaulting statues.

One of the greenskins leapt from the ground and hurled its spear at Arulos. He cut the projectile down with a swipe of Arphax then hacked the sword down towards his attacker. The monster raised its shield but the painted grin turned to splinters as the greenskin died. Arulos sliced and parried his way through the mob, downing dozens of the monsters as he made for the top of the hill. He looked for a leader, determined to find out who had led him to such a merry dance, but then more greenskins rushed over the brow of the hill, all carrying the same spears and shields as the others. They flooded down the slope towards him, wailing and screaming.

Arulos halted, planted a boot against a rock and raised Arphax, ready for the impact.

A tide of blue and gold surged past, rushing up the slope. It was the Vindictors, spears raised in a perfect phalanx as they shredded the greenskin lines, driving the creatures back up the rocks. They drove their spears into the enemy then drew swords, splitting skulls and shields in a flurry of glinting blows. Then the Annihilators stomped up the slope and added their hammers to the slaughter, pounding the greenskins as they tried to flee.

Arulos powered up the rocks and looked across the hilltop, but there was still no sign of a leader. Greenskins were always in thrall to the largest member of their tribe, a brutish dictator who had proven itself to be more savage than the rest, but Arulos could only see the hunched rank and file troops. He had entered a long, sunken hollow where the fog pooled like a lake, making it impossible to see more than a few feet in any direction. Arulos cried out, swiping his sword at the mist.

'Show yourself!' he bellowed, stomping up the slope of the hollow to see if he could spot a creature running down the other side of the hill. Behind him, the battle was still raging, shouts and clangs echoing through the fog, but there was no sign of a leader.

Arulos cursed and clambered up another rock, trying to see further down the slope. For a moment, he thought he saw a green-skin that had escaped the battle, but then he realised that the fog was playing tricks on him. The figure he could see was far away, but so massive that even the dreadful weather could not entirely hide it from view.

Arulos looked back at the fighting. Varek was leading the others with his standard raised in one hand and his sword flashing in the other. He cried 'Anvil born!' as he advanced, driving the rest of the Anvilhearts on. The greenskins were routed. Those that could were already fleeing into the fog and the rest were being butchered. Seeing that he was not needed, Arulos headed down the other side of the slope, intrigued by the figure in the fog. He kept his sword raised as he descended the hill, conscious that the greenskin leader was still out there. The slope was more gradual on this side and he was able to jog down it with ease, keeping the distant figure in view.

'Knight-Arcanum!' cried Varek, appearing at the top of the hill.

'This way,' he called back, waving for Varek and the others to follow. He crossed a weed-filled stream and entered another boggy field. Then he paused under a grove of trees, waiting for Varek and the others to reach him. 'Do you see?' he said as Varek approached. 'I have a feeling this is what they didn't want us to find.'

Varek looked through the fog. 'They certainly wanted to keep us on the other side of that hill.'

Arulos nodded and marched on. 'Let us see what they were so keen to keep us away from.'

It only took a few more minutes of walking for Arulos to realise that he was approaching a statue. The raised hammer and trailing beard were unmistakeable.

'Sigmar,' he muttered, wondering who would have built a likeness of the God-King in such a forsaken spot.

'It must be one of the other crusader settlements,' said Varek.

It was a sensible suggestion but Arulos was unconvinced. There was something familiar about the statue's pose. He was sure he had seen it before. He picked up his pace, rushing through the muddy field until he reached the top of a slope overlooking a broad valley. From there, he saw that the statue was not part of a ruined town or fortress, but perched on the sloping surface of a ruined metalith. The floating island had crashed into a cliff and split down the middle, losing its buoyancy and toppling to the ground. There was wreckage everywhere: shattered rock, broken crates and piles of duardin machinery heaped all across the valley, and trailing like a tail from the fallen metalith were the huge chains that had once tethered it to a gall tusk.

'It's one of ours,' said Varek, pointing to a banner hanging limply from its side. A symbol was just visible on the sodden cloth: the circled tower motif that had been designed for Ardent Keep.

Arulos rushed down into the valley and began picking through the wreckage. Everything useful had been taken, by greenskins, he guessed, and there were human remains scattered in the mud – crusaders who had been riding on the metalith when it crashed.

'Why would the greenskins have wanted to keep us away from this?' asked Varek. 'There's nothing here of any value now. Perhaps you were wrong, Knight-Arcanum.'

Arulos shook his head. 'I was right. They did not want us to see this. Everything they did was to keep us on the other side of that hill. I imagine we were often close to this place but their fog blinded us to the fact.'

'How can you be sure that's what they were doing?'

'Listen.' Arulos looked back the way they had come. 'What do you hear?'

'Nothing.'

'Exactly. No laughter. They're not finding us amusing any more. As soon as we headed to that hill and fought our way to this wreckage, they stopped laughing.' He picked through some more of the rubble, lifting sacks and turning over barrels. 'But I'm damned if I can work out why.'

He reached one of the enormous chain links that were hanging down from the underside of the rocks and patted it with his hand. Then, as he looked down the chain's length he saw the great channel it had gouged as it dragged through the earth.

'Of course,' he said, leaving the chain and hurrying over to the ditch it had made.

'What?' said Varek.

Arulos pointed down the ditch. It snaked off into the fog, disappearing from sight hundreds of feet away. 'This metalith has come here all the way from the tor. If we follow the tracks made by these chains we could return to the Dawnbringer and her crusaders.' He turned to Varek. 'The greenskins did not want us to find this because it can lead us back to Ardent Keep.'

Varek cursed. 'So they can attack it.'

Arulos nodded. 'They just wanted us to leave the settlement undefended. And we've done exactly that.' He paced back and forth as the face of his wife flashed across his thoughts. 'We've left them all to die.'

'But we might still be in time to save them,' said Varek. 'The greenskins were still trying to keep us from finding this metalith. If they'd already butchered everyone on the tor I can't see why they would bother to keep us out of the way.'

'Agreed. If they are still trying to keep us away, there may be some time left.' He looked again at the tracks the metalith had made. 'But there is no way of knowing how much.'

He turned to the rest of the Anvilhearts who had all gathered around him.

'We must be fast. Hundreds of lives hang in the balance.'

The Anvilhearts were a mess. Their armour was buckled and blackened from the tar pits and the parts that were undamaged were covered in blood and muck. They were not the proud host Arulos had seen in his storm dreams. They were not the gleaming heroes he saw breaking the siege at Delium. But when they pounded their weapons against their chests he felt a rush of pride.

He raised his sword to them then turned and ran, sprinting down the track, his head filled with echoes of Zagora's hymn.

CHAPTER NINETEEN

'Sigmar be praised,' said Chiana as Kolgrimm and Niksar led her round the battlements of Ardent Keep.

It was less than a week since Niksar gave Kolgrimm the silver talon, but the settlement had already been transformed beyond all recognition. The initial calm that greeted the crusaders only lasted a day. There had been a stream of attacks since then, but as the scouts and sentries dealt with roving predators and bands of orruks, the bulk of the crusaders had kept working.

And the results were impressive. It was a cool, grey dawn and curtains of drizzle filled the air, but even that could not dim the triumph in Chiana's eyes as she looked out from the walls. The original perimeter had been completely changed, expanded from a neat circle crowning the hilltop to a rambling, much larger structure that circled most of the tor. The walls were covered in scaffolding and still only half built, but the ambition of the building work was clear. Even at this early hour, people were working. Hundreds were on the walls, lowering huge, stone blocks into place or working at braziers and forges. Others were streaming through the front gates, driving carts laden with soil from the surrounding hills. Kolgrimm's forge, the imposing, bronze structure forged in the shape of a duardin head, was roaring constantly, spewing smoke and embers, while gangs of grimy, sweating labourers hauled blocks of mud through one entrance and stone blocks from another.

'It's more glorious than I ever imagined,' said Chiana. 'From the drawings you showed me, I pictured something much humbler.'

Kolgrimm was glaring at a distant section of wall. 'Eh?' He turned back to Chiana.

'It looks glorious.'

'Oh, aye.' He seemed distracted, looking back at the construction work and muttering.

'This way,' said Captain Tyndaris, a stern expression on his face as he waved them along the wall to one of the few turrets that were finished. He was accompanied by some Freeguild soldiers, including Haxor and the noble, Taymar. Zagora was there too, standing with Chiana and some of the other Sigmarite priests.

As they moved on towards the tower, Niksar shifted closer to his sister. 'What's the matter?' he whispered. 'Look at this place. It's better than you could have hoped for. You're a hero. Why do you look so worried?'

'I'm fine,' she said, but her voice was hesitant and she did not meet his eye. She was gripping the augur stone so tightly her knuckles gleamed.

'Quickly,' said Tyndaris, waving his cane at the steps and ushering them all up the turret. There were more soldiers waiting at the top and one of the Anvilhearts was also there, standing alone, a dozen feet from everyone else. When everyone had gathered along the battlements, Tyndaris turned to face them.

'It's been a week since we heard from Arulos Stormspear. Or anyone else. There's no sign of the White Angels or any of the other crusades we're meant to join forces with. So, yesterday, I sent out another group of scouts.'

Zagora frowned. 'None of the others have returned. We agreed no more. You can't keep sending people to their deaths.'

'I'll send us all to our deaths if I don't find out what's out there. The attacks we've seen so far are nothing to what will follow. I have to do *something*. We can sit here as long as we like, congratulating Kolgrimm on the size of his walls, but we're still going to be butchered if we don't have the backing of Stormcast Eternals or the other Freeguild regiments.'

Chiana touched Zagora's arm and smiled at her. 'And your scouts,' she said to Tyndaris. 'Have you heard something back from them? I presume that's why you interrupted our morning prayers.'

'I heard nothing. Just like every other time. And then, this morning, I woke up to find this.' He took a spyglass from his belt and handed it to Chiana.

'By the God-King,' she whispered, looking out into the dawn. 'What is that? Is he dead?'

'No,' said Tyndaris, his voice flat. 'Not yet.'

'Who's not dead?' muttered Kolgrimm, but he was looking at the forge in the centre of the keep, his mind clearly elsewhere.

Niksar had a spyglass of his own and as the others took it in turns to use Tyndaris', Niksar used his own lens to look in the direction Tyndaris had pointed. The rain was getting heavier by the minute, and at first he thought the distant, blurry figure was some kind of scarecrow. It was man-shaped, but with a perfectly circular head that wore an absurd, ear-to-ear grin.

'It's Sergeant Drannon,' said Tyndaris. 'I think the thing covering his head is some kind of fruit or vegetable. Someone has carved that smiling face into it. I think it's the scent of the fruit that brings the animals out.'

'Why aren't you doing something?' gasped Haxor, leaning out

over the battlements. 'Why are you just leaving him there? Cut him down!'

'What do you mean, brings out the animals?' asked Niksar.

'He's alive,' said Tyndaris. 'Exhausted, but alive. When the animals come, you'll see. He'll move then. He'll try to get himself off that pole. But whoever put him there has tied him securely.' He turned to Haxor. 'And the reason I'm leaving him there is because, after the first few attempts, we realised what the game is.'

'Game?' Kolgrimm finally gave Tyndaris his full attention. He used a lens of his own to study the bound soldier. 'What are you talking about? Get the man down from there.'

'We tried.' Tyndaris pointed east, across the rolling hills. 'But that's what will happen if we try to cut him down.'

Niksar peered through his spyglass and saw another round-headed figure slumped on a stake. This one was clearly dead. His body was little more than a bloody skeleton, dangling from the grinning fruit. Not far from where he was hung, there was a long, dark gash in the earth, a deep trench lined with spears. From his high vantage, Niksar could see the bodies at the bottom of the trench: Phoenix Company soldiers, lying broken and motionless, their bodies skewered.

'Whichever direction we approach the prisoners from,' said Tyndaris, 'the ground drops away onto those traps. Sigmar knows how long those trenches have been out there. But the triggers weren't active when we came down into this valley. Someone has activated them since we got here. There are scouts strung up like that right across the valley. I sent people racing to help them before I understood what was happening.' He stared at the trench. 'I've lost nearly twenty soldiers this morning. And that's not counting the poor souls left out there as bait.'

'But who's done this?' asked Haxor. 'That's not the work of animals. Is it greenskins?'

'Greenskins don't go in for mysteries and ploys,' said Kolgrimm. 'They're not patient enough. If there are greenskins in this valley they'd be slamming their thick skulls against our walls. Like all the others we've seen.'

'I don't understand,' said Chiana. She looked back at Sergeant Drannon. 'If we go out to help him, we'll trigger a trap, but what danger is he in? You said animals?'

Tyndaris nodded. 'Look at his legs. See the blood? He's already fought a few off. He must have kicked them away.' Tyndaris pointed his cane at the ground not far from the bound man. 'These are the wildlands. Put some meat on a stick and the local fauna won't take long to notice. Look, something else is already coming to take a look at him.'

At first Niksar thought he could see a snake, coiling quickly through the mud, but then he saw it had rows of legs rippling along its length, like a centipede. The thing was at least twelve feet long, perhaps longer, and its head was avian, with a long, curved beak.

'It's heading towards him,' gasped Haxor.

'Help him!' demanded Kolgrimm, gripping his axe as though he meant to hurl it from the wall.

'I will,' said Tyndaris. 'I just wanted you to understand.'

'Quickly!' cried Zagora. 'It's almost reached him.'

Tyndaris nodded to one of the archers. The soldier loosed a single arrow, sending it hissing through the rain. The arrow landed neatly in the man's left eye. He twitched briefly, then slumped in his bonds.

There was a stunned silence.

'Why didn't you shoot the serpent?' cried Haxor.

Tyndaris pointed out another one of the creatures, then another, and then another until he had made it clear that the ground near the corpse was teeming with them. 'We can't stop them all. I've seen enough scouts being eaten by those things this morning. I'm not doing it again. Drannon wasn't in any pain, or I'd have done this before you even got up here.'

They all watched in dismay as the creatures reached the sergeant's corpse and began pecking at it, filling the rain with splashes of crimson.

'I went out there,' said Tyndaris, 'when we found the first few, and do you know what I heard?' He glared at each of them in turn, as if he held them personally responsible. 'I heard laughter. From somewhere out in the darkness, I heard laughter. And then, when I tried to save the scouts and sent more people to their deaths, the laughter got louder.' He was shaking, tapping his cane on the flagstones. 'Someone is out there, mocking us, waiting to bring all these pretty walls down. And these are no wild beasts. There's someone clever in these hills.'

Niksar shook his head. 'That makes no sense. If someone wants to take the keep, why are they hiding out there laughing? Why not just attack?'

'I've seen this before,' said Tyndaris. 'It's an old trick. Someone's playing mind games with us. They want to sap our will. They want to demoralise us before they strike in earnest.'

There was a long pause as everyone digested what they had just heard. Then Chiana whispered a prayer and shook her head.

'We must hold our nerve, whatever happens out there. The Dawnbringer brought us here, exactly as Sigmar wished her to. The augur stone clearly showed this place. Am I correct, Zagora?'

Niksar noticed a strange hesitation before his sister replied, as though she wanted to qualify something, but then she nodded and looked at the ground, touching the stone at her brow. No one seemed to notice her uncertainty but Niksar found it troubling. He decided he had to speak to her alone as soon as he could.

Chiana waved her sceptre at the Stormcast Eternal standing a few feet away from them. 'Soon, Arulos and the rest of the

Anvilhearts will return. And the White Angels will be here any day. It doesn't matter who's waiting out there, laughing at us. We have the God-King's mightiest warriors watching over us.'

'Forgive me, high priestess,' said Tyndaris, 'but that's nonsense. Stormspear was meant to return after one evening. It's been a week. Either Arulos has abandoned us, or he has been killed.'

'Abandoned us?' Chiana shook her head, laughing.

'You know as well as I do that this crusade was never his primary concern,' said Tyndaris. 'His orders were to reach the great muster at Delium. He swore to get us this far but after that we are under the aegis of the Knights Excelsior, who are conspicuous by their absence.'

The Anvilheart on the wall turned to face them. His voice was calm and sure.

'Stormspear said he would return. The Knight-Arcanum will not break his word.'

Kolgrimm nodded, waving at the Stormcast Eternal. 'He'd hardly go to the coast and leave half his men here, would he?'

'Half?' said Tyndaris. 'He's left us with ten Anvilhearts. *Ten*. However mighty they are, ten Stormcast Eternals are not enough to hold back the whole of Ghur. And how long can we go on pinning our hopes on the White Angels? What if they don't get here for another month?' He nodded to Sergeant Drannon's corpse. 'Whoever's doing that won't wait forever. Whatever game they're playing, they'll soon tire of it and make their move. My guess is that they're the vanguard of something much larger. They're just killing time while they wait for the bulk of their troops to arrive. Softening us up.' He tapped his cane on the ground, giving them all a pointed look. 'I think we might only be hours away from a full-on attack. My suspicion is that they will strike when darkness falls tonight. And, even if I'm wrong, there are all the other predators we've seen over the last few days. If the scout killers don't attack, the banshees will return, or gargants, or the krakens or whatever else the land decides to throw at us.'

'You paint a bleak picture,' said Chiana, her smile growing more brittle. 'But what exactly are you suggesting we do?'

'I'm suggesting that Master Kolgrimm finish the job he was sent to do and stops indulging himself with grand follies, leaving us with one watchtower and a set of half-finished walls.'

'What do you think that is?' boomed Kolgrimm, pointing at the lines of people carrying mud and stone across the hillside. 'I'm building the keep in the way I see fit. And trust me, when it's finished you'll thank me for every inch of the extra fortifications.'

'When it's built we'll all be dead.' Tyndaris was white with anger but he kept his voice level. 'Unless you follow the plans that were laid down in High Azyr.' He looked at Zagora. 'Have you studied any copies of the Decree Sigmaris? I have. If we had followed the plans as written these walls would all be finished. The keep might not be as impressive as Kolgrimm would like but the walls would be up. They would keep things out. We would have something to defend instead of a heap of mud and scaffolding.'

'Mud and scaffolding?' Kolgrimm glared through his goggles. 'Exactly how much do you know about engineering, Captain Tyndaris? How much did you understand when you studied the Decree Sigmaris? Perhaps we should hand the construction work over to you? Perhaps you're better at building than you are at keeping your men alive.'

Tyndaris tensed but it was Haxor who looked the most outraged. She gripped the hilt of her sword and pointed at Kolgrimm.

'If you weren't so concerned with your own legacy this place would be finished and Captain Tyndaris might not have to send people out to look for help.'

Kolgrimm did not deign to reply, staring furiously back at her. Haxor looked shocked by her own words and Niksar had the horrible sense that a fight was about to break out. He spoke up quickly.

'We're very close. In a few more days the walls will all be finished. Four days, at most.'

Everyone other than Kolgrimm looked at him in surprise.

'What do you know about it?' asked Haxor, still gripping the handle of her sword.

Zagora frowned. 'You've never built so much as a bookcase, Niksar. How can you know how long things will take?'

'Your brother has been an invaluable aid to me,' said Kolgrimm. 'He's one of the few people here who actually seems to know his arse from his elbow. And he's right, dammit. These walls will be finished in four days. Five days at the most. And they will be big enough to keep out anything this place throws at us.'

'Five days?' Tyndaris laughed and looked at Zagora. 'Can you hear this? Five days. Did your visions show us taking so long to build the place? The whole idea of the strongpoints is that they are designed to be assembled in a day or so. That's the only chance anyone has of surviving out here. The miracle is not that we've managed to assemble a few buildings. The miracle is that we've only faced one serious attack. Any moment now, something out there will catch our scent and decide we're a meal. These are the Thondian wildlands. Five days is a lifetime. And we've already been here over a week.' He kept his gaze locked on Zagora. 'What did you see happening? When you looked in that stone did you see us spending weeks labouring over a vast fortress filled with temples and guildhouses?'

'No.' Zagora sounded oddly hesitant again. Niksar wondered what had happened to change her so drastically. 'No, I did not see Ardent Keep taking so long to build. Or that Master Kolgrimm would work on such grand buildings. And I am surprised we have been left to our own devices even for this long.'

Chiana pursed her lips and looked from Zagora to Kolgrimm, then back at Zagora again. 'This is your crusade, Dawnbringer. What do you wish us to do?'

There was an expectant silence as everyone waited for her to reply. Even the Stormcast Eternal looked over. To Niksar's eyes, Zagora seemed to have shrunk. For a horrible moment he thought she would refuse to speak. But then she nodded.

'Two days, at most.'

Tyndaris hissed in frustration. 'Two days? These things are going to make their move tonight, I'm sure of it. That's why they wanted to lure us out into the fields with those scouts. We need to find a way to finish things today.'

'Two days?' Kolgrimm laughed. 'Is that supposed to be a joke?' He waved at the crowds clambering over the walls, placing blocks and heaving on pulleys. 'How can we finish that in two days?'

'You could revert to the original plan,' said Tyndaris. 'The plan that was prescribed by the Decree Sigmaris. The plan we all thought you were following. It would be half the size of the work you're currently planning and you could easily have it finished in two days – earlier, probably, if you worry less about the details.'

'Worry less about the details,' breathed Kolgrimm as though someone had just suggested he trim his beard. He sounded too dazed to even be angry.

'Two days,' said Zagora. She looked at the corpse on the hillside and grimaced. While they had been talking it had almost been stripped to the bone. 'Whatever is out there, we have to assume we might be facing it alone. You will finish Ardent Keep by nightfall tomorrow.'

'Madness!' snarled Kolgrimm. 'You'll doom us all with this needless haste. Think about what's happened since we got here – a few small skirmishes with greenskins and some wild animals jumping over the stockade. Then these traps. A few dead scouts.

That's not a reason to abandon everything I have… Everything *we* have worked for.'

'No one's telling you to abandon anything,' said Tyndaris. 'We're just telling you to finish it.'

'You've been against me from the start!' roared Kolgrimm, levelling his axe at Tyndaris. The conversation had been tense until this point but not outright confrontational. Even Kolgrimm's apprentices looked shocked.

Tyndaris placed his hand on his sword and the two old warriors glared at each other.

'No one is against you, Master Kolgrimm,' said Zagora. 'But we have already taken far longer than anyone expected.' She nodded to the distant corpse. 'And I fear that Tyndaris is right – these cruel jokes seem like a warning, or a threat. I think this is the start of our greatest test. And without Arulos or the White Angels, we'll face it alone. So we must at least have walls that are ready to withstand an attack.'

Tyndaris nodded furiously and Chiana reached out to Kolgrimm, looking sympathetic.

'Master Kolgrimm, you have done so much already. You must be exhausted. I haven't seen you rest since we left Excelsis. I know how much you care about the design of the keep, but perhaps it's time to let someone else carry this burden for a while? There may be others amongst us who can find a way.'

'Madness,' muttered Kolgrimm, shrugging off the high priestess and glaring back at his forge. Then he rolled his head on his shoulders and slammed his axe on the flagstones. 'But I'll do it.' He looked at Niksar. 'I have the means. There are ways to accelerate the process.'

Zagora visibly relaxed, giving a deep sigh. 'Thank you, Master Kolgrimm. We all appreciate what you have done. I know that you are the only one who could have achieved all this.'

Kolgrimm nodded and sounded slightly mollified. 'I will not be able to achieve everything I planned, but that can come later. Let there be no talk of reverting to the original size though.' He glared at Tyndaris. 'I will finish *these* walls.'

Before anyone could challenge him, Kolgrimm turned and stomped from the tower, muttering to himself as he hurried back down the steps with his fellow engineers rushing after him. Niksar moved to follow but then he paused, looking back at his sister, remembering how hesitant she was at the start of the conversation. Zagora caught his eye and nodded, but she was clearly troubled. He was about to ask her for a moment alone when Chiana gripped her shoulders.

'We must finish our prayers, Dawnbringer. If Captain Tyndaris is correct, and today is the day of our great trial, it is more important than ever that we sanctify every inch of this keep. There is no time to lose.'

Niksar called out to Zagora as the priests bustled past him but she gave him a helpless shrug as they led her down the steps and back towards the temple.

'I saw that too,' said Haxor, once Tyndaris and the other Freeguild officers had left.

'Saw what?' replied Niksar.

'That look in your sister's eyes. Something's wrong. She looks troubled.'

Niksar looked around the top of the tower. The guards were looking out from the battlements and the Stormcast Eternal seemed oblivious to everyone, but he still led Haxor to the opposite side of the tower before replying.

'But why now?' he whispered. 'Think what we faced on the river. Everyone else was too terrified to think but she was magnificent. And she got us here, just as she said she would.' He waved at the distant hills surrounding the valley. 'I know there's more to come, but she should be feeling more confident rather than less. Why does she look so worried now?'

Haxor shrugged. 'Sometimes, the more you learn, the more you realise you don't know. Perhaps it's only now she's got us all out here that she realises how big the challenge of surviving will be. Perhaps she's finally realising the scale of what she's signed herself up for.'

'No, it's not that. I know her. Something specific is bothering her. She was keeping something back from everyone.'

Haxor nodded. 'I know what you mean. I saw it.'

'What are we going to do?' said Niksar. 'I have other concerns, too.'

'Kolgrimm?'

'Yes. He's obsessed with making this place bigger and better. I need to make sure he really does get it finished.'

'Then let me see to your sister. Chiana has to let her rest at some point. I'll loiter near the temple until they break from their prayers, then I'll try and prise her from Chiana's grip and find out what's worrying her.'

'Good. I'll be at the forge with Kolgrimm. Come and find me when you have news.'

They left the tower and, as Haxor rushed off towards the temple, Niksar turned to face Kolgrimm's forge. The fumes pouring from its nostrils were thicker than ever and they were flecked with splashes of colour: pinks, greens and blues that coiled through the smoke like oil in water. The cogsmiths were racing back and forth, bellowing commands at the gangs of labourers who were hauling mud towards the forge's gaping mouth. The scene was even more frenzied than it had been the day before and there was a droning sound radiating from the metal head, like the wail of a hunting horn.

Niksar was still a dozen feet away when a familiar shape came towards him, weaving through the miasma.

'Ocella,' said Niksar as she hobbled towards him. He tried to sound pleased to see her but he could not help backing away as she reached out to grab his arm. She looked filthier than ever and her skin was covered in ash and soot.

'I've been waiting to speak with you,' she said, looking even more distracted than usual, pulling at the mound of animal skins that passed for her clothing and scratching at her skull-knotted hair. 'You need to watch him.'

'Who?'

'Master Kolgrimm. The aetheric alkahest is like a drug, you know. It's addictive.' She looked around at the various half-completed buildings that had appeared in the last two days. 'Did he always mean to build so many things?'

'No. Not exactly.'

Ocella looked pained. 'You see, the alkahest, it can give people a chance to do great things but, historically, that has not always gone so well.'

'What are you talking about? Why didn't you mention this before? You said it's not evil.'

'It's not! But... If you give someone the chance to make anything they want, to realise their most cherished ambitions, it can be hard for that person to know, well, to know when to stop.'

'Dammit!' Niksar paced around her in the mud. 'That's exactly what we don't need. He has a *lot* of cherished ambitions. He was already being unrealistic. Now you're telling me that thing will make him even worse.'

'Well, wouldn't it make you worse? If you could produce any material you desired, in any quantity? Wouldn't you be at risk of losing your way?'

Niksar pictured himself, surrounded by precious metals and gems. 'Perhaps. But Kolgrimm's the one we need to worry about. He's obsessed with making this place more impressive than all

the other crusader settlements. He wants it to be the jewel in
Sigmar's crown. How can I keep him on track? He's got until
tomorrow night to get these walls finished. And if you listen to
Captain Tyndaris, he hasn't even got that long. Tyndaris thinks
we're going to be attacked today.'

Ocella frowned and pulled at her hair, causing the bird skulls to
rattle musically. Then she grinned. 'I know what you should do.
Tell him he needs to let the thing cool. Tell him it's something to
do with its magical properties. Tell him, if the alkahest is over-
used, without rest, it starts to lose its shape.'

'Which would be bad?'

Ocella gave a 'haw haw' and tapped her nose, still grinning.
'It won't *really* change shape. The alkahest is a divine talisman.
It couldn't be altered by anything Kolgrimm possesses. His art
is only a shadow of the art that came before. The alkahest was
forged in the Spiral Crux, in another age. In the times before the
Mortal Realms were diminished by the coming of Chaos. But
Kolgrimm does not need to know any of that. Tell him he must
rest the thing and work with the stone he already has, or it will
have results we cannot foresee. Do you see? Tell him he needs
to let the alkahest cool down, that he must not keep that furnace working at this pace.' She looked over at the forge. 'Look at
that. When he came back from talking to the Dawnbringer, he
must have told his apprentices to stoke the flames even more. He's
making it even hotter in there.' She briefly met Niksar's eye. 'Is he
unwell? I mean, in his mind.'

Niksar struggled not to laugh at the idea of Ocella questioning
someone's sanity. 'He swore to finish the whole keep by tomorrow
night, just a few seconds after he'd told everyone that was impossible. I wondered how he meant to do it. It sounds like his plan
is just to work the furnace harder and produce the stone much
quicker.'

Ocella performed an odd kind of dance, stamping her feet in the mud, fiddling with her furs.

'What are you doing?' asked Niksar. She seemed even more distracted than usual.

She looked around to make sure they were not being watched, then she turned to the side and pulled back her sleeve so that Niksar could see under her furs. 'Don't tell anyone,' she whispered as a pair of round, glossy eyes gazed out at Niksar.

'What in the name of Sigmar is that?'

She grinned. Then she reached into a bag at her belt, took out a tiny, dead rodent and dangled it near her armpit. An arrow-shaped head lunged from under her furs and swallowed the rodent whole. It was a serpent with small, gleaming white horns jutting up from its scales and a curved avian beak. It gazed sleepily at Niksar as it ate, then it coiled back under Ocella's clothes.

Niksar stepped away from her. 'I've just seen some of those things eat a man. What are you thinking? It's right next to your chest. Are you insane?'

'This girl won't harm me. I've had her since we first reached the valley. She seems quite taken with me. She's my guardian.'

Niksar could not decide whether to be horrified or amused. Of all Ocella's perversities, this seemed the most absurd. 'You need to get that thing out of here before it rips you open.'

'Not all creatures in Thondia are evil.' Ocella patted the serpent's head and gently hid it back under her furs. 'She needs to eat, but don't we all? Some things in the wilds are unnatural, but the desire to stay alive is quite understandable. Besides, this girl's only young. I think she's adopted me as her mother.'

Niksar stared at her.

Ocella shrugged, still stroking the thing coiled under her clothes. Then she looked panicked again. 'You have to stop the duardin. Tell him he has to let the talon cool down.'

'That won't be easy.'

Ocella frowned. 'He does seem proud. Nothing good ever comes from that. Ambition can be a curse, unless it's tempered by humility.'

The thought of Kolgrimm being slighted by someone as wayward as Ocella grated on Niksar's already frayed nerves. 'There's nothing wrong with ambition. If it wasn't for Kolgrimm's pride we'd all be digging holes to sleep in. He's the engine of this crusade.'

'You have to slow him down.' Ocella looked at the workers hurrying past. She lowered her voice to a whisper. 'We should never have let him have the alkahest. I had no idea he would use it like this. Perhaps he's one of them.'

'One of who?'

'You know. *Them.*'

Niksar resisted the urge to ask for an explanation. Ocella's paranoia was all consuming. He would be there for hours if he asked her to list all the people she thought were trying to kill her. 'I'll see what I can do,' he said. 'Kolgrimm won't want to break the talon. If I can convince him that's a possibility he should stop.'

'The more he uses it, the more ambitious he will become. It will feed his pride and his desire.'

Niksar closed his eyes, wondering what had possessed him to work with Ocella again. 'I'll talk to him.'

Niksar spoke more harshly than he intended and the serpent uncoiled from Ocella's furs again, hissing and curling its head back, preparing to attack.

'I'll talk to him,' repeated Niksar in softer tones, holding up his hands and backing away.

Ocella nodded and petted the snake as Niksar left her and rushed on through the mud towards the forge.

Kolgrimm was howling at one of his engineers as Niksar entered the building. There was so much smoke it was impossible to distinguish one cogsmith from another but it was easy to locate Kolgrimm from his booming voice. He had grabbed one of his apprentices and slammed him against the wall, spitting vitriol at him.

'Get more soil or don't come back! I have no time for half-a-job layabouts.'

Niksar hesitated at the threshold. Ocella was right: Kolgrimm looked unhinged. He had always seemed driven, but since he started using the alkahest he was frantic, his voice cracking as he rounded on his engineers, hurling abuse at them.

'Get out! The lot of you! Come back when every wagon is loaded with soil. Or I'll put *you* in the furnace!'

Niksar stepped aside as most of the duardin rushed out, leaving just Kolgrimm and a few gun-wielding guards.

'Don't just stand there!' cried Kolgrimm, shoving his guards to the piles of mud heaped in front of the furnace. 'Load it!'

The guards rushed to obey and as they tipped the mud into the prismatic flames, Kolgrimm cranked a pair of mechanised bellows, wheezing more smoke into the room.

'Master Kolgrimm,' said Niksar.

'What?' barked Kolgrimm without turning from his work.

Niksar could see the cogsmith's eyes through the lenses of his helmet. They were bloodshot and strained. He hesitated. Then, remembering Ocella's warning, he forced himself to speak.

'The alkahest will overheat.'

Kolgrimm kept turning the crank, filling the room with embers and smoke. 'Eh?'

'The talon. It's not meant to be used for such long stretches. You need to let it rest.'

'Let it rest?' Kolgrimm paused and stared at him. 'Is that meant to be some kind of joke?' His voice was low and dangerous.

'No, I'm afraid not. If you keep using it without pause it will warp. And if it changes shape, the results will not be...' He shrugged, trying to remember what Ocella had said. 'It will not work in the way you expect.'

Kolgrimm glared at him. Then he tapped a book on his desk. 'I have studied this thing. I know a lot more than you might think. The alkahest could *never* overheat. Not in any fire I can create.' Suspicion crept into his voice. 'So why are you claiming it will?'

He lifted a ratchet that was lying in the coals. The metal glowed angrily in his gauntleted hand as he waved it in Niksar's face.

'He sent you, didn't he?'

'He?'

'Ulfarsson.' Kolgrimm started pacing around the room, swinging the ratchet and muttering to himself, surrounding himself with fiery contrails. 'I should have seen it. You're one of his spies. That's why you've been hanging around, asking so many damned questions, giving me advice that I'm starting to think was bad advice. Ulfarsson sent you to hinder me, didn't he?' He slammed the ratchet into the wall near Niksar's face, making the forge clang like a bell. 'Isn't that right?'

'No!' gasped Niksar, trying desperately to remember who Ulfarsson was. 'I gave you that alkahest in good faith. None of this would be possible if I hadn't helped you.'

Kolgrimm glared up at him, muttering and grunting. 'Aye, you did get me the alkahest.' He shrugged and went back to turning the crank. 'Perhaps you're not working for Ulfarsson. But you're still talking nonsense. I know more about metallurgy than anyone in Thondia. That talon's sound. Nothing could warp it. Even this furnace.'

Niksar stepped as close to the furnace's opening as he could, raising his voice over the noise of the flames. 'Master Kolgrimm, I assure you, you need to let the thing cool for a while. If you don't, there will be–'

'Get him out!' snarled Kolgrimm, waving his guards towards Niksar. 'I can't think with all this prattling.'

'Wait!' gasped Niksar, but Kolgrimm kept his back to him as the guards bundled him to the door and out into the morning light.

The door to the furnace slammed shut and Niksar stood there in the rain, staring at the riveted copper. Then someone thudded into him and he saw that teams of workers were rushing in every direction. As the forge's output increased, the duardin engineers had rounded up dozens more crusaders and carts. Stone blocks were being rushed through the rain, heading to every corner of the keep. But only half of them were going to the walls. Everywhere Niksar looked, new foundations were being laid, the footings of buildings even grander than the nexus syphon or the temple.

Niksar stumbled through the mud, filled with a sense of unease. Then he shook his head and sighed. He had done nothing wrong. He had simply given Kolgrimm the means to build Ardent Keep. And if Kolgrimm thought he could build more than he originally planned, perhaps he was right. He was a venerated, duardin cogsmith. And Ocella was a… He did not know exactly what Ocella was, but she was no engineer. He looked around but could see no sign of her in the crowds of labourers. She would probably be off somewhere talking to a lizard.

He watched the workers for a while, trying to convince himself that all was well. At least some of the workers were focused on finishing the walls. But Niksar kept thinking of the troubled look he had seen in his sister's eyes.

He headed for the shelter of the Phoenix Company's newly built barracks, and looked up at its absurdly grand portico, unable to shake a growing sense of dread.

CHAPTER TWENTY

'Days have passed,' said Arulos, as they reached the top of a rise and saw the stars spread overhead. It was early evening, and from the top of the slope he caught his first clear glimpse of the sky since they entered the swamps. 'Look at the moons.'

Varek climbed up beside him and looked up at Gnorl and Koptus. The conjunction had passed and the moons had resumed their normal place in Ghur's heavens. 'How is that possible?'

'The fog.' Arulos looked back the way they had come. The marshes and bogs behind them were still shrouded in impenetrable mist. 'The greenskins have altered it. I have known even the most savage of Ghurite beasts employ a crude form of sorcery. Some of their shamans are able to tap into the pulse of the land and direct it. They can commune with bestial gods. I think that is what has been done here. They have harnessed the weather to their will. They have laced the fog with magic that has robbed us of our senses. And while we were in their clutches, days have passed out here.'

'But it has not worked,' said Varek as the rest of the Anvilhearts gathered around them on the ridge. 'We have emerged sooner than they expected. They were still keen to avoid us finding that metalith.'

Arulos nodded. 'We may still be in time.' He held up a hand for silence and peered through the renunciation crystal. With a flood of relief, he saw Sigmar's tempest. The might of the God-King, hidden from him for so long, finally flooded his mind again. He held his aetherstave aloft and allowed some of the majesty to spark around the metal.

'He sees us,' he said. 'We are in Sigmar's sight. We are lost no longer.'

The others clanged their weapons against their chest armour, muttering prayers and oaths, but Arulos barely heard them as the storm hurled him through the aether-clouds, his spirit tumbling and raging through the squalls. He saw the shrouded lands behind them to the north, where the Great Excelsis Road had been swamped in fog for miles, hiding the massacres at the crusader outposts. Then he looked the other way, letting the rain carry his thoughts south, across the bogs and muddy fields until, gleaming in the rain, he saw Ardent Keep, rising defiantly from the tor. It was far more impressive than he would have expected. The walls were huge and punctuated by dozens of soaring turrets. All along the battlements, banners were snapping in the storm, bearing the sigils of Sigmar, Excelsis and the circled tower of Ardent Keep. Despite the ambition of the construction, almost all of the walls were complete, with just a few sections still to be finished.

'The cogsmith has excelled himself,' said Arulos. Even as he took in the glory of the building, Arulos' vision started to dim. The fog that had baffled him for so long was washing south across the landscape and pouring into the valley that cradled Faithful Tor. 'Our enemies are preparing to attack,' he said. 'But they are only making their opening gambit. We are just in time.'

He was vaguely aware of Varek saying something, announcing his relief that the crusaders could still be saved. Then, as the fog gathered in hollows and began to obscure his stormsight, he followed it back up the valley to its source. In his fading vision, he saw an unruly mob: tall, rangy greenskins, like the ones they had just fought, all carrying the same grinning shields and spears.

'Two hundred,' he said, letting his thoughts glide over the jeering monsters. 'No, far more.' Varek spoke but Arulos did not catch the words. 'That was just vanguard. A host is gathering, rising from all the surrounding swamps. There could be as many as two thousand. But they are not attacking yet.' The fog was flooding his thoughts again, clouding the figures at the end of the valley, but he had time to notice something odd. 'They have animals. In cages. Hundreds of them. They are goading them. Cutting them with knives. Why would they do that? Why waste time when the keep is laid out beneath them? The walls are almost complete. If they do not strike soon, they will face an impregnable fortress, but they are wasting their time tormenting animals.'

In his final glimpse of the greenskin lines, Arulos saw something that made him smile. 'I see the leader. A tribal chieftain. Larger and more heavily armoured. Riding some kind of steed. A horse? No, a hound. An attack dog. Larger than a horse. The chieftain is carrying something.' As the scene faded, Arulos realised what was hanging from the leader and its steed. 'Body parts,' he said, turning to face Varek. 'The chieftain is covered in heads and limbs. The leaders of the other crusades.'

'How far away are they?' asked Varek.

'No more than a couple of hours if we run.' He shook his head, confused. 'This is a peculiar breed of greenskin. None of them are behaving how I would expect. The chieftain has a chance to storm the keep, but it's holding back, working on a plan that revolves around animals in cages. What kind of greenskin ever held back from an attack? There is something odd about this whole region.' He looked around at the sodden fields. 'It is something to do with these swamps and bogs.'

'Knight-Arcanum. How clearly did you see? Are there really two thousand?'

'At least. Perhaps more. But once we reach the keep no amount of greenskins could take it. Once we bolster the Freeguild regiment that hill will be secure.'

Varek studied him in silence, then shook his head. 'If we enter the keep we could be there for weeks, trapped in a siege here when we should be relieving the one at Delium. Is that really what the Lord-Imperatant would want us to do? Are we going to risk Delium and the whole coast so we can protect these crusaders?'

Arulos gripped his aetherstave in both fists, as though he could squeeze an answer from it. 'We have to do both, Varek. We can't let Zagora fail.' He shook his head. 'But the storm has shown me that we will strike a decisive blow at the siege. We need to solve this problem quickly. We need to defeat this horde before they even reach the keep. We need to slay that chieftain and behead the army.'

Varek looked around at the battered, limping Anvilhearts. 'You know I will follow you wherever you lead, old friend, but two thousand greenskins sounds a tall order.'

'We can do it,' said Arulos. 'The numbers are irrelevant. The storm is with us. Sigmar is with us. It will work exactly as it did when we fought the greenskins on the banks of the Claw-water. I will turn the hunger of the land against them. Once I cut down the leader, they will become even more of a rabble. They will turn on each other and try to vie for power.

'It's the only way, Varek. You're right that we can't risk a lengthy siege. A week, at least, has passed while we were in that fog. We swore an oath to the Lord-Imperatant. We have promised to aid Yndrasta. We cannot let ourselves be trapped here.'

An image flashed through his thoughts. It was the memory that escaped from his renunciation stone: his wife, begging him not to abandon her.

'But I will not leave the Dawnbringer to die at the hands of these creatures. We have to strike. And strike fast. Luckily for us, the greenskins seem deranged. And their own fog means that they will not see us coming.' He thought of the chieftain on the massive hound, draped in gruesome battle trophies. 'We have a chance to make them pay for what they have done.'

CHAPTER TWENTY-ONE

Niksar had slept for hours. He had only meant to rest for a few minutes but as soon as he lay down in the barracks he fell into a profound slumber. He had not had so much uninterrupted sleep since the start of the crusade and he felt dazed as he stumbled back outside. The whole day had passed while he slept and the stars were already glittering overhead.

He yawned and strolled over to a recently lit campfire where Taymar and some younger soldiers were heating broth in a copper pot. Taymar was making sketches of the soldiers as they slumped, exhausted, on the ground, huddled in dirty blankets and leaning against each other. He was regaling them with a story but he had lost some of the fervour that usually made his face so bright and animated. His words sounded flat and disjointed. He smiled as he saw Niksar approaching and sat up straight, regaining some of his spark.

'And Niksar was there at the beginning, when the Dawnbringer first beheld the augur stone. Tell us about it. Where were you when Zagora first touched the glimmering?'

The younger soldiers stirred, looking up at Niksar. All of them carried wounds of some kind, from cuts and bruises to bandaged limbs, and they all looked dreadful – weeks without a decent night's sleep and days of endless labouring had left them with shadows under their eyes and sunken cheeks.

'Aye, tell us,' said one of them, smiling weakly. His eyes looked huge in his gaunt, dirty face, flashing in the firelight as he held out a piece of bread to Niksar. 'You saw the start. You saw how it all began.'

Niksar grunted and shook his head. He was stiff and groggy and he had awoken with the same sense of dread that had been plaguing him when he fell asleep. In fact, if anything, it was worse. He took the bread and sat near the fire with a muttered thanks, looking around at the walls of the keep. They were glorious but still not finished. Kolgrimm had even begun several fresh additions, including new towers and what looked suspiciously like a drinking hall. At this rate, the walls would never be finished.

'Isn't it incredible?' said Taymar, looking past the fires that littered the tor and gazing at the towering walls. 'Your sister is not the only one blessed by a god. Grungni himself must be working through Master Kolgrimm. Look at what he's achieved. We will be ready to face anything by the time he's done.'

Niksar remembered Tyndaris' warnings about the dead scouts and muttered something noncommittal.

'Tell us about the day Zagora found the stone,' said another one of the soldiers. It was the hulking youth called Brod – a friend of Zagora's from the days when she was just another Freeguild soldier. One of his arms was wrapped tightly to his chest in a blood-sodden bandage and his face was mangled by bruises, but he smiled eagerly at Niksar.

Niksar looked around at the youths. They were so caked in mud that they seemed to be becoming part of the landscape. Becoming less human. He pitied them but he was reluctant to play the part Taymar was trying to give him. He did not want to be used like Zagora – as a sacrificial figurehead, inspiring people to attempt the impossible. He did not *believe* in the way she did.

'She was crawling in the dirt under my bed,' he snapped. 'Helping me dispose of stolen goods.'

Brod's grin froze and the other soldiers all looked shocked.

'Stolen goods?' asked one.

'Really?' said another.

'Are you joking?' asked Brod. 'Zagora?'

Niksar saw hope waver in their eyes. They were on the point of collapse. And what would they be without hope? As much as it annoyed him to admit it, he realised he could not rob them of the one thing that was keeping them alive.

'Of course I'm joking. She's always been a bloody saint.'

The soldiers laughed in relief and glanced at each other as though they could not believe their luck encountering Niksar. He leant back against a grain sack.

'Even when we were children, she was different. We grew up in the slums, in the Veins, and I was always desperate to prove I was better than everyone else. I was always trying to compete, to show I could be more than where I came from. I made deals and I tricked people. I invented scams so that I could dress in clothes that made me look like a noble, like I was from somewhere else in the city. I made friends I thought could be of use to me. I made plans. I craved wealth. And power.

'But Zagora never cared about any of that. All she has ever wanted is to help those who can't help themselves.' He looked around at the crusaders. 'She was born for this. Born to lead. She doesn't care what those priests do to her. She doesn't care what happens to her. All she cares about is finding a way to keep people alive, to keep the wolf from the door.' The words tumbled out of him. 'She's better than all of them – all those priests and nobles with their big words and their fine clothes. They're no better than me, only thinking about what they will get out of this. Thinking about what scams they can pull. But Zagora actually means what she says. She's…'

His words trailed off as he noticed how the soldiers were staring at him. They looked like they were witnessing a miracle. It was the same way people looked at his sister. He shuddered.

'Anyway, that's it.' He continued eating his bread. 'That's Zagora. You're right. She's worth something. Worth following.'

There was a stunned silence, then Brod patted Niksar on the back. There was such pride and hope in his eyes that Niksar resisted the urge to snap at him. Taymar gave Niksar a look that was hard to read. Rather than fawning and praising him, as Niksar would have expected, the old noble looked thoughtful.

'Your sister's an inspiration,' he said. 'But we do not all need to measure ourselves against her. There are other ways to do good.'

'What do you mean?' Niksar was surprised by Taymar's tone. It was as if he pitied him. 'Why did you say that?'

Taymar shrugged. 'I thought, perhaps, that it might be hard for you – living in her shadow. But you have your own strengths. We are *all* worth something.'

Niksar shook his head, unsure how to reply. Taymar had gauged him with surprising accuracy.

Taymar looked like he might say more, but then he returned to his pieces of parchment and began writing, no doubt recording the moment for posterity.

For a few moments, Niksar allowed himself to relax, eating in quiet comradery with the wounded soldiers. They began to crack jokes and seemed to forget their awe of him, treating him like he was just another member of the regiment.

'Has anyone seen Haxor?' asked Niksar when he had finished eating.

Taymar nodded and waved at one of the other campfires further up the hill. 'Shall I take you to her?' he asked, putting his papers away and standing. 'I could use a walk.'

The other soldiers all prepared to rise and come with them.

'No.' Niksar held up his hands. 'Please. Get some rest. It might be your last chance. I'll be fine.' He thanked them for the food and rose to leave. 'Is that drumming?' He hesitated at the edge of the firelight. There was a vague juddering sound drifting through the air.

The soldiers shrugged and shook their heads, settling back down around the fire, so Niksar headed off through the endless drizzle to speak with Haxor. The noise got louder as he walked and he frowned, trying to see the source. There were several musical troupes accompanying the crusade, but it seemed unlikely any of them would be performing. He walked higher up the tor, trying to get a clear view of the whole keep but, even from a better vantage point, he could not see any drummers. The sound was oddly loud and getting louder by the second. He squinted through the rain and saw some Phoenix Company soldiers rush away from their campfires and dash through the mud, heading towards the front gates. Near the wall, at the bottom of the hill, gold flashed in the rain as Stormcast Eternals left their posts and strode towards the gates to join the Freeguild soldiers.

'What's this?' he muttered.

The drumming grew so loud that the ground was juddering under his feet and then, just as he was about to head back to the campfire, horns rang out along the walls, causing people to cry out and leap to their feet.

'Niksar!' cried Haxor, running past him with some of the other Freeguild soldiers. She had drawn her sword and her expression was grim. 'It's starting! They're attacking! This is it!'

Niksar looked around at the walls. They were incomplete in

several places, only a few feet tall at some points. 'Damn you, Kolgrimm,' he muttered.

He raced after Haxor and soon found himself in a tide of crusaders who were grabbing weapons and donning armour as they rushed to the gates. As the sound grew louder, Niksar realised it could not be drums. It was a continuous rumble, more like a landslide or a waterfall.

There was a crush as they all reached the walls and tried to clamber up the steps. The walls around the front gates were finished and Kolgrimm had built them absurdly tall, so it was pain-fully slow going trying to reach the top.

'This way!' cried Haxor, leaping from the steps to some scaffolding. Niksar and several other soldiers jumped after her, clambering up ropes and gantries as the horns continued to blare overhead. Niksar had spent his teenage years climbing rooftops in the Veins, so he bounded easily up the rattling planks and dragged himself up onto the walls ahead of Haxor and the others.

Captain Tyndaris was there, limping up and down the wall, waving soldiers into position with his cane in one hand and his sword in the other. 'Wait!' he bawled, straining to be heard over the roaring sound. 'Hold your fire! Do not shoot until I give the order.' He caught sight of Niksar and glowered at him. 'Don't let your duar-din friend come anywhere near me. Or I'll turn these guns on him.'

As the marksmen jostled for position along the battlements, Niksar wondered what they were taking aim at, battling through the crowds of soldiers to try to get a view of the rain-whipped fields beyond the walls. He reached some steps directly above the gates and scrambled up into a watchtower.

'Sigmar's crown,' he whispered as he squinted out into the rain. 'Is it a flood? Maybe a river has burst its banks?'

Haxor shook her head. 'If it was a flood, Tyndaris would have us all running for the high ground.'

Niksar wiped rainwater from his eyes, trying to see more clearly. The valley was covered in a thick fog that made it hard to see very far, but he could feel the ground shaking. The valley seemed to be moving. There were hundreds, perhaps thousands of shapes rushing towards them, rushing through the downpour.

'It's an army,' he muttered.

'Orruks?' said Haxor, leaning out over the parapet.

'No,' he said. 'Something else. I think it's… I think they're animals.'

As the wave of shapes rushed towards the keep, Niksar started to make out details. Some of the creatures were four-legged, broader and more muscular than horses, but with long, trailing manes. They had sweeping, bovine horns and their hooves were the source of the noise Niksar had mistaken for drums. Then he made other shapes out in the crush: lithe, fast-moving ruminants and huge, rangy hounds almost as big as the horned beasts. There were other, smaller creatures weaving between the larger animals. All of them, large or small, were horribly frenzied – spit was foaming at their muzzles and their heads were jolting and convulsing in a way that reminded Niksar of Ocella.

'It's a stampede.'

Below them, on the wall, Tyndaris was waving people back the way they had come, ordering them down the steps.

'The gates will hold, damn it! Get to the *unfinished* parts of the wall! Man the gaps!'

The sound of the stampede was deafening and not many people heard Tyndaris, continuing to crush around the steps at the side of the gates.

'Man the other walls!' howled Tyndaris, waving his cane at the few sections of the wall that had not been finished. 'Block the holes!'

Finally, the people nearest to him understood, but when they tried to turn they faced a mob of people attempting to climb up the steps. There was chaos as people grappled and cursed, shouting at each other to move aside.

The stampede slammed into the gates. The watchtower shook so violently that Niksar was thrown backwards from the battlements. If Haxor had not managed to grab him by the wrists he might have fallen to his death. She shouted something in his face but the sound of the beasts drowned out everything else. There was a chorus of screeches, howls and lowing, accompanied by the thud of bodies slamming into wood and stone.

Haxor swung Niksar onto the scaffolding and then climbed out to join him. They scrambled quickly down and backed away, staring at the juddering gates.

Screams came from dozens of directions at once. Niksar whirled around, slipping in the mud, and he saw that Tyndaris' warning had come too late. All across the tor, animals were leaping over the unfinished sections of wall, thundering into the keep. There was a rattle of gunfire. Freeguild soldiers were shooting at the beasts but it was useless, the animals had too much momentum from charging down the hill. After the first few fell, hundreds more thundered over the carcasses and flattened the soldiers.

People tried to fight the stampede in the same way they would have fought an army, lashing out with swords and firing pistols, but it was a farce. The animals bucked and gored or simply crushed people under hooves. The more the crusaders fought, the more frantic the animals became, throwing themselves against walls, more panicked than aggressive.

'Niksar!' cried Ocella, rushing across the hillside towards him. She had to dodge animals and people to reach him but her lurching, juddering gait seemed to help, enabling her to weave and duck through the mayhem. 'These animals aren't predators!' She waved her bone staff at the carnage. 'We don't need to attack them!'

'Attack them?' Even for Ocella this was deranged. 'We're not attacking them!' cried Niksar. 'They're attacking us!'

'Who *is* this?' cried Haxor, staring at the hunched, ragged woman. Niksar tried to make his way past Ocella.

'Something made them do this!' cried Ocella. 'This is not natural.'

People were being trampled all around them. Niksar turned and glared at Ocella. 'What are you talking about?'

'Look!' she cried. 'They've been poisoned!'

Niksar shook his head and was about to move on when Haxor grabbed his arm.

'Wait,' she said. 'She's right. Look.'

They all had to leap aside as one of the bull-like creatures thudded past, snorting and trailing corpses from its horns and hooves. It came so close that Niksar saw something jutting from its flank. It was a knife – a curved, rusty blade that was hissing with the same yellowish froth that was bubbling at the animal's nostrils.

'So what?' he said, realising that all the animals were injured in the same way, froth-covered blades jutting from their sides. 'What difference does it make? Who cares *why* they're killing us? They're still killing us.' He pointed his sword at the walls. 'We need to help block those gaps.'

The hillside was already crowded with animals and Niksar was about to point out that it was too late, when one of the beasts charged directly at him. It was a stag, taller than he was and crowned with a tortuous mass of antlers. It lowered its head as it charged up the slope towards him, its eyes rolling and its fur lathered with sweat. Niksar leapt aside as the stag rushed past, thundering off into the darkness. Niksar stared in disbelief as the stag raced off into the banks of fog, disappearing from view.

'They're not predators,' said Ocella, looking at the slaughter taking place all around them.

The crusaders were being butchered. The more they fought the animals, the more violent the creatures became. Every sword strike and gun volley added to the carnage and the stampeding animals were still pouring through the gaps in the walls, trampling the soldiers trying to halt them. Only the Anvilhearts were holding their ground. The Vindictors had formed a wall of shields near the largest hole and there was a mound of animal carcasses heaped in front of them as they leant into the stampede, holding back an incredible weight of bodies.

'Why are you babbling on about whether they're predators or not?' cried Haxor, glaring at Ocella.

'Because they're not attacking us. They're stampeding. There's a difference.' Ocella looked at Haxor as if she were an idiot. 'Don't you see? If we try to fight them we'll only make it worse. They're not soldiers. If we trap them in here we'll just make them more dangerous.'

Haxor narrowed her eyes. 'That does actually make a kind of sense.'

'What?' said Niksar, still dazed by the scale of the carnage.

Haxor waved at the beasts crashing into the line of Anvilhearts. 'If this is a stampede, we need to let it move on, not lock horns with it.' She looked at the other side of the keep, where Kolgrimm had been building another set of gates. 'We need to open those gates and drive the animals that way. Stampeding animals follow the leaders of the herd, don't they? If we could drive even a few of them that way, to the gates, the others might follow.'

'You want to herd them?' laughed Niksar.

'Look at that!' cried Haxor, pointing at the fighting.

Soldiers and civilians were forming lines near the Stormcast Eternals, trying to hold their ground in the same way as the Anvilhearts, but it was a gruesome farce. Some of the Freeguild knights were there, wielding lances from the backs of their huge, demi-gryph steeds, but even they looked absurd, battered and trampled by the waves of creatures, sent tumbling from their saddles. The more people attacked the animals, the more frenzied and confused they became, bucking and goring with so much savagery that even the demigryphs were caught up in the mania, rearing and snarling as their riders battled to control them.

'Is herding them as insane as trying to draw up battle lines against them?'

'We have to let them keep moving,' said Ocella. 'Or they'll kill everyone.'

Niksar nodded, slowly. 'Perhaps there is a mad kind of logic to that. We'd have to tell the captain.' He looked at Haxor. 'And all the others.'

'I'll head back to the gates,' said Haxor, 'and tell the guards to open them. Then I'll spread the word that we have to change our approach.' She nodded at the fighting. 'You let Tyndaris and the others know.' She gave Ocella a wary look. 'But I wouldn't mention whose idea this was.'

As Haxor ran off, Niksar dashed through the rain, jumping and sidestepping as shapes rushed at him from every direction. Ocella hobbled after him for a while then vanished from view behind a wave of animals. Niksar halted and looked back, thinking she had been flattened, then he saw her scramble up a muddy slope and head back the way she had come.

He left her and raced towards the wall, making for a breach. There was a huge crowd of crusaders gathered behind the Anvilhearts where animals spilled into the keep. It was a chaotic scene. Some people were howling orders but most were lying broken in the mud, crushed by the animals that had made it past the Stormcast Eternals. There were a dozen or so Phoenix Company halberdiers nearest to the wall, trying to hold their place, halberds raised, as a massive, bull-like creature thundered towards them.

There was a flash of white as Zagora leapt through the rain, slamming her hammer into the creature's head just before it hit the soldiers. It stumbled off course and crashed into a building, causing the whole structure to slump and crack.

The soldiers cheered as Zagora turned on her heel to face the beast. It shook its head, clearly dazed, and stumbled away. Zagora nodded to the soldiers and began heading towards the Anvilhearts.

'Wait!' cried Niksar, sprinting through the mud and grabbing his sister.

'What are you doing?' Zagora stared at him in disbelief.

'Fighting them only makes it worse!' he gasped. 'They don't want to attack us. They just want to get past us. Look at the knives in their flanks. They've been goaded into this.'

'Knives?' said Zagora, whirling around and looking at the beasts racing across the tor.

'They've been poisoned!' cried Niksar. 'They're just panicked. We need to let them keep moving. Fighting them is madness.' He pointed to the rear gates of the keep. 'Haxor's getting those gates opened. If we can drive some of the animals that way the rest should follow.'

Zagora stood, swaying in the mud, watching the stampede for a moment, then she wiped some of the blood from her face and laughed.

'Damn it. You're right, brother.' She raced through the tumult and leapt up onto the side of an overturned cart. 'Drive them on!' she howled, her voice carrying somehow over the din. She pointed at the gates on the far side of the hill. 'Let them pass!'

People stared at her in confusion, faltering but not backing away, so she leapt down into the mud and rushed to the front lines, dragging people back from the fighting. 'Let them pass through!' she cried.

'Let them pass through!' echoed Niksar, shouting her call and pointing his sword at the gates. To his delight, he saw that they were already swinging open. Haxor had either convinced the guards or found the gates unattended and done the job herself.

Gradually, as people understood what Zagora was trying to do, they repeated her cry and began backing away from the animals, driving them on across the keep rather than trying to hold them back. At first it made no difference and the beasts continued tearing through armour, wood and flesh, but finally the Anvil-hearts seemed to grasp what Zagora was trying to do and backed away from the wall, letting the bulk of the creatures surge forwards.

The Stormcast Eternals rushed to help Zagora, and when they had driven enough of the beasts in the right direction, the others started to follow. A trickle quickly became a stream, and then, after a few minutes, the crusaders and Anvilhearts had to dive for cover, clambering up the tor as the stampede formed into a single, deafening torrent of fur and tusks, pounding through the mud towards the gates.

CHAPTER TWENTY-TWO

The fog was so thick that by the time the greenskins caught sight of the Anvilhearts they could do nothing but stand and fight. They were gathered along the northernmost ridge of the valley and as Arulos marched out of the mist to face them, he saw them clearly for the first time.

The front ranks were made up of wizened little creatures, no bigger than children, and they were gathered around rows of empty cages. These were the cages that Arulos had seen in his stormsight, crowded with animals, but they were now empty and the ground before them had been churned up by the passing of many hooves and claws. Behind the animal handlers were the creatures that had been tormenting the Anvilhearts: grubby, sinewy greenskins with tall heads and crudely made spears. They all carried the same leering shields. It was an impressive host, and further back Arulos saw greenskins clad in thick plates of armour and carrying crossbows that were almost as big as they were. The rabble screamed and howled as the Anvilhearts strode towards them, but

Arulos ignored the din, looking over their heads at his prize: the chieftain on the giant hound.

There could be no doubt that it was their leader. It was by far the largest of them and, although it carried a spear and shield that was similar to all the others, its armour was far more impressive and its steed was draped in the remains of human victims: heads and torsos that had been washed by the rain so that they gleamed horribly in the darkness.

Beyond the chieftain, at the rear of the army, wheeled war machines of some kind loomed over the rabble. They were too hidden in fog for Arulos to make out clearly, but he guessed they were siege engines. The greenskins meant to break through the walls Kolgrimm had spent so long crafting.

The Anvilhearts advanced in silent ranks, lashed by the rain, coolly observing their foe. The greenskins began shaking their shields and laughing. It was only now that Arulos realised some of the laughter was actually coming from the shields. As the greenskins shook them, some quirk of their design produced a keening wail, like a cross between human laughter and the call of a wounded animal. The greenskins were laughing too, though, and as he heard the sound, Arulos felt a rush of doubt. Why were they so amused? Perhaps they simply did not understand what they were facing. They did not know that the Anvilhearts were Sigmar's thunderstrike. They thought they were facing mortal warriors. They did not know they were facing the fury of the storm.

'As before,' said Arulos calmly, ignoring the riotous scene up ahead. He looked at the Annihilators. 'Race to their leader. Do not be drawn by anything else. Cut a straight path to the chieftain and then hold your line. I will do the rest.' He turned to Varek. 'You will draw them out. Take the Vindictors straight into their front ranks. You will be massively outnumbered but numbers will not matter. You will only have to face them for a short time.'

He gripped his aetherstave and held it to the rain. Lightning danced along its length, bathing them in blue light.

'The storm is our blood!' he cried and the Anvilhearts roared his words back at him.

'Sigmar is our armour!'

Again, their cries tore through the fog.

'Once I have slain the chieftain,' he said, 'the God-King will raise a tempest. The greenskins will be deranged. Just as they were at the Claw-water. They will turn on each other. All we have to do is light the fuse.'

Since reaching the break in the fog, Arulos' stormsight had returned to him with more power than ever before. He could see his moment of glory so clearly now that there was no way he could doubt it. He saw himself consumed by power and light, united with the tempest as he levelled the enemy forces at Delium and broke the siege at Yndrasta's side, finally fighting as her equal, pounding Sigmar's wrath into the beasts that sought to devour his people. He would not fail Sigmar or Yndrasta. He would reach Delium.

'This is the only way,' he said. He tried to speak softly, despite the energy that was raging through him. He wanted Varek to know that he valued his opinions. 'A fast strike is the only way we can help the crusaders and still reach the muster at Delium. Do you understand, Varek?'

Varek nodded. 'I do, Stormspear.' He looked at the greenskins who were readying themselves for an attack, still howling and jeering. 'And I will make sure you have enough time to knock that savage to the ground.' He looked back at the greenskins. 'What are they doing now?'

Arulos assumed the greenskins were about to charge but, rather than rushing across the hillside, they were passing something forwards through their ranks as the chieftain howled commands, waving his spear in the direction of Ardent Keep. The front ranks parted their shields and more cages appeared, pushed forwards to the smaller, goblinoid creatures. The cages were much smaller than the empty ones heaped in front of the army and the goblins grabbed them and began stuffing things between the bars, giggling and screeching as they worked. The troops behind them shook their shields again, filling the valley with ululating laughter.

'Move now,' said Arulos, turning to Varek. 'I do not want–'

Before he could finish, the small greenskins opened the cages, grabbed the contents and hurled them down the hillside. As the objects left their hands, they looked like balls of feathers, but then they pounded wings and managed to right themselves as they hurtled into the valley.

'Birds?' Varek laughed. 'They're attacking the crusaders with birds?'

Arulos shook his head. 'Birds that are carrying something. Look. Bottles? Attached to their bodies.'

'Bottles?' muttered Varek, but before Arulos could reply, the greenskin chieftain howled again. This time it pointed its spear at the Anvilhearts. There was a thunderous din as the greenskins finally attacked, shields howling, charging across the turf on a wave of mud and laughter.

CHAPTER TWENTY-THREE

Niksar spotted Zagora near the nexus syphon. She was picking her way through bodies, her armour drenched in blood and her hammer hanging limply in her hands. He ran across the tor, battling through the crowds to reach her, but the Ardent Keep was in chaos.

Thanks to Ocella's insight, most of the animals had been driven away, but not before many hundreds of people had been gored. It was a massacre. Crusaders were sprawled all over the muddy hillside, either dead or howling in pain, clutching dreadful wounds and crying out for help. Priests and soldiers were rushing back and forth trying to help those they could, but most of the able-bodied were working frantically at the walls, hauling carts of blocks and mortar towards the unfinished sections of the fortifications. The rear gates had been closed and people were trying to work on, despite the dreadful sounds of the dying.

Niksar paused as he saw Kolgrimm, sitting near one of the groups of labourers. The cogsmith looked like he had been crushed. Rather than howling and berating the workers, he was slumped on one of the blocks, ignoring them and staring at his upturned palms. People were trying to talk to him but he did not seem to hear. He was barely recognisable.

Niksar considered heading over to him. His fury at Kolgrimm faded as he saw how broken he looked. Then he saw that Zagora was almost out of sight so he climbed onto an overturned cart and leapt over another group, landing heavily in the mud, and ran to a patch of open ground, trying to reach his sister before she vanished.

As everyone else tended to the wounded or fixed the walls, Zagora approached one of Kolgrimm's engineers, pointing to the columns of the domed building that held the nexus syphon. She seemed to be asking him something, pointing to the centre of the building. The stampede had had no effect on it. The columns were still shimmering with aetheric power and hurling it across the ground to each of the statues that guarded the walls. The light was burning brightly under the nexus syphon's dome and in the statues' chests, blazing out into the fog and rain. It should have been a glorious sight, but as Niksar clambered over the dying and the dead, he felt as though the light was mocking him, mocking them all.

He had almost reached Zagora when he noticed a familiar face in a pile of corpses. He stumbled, almost falling, as the strength went from his legs. It was Brod, one of the youths he had been chatting to less than an hour ago. They were all there, their bodies heaped in awkward, unnatural shapes. He stared at their grimacing faces, remembering how excited they had looked when he told them of Zagora's piety. He had filled them with hope. And this was where hope had led them. Taymar was there too, his fine, filigreed armour ripped open by a claw and the pages of his notebook scattered in the mud, but it was the young men that caused

Niksar's mouth to fill with bile. Taymar had come here looking for glory, but the boys hadn't. They were just ordinary soldiers. Simple lads from the city, probably born in the Veins.

'You should have left,' he whispered. 'I should have told you to leave.'

He stooped down and picked up one of Taymar's papers. It was a drawing of Sigmar, hammer raised as he led the crusaders to victory. From Taymar's age and manner, Niksar had assumed his drawings would be skilfully rendered, but the picture was pitifully amateurish. It looked like the work of a child.

He dropped it into the mud, shaking his head. All of this had begun when he told Zagora to try to sell the glimmering. All this death was on his head.

'Niksar!' Zagora slipped and stumbled down the muddy slope towards him. 'Are you hurt?'

He rose to meet her and they embraced, holding each other in silence for a long time, unable to speak. She backed away from him and looked him up and down. Her hair was growing back, coating her head in a downy fuzz, and the circlet was as encrusted in mud as the rest of her. Her face was skeletal and her eyes had a piercing intensity, as though she were staring at something far away.

'You saved us,' she said. 'If you had not mentioned the poison knives, we would never have known what was happening. We would have kept fighting them.'

Niksar looked around at the mounds of corpses. He guessed that half of the crusaders who reached the tor were now lying on it, either dead or dying. 'Saved us?'

She gripped his shoulder. 'You saved us. And we're close now. Look at the walls. There are only a few holes left to fill and Kolgrimm will have that sorted in the next hour or two. We have...' Her voice faltered and she looked hesitant, as she did in the morning when they were talking to Tyndaris.

Niksar peered at her. All the conviction had gone from her face.

'You've lost it, haven't you? Lost your faith in all this. You don't believe what you just said. You're just saying what you think you're supposed to say.'

Anger flashed in her eyes but it faded as quickly as it came and she looked away.

'What is it?' demanded Niksar. 'Tell me, by the God-King. Chiana's not here now. There's no one watching. Just tell me. What are you hiding from them all?'

She shook her head, colour draining from her face.

'I saw it in your eyes,' he said, 'this morning. You can't fool me. I know you, Zagora. None of the others out here do but I can see when you're lying.'

She collapsed, as if she had been punched in the stomach, and sat down heavily in the mud, slumping against her hammer and staring at the corpses of Brod and Taymar and the others, mouthing their names.

Niksar sat next to her and they leant against each other. 'I was just talking to them,' he said. 'Before the stampede. I told them how glorious all this is.'

He felt Zagora stiffen and then shake her head. 'This is not it,' she whispered.

'This is not what?'

'This is not the tor.'

Niksar turned to stare at her. 'Of course it's the tor. What else could it be?'

She nodded to a shape in the distance, beyond the walls of the keep, further down the valley. 'That is Faithful Tor. We've built in the wrong place.'

Niksar laughed, but when he realised she was being serious he shook his head. 'What are you talking about? How can it be wrong? We're near the Great Excelsis Road and Kolgrimm has

built a strongpoint. That's what we set out to do. How can it be
wrong? How can it matter which hill we're on?'

'It matters.' Her voice was flat. 'I couldn't see clearly. I've never
seen any of it clearly. Chiana told me not to show doubt but I've
doubted everything.' She placed her palm at her forehead, covering
the augur stone. 'Sigmar speaks to me, Niksar, he really does, but
he's hard to hear. *So* hard. His words make no sense. We reached
the valley, as we were meant to, but when I had to choose between
the tors Sigmar's voice was too faint. I had to choose. I couldn't
show any doubt.'

Niksar's belief in the crusade had died when he saw the dead
youths, but he could not bear to hear the pain in Zagora's voice.
'You've done everything those damned priests asked of you. You
got us here. You got us to this valley. And you got us to a place
where Kolgrimm could build his glorious palace.'

She turned to face him, her face rigid. 'I've seen what will happen,
Niksar. The nexus syphon was not built on the right location. We
are *near* the intersection of ley lines but not on it.' She nodded to
the lights in the statues. 'We harnessed power, but not enough.
Which means these walls will not hold even if Kolgrimm finishes
them.' She spoke so quietly he could barely hear. 'I have not been
true to the vision. That's why everything has gone wrong. That's
why the White Angels weren't here to meet us. That's why Arulos
and the Anvilhearts never came back. I have not acted in accordance with Sigmar's wishes. The walls will fall. The keep will not
survive. We built in the wrong place.'

'It can't all just be about faith and fate. Surely it matters what
we do. Surely it's about determination and courage too.'

'I brought us to the wrong place,' muttered Zagora. There was
such a terrible finality to her words that Niksar's arguments stalled
in his mouth.

Besides, he knew she was right. He had felt it when he saw

Taymar and the dead youths. Ardent Keep was doomed. They sat for a while, watching the miserable scene they had helped create. Then Niksar wiped the blood from his face and shook his head.

'None of this is our fault. Chiana and the others forced you into a role they invented. They probably knew this stupid crusade could never work. I imagine it was only ever a decoy. They just needed you to paint a veneer of holiness over what they were doing. We should go. We should leave them to the mess they've made.' He grabbed her wrist. 'We were born out here. We can survive in the wilds. Let's leave these fools to their prayers and head back to the city.' He felt his despair leaving him as the idea took shape. 'We could make it. Together, just me and you, we could get back to the city. And when we get there we'll never go near another damned crusade. What do you say?'

She gave him a sad smile and shook her head.

'Why not?' he demanded. 'Why should we stay? They tricked us into this. None of this is our fault. And now the whole place is coming down around their ears. It's over. You've seen it. And even if you hadn't I already knew it. Why should we stay here and die with them?'

'I won't leave them.' She spoke quietly, looking at the crusaders stumbling past, pulling carts laden with bodies and building materials. 'They put their trust in me. I won't betray them now.'

'Don't be a damned fool!' Niksar stood and glared down at her. 'Stop playing the blessed martyr. You've just told me we've failed. None of them are going to survive. What good can you do by dying with them?' Niksar stumbled back and forth, shaking his head, his pulse hammering in his temples. 'Let it go, damn it! You're only here because of my stupid greed.'

'They came here because they believed in me.' The more Niksar raged, the calmer Zagora became. 'They left their homes to follow me. I will stay with them until the end.'

Niksar gripped his head and shook it, as though trying to wrench it from his neck. 'You're insane!' He stopped and jabbed a trembling finger at her. 'No, you're not insane, you're addicted – addicted to this role they've given you. You can't bear the thought of being ordinary again. You'd rather be a dead Dawnbringer than a living Zagora.'

She was no longer looking at him, staring at the crusaders instead. The hopelessness had faded from her eyes and Niksar saw the same ecstatic expression she wore when she was onstage in Excelsis.

'I still have a role to play. Sigmar still has work for me here, I can feel it. I can still help them. Even now, after all of my mistakes, I can still do some good.'

Niksar's rage boiled through him, exploding from his lungs, producing a howl that made the nearest crusaders look round in surprise. He grabbed Zagora, dragged her to her feet and tried to pull the circlet from her head.

'I won't let you!' he cried, clawing at the glimmering as she tried to get away from him. 'I won't let it happen!'

'Let go, Niksar,' she said calmly as they wrestled, locked together, slipping and sliding down the hill.

'You're coming with me!' he cried.

Pain exploded on the side of his head and he found himself struggling to breathe, his mouth full of cold mud. He choked and coughed, then lurched up from the muck, gasping for air. He tumbled backwards and rather than Zagora, he saw the brutal, tattooed face of a zealot. The fanatic was gripping the piece of scaffold he had just used to knock Niksar to the ground. Zagora was a dozen feet back up the slope, struggling with more zealots who were leading her away from Niksar. A gang formed around him wielding clubs and iron balls on chains.

'Heretic!' spat one, landing a punch to Niksar's face. His head snapped back and he rolled down the hill with the zealots chasing after him.

'He attacked the Dawnbringer!' cried one of them, dragging howls of disbelief from onlookers. 'He tried to take the augur stone!'

Another zealot ran forwards and planted an ironshod boot in Niksar's stomach. A flurry of blows rained down on him until one of the zealots howled in pain and a familiar voice cried out.

'Back off! He's her brother. Get off him, you morons!'

Rough hands grabbed Niksar and dragged him, coughing and gasping, away from the mob.

'Stay back or the rest of you will get the same treatment!' yelled Haxor as she led Niksar to safety, her sword held before her. There was blood flowing down Niksar's face. As he wiped it away he saw that Haxor had wounded one of the zealots, leaving a deep gash across his chest. Zagora was far in the distance, being bundled away through the rain, so Niksar let Haxor lead him away, leaning on her as she waved her sword menacingly at the zealots before turning and pulling them both through the crowds.

'You're making so many friends,' she muttered, reaching a patch of dry ground under a tarpaulin and dropping them both down onto it.

Niksar was hurting too much to reply. He lay there for a few minutes, panting and staring at the stars while Haxor looked around to see if they had been followed. Then, when she sat back down next to him, he finally managed to sit up and speak.

'Thanks.'

She shook her head in disbelief. 'Fighting with the Dawnbringer. Trying to steal the glimmering. Does any of that seem wise to you?'

He groaned, clutching his head.

'You don't seem too badly hurt.' She patted down his clothes and turned his head from side to side. 'You're lucky. Those people love an excuse to burn somebody.' She laughed. 'Even when the world's already bent on killing us all.'

She handed him a flask of water and looked around at the corpses. 'What an unholy mess.'

'I'm getting out of here,' said Niksar through punch-swollen lips. 'I'm going.'

She looked shocked. 'Are you mad? That's a death sentence.' Then she narrowed her eyes. 'What did you talk about with your sister? What did she tell you?'

Furious as he was, he found it hard to tell Haxor the truth. It was breaking a confidence. His sister would hate him for it. But the words came anyway.

'It's all over. Zagora made a mistake. We're not meant to be here. This is the wrong hill so her prophecy counts for nothing. The walls are coming down. Whatever we do, this place is damned.'

'The wrong hill?' She stared at him. Then tears glinted in her eyes and she looked away. When she looked back at him the tears were gone and her expression was hard. 'Are you telling me the truth?'

He slumped back onto the ground. 'It's the truth. Zagora is going to stay to the bitter end because she feels guilty. But everyone here is going to die.'

Haxor punched the mud. 'Damn them all. The wrong place! It's like a bad joke.' She looked across the mounds of bodies to where Kolgrimm was slumped despondently near the unfinished wall. 'I believed in them. Especially Zagora.'

Niksar wanted to defend his sister, but there was nothing he could say. 'Come with me. I'm going to find a way back to Excelsis.'

'Across the wilds? On your own? You wouldn't last a day.' Despite her mocking tone, she looked closely at him. 'And even if you did, how would you sail back up that river?'

'I'm not going anywhere near the river. That was just a way to travel quickly. In a small group we could take other routes, on foot, hiding from predators.' He looked out into the darkness. 'If we can find Ocella, she would probably come too. I'm the only person she trusts. And she would be a big help.'

'The mad woman in the furs?'

'She understands the beasts that live out here. With her knowledge and your sword arm we'd have a chance.'

'What about your sister?'

He touched the blood that was still running down his face and shook his head. 'I can't...'

Words failed him so he simply shook his head.

'It's suicide.' She shrugged. 'But perhaps we should go. If your sister says this place is coming down, clearing out first might be our only chance.' Haxor looked out into the darkness. The fog was spreading over the tor, making the survivors look like spectres. 'Sigmar knows how we'd find your friend, though. It might have to be just the two of us.'

Niksar stood, leaning on Haxor and wincing at his various bruises. Then he limped out from under the tarpaulin, trying to guess where Ocella might be. The light from Kolgrimm's forge was fading and it was pumping out less smoke as the engines slowed.

'She might go there. There's something she would want to take back.' He was about to head in that direction when shapes started whistling overhead, cutting through the fog and smoke.

'Are they arrows?' asked Haxor, hurrying to his side and looking up. 'Bullets?'

One of the shapes turned above their heads and Niksar heard a flutter of wings. 'Birds?' Soon there could be no doubt as the air filled with the sound of flapping wings and harsh, crow-like cawing. 'This must be more of the same. They're attacking us with animals.'

Haxor laughed. 'With birds?'

They climbed up the slope, to a break in the fog, and looked across the tor. Lots of the crusaders had noticed the birds and were looking up at them, but no one seemed sure what to make of it. Then, near the gates of the keep, a mushroom of green fire blossomed in the darkness, hurling people through the air and causing flat-tusks to bolt. A fresh wave of screams followed the blast and Niksar heard the dull thud of body parts landing on the hillside.

He was about to say something when another blast ripped through the walls, billowing over the stonework. The lights in the statues pulsed and the walls did not break, but more bodies were thrown through the night. Three more detonations rocked the hill in as many seconds and people abandoned their carts, diving for cover as rubble and corpses rained down.

'This is it!' said Niksar in a pause between explosions. 'We have to go.'

'What about your friend?' replied Haxor, flinching as another blast lit the tor.

Niksar shook his head. 'We have to go.' He waved at one of the unfinished sections of wall. In the wake of a nearby blast, the workers and soldiers had scattered, leaving only a small group near the opening. 'We could get out that way.'

Haxor had to wait to reply as another explosion caused them both to crouch and cover their heads. Then she grabbed Niksar's arm. 'This looks like they're softening us up for the main event. What are we going to find on the other side of that wall?'

'A chance. And there's no chance on this side.' Niksar was filled with adrenaline and he knew his only hope was to let it carry him. If he stopped to think, his anger at his sister would fade and he would find it impossible to leave her. 'Now!' he snapped and ran down the hill.

There were hundreds of birds wheeling overhead and the

explosions were lighting up the hillside, bathing it in a green light that revealed the crusaders in horrible detail. They were routed, crashing into each other and trampling people underfoot as they tried to escape the explosions. Some of the soldiers tried shooting the birds down but it was no help: bullets triggered explosions in the air and arrows dropped birds from the sky, causing their bottles to explode when they hit the ground.

Niksar was still a hundred feet or so from the wall when Haxor called out and caused him to stumble to a halt.

'Is that her?'

Cowering under the porch of a building, staring at Niksar, was a hunched figure in rags.

'Ocella?' he called out. 'Is that you?'

She edged out into the panicked crowds, flinching and twitching as she crept towards him.

'Quickly!' cried Haxor, waving her over.

There was an explosion, only thirty feet from where Niksar was standing. He felt his feet lift from the ground. Then he thudded into the side of a building and cried out as bricks landed all around him.

He ignored the pain and heaved the bricks aside, staggering clear of the toppling building. Haxor was still standing and she rushed over to him. Her face was covered in soot and she shook her head.

'We really are out of time.'

He nodded and looked around. Ocella was nearby, cowering and staring up at the sky, holding her bone staff over her head as though it would protect her from falling rocks.

'Now!' cried Niksar, waving the two women on and continuing through the smoke.

They both followed, and as Niksar reached the wall he saw that the way was clear. Everyone had either been killed or had run for cover as more birds sliced overhead.

'Where are you going?' cried Ocella as she reached Niksar and grabbed his arm. She looked frantic, shaking and flinching as she stared back into the green fires. 'Were you going to leave without me?'

'No. Of course not. I knew you would be here.'

She nodded, accepting the lie without question.

'We're leaving,' he said. 'Everything is lost.'

'Not everything is lost,' she said.

'What?'

She nodded. 'I'm with you.'

Niksar was surprised at how relieved that made him feel. 'Good. Then let's move.'

Despite the force of his words, he hesitated, looking back into the carnage, trying to spot his sister in the flames. He could see priests near the temple, but Zagora was not with them. Then another explosion erupted nearby and Niksar climbed the wall, swung over the top and dropped into the darkness on the other side.

CHAPTER TWENTY-FOUR

Varek raised his standard to the wind as greenskins crashed into the shield wall. The Vindictors braced against the impact in stoic silence, digging their boots into the mud, their shields locked together. Then Varek led them forwards, a wedge of tarnished gold slicing into the filthy mobs of greenskins.

Arulos watched the fighting from further up the slope as he led the Annihilators to the ridge. With every step of the climb he felt the storm build in his bones. Sigmar was breathing new life into him. It flowed through the darkness, gilding the souls of his men. As he gathered the Annihilators at the top of the slope, their amour was already sparking. The aether burned brightest in their hammers and shields but every inch of them was aglow, hiding the damage wrought by the tar pits and making them look whole again.

'On my command,' he said, as the bulk of the greenskins poured down the hillside to Varek and the Vindictors. Their spears glimmered with the same fire. Rather than holding the line, Varek was leading the Anvilhearts relentlessly onwards, cutting into the greenskins so fast the creatures were already in disarray.

The chieftain was watching from afar and could clearly see what Arulos was doing. It was looking in his direction and giving commands to its subordinates, pointing its spear at Arulos but not actually pursuing him. Further down the hill, the smaller creatures were still hurling birds from their cages and, with his stormsight regaining its full potency, Arulos could see the results, looking through the fog at the destruction that was tearing through Ardent Keep. The crusaders were dying fast. And now the chieftain was waving the bulk of the army on, sending them down the slope to attack the keep in force. Again, the greenskins had shown a cunning he had never seen before. The assault proper was about to begin. Arulos had to make his move quickly if it was going to achieve anything.

'That is our line,' he said, pointing out the most direct route to the chieftain. 'Do not waver. And do not halt until we reach the chieftain, but do not overshoot your mark. I need you around me.'

The Annihilators pounded their chests. 'Anvil born!'

'Anvil born,' he replied, drawing his sword and starting to run.

The greenskins laughed as they saw him coming, but now that Arulos knew the sound was produced by their shields, it had lost its hold over him. He crashed into the front ranks. They toppled, shields exploding into splinters, spears buckling against his armour. Arulos swiped Arphax back and forth as he ran, surrounding himself in a whirl of body parts and broken armour. The renunciation stone pulsed, itching to be unleashed, but he left his aetherstave on his back, saving it for the chieftain.

The greenskins were not as broad as the orruks he had fought before but there was surprising strength in their wiry limbs. Arulos felt no fear as he fought them, and he was able to gauge them with cool disinterest, noting how they fought and moved.

It was not just their anatomy that seemed unusual; they fought more like men than greenskins: wily and cunning, trying to avoid facing him directly, crouching and cowering then lunging at the damaged parts of his armour. All around him, the Annihilators were swelling with the valour of Sigmar's storm. As they ran faster, their massive plates of armour grew indistinct, hazed by rivulets of lightning, burning with inner fire. Greenskins died before the Annihilators even reached them, trampling each other in a desperate frenzy to escape their inexorable force.

'Anvil born!' howled Arulos, his equilibrium finally broken, washed away by the magnificence of the charge. The Annihilators echoed his war cry, swinging their hammers with even more ferocity, blasting whole mobs of greenskins aside, flinging their wiry frames through the darkness and bejewelling the night with embers, unleashing constellations that danced and whirled around Arulos, until he felt as though he were falling through the heavens, just as Sigmar had done when he first reached the Mortal Realms, guided by the Great Drake, Dracothion.

Arulos was so lost in the wonder of Sigmar's wrath that he was surprised when he realised they had almost reached the chieftain. As most of the greenskins poured down the hillside towards Ardent Keep, the chieftain had held its position at the top of the incline, waiting for Arulos. The creature was slumped casually in its saddle, watching Arulos approach but making no attempt to defend itself. There were dozens of the heavily armoured, crossbow-wielding greenskins gathered around their chieftain, but even they seemed unconcerned by the golden thunderhead racing towards them. A momentary doubt needled Arulos but he shrugged it off, swinging Arphax with ever faster strikes, slicing through the final lines of creatures between him and the group at the top of the hill.

By the time they reached the chieftain the Annihilators were barely recognisable as individual warriors. The lightning playing over their armour was so fierce that they looked like a wall of aetherfire and Arulos had to howl to make them hear his command.

'Anvilhearts! Halt!'

The Annihilators dimmed and slowed, finally coming to a stop twenty feet from the chieftain and its honour guard. Arulos marched out in front, taking his aetherstave from his back.

Seen at close quarters, the chieftain was even more repulsive than Arulos had expected. It was as rangy and hideous as its troops, but it wore an absurdly grand, horn-crested helmet and its armour was draped in bloody trophies: teeth, half-decayed skulls and necklaces of human hands. Its steed was equally repulsive, four times the size of a normal hound with grotesquely enlarged muscles and a thick, scarred hide. Its snout was as big as a man's chest and its lips were curled in a rabid snarl, revealing teeth like sharpened stakes.

'By the God-King,' muttered Arulos as he felt the storm jangling through his bones. 'You will pay for what you did to Sigmar's people.'

The chieftain leant forwards in its saddle and laughed. The sound did not come from its shield but from its ragged, glistening mouth. The other greenskins did the same, pointing at Arulos and the Annihilators and howling.

Arulos looked around, confused. At the bottom of the slope, the greenskin army had reached Ardent Keep. Green flames were flickering on the far side of the walls and he could see figures silhouetted on the battlements. Despite the green pall, though, he could still see the light of the guardian statues burning around the walls. As far as he could make out, Kolgrimm had built a fortress worthy of Sigmar's people. With the power from the ley lines flooding the statues the walls would be impregnable, tempered by the wildness of Ghur itself.

'You will not take that keep,' he said, approaching the chieftain, his aetherstave raised before him. 'However many troops you throw against it.'

The chieftain yawned, then laughed again, fixing Arulos with its crimson stare.

'You…' it said, the word horribly mangled by its bestial mouth. 'Are… A… Fool.' As it spoke, the chieftain kicked its enormous hound in the flank so that it took a few steps sideways up the hill.

As the beast moved, it revealed another greenskin that Arulos had not seen, neither with his mortal eyes nor his stormsight. Anger knifed through him as he realised that the greenskins had managed to hide something from him for all this time. Even with the power of his god-given sight, he had never glimpsed the hunched, robed creature that was cowering behind the chieftain.

It was a shaman, draped in tribal fetishes, strings of bones and bundles of small, cloudy bottles that clinked as it moved. It was surrounded by a circle of iron cauldrons that were seething with pale fumes. This was the source of the blindness that had dogged him since he left the Claw-water. Fog was coiling from the iron pots and from the shaman's robes as it turned to look his way. The thing's face was hidden by the fumes but Arulos knew, instantly, that it was the shaman, not the chieftain, that had confounded him for so long. He rushed forwards, but as he tried to attack, he found that his feet were hanging over a void.

He cursed and tried to turn, trying to reach back towards whatever ledge he had fallen from. But there was no ledge. His hands grasped at nothing. All he could see was a seething miasma. The Annihilators had gone. So had the greenskins. Even the valley was gone. He was tumbling. He tried to look through his renunciation stone, to see into the storm, but there was only the fog.

Pain splashed across his side and he whirled around to see a quarrel jutting from his armour. The shot had landed in one of the places where his war-plate had been warped by the tar pits.

Sparks and blue flames danced around the ruptured metal. He cursed and wrenched the quarrel out, spilling sparks and blood.

'Face me!' he cried, whirling around, his feet standing on nothing. His fury was directed at himself. He could not bear the idea that he had let himself be drawn into another trap. He *would not* bring dishonour on the Hammers of Sigmar.

The only reply was waves of sneering laughter and another crossbow quarrel. This one slammed into the side of his chest. Again, it landed in one of the spots where the sigmarite had been corroded. The bolt sank deep. Pain jolted through him. He staggered, blood and lightning spilling from his ribs.

CHAPTER TWENTY-FIVE

'Watch out!' cried Haxor as a figure rose up from the darkness.

Niksar raised his sword, thinking she had spotted a predator, but then he saw it was a corpse, one of the Phoenix Company halberdiers, dangling from a post, little more than a skeleton and some rags.

'Into the trap,' said Haxor, pointing out the trench that gaped, mouth-like, in front of the corpse.

An ocean of monsters was thundering down the hillside. Greenskins and feral hounds were charging from the mist in their hundreds, perhaps thousands, racing towards Ardent Keep. Niksar and the others had only been outside the walls a few minutes when they realised they had walked right into an army. And this time it really was an army, full of armoured, hunched warriors clutching spears and swords. Haxor had suggested heading back but Niksar had refused. The keep was a death sentence. Zagora had made that clear. At least out here they had a tiny chance of escaping.

'We can hide in it,' said Haxor, shoving Niksar and Ocella towards the opening. They clambered down into the muddy pit. It was lined with crude, wooden spears that had been thrown up when the trap was sprung. There were three more corpses in the hole, hanging from the spears, their bodies as mangled as the soldier they had died trying to reach.

Niksar grimaced as he squeezed into the hole, hunkering down in the mud next to the corpses, but he saw that Haxor was right. The greenskin army was flooding towards the walls, frenzied and deranged; they were not likely to start rooting around in holes.

Ocella was crushed so close to him that he could feel her pet animals shuffling under her robes, snuffling and clawing. He could also smell them. The stink was even worse than the stench of death. He tried to back away from her but Haxor was pressed against his other side, trying to load her pistols in the dark.

'Why didn't the traps open until this morning?' asked Ocella.

He was only half listening to her, his mind full of thoughts of Zagora. Of all the wretched things he had done in his life, abandoning his sister was the lowest. She had saved his life countless times since they were children. His father had always made them swear to remember that family meant everything. 'The chain will be unbroken,' he muttered.

'They must be controlled manually,' said Ocella, babbling to herself. 'Rather than triggered by pressure.'

'What?' whispered Haxor. She looked at Niksar. 'What is she talking about?'

'The traps,' said Ocella. 'When we arrived in this valley we marched all over it. And none of these traps opened. They must be controlled manually. There must have already been greenskins hiding in this valley somewhere. They must have been watching us the whole time.' She continued chatting to herself, despite the fact that the other two were ignoring her. 'Or, perhaps, the controls were left unattended until this morning. I don't think even a greenskin could have lived in the mud all this time, watching us from underground while we built the keep.'

'None of it matters now,' snapped Niksar as cold blood and water seeped through his clothes. 'Don't you see? It was all for nothing. All these heroes and martyrs. Pointless.' He gripped his skull, trying to quell the madness that was trying to overcome him.

The drumming sound of the approaching army was growing louder. The hole would soon be overrun.

Haxor frowned at Ocella, clearly intrigued by what she had said. Then she looked out into the darkness. 'We should move further from the keep. They're going to pass right over this pit.' She pointed at a vague shape in the gloom. 'Look, there's another one, further down the valley. If we move now we can reach it before they get here. They won't see us in all this rain and fog.'

Niksar nodded, not really following her words but glad that at least one of them was still able to think. They clambered up the muddy slope and sprinted away from the keep, keeping their heads low as they ran. Birds were still fluttering overhead and green light was spilling from the keep as the flames continued to spread. Niksar could hear shouts from the battlements as the defenders readied themselves for the attack. Even now, some of the crusaders were not accepting defeat. He stumbled to a halt, looking back at them, unable to understand how they could face such a multitude and not despair.

'Look,' gasped Haxor, pulling him forwards and pointing something out. 'They're all linked.'

Niksar looked down at the mud and saw what she meant. The stampede had disturbed the ground so much it had uncovered stretches of pipe that ran under the mud, linking each of the traps. 'What of it?'

Haxor looked at Ocella. 'I'm just thinking about what she said.'

Light flashed nearby and they rushed on, stumbling and slipping until they reached the other trap and dropped down into it. There were more corpses slumped on spikes and, unlike the others, these bodies had not been mauled by anything. Somehow, this made them even more disturbing, their last pained cries still visible on their faces. This hole was at least a little larger and Niksar managed to keep clear of Ocella as she muttered to the shapes bustling in her furs.

Niksar and Haxor looked back across the hillside. The fog was growing thicker by the moment and the attacking army was wearing it like a vast cloak, trailing strands of mist as they reached the walls of the keep and hurled ladders against the bricks. They were met by a roar of defiance from the battlements and a storm of arrows and bullets.

'Is that her?' asked Haxor, pointing out a figure on the walls.

Niksar nodded. His sister was unmistakeable. Her white armour was flickering in the firelight and her hammer was raised to the clouds. Niksar could not hear her words but he could tell from her posture that she was crying out, not in fear but in determination. Banners gathered around her as the barrage of shots grew in ferocity. Niksar was hypnotised by the scene. Zagora knew that the keep would fall. She knew the crusaders could not win. But it did not matter to her. She was fighting with more passion than ever. Even from here, hundreds of feet away, he could feel power emanating from her; he could see it radiating through the other crusaders. There were Anvilhearts near her on the walls, but even the gold-clad immortals seemed shadowed by her. It was the most incredible thing Niksar had ever seen.

'I can't leave her,' he whispered.

'What?' Haxor stared at him. 'What are you talking about?'

'I can't betray her.' The realisation hit Niksar with a strange kind of relief. He was afraid, but he was not a coward. He was a cynic, but not a scoundrel. He could not do this. 'I can't leave.'

'We've already left!' Haxor looked like she might hit him. 'Look at those greenskins. Can you see the size of that army? Did you hit your head in that last hole? We couldn't get back through that lot even if we wanted to.'

Niksar felt more composed than he could remember feeling before. 'I can't do it. I can't leave her to face this alone. She's the better part of me. I have to fight for her. Even if it's useless, I have to fight for her.' He waved to the darkness at the far end of the valley. 'You go. I brought you out here. It's not fair to drag you back. If you take Ocella with you, you could reach Excelsis, I'm sure you could.'

Ocella looked up, alarmed. She had been talking to one of her animals but she stuffed it under her clothes and scrambled over to Niksar. 'Take me with her? What are you talking about? I'm staying with you.'

He shook his head and pointed at the army crashing around the keep. 'I'm headed back through that. I wasn't thinking clearly before.' He touched the cuts on his head where the zealots had injured him. 'I was angry and afraid. But now I understand. My place is with Zagora. I don't know how I'll get through all those greenskins, but I'm going to try.'

'I know how you can get through them!' cried Ocella, shaking and clutching at him. 'I'll tell you if you let me stay with you.'

'Just tell me,' he said. 'How can I get back through that army?'

'She means trigger the traps,' said Haxor. 'Don't you, Ocella?'

Ocella nodded. 'Only a few of the traps have been sprung. If we opened up the rest of them it would create a distraction. Lots of the greenskins would fall in holes. There would be confusion. And while the greenskins look around for the controls we would have a chance to get through them and back to the keep.'

'Don't sound so pleased with yourself,' said Haxor, glaring at Ocella. 'Think about what you'd be doing, heading back into that hell. The fight is over. Zagora said so. Niksar's only going back there to die with her. Why would you want to go with him?'

'He's not going to die.' Ocella spoke with a certainty that surprised Niksar. He studied her, trying to understand how she could sound so convinced. He could never quite tell if she was deranged or inspired.

'Those pipes you saw,' he said, looking at Haxor. 'They'd probably lead back to the controls, wouldn't they? That's what you were thinking, isn't it?'

She clutched her head in her hands, but nodded. 'How did I end up with you people?'

CHAPTER TWENTY-SIX

Arulos ignored the laughter and fought to calm his mind. If he gave in to his mortal emotions he would be lost. He had to remember who he was. He was anvil born. An avatar of the God-King. Memories of his training in Azyr steadied his nerves and he reassured himself that this must be an illusion. The greenskin shaman could not have dissolved the whole valley into mist. The ground must still be there. The hillside must still be there. The shaman had simply mesmerised him. Whatever his senses might tell him, he was still standing in the valley near the chieftain.

He thought back over the last few seconds and realised that he had not turned and had barely moved since being blinded by the greenskin sorcery. He was still facing in roughly the same direction, so, even though he could not see them, he must still be facing the chieftain and the shaman.

Arulos raised his aetherstave and pointed to where he thought his enemy should be. Calm certainty reunited him with the storm. Sigmar's blood filled his veins, sparking beneath his skin. He cried out and the aetherstave bucked in his grip, rattling his gauntlets, hurling lightning through the fog.

There was a shocked howl and the hillside flowed back into view. Arulos' aim was true. The shaman was lying on its back, blackened and scorched, struggling to stand. The howl had come from the chieftain. The warlord's face was contorted with rage and it pointed its spear at Arulos, roaring a command.

Arulos stumbled backwards as another crossbow bolt slammed into him, punching through a hole in his armour just below his diaphragm, lodging into his stomach. His stormsight remained vivid, giving him glimpses of combat from right across the valley, but his physical sight started to fade. He tried to raise his staff again, but the strength had gone from his limbs and he dropped to one knee.

At the bottom of the valley, the greenskins had reached the keep and were hurling ladders against the walls, but the chieftain paid them no attention, riding towards Arulos, trembling and spitting with rage. Arulos looked around and saw that the Annihilators were now scattered across the hillside, their perfect ranks broken. The fog must have beguiled them in the same way it had him. They were isolated from each other. The momentum that had carried them forwards with such force was gone and they now looked like proud bastions, towering over the jabbering mobs that were crashing against them. If they had noticed Arulos' injuries, there was nothing they could do to help him. The crush of bodies around them was dozens deep. They were trying to deal out hammer blows, but there were so many of the greenskins heaped against them they could barely move.

The shaman died with a grunt and the effect on the valley was instant: the fog immediately began dissipating, leaving a clear, starlit battlefield. He saw the battle clearly. Arrows were raining down from the walls of Ardent Keep, but they were landing on a roof of tightly packed, grinning shields.

Arulos tried to stand as the furious chieftain reached him, but his legs refused to obey.

The chieftain reared up in its saddle and pointed its spear at the walls of the keep. Waves of greenskins were swarming up towards the battlements, climbing ladders that had been locked somehow to the stonework.

'End!' roared the chieftain, spitting and shaking its head. 'Of empires!' Then it dropped from its saddle, gripped its spear in both hands and ran through the mud.

Arulos finally managed to stand, leaning heavily on his aetherstave, but his head was spinning, dazed by blood loss, and he struggled to focus on his enemy.

'Anvil born!' howled Varek as he and the Vindictors smashed through the enemy lines and raced up the hill, spears lowered and shields raised.

The chieftain wavered, then backed away and leapt back up onto the giant hound, kicking it so that it reared up and howled. It looked back, shivering with rage, still glaring at Arulos.

'I will have... Your... Head!' it snarled. Then it kicked its heels into the hound's side and raced off into the darkness.

The greenskins with crossbows only managed to loose a few shots before the Anvilhearts collided with them, plunging storm-bright spears through crudely wrought armour. Pride and relief gave Arulos a rush of vigour and he waved his aetherstave with such force that thunderbolts fanned out through the mayhem, incinerating and rending as they blazed through the darkness.

The chieftain charged back into view and the hound locked its jaws around Arulos' armour, grabbing him by the arm and shaking its head, trying to hurl him through the air. Arulos cracked his aetherstave across the monster's muzzle with a flash of power. The hound reeled away from him, howling and rearing up on its hind legs. The chieftain cried out, yanking furiously at the reins.

Arulos staggered after them, drawing back his staff to hurl another bolt, then he toppled to the ground, blood and embers tumbling through the holes in his armour. His vision swam. It seemed as though lightning bolts were landing all around him, tearing down from the stars and thudding into the hillside.

Spears slammed into the hound as Varek and the Vindictors rushed through his peripheral vision. The hound reared again, then collapsed onto its haunches, snarling and coughing blood. The chieftain leapt clear and bolted into the crowds of greenskins, vanishing from view with another outraged howl.

'Knight-Arcanum!' cried Varek, racing over to him and helping him to stand. 'Sigmar's throne! You're wounded.'

Arulos shook his head. 'No matter. It is not my time, Varek. I am not destined to be slain by this rabble.'

'We have to get you to safety,' said Varek, sounding unconvinced, looking at all the crossbow quarrels that were jutting from his armour. 'We will have to get into the keep. We could treat your wounds there. They will have healers.'

'No!' Arulos looked around. The Vindictors had formed a circle and were lunging at any greenskins that came close, but most of the enemy were already halfway down the hill, racing to join the legions that had gathered around the keep. 'You were right. We can't be drawn any further into this.' He tried to shrug Varek off and walk away, but he almost fell again and had to reach out for Varek's shoulder. He stood for a moment, his breathing laboured as he looked out into the darkness. The fog was almost entirely gone now, from the top of the slope, and he could see the greenskins clearly. 'Where is Gerrus? And the other Annihilators?'

Varek shook his head. 'Did you not see the lightning?'

'What are you talking about?' demanded Arulos with a growing sense of dread as he recalled the flashes of light he had seen when he was fighting the chieftain.

'They fell, Arulos. Even they could not stand alone against so many.'

'They fell?' Arulos laughed. 'Rubbish.'

Varek shook his head and pointed his sword to dark, smouldering craters that peppered the hillside. Each blackened hole was surrounded by mounds of greenskin dead. 'They died bravely, Knight-Arcanum. They re-joined the storm with their honour intact.'

'No. It cannot be.' Arulos managed to stand unaided and limp down the slope, staring at the craters. 'All of them?'

Varek nodded.

Anger threatened to overcome Arulos. He had to stare into the heart of the renunciation crystal to centre himself. Even then, with the full might of the stone shining into his thoughts, Arulos teetered on the brink of fury. The Annihilators had been destined to aid Yndrasta. And now they would never be able to lend their might to her cause. They would never answer her call. They were immortal, as all Stormcast Eternals were, but their journey back to High Azyr would be long and hazardous. Who knew what form they would take if they were remade on the Anvil of Apotheosis? And whatever shape they took when they were reborn, it would be no use to Yndrasta. By that time, her battle would be a matter of history.

'I have to find that chieftain,' he said, managing to keep his voice level as he strode towards the receding greenskin army. He had only taken a few steps when the ground seemed to rush up and slam into him.

'We have to join the others in Ardent Keep,' said Varek, helping him back up and waving some of the Vindictors over to help.

'No. We can't let ourselves...' Arulos' mouth filled with blood and bile and he could not finish his words.

'We have no choice,' said Varek, helping him across the mud. 'I will not let you die on this hill.'

CHAPTER TWENTY-SEVEN

Niksar scrambled across the hillside, pawing at the muddy turf, following the route of the pipes as Haxor and Ocella stumbled after him. With every moment that passed, the greenskin army seemed to double in size. And as it spread out across the hillside, it moved ever closer to them. The fighting on the walls was already desperate. Dozens of greenskins had managed to scale the embrasures and some of them had formed groups on the top of the wall, holding their position however furiously Zagora and the crusaders tried to drive them back.

'It could be anywhere,' he muttered, peering into the darkness. 'We should split up and see if we can—'

His words were cut off as a figure loped into view. It was a crook-backed, greenskinned horror, as tall as Niksar and gripping a spear in its bony hands. It sniggered as it padded across the mud, followed by a second equally hideous creature that swaggered in its wake.

It was the first time Niksar had seen one of them close up and he realised how different these monsters were from the ones they had fought on the banks of the Claw-water. The thing was tall and wiry, with gaunt, almost human features and there was a look of hard cunning in its eyes. The creature howled with laughter as it leapt at Niksar, jamming its spear at his chest.

He sidestepped and drew his sword in time to parry a blow from the other greenskin.

Then there was a bang and a flash of light and the first greenskin toppled back into the mud, a blackened hole where its face had been. Haxor rushed forwards, her pistol smoking as she drew her sword. The second greenskin hesitated long enough for Niksar to lash out with his sword and send the monster tumbling back in a shower of blood.

A third greenskin rushed towards him, drawing back a sword to strike, but it crumpled to the ground, knocked senseless by a blow from Ocella's staff. The three of them stood back-to-back, looking around for more attackers, but none came.

'Keep moving,' said Niksar. They raced on, still following the pipes through the mud.

'It's there!' cried Ocella a few minutes later, letting out one of her abrasive laughs as she pointed out a large rectangle of grass.

The other two rushed to join her, and together they pulled the hatch back and revealed a deep, crypt-like chamber under the sod. It was bare apart from a wooden frame at one end that bristled with levers. They dropped the hatch onto the grass and jumped into the hole. Niksar landed awkwardly and grimaced, his bruises reminding him of his encounter with the zealots. Even with the sounds of battle raging all around them he found himself staring at the machine in disbelief. Lightning flickered somewhere in the darkness, at the rear of the greenskin army. There was a chorus of distant laughter and jeering.

'Let's get on with it then,' said Haxor, looking at Ocella. 'What do we do? Just pull them all back?'

Niksar shrugged, grabbed a lever and yanked it back. Outside, somewhere in the distance, they heard howls of surprise.

Haxor nodded, grabbing one of the handles.

CHAPTER TWENTY-EIGHT

Pain and blood loss combined to give Arulos the impression he was gliding down the hillside. He could feel Varek under one of his arms and a Vindictor under his other, but the thought of being carried was a distant one. Since the Anvilhearts had started their rush towards Ardent Keep, Arulos had fallen deep into the whirlwind. The shaman's fog was gone, leaving him free to embrace the aether tides. He was searching furiously for the fate he had beheld so many times before. But when it came, it was a torment.

He saw it just as vividly as he had always done. He was with Sigmar's angel, Yndrasta, her wings spread across a great battle as she drove the God-King's enemies from Delium and freed the souls trapped within its walls. The Anvilhearts were with him, but that was the torment: they were clad in perfect, gleaming sigmarite, and he knew that was a lie. All of them had been ruined by the tar pits. Their armour, in truth, was tarnished and twisted into ugliness. So his vision of gleaming triumph, at Yndrasta's side, the vision he had pursued for so long, was false.

'What is this?' cried Varek, stumbling to a halt.

The other Anvilhearts cried out too, pleased and delighted, so Arulos dragged his thoughts back to his shameful wreck of a body and tried to see what had excited them.

The ground was devouring the greenskin army. For a moment, Arulos thought it must be a hallucination brought on by pain, but he could hear from the cries of his warriors that this was reality. He tried to focus, staring at the confusing scene. All around Ardent Keep, sections of the greenskin army were dropping from sight. Then Arulos saw the reason: platforms were sliding from beneath their feet, revealing spear-lined pits.

'How?' he managed to croak.

'Traps!' cried Varek. 'The crusaders must have put them there in preparation. They must have known the greenskins were coming. Stop here!' He halted and waved for the others to do the same. 'We don't want to fall foul of them ourselves. Wait here.'

The small number of greenskin stragglers nearby were not brave enough to attack the Anvilhearts alone, so Arulos and the others were able to watch the scene unfold in relative peace. Whole swathes of enemy troops were falling from view, and none of them re-emerged from the holes. The host quickly lost its momentum as greenskins tried to flee back up the hill and escape the traps, only managing to fall into identical traps on the higher slopes. Fights broke out among the enemy lines and Arulos tried to spot the chieftain. A leader of any worth would be rallying his forces and regrouping them, but the chieftain was nowhere to be seen.

'They need to attack,' he gasped, leaning closer to Varek and trying to raise his voice above a croak.

'What, Knight-Arcanum?'

'This is their one chance, while the enemy is in disarray. The crusaders need to attack. Once the traps have all been triggered, the greenskins will regroup and attack.'

'But we have no way of signalling to them.'

'If they see us attack…' Arulos was struggling to breathe and he had to scrape his words from his throat. 'If they see us charging… They will follow suit. They will understand. Zagora will understand. She sees me. She sees into the storm.'

'That would be our last move.' Varek did not sound afraid, he simply wanted to clarify. 'If we lead the Vindictors into the centre of that host, we will not come out the other side.'

Arulos remembered his vision. 'It was a lie, Varek.'

'A lie?'

'I saw us reaching Delium. I saw us fighting with Sigmar's winged angel. But that can never come to pass.' He stood erect, managing to straighten his back and lift his chin. 'So if this is to be our end… Make it worthy, Varek. Make it count.'

'Here? We make our stand here?'

'This is where we are meant to be, Varek. I see it now. This was never a detour. This was never a delay. *This* is our purpose. This moment.'

Varek stared at him, then looked up at the stars, rain flooding over his ruined amour. 'Then we will make it a glorious moment.' He turned to the other Anvilhearts. 'Gather round.'

As the others approached he planted his standard in the ground and called out to the storm, his voice chiming like a great bell.

'For Sigmar!' he cried.

'For Sigmar!' cried the other Anvilhearts, as the threads in the banner rippled with an inner fire.

'For the Anvil!' cried Varek.

'For the Anvil!' they all cried together and the banner flashed so bright that even Arulos was dazzled. For a moment he saw all of them with him in the storm, weapons raised as the tempest howled around them. Then he was back in the rain-lashed mud. But not everything had returned to how it was.

Arulos looked down at his armour in disbelief. The black marks had vanished and the rents had healed. Beneath the sigmarite his body was still ruined, but his battleplate was restored, as glorious as the day it was first forged. The others were the same. He was surrounded by a circle of gleaming, noble heroes, their shields blinking with strands of aetherfire and their spear tips shimmering.

The sight of the Anvilhearts renewed gave Arulos a burst of strength. He shrugged off the Vindictor who was helping him to stand, raising his sword to the heavens.

'When the last traps have been sprung, we charge.'

They moved to pound their chests but he held up a hand.

'A last chance. Do you understand? Who can say what plans Sigmar has for our souls, but this will be where we lay down our bodies for him. Here, in this mud, among this vile host, we will show the God-King our worth.'

They bowed their heads, whispering prayers.

The wind rose around them, lashing against their flawless armour, hurling rain through the night.

CHAPTER TWENTY-NINE

Niksar fell every few seconds as he tried to reach the keep. The advancing army had churned up the mud, making it impossible to find purchase and, as he neared the gate, he abandoned all attempts to stay hidden. The greenskins were in a frenzy anyway, struggling to avoid the pits he had opened and battling against each other to reach the patches of safe ground. It looked more like a riot than an attack. The traps had killed dozens of greenskins, but their panicked response was going to kill hundreds. Their superiors waded through the mayhem, lashing out with whips and clubs, barking commands, but no one could hear them over the tumult.

'They're deranged!' gasped Haxor, struggling to keep up with him while stopping Ocella from wandering off in the wrong direction. 'I didn't think it would panic them quite this much.'

A greenskin noticed them and lunged in their direction, snarling and raising a jagged knife. Niksar drew back his sword to strike but Haxor had already thrust forwards, impaling the thing with her blade. It called out to the others as it died, but they were growing more frenzied by the second and none of them paid any heed.

'Look,' said Ocella, pointing her staff back up the hill. 'It's not just the traps that have unnerved them.'

Further up the slope, golden light was flickering through the rampaging greenskins and Niksar caught a glimpse of gleaming armour.

'Arulos! He came back!'

For a moment, the three of them stood and stared, hypnotised by the glorious sight of the Anvilhearts charging down the slope, Varek's battle standard held high and lightning flickering across their shields. It looked like Sigmar had hurled a golden blade through the enemy ranks. Ocella was right, it was the sight of Stormcast Eternals, combined with the opening of the traps that had created such turmoil in the greenskin army. For a few, glorious minutes it looked as though Arulos and his small band of warriors were going to rout the entire greenskin host but, slowly, as the greenskins realised that no more traps were going to open and that they outnumbered the Anvilhearts more than ten to one, they began to slow their advance.

The charge of the Anvilhearts stalled and finally stopped as they became mired in the crush. Greenskins attacked from every direction and the Stormcast Eternals formed a circle, fighting back-to-back as greenskins clambered towards them in droves, hurling spears and swinging swords.

As they grew less panicked, more greenskins noticed the humans in their midst and began rushing at Niksar and the other two, forcing them to fend off blows and stagger backwards through the mud. As he fought, Niksar saw one of the Anvilhearts vanish under a wave of greenskins then, moments later, the night turned silver as lightning slammed into the hillside, landing where the

Stormcast Eternal had fallen. The blast washed through the enemy lines, hurling greenskins through the night.

'Sigmar has taken him,' gasped Ocella, clubbing a greenskin to the ground with her staff then pointing to where the lightning had struck.

Niksar struggled to see, blinded by the afterglow. Then another bolt slammed down followed by two more in quick succession. The glare was blinding and each blow had the same effect as the first, hurling waves of lightning through the enemy and obliterating dozens of greenskins.

'Is that a weapon?' he asked. 'How are they doing that?'

'They're dying,' said Ocella.

'They're immortal,' said Haxor, parrying a spear and cutting down her attacker. 'They don't die. They're leaving the Mortal Realms. Returning to the God-King.'

'Sounds like dying to me,' grunted Ocella, lashing out at another greenskin with her staff.

As they watched thunderbolts rain down, Niksar fought with less fury, his blows weakened by exhaustion, but also by the misery of the scene. Sigmar's invincible warriors were being torn down. And Ardent Keep would be next. He sensed the final moment of his life fast approaching and wished he could have spent it at his sister's side.

'I'm such a fool,' he muttered.

Ocella paused to look his way, about to say something, but before she could speak a new sound echoed across the valley. It was almost as loud as the lightning had been but it was different: a deep, resounding clang.

'The gates!' cried Haxor, laughing.

At the foot of the keep, the gates had sprung open and the crusaders were spilling out into the night. There was a column of the high-born knights mounted on their armoured demigryphs and they were flanked by the Anvilhearts who had been watching the walls. Behind them came a great host of Freeguild soldiers, warrior priests, chain-swinging zealots and civilians carrying torches and clubs – every one of the crusaders who could still stand. And at the head of the charge was Zagora. She was riding a white stallion clad in battleplate and she was standing in the saddle, hammer raised, howling in defiance. The augur stone at her brow caught the firelight, glinting like a fallen star.

'For Excelsis!' she roared, her voice carrying across the tumult. 'For Sigmar!'

'For Sigmar!' echoed every man, woman and child who could still draw breath, hundreds of ragged throats that sounded like thousands.

Niksar reeled from the sight, shaking his head in wonder, then he answered his sister's call, crying, 'For Sigmar!' as he leapt into battle.

The counter-attack was so unexpected that the crusaders tore straight up the side of the valley, hacking and pounding the greenskins into the mud as though they were an army twice the size. Niksar leapt, sliced and punched his way through the press, moving so fast that Haxor and Ocella struggled to keep pace. As he fought he saw Zagora lead her host straight towards Arulos and the few Anvilhearts who were still fighting with him.

Then Niksar found himself back with his own kind, surrounded by gaunt, grim-faced humans rather than leering, frenzied greenskins. He knew, immediately, that he had made the right choice. Whatever happened now, he had done the right thing. He had come back. He called out to Zagora, wanting her to know he was there, wanting her to know that he had not left her, but she was too far ahead. The noise of battle was too fierce. Captain Tyndaris saw him though, nodding in recognition as he galloped past, firing his pistol into the howling greenskins. The captain was grinning savagely as he fought, shoving his gun back in his belt and drawing his sabre, cutting down everything in his way, riding his steed furiously up the hill.

Finally, as the crusaders reached the remaining Anvilhearts, Zagora reined in her horse and leapt from the saddle to speak with Arulos. This was Niksar's chance. He sprinted through the battle, not pausing to exchange blows, determined to let Zagora know he was with her.

Freeguild soldiers and Stormcast Eternals had formed a circle around Zagora and Arulos, but they did not challenge Niksar as he ran through their lines, heading for his sister. It was only as he reached the crusade leaders that he saw Arulos had been wounded. His armour was unmarked but he limped as he fought. Niksar could only see ten Anvilhearts, including Arulos, but they were such a magnificent sight in their flawless armour that he could almost imagine them defeating the entire greenskin army.

Chiana was wounded too, leaning on two priests for support, her robes dark with dried blood. He was relieved to see that Zagora was unharmed, her white armour shining through the gloom as she talked urgently to Arulos.

The circle of warriors surged and swayed as the greenskins tried to break through, but they held their line, buying enough time for their leaders to exchange a few quick words.

'Zagora,' cried Niksar as he rushed towards her.

Relief flashed across her face as she heard his voice and looked around for him. She waved briefly but seemed desperate to explain something to Arulos. He was shaking his head, as though he could not grasp her meaning, and Zagora kept looking up the slope and back at the keep. As he got closer, Niksar saw that there was a change in her. The despair had left her eyes. Her expression was grim but determined. *She has hope again,* he thought. *This is not just a last stand. She sees a way out.*

Finally, as Niksar reached the centre of the circle, Arulos nodded, grasping whatever Zagora had been trying to explain.

'I need a small force of soldiers,' said Zagora, turning from Arulos and calling over to Tyndaris. 'Twenty. The bravest you have. To accompany me and the Anvilhearts.'

Tyndaris nodded, backed his horse away from the fighting and waved at a group of soldiers, sending them over to Zagora.

'Let me help,' cried Niksar, grabbing his sister's hand.

She stared at him, her eyes wide, as if he were the most glorious prize she could have imagined. 'The chain...' she said, her voice wavering.

He nodded and hugged her. 'What now? What do we have to do? I can see you have a plan.'

She nodded to where Chiana and Kolgrimm stood a short distance away. 'You will go with them.'

'Go with them where? I'm not leaving you again.'

There was an explosion of noise further up the incline and some of the crusaders began staggering backwards as the greenskins surged down the slope towards them.

'We have to move quickly!' cried Varek, fighting furiously alongside the other Stormcasts to maintain the circle around them.

'It's here!' cried Arulos, shrugging off the people who were holding him up and gripping his staff. 'I see it, Dawnbringer! The chieftain is here.'

She nodded and turned back to Niksar. She pointed her hammer at a hill further down the valley. 'That's where we have to make our stand. That's where we were always meant to be. I made a mistake, but now I see that it's not too late. You and Kolgrimm and Chiana are going to lead the crusaders to that hill. Once you're there, everything will be right. We will be acting in accordance with Sigmar's will, just as the glimmering showed. The crusade can still succeed. These people can still live. I understand it now. I have seen the way.'

'But you're not coming with us?'

'I have one last thing to do.' She pointed down to Ardent Keep. 'Without Kolgrimm's keystone there is no way to rebuild. I have to…'

'Rebuild?' Niksar's mind baulked at the idea.

'Yes. Rebuild. On the tor that was prophesised. Ardent Keep must be built properly, where it was always meant to be built.'

Soldiers fell back towards them as greenskins broke into the circle before being brutally cut down. Arulos staggered up the slope and hurled lightning across the hillside. There was a brief, distant flash. Bodies tumbled through the rain.

'Now!' growled Arulos, lurching past Zagora and staggering down the hill.

'I'm coming with you too,' said Niksar.

Zagora rounded on him, furious. 'Do not fail me, brother! Not in this. I *need* you to get these people to that damned hill. I can't do it all by myself, Niksar. I need you.'

In that moment, he did not know her. She was magnificent. And terrifying. He stumbled away from her.

'I will… Of course…'

The fighting grew in ferocity and Tyndaris howled orders, directing nobles and soldiers across the valley, sending them to the tor that Zagora had pointed out. Niksar hesitated, watching his sister and the Anvilhearts rush in the other direction, rushing towards the burning keep. Then he went where Zagora had ordered him.

CHAPTER THIRTY

Arulos was adrift in the storm. Thunderheads crashed, filling his lungs. Lightning coursed through his eyes, revealing the heart of the land. Revealing truth. As he fell through the clouds, he saw the Dawnbringer ahead of him, hammer blazing in the starlight as she rode the storm. In another place, in another life, he knew he was broken, limping and staggering through flaming corpses, moments from death, leaning on a mortal soldier for support as he followed Zagora through clouds of sparks. It was a wretched dream. Reality was in the firmament, where his mind was intact and his body still whole. Where he would never die. But he forced himself to focus on the shadows below.

'Are they following?' he asked, looking back through the flames at the other Anvilhearts.

'All of them,' said Varek. 'They are barely even harrying Tyndaris. They're sending everything after us. I can't understand it. They could be butchering those people.'

'It's me the chieftain wants,' said Arulos. 'All this time it's had me hunting it down, but now the tables are turned. I robbed it of its best weapon and now it can't bear the thought of letting me go.'

The keep was collapsing all around them as Zagora led them on through the fumes. Arulos slipped between realities until he could no longer distinguish between them. A temple appeared ahead of them in the clouds: grand columns supporting a dome, painted with frescoes and edged with sigmarite. The God-King was there. He was waiting for them. Arulos could feel Sigmar's wisdom. And his omnipotence. It blazed through the columns and flagstones. Sigmar was in the mortar and the air. The temple burned with his will.

'I know where to go,' said Zagora, rushing up the steps onto the dais.

Arulos was about to follow her into the light but the other reality clouded his vision. He saw corpses on a muddy hill and mobs of greenskins gathering outside burning buildings, laughing as they approached.

'For Sigmar!' bellowed Varek as the Anvilhearts rushed at the enemy. Thunder rolled as the Stormcast Eternals ripped into the greenskins, shimmering as they fought, mercury poured through oil.

Arulos raced into the fray, sword raised, answering Varek's call. Alongside the Stormcast Eternals came the mortal soldiers – Freeguild halberdiers and nobles on lionine steeds who fought with the same fury as the Anvilhearts, howling prayers and battle cries. The greenskins crumbled before them, shocked by the amount of havoc that could be wreaked by such a small group of warriors. For several, glorious minutes, the Anvilhearts and the mortals drove the greenskins back through the burning buildings, cutting them down in swathes. But slowly, as hundreds more of the monsters crowded into view, teeming like rats over the broken walls, they started to slow the crusaders' advance, overwhelming them with dozens upon dozens of bodies until Sigmar's chosen could barely move for the crush. The mortals showed no fear as they died, torn apart by the greenskins, howling in defiance even as they fell.

Varek was the first Anvilheart to fall. The explosion was so fierce that dozens of greenskins were thrown back, bones shattered and skin burned away by Varek's death blast. Then others followed, filling the night with seismic booms as they fell.

Arulos fought on, not stopping to consider the losses, thinking only of how many greenskins he could slay in Sigmar's name. Finally, he was alone, driven back towards the domed temple, his armour drenched in blood and mounds of bodies heaped around him. Greenskins began to land blows on his armour, singling out the places where he had already been wounded, sensing his weakness. Then, finally, as Arulos staggered back up the steps, gasping for breath, he saw the chieftain shoving its way through the mob. The creature had no steed but it was far bigger than all the other greenskins, tall enough to stand face-to-face with Arulos as it reached him. It leered at him, drool hanging from its jaws as it waved its spear at the destruction it had wreaked on the keep.

'End. Of. Empires,' it spat.

'Not the end,' said Arulos, too quietly for the creature to hear. 'Just the beginning.'

As the chieftain frowned, straining to catch his words, Arulos thrust his aetherstave forwards and hurled lightning through the fire, summoning all his last reserves of energy for a final attack.

The chieftain raised its shield to catch the blast. To Arulos' surprise, the shield held and the aether washed harmlessly over its grinning surface. It must be warded by greenskin sorcery, he realised, perhaps by the shaman he had killed. Arulos dropped to his knees, exhausted, blood rushing from the joints of his armour. As the lightning died away, the chieftain laughed and swaggered towards Arulos, preparing to hurl its spear at his chest.

There was a blur of movement and the chieftain stumbled sideways, sending the spear wildly off target so that it missed Arulos entirely and thudded into a door.

The chieftain roared in frustration as it saw its attacker was one of the Freeguild soldiers who had returned to the keep with Zagora and the Anvilhearts. The greenskin broke the man's neck with a single wrench and hurled him through the smoke.

But as the chieftain turned back towards Arulos it snarled in shock. Arulos had seized his chance, using the distraction to lurch back to his feet and draw his sword. The chieftain barely had the chance to howl before Arulos lashed out, beheading it with a single swipe.

'This way!' cried Zagora from behind him as the greenskins turned on each other, incensed and excited by the death of their chieftain. A savage fight broke out as the monsters vied for power.

Arulos was drowning in pain from countless wounds but he managed to turn and stumble back up the steps of the dais. His armour was sparking and breaking, leaking light and blood as it came apart. He was close to the storm now. He could feel it. It was rising in his chest.

'Quickly!' cried Zagora.

Arulos struggled to follow her words as music swelled around him. A hymn. A hymn he had learned in Azyr, before he was remade on the Anvil. He whispered the words. 'He rides the storm to conquer.' The music consumed him, robbing time of its meaning.

Finally, after what seemed like years, he was reminded that he was not alone.

'Now,' said Zagora, stepping through the light. 'It is time. They are all here. The entire host.'

Arulos caught another glimpse of the burning keep. Hundreds of monsters had surrounded them, jeering and pointing.

He dropped to his knees and looked up into the dome. It was not architecture any more. It was a comet, burning impossibly bright, trailing two tails of golden fire. As his armour fell apart, aetherfire poured from his wounds and rushed into a stone in the centre of the floor, filling it with light.

'We must ascend.' Arulos could not tell if they were his words or Zagora's. 'Soon, we will see the God-King's face.'

Arulos remembered something. A mistake he had once made. 'It was you,' he said, looking at Zagora. She was standing over him, her hammer raised to the tumult and, as the flames rose behind her, they looked like vast, spreading wings. This was the moment Arulos had sought for so long. Not at Delium but here, at Ardent Keep.

'It was you,' he said. 'All along. Not Yndrasta. It was you I was sent to join. *You* are my destiny.'

Zagora smiled. 'Sigmar knew you would stop that chieftain before it stopped me.'

The greenskins' jeers grew louder, threatening to ruin the sanctity of the moment.

'Time to leave,' she said, looking at Arulos' fragmenting armour.

'But you are mortal.'

'I am not afraid.'

The light grew, passing through them, spreading into the cosmos. And then it became a roar.

A wordless cry of vengeance.

CHAPTER THIRTY-ONE

The crusaders were halfway down the valley when Ardent Keep exploded. Almost all of the greenskins were inside. The blast rocked the hillside, shaking the whole valley. Niksar and the others halted, staring in disbelief. A column of pure white lanced up into the clouds, brighter than any of the preceding thunderbolts. Then it vanished and a fireball rushed to take its place. One by one the guardian statues detonated, adding their light to the inferno before turning dark and toppling into the flames. There were no screams from the keep. The blast was too fast. Too fierce. But as the crusaders on the hillside registered the loss of Zagora, they began to wail.

'She must have got out.' Niksar's skin turned cold with shock. The blast had been so powerful. Even the walls had been vaporised. There was nothing but fire and smoke where the greenskin army had been. 'She must have primed some explosives. And then left.'

Haxor and Ocella were at his side. They both looked away and did not reply.

At the front of the group, Tyndaris cried out commands, warning people that there might still be greenskins lurking in the darkness, ready to attack, but no one listened. Then even Captain Tyndaris fell silent, rigid in his saddle, staring at the flames.

'She must have got out,' repeated Niksar as the howls of despair grew louder. Most people were too consumed by panic or grief to register what he was saying but as Niksar scoured the crowd, searching for someone to agree with him, he saw Kolgrimm looking his way. The old cogsmith had removed his helmet and his eyes were glinting darkly under his brow.

Somehow, as he met the duardin's gaze, Niksar felt the truth. His sister was dead. And she had tricked him. *This* was her plan. She had given her life so that everyone else could live.

'You knew,' he howled, rushing at Kolgrimm.

Kolgrimm did not flinch as Niksar punched him. 'She swore me to secrecy,' he said, backing away and wiping blood from his beard. 'The priests would have stopped her. But she had to tell me.' His tone was flat. 'She needed to know how to overload the nexus syphon. I had to tell her where the keystone was. She had to get Arulos there before he died. It was his death blast. He triggered it.'

Niksar cried out again and drew back his fist for another punch, but when the duardin grabbed his arm, Niksar did not struggle. He sat down heavily in the mud.

'For what?' he moaned, clutching his head. 'Why did she do it? What was the point? We have nothing left. We'll die out here anyway without the keep.'

Kolgrimm sat down next to him. 'Your sister thought not.'

Niksar was overwhelmed by grief and despair, but something in Kolgrimm's voice forced him to listen.

Kolgrimm took a small object from his armour and passed it to Niksar. It was the augur stone, removed from the delicate circlet and looking just as it did when Ocella first gave it to him.

'She didn't think you'd suit the crown,' said Kolgrimm.

'I don't understand.' Niksar shook his head. 'What did she want me to do with this?'

'I still have the alkahest, Niksar. And the Decree Sigmaris.' He nodded to a shape looming behind the flames. 'We still have building materials on that last metalith. It will take longer, making things from scratch, but if it was smaller this time, we could build again.' He hesitated, looking away, his voice brittle with shame. 'Your sister said it should be me. That I was the one to build it. But how could she think that after what I did? After the way I failed everyone?'

'Build again.' The words sounded like madness to Niksar but, even through his pain, there was something in Kolgrimm's words that touched him. He could hear his sister's voice beneath Kolgrimm's rough tone. 'Perhaps,' he said. 'Perhaps it could be done. If we believe in her.'

Kolgrimm closed his eyes, then gripped Niksar's hand, crushing it in his battered gauntlet. He nodded. 'They would need someone to follow, though.' Kolgrimm nodded at the augur stone in Niksar's hand. 'Someone chosen by their god.'

As the howls of grief washed through the valley, Niksar stared deep into the heart of the glimmering. He was surprised by the face it reflected back at him.

CHAPTER THIRTY-TWO

'Lord-Celestant Volk,' said Retributor Mazura, marching back through the ranks towards the Lord-Celestant. It was just after dawn and pale light glimmered over the Knights Excelsior, flashing on the greaves of their perfect, white armour. Mazura pointed to a shape on the horizon. 'More ruins, my lord. Possibly the remains of a stormkeep.'

Volk steered Kurtha on with a tap of his heels. The dracoth snorted beneath him as she padded along the rubble-strewn remains of the Great Excelsis Road. 'There were never any storm-keeps along this stretch of the road.' Volk peered through the fog at the distant shadows. 'It must be another greenskin settlement. It looks abandoned, though.'

As they travelled on, Volk rode ahead of his ranks of Paladins, intrigued by the ruins. He quickly realised his guess was wrong. The shapes were too warped and fluid to be the work of orruks.

'There's something odd about this,' he muttered, turning Kurtha to face down into the valley. He gestured for the others to follow and left the road, riding slowly down the slope into the muddy fields. When he reached the ruins and saw the imposing gates he laughed in surprise. 'It's one of the crusader strongpoints. I thought the ones along this stretch had been levelled a long time ago.' He glanced back at Mazura. 'In fact, I didn't think any of them got as far as building walls.'

It was nearly six months since Volk had told the High Arbiter the crusades were a mistake, and since then he had been proved right. There was an endless stream of reports flooding into Excelsis describing the miserable fate of those who took the Coin Malleus. The people who travelled to this stretch of road had been slaughtered in particularly horrific fashion.

He dismounted, ordered Kurtha to keep watch at the gates and headed into the ruins with Mazura at his side. He gestured for the rest of the Paladins to fan out through the buildings and keep spaced apart. Since leaving Delium, the Knights Excelsior had been attacked several times. And these ruins looked like exactly the kind of place the greenskins would spring an ambush. There were charred remains everywhere. He could see the skeletons of humans and greenskins, mangled together like a work of grotesque art, skulls and limbs fused into a revolting mess.

After several minutes of searching, however, there was no sign of the enemy and Volk allowed himself to examine the strange architecture. It was based on classical, Azyrite designs but it had been twisted and moulded in a peculiar fashion. It took him a while to realise that it had been melted.

'There must have been an explosion of incredible power to do something like this.' He snapped off a tusk-shaped piece of stone and stared at it. It had a dark lustre, as though it had been turned to glass. 'They must have been impressive structures,' he said, looking up at the remains of the walls. 'This was once a large settlement.'

'It looks like the centre of the blast was that way,' said Mazura, pointing between some of the toppled buildings. 'Look at those shapes in the mud.'

The ground was churned up in circular waves. As they trod over the ridges Volk paused and crouched down, rolling dust between his fingertips.

'This is not the work of greenskins,' he said, looking up at the clouds.

'Sorcery, then?' said Mazura. 'Do you think followers of the Dark Gods did this?'

'No.' Volk frowned. 'This was a different kind of power altogether. I sense the hand of the God-King in this.'

'Greenskins were definitely here, though,' said Mazura, picking something from the rubble and handing it to him. 'Look. The same as all the others.'

It was a circular shield and, as Volk turned it over, he knew what he would see: a leering, hysterical face that grinned at him as he examined it. He grimaced and threw the thing back onto the ground.

'Kragnos,' said Mazura.

Volk nodded. 'Everywhere we go, he is there before us.'

The name had been on the lips of every dying mortal they encountered and every greenskin that hurled a curse at them. *End of Empires* they called him, and Volk was more troubled by the words every time he heard them. The greenskins had always been erratic, a disorganised rabble. But the ones who prayed to Kragnos were different, laying traps and showing a cunning unlike anything he had seen in orruks before. More worrying still was the rate at which they were spreading. Everywhere Volk went, the old orruk tribes had been swept away by the greenskins who followed this new god. And all of them seemed bent on the destruction of Excelsis.

He walked to the centre of the blast and dropped to one knee, picking something from the ash. It was a golden fragment – a piece of sculpted sigmarite. 'The Hammers of Sigmar were here,' he said, peering at the shard.

'The Anvilhearts?'

'Perhaps.' He looked around at the ruins. 'Which would make this Ardent Keep. And it would explain why Arulos never reached Delium.' He shook his head. 'The crusaders did well to achieve so much. I would never have dreamt they came this far. And surviving long enough to build a settlement is even more impressive.' He stood and flicked the shard of sigmarite into the dust, considering how much he had misjudged the crusades.

'My lord!' cried another one of his men from further into the ruins. 'Look here.'

As Volk strode through the wreckage, he thought the poor light and the dust must be playing tricks on his eyes. The Paladin who had called him over was pointing beyond the ruined walls, down the valley to another set of buildings. These ones were not ruins. They rose from the summit of a hill half a mile away, silhouetted by the rising sun, and they looked magnificent.

'Is it a city?' said Mazura, rushing over.

'Almost,' said Volk, shaking his head as he realised how tall and well-defended the walls were. There were towers inside that looked as grand as anything in Excelsis and he could see Freeguild soldiers patrolling the battlements as colourful pennants fluttered overhead. Outside the main structure there were watchtowers and smaller fortifications, along with what looked like farmsteads. 'Impossible,' he muttered. 'No one can have survived out here.'

'That symbol on the banners, my lord, do you recognise it? A tower in a circle?'

Volk looked at the melted rubble lying around him then back at the imposing fortress further down the valley. 'They made it,' he said, struggling to believe his own words. He shook his head and laughed. 'They *survived*. That's Ardent Keep.'

EPILOGUE

The children ran through the night, clambering up muddy banks and wading through brackish pools. Grief hit them in waves. Sometimes they sobbed wildly as they ran, unable to console each other, at other times they were numb with exhaustion and shock. The laughter was always there, on the far side of the river, following them through the night, mocking them for their loss. For the first few hours it had sounded distant, but in the false light before dawn, the sounds moved closer, too near to be on the other side of the water. The children knew what it meant: the greenskins were racing to cut them off; they were going to intercept them before they could reach Excelsis.

The city loomed on the horizon, taunting them as cruelly as the laughter. It was so close they could see soldiers on the walls and ships bobbing in the harbour. They could even make out the vast spear of rock that rose from the bay, marking the city as Sigmar's domain. Thousands of lights shone from windows, glittering across the surface of the sea, speaking of safety and peace. It was the most beautiful sight either of them had ever seen.

'We *will* make it,' said the girl, but her voice trembled and she was glancing anxiously from side to side as she ran, peering into the shadowy groves that lined the road. Travelling on the road was risky, but the land either side was so marshy they could barely walk, never mind run, so the road had seemed the better option.

The boy nodded, then halted, grabbing the girl's arm. The road was climbing a small hill and, on the other side, he could hear something: heavy boots rushing across stone, headed towards them.

'It could be soldiers from the city,' said the girl, hope flashing in her eyes. 'Mother said these lands are patrolled by the White Angels. Perhaps we should wait and see if–'

There was an explosion of noise: bestial snorts, howls, clattering metal, horribly familiar laughter.

The children turned and bolted from the road, sprinting towards the nearest clump of trees. The sounds of fighting rushed after them. They heard the hacking of flesh and the snapping of bones. The greenskins howled and giggled hysterically and lights flickered through the trees, illuminating the children's filthy, tear-stained faces.

'They're lighting a fire,' groaned the boy. 'To block our way.'

'Across the fields!' said the girl, dragging him on through the trees and out into the moonlight on the far side. They waded through the mud, dragging each other along as the laughter came closer. The ground descended, falling sharply into a steep-sided gully, and the boy fell, sliding and landing at the bottom of the narrow ravine, hitting the ground with a painful jolt.

His sister rolled and fell after him, landing almost as heavily as he had done. They lay on their backs for a moment, gasping, looking up through the top of the gully at a narrow strip of stars. Then heavy, quick-moving feet rushed towards them.

They struggled to their feet as shapes emerged from the shadow at the southern end of the gully. They were tall, wiry and hunched, gripping crudely forged weapons and giggling. As the monsters lurched into the starlight the children saw that it was the same creatures who had killed their parents: stooped, leering, goblinoid things with elongated heads and hide the colour of riverweed.

The children turned to run and found themselves facing a sheer, rocky wall. They were trapped. They had landed at the end of the ravine. The only way out was through the greenskins. The boy shook his head, too terrified to think, but the girl grabbed a stick from the ground and levelled it at the greenskin leader. She was crying as she spoke and her arm was shaking, but her voice was iron.

'You will pay. You will suffer for what you did. You might take our lives but I swear, on Sigmar's throne, you will die too.'

The boy stared at her in disbelief. Then fury rushed through him and he grabbed a rock and stood at her side. 'By the God-King!' he cried. 'We defy you!'

The leader of the greenskins halted, surprised by the strength of their cries. It was larger than the others and it was gripping a rusty meat cleaver as big as its arm. It stared at them with nightmarish eyes. Then it laughed. The other greenskins joined in, pointing at the children and howling in delight. There were at least a dozen of them. Some were bleeding from fresh wounds and one was limping. The boy sensed that they were pleased to have found easy prey.

The leader stopped laughing and put the cleaver on its back. Then it took out a long, thin knife and swaggered towards the children, grinning, revealing a mouthful of black needle-teeth.

The children leant against each other, sticks raised, whispering prayers.

Then another, larger monster dropped into the crevasse, landing at the head of the others. It was huge, clad in plates of metal armour, and as it raised a hammer light flashed from the weapon, filling the gully and dazzling the children.

The noise that followed was horrific. The boy clamped his hands over his ears, trying to drown it out: a savage din of howls, screams and crunching bones. As the sounds of slaughter grew, the light increased, filling the air with strands of energy and painting the gully white.

Finally, it was over, and the light dimmed. The children cowered against the rocks as the armoured figure turned from a pile of corpses to face them. Its hammer was drenched in blood. Runes written in blue fire glimmered across its golden battleplate. As it moved closer, the children raised their sticks, but all hope had left them. This thing was more terrifying than anything they had faced before. Sparks flickered up from its boots as it reached them. The air shimmered with unearthly power. *It must be a daemon,* thought the boy. He was too scared to breathe.

The monster placed its hammer on the ground, removed its helmet and knelt on one knee to study the children. They were astonished to see that it was a woman. Unusually tall and clad in outlandish armour, but a woman, nonetheless. Her face was fierce and covered in scars, but she spoke to them in a surprisingly soft voice.

'Are you able to walk?'

For a moment, neither of the children could speak. Then the boy managed to nod.

'I… I think so.'

'Yes,' said the girl, wiping tears from her face, smearing her cheeks with mud.

The warrior nodded. 'None of the roads to Excelsis are safe. I will escort you.' With that, she fastened her helmet back on, picked up her hammer and strode back down the gully, her boots crunching over the dead greenskins.

'What are you?' gasped the boy, stumbling after her.

'Zagora,' said the woman, without looking back. 'The Dawn-bringer.'

ABOUT THE AUTHOR

Darius Hinks is the author of the Warhammer 40,000 novels *Blackstone Fortress, Blackstone Fortress: Ascension* and the accompanying audio drama *The Beast Inside*. He also wrote three novels in the Mephiston series: *Mephiston: Blood of Sanguinius, Mephiston: Revenant Crusade* and *Mephiston: City of Light*, as well as the Space Marine Battles novella *Sanctus*. His work for Age of Sigmar includes *Hammers of Sigmar, Warqueen* and the Gotrek Gurnisson novels *Ghoulslayer* and *Gitslayer*. For Warhammer, he wrote *Warrior Priest*, which won the David Gemmell Morningstar Award for best newcomer, as well as the Orion trilogy, *Sigvald* and several novellas.

An extract from
Stormvault
by Andy Clark

WHUMP – WHUMP, WHU-WHUMP!

The beat of the Big Drum rolled through the still air of the evening like the colossal heartbeat of a godbeast.

WHUMP – WHUMP, WHU-WHUMP!

Brognakk the Skinner felt its basso boom vibrate in his barrel chest. The sound sent a surge of exhilaration through the old megaboss. A spike of aggression tightened his fist instinctively around his massive double-bladed choppa, Krump, until its gnarled leather bindings creaked.

WHUMP – WHUMP, WHU-WHUMP!

The sound bounced off the mountains that towered like Gorkamorka's tusks to the north. It boomed like thunder over the ruined cityscape that sprawled before Brognakk, its sunken streets and canyons black with shadow, the hard planes of its ruined buildings daubed bloody down one flank by the setting light of Hysh.

WHUMP – WHUMP, WHU-WHUMP!

The Big Drum itself had been hauled to the top of the ruined watchtower that overlooked the road north of the city. Crude block and tackle winches and a great deal of gargant muscle had got the drum into position, and now a pair of hulking ogors pounded away at it with double-handed beaters made from obsidian and monster-bones.

Beneath him, Brognakk's maw-krusha steed shifted restlessly. It hunched on a crag overlooking the watchtower and the drum. He had named the enormous beast Smash; this was in part because of what Brognakk had seen it do to Boss Graznak's 'ardboyz the day he killed Graznak and took the monstrous steed for his own, and partly because he didn't have time for all that imaginative mucking about. Let the weaker races mess around with fancy names for their weapons and mounts and what have you. While they were wasting time with such nonsense, the orruks would be kicking down their castle doors and smashing their teeth in.

'Steady, lad,' growled Brognakk as Smash stirred again. The maw-krusha pounded one huge, scaly fist against the lip of the crag, dislodging a spill of scree. Brognakk gave his steed an affectionate whack on the back of the skull with his own clenched fist, asserting dominance as naturally as he breathed air. 'It's da drum, innit? You feel it too,' he said. His maw-krusha gave a deep, rumbling snarl that sounded like wet rocks grinding together deep beneath the earth. Brognakk chose to take that as assent. It was the Big Drum, he thought, the war beat of Gorkamorka pounding out until it filled the valley. How could Smash not respond to that? How could any of them not?

At the thought of Gorkamorka, Brognakk spat superstitiously, first right then left. One for each head of the Great Green God.

'Come on, lad. They'll be gavvered by now,' said the leathery old megaboss, and gave his steed another whack to get it moving. Smash let out a deafening roar then launched itself from the lip of the crag and spread its wings wide. Maw-krushas couldn't really fly, per se, not like the fancy winged beasts of Sigmar's storm ladz or the twisted-up terrors that the biggest Chaos boyz rode to battle. They were too big, too tough, solid lumps of muscle and bone that even the widest wingspan wouldn't keep aloft indefinitely. Instead they leapt and glided, as Smash did now, launching itself high into the air with a tremendous shove of its heavily muscled forelimbs then catching the air and soaring upon it with the wide flaps of skin that stretched bat-like between its wrists and hind legs.

Brognakk grabbed onto the pommel of his saddle and enjoyed the sensation of acceleration. Smash shot over the watchtower where the Big Drum still pounded, greenskin shamans and war-chanters gibbering, dancing and adding their own drumbeats about its base. The maw-krusha sailed down over the lower slopes and as it went its shadow swept over a sea of shanty-encampments. Fire smoke billowed around Brognakk, parting in a whirl as Smash plunged through it. Crude idols to Gorkamorka jutted up everywhere, ramshackle agglomerations of rubble, hewn wood, war trophies and dung daubed with vibrant colours and jangling with cheap bells and trinkets. Smash clipped a few of the tallest and Brognakk leered at the cries of shock from below as rubble crashed down on surprised orruks and ogors. Thousands upon thousands of warriors marched beneath Brognakk's flayed-skin banner, and they teemed underneath him as he rushed like an angry wind towards the valley floor.

The slopes raced past below, thick with grass, undergrowth and giant emerald-green ferns that broke like green waves against the rocky outcroppings jutting amidst them. Ahead, the ruins of the city swelled larger with alarming rapidity as the horde's forward positions approached.

'Dat way,' barked Brognakk, wrenching Smash's head around as they whipped past a hillock crawling with chanting Bonesplitterz and the Morkagork hove into sight. The enormous war fort had been wheeled all the way to the fringe of the city's crumbling northern districts and now loomed, huge and menacing, as its two wood-and-iron visages watched the city sink into twilit shadow. Brognakk's black old heart swelled with pride at the sight of the Morkagork, as it always did when he saw the colossal war engine. He had enslaved an entire nation of Spiderfang grots to build it, working most of them to death as they hacked down the web-festooned trees of their dank valleys and mined their shadowy caverns for the materials to make Brognakk's rolling tribute to the Great Green God. It was a veritable castle on iron wheels, moved by gargants chained into its lowest level, bedecked to resemble Gorkamorka and loaded up with deck upon deck of spear chukkas. For now, its presence was a brazen challenge to any enemy entering the valley. It said, 'Orruks is 'ere, get gone or get ready fer a fight.'

It would rain spears down upon the enemy in support of his horde when the big fight came, as it always did.

And there was a *big* fight coming, thought Brognakk.

Of that he was sure.